Acclaim for Emily Gunnis's emotional thrillers

'Utterly gripping, taut and powerful . . . emotionally charged, co[mpelling]'

'A g[reat . . .]'
Wom[an's Home]

'I really loved it! Tense, emotionally charged'
Jenny Ashcroft

'I was gripped. The story is compelling, twisty, heart-wrenching and thought-provoking. A novel that stays with you'
Sophie Kinsella

'A great book, truly hard to put down. Fast paced, brilliantly plotted and desperately sad at times – all hallmarks of a bestseller'
Lesley Pearse

'Gripping. A great read to curl up with for the afternoon'
Fabulous magazine

'A truly brilliant and moving read. I loved it'
Karen Hamilton

'A hugely addictive story . . . full of twists, turns and deceit. An engrossing read'
Heat

'Captivating and suspenseful'
Jessica Fellowes

'A gripping story that will take you on an emotional rollercoaster'
My Weekly

Emily Gunnis is the internationally bestselling author of *The Girl in the Letter*, *The Missing Daughter* and *The Midwife's Secret*. Her novels have sold in twenty languages. Emily previously worked in TV drama and lives in South Wales with her young family. She is one of the four daughters of *Sunday Times* bestselling author Penny Vincenzi.

Also by Emily Gunnis

THE GIRL IN THE LETTER
THE MISSING DAUGHTER
THE MIDWIFE'S SECRET

The
Girls Left Behind

EMILY GUNNIS

REVIEW

First published in 2023 by Headline Review
An imprint of HEADLINE PUBLISHING GROUP

3

Cataloguing in Publication Data is available from the British Library

Paperback ISBN 978 1 4722 7209 6

Typeset in 12.5/14.75 pt Adobe Garamond by Jouve (UK), Milton Keynes

Printed and bound in Great Britain by Clays Ltd, Elcograf S.p.A.

Headline's policy is to use papers that are natural, renewable and recyclable
products and made from wood grown in well-managed forests and other
controlled sources. The logging and manufacturing processes are expected to
conform to the environmental regulations of the country of origin.

HEADLINE PUBLISHING GROUP
An Hachette UK Company
Carmelite House
50 Victoria Embankment
London EC4Y 0DZ

www.headline.co.uk
www.hachette.co.uk

*For my mother-in-law, Sue Kerry, aka Nanny,
for all your invaluable help with this book.
In the words of Grace and Ellie, love you
to the moon and back.*

'You never fail until you stop trying.'
Albert Einstein

'Grief is the price we pay for love.'
Queen Elizabeth II

Prologue

Jo

14 December 1975

Any unit to attend 42 Wicker Street, Saltdean. Report of a violent domestic by the neighbour, Mrs Brook.

WPC Joanna Hamilton let out a puff of adrenaline into the cold cabin of her Morris 1000 as she reached down for the radio cradled to the left of her steering wheel.

'Whisky four zero one. I'm only single crew but I'm four minutes away,' Jo said, taking a last gulp of the warming tea Martha in the all-night launderette on Saltdean High Street had made for her – a place her brother had tipped her off about to get a much-needed cuppa on a long night shift.

Roger, if you start to make your way, I'll get another unit to attend.

The reply came as Jo flipped down the button switch on the dashboard to start her blue lights, waving to Martha who was folding linen at the counter in the warm fog of the tumble dryers. As she pulled away, Jo decided against putting on her siren; it was a bitterly cold night, the roads were fairly empty, and she didn't want to wake the whole housing estate on her approach. She pressed down on the accelerator, and glanced at the face of her small leather watch which told her it was midnight; pub closing time, and – in her limited experience – the hour when violent husbands came home and started on their wives.

1

Pulling out onto the A259 seafront, the small baby-blue panda rattled in the freezing gale coming in from the English Channel over the Saltdean Cliffs. She felt her heart start to race, knowing she shouldn't be attending domestics on her own, but hoping the sight of the police car would be enough to stop a fight kicking off until backup arrived. Before the recent changes at the station, she would never have dreamed of being in such a vulnerable situation on her own. She, like most of her female colleagues at the station, resented the arrival of the 1975 Sex Discrimination Act. Its aim had been largely to protect women, which in the police force meant an end to the division of crimes into 'blue' for the men: major crime and fraud; and 'pink' for the women's police department: petty crime, shoplifting and dealing with female prisoners and their children. In reality, however, they had all been left with a lot of blurred lines, and life was now even harder than before. All the women on the force still ended up doing all the 'pink' jobs, but with the addition of being put on very risky night shifts on their own. Jo had been terrified, the first night she went out on the beat alone, but she knew better than to complain; her Detective Chief Inspector, Bart Bailey, would have just sent her packing. To her intense relief it seemed that just the presence of a woman when a fight was kicking off could be enough to cool things down. And she soon found she had a gift for calming frayed nerves; by being non-confrontational, talking quietly but firmly, and getting any children out of harm's way, she could usually buy herself enough time until backup arrived.

Jo changed down a gear, accelerating hard, as she reached the peak of the cliff face where, to her right, stood Morgate

2

House Children's Home, an imposing Victorian red-brick building which for the past century had homed children in care from the ages of three to seventeen. It towered over the Saltdean Cliffs, visible from miles out to sea, but for the past decade had been inching perilously close to the jagged white cliff face which was falling away onto the beach below at an increasingly alarming rate. With only a small white picket fence separating the grounds of Morgate House and the two-hundred-foot drop onto Saltdean Beach below, it had become a magnet for waifs and strays wanting to take their own lives. Runaways like Gemma Smith, a fifteen-year-old resident of Morgate House, whose bloated and twisted body Jo had been sent to cordon off on the beach just the month before. Jo felt goosebumps prickle up her arms as she drove past the vast Gothic mansion, the memory of Gemma's lifeless limbs sprawled over the rocks below like a jellyfish's tentacles; Gemma's long dark hair tangled with fishing rope, her clothing torn from her body in the stormy sea. It had been a bitterly cold day as Jo tried to hammer stakes into the ground to wrap the police tape around. She had stood guard to stop the general public from drifting too close, waiting a painfully long time before her male colleagues arrived. In the bitterly cold sea gale, she had to keep prying eyes back as the scene of crime officer took photos of Gemma's broken body, before two undertakers lifted her onto a stretcher and took her away to the mortuary to be examined by the pathologist.

She had tried not to stare at Gemma's body herself, but the girl's green eyes, framed with thick dark eyelashes seemed to watch her as she went about her work. It had not been the first time Jo had seen those eyes, but the last time there had been life behind them – when Gemma had been caught stealing biscuits from Jenkins' minimarket, in Rottingdean High Street, and Jo had been radioed on her shift to attend. Gemma, a petite girl, wearing a grey woollen jumper, her long dark hair cascading in waves around her pretty face, had been sitting in the back office of the small grocery shop, staring down at her hands, while the owner and his wife sat scowling at her.

'Those bloody Morgate House kids, they're always in here trying to pinch stuff. I've had enough of it. Why can't you lot go up there to the people that run it, and read them the riot act. The kids are out of control, out till all hours up at the grain store on the Tye. Stealing, drinking.'

'I'll pop up to Morgate House today, Mrs Jenkins, I'm sorry for the inconvenience. Do you want to prosecute?'

'No, I don't want to prosecute, I don't have time for all that, and the kid is hungry is all, but it's not our job to feed them. We're hardly breaking even here as it is.' She had wiped her dirt-covered hands on her brown apron and scowled down at Gemma who hadn't looked up once.

The girl had refused to answer any of Jo's questions in the car, about her life in care, and why she was stealing food. 'I want to help, Gemma,' she had said, 'if they're not feeding you properly, you can tell me.'

Gemma had opened the door to get out, then fixed her green eyes on Jo. 'You think you care, but you don't. You'll go home to your family and forget about me in a day or two. Everyone wants us to disappear. Well, maybe one day I will. Me and my man, we're getting out of here.'

'Mrs Price?' A grey-haired lady in her fifties had answered

the door, ushering Gemma in and giving Jo fairly short shrift. 'I wondered if we could talk about the meals you are giving the children. Gemma says she's very hungry.'

'They are given plenty to eat,' the woman had snapped. 'You are welcome to come back at any mealtime and see for yourself. If you want to raise a complaint, you can do so with the council.'

Gemma had glanced back at Jo as Mrs Price closed the door on her. The same unblinking stare which had fixed on Jo on Saltdean Beach.

Indeed, it was those eyes which had haunted Jo's dreams ever since, and made her want to attend the inquest into Gemma's death. Jo's brother Charlie had gone with her – he was ten years her senior and also a serving police officer. Despite her terrible start in life, Gemma had seemed to Jo to have spirit. She was looking to the future and Jo could not fathom how someone so vital and beautiful would feel so desperate that she would take her own life, so young.

She and Charlie had sat on the cold, hard wooden benches at the Coroner's Court in Brighton while her superior officer Detective Inspector Bart Bailey had given his account of Gemma's difficult life, including countless arrests for shoplifting, abusive behaviour, and being returned to Morgate House when she ran away. There had been no questioning the coroner's suicide verdict from her police colleagues, who knew Gemma Smith as a troublemaker and one who had threatened to take her own life many times. 'Morgate House broke her spirit,' Charlie had told her as they shuffled out of the inquest into the cold December day. 'If anyone is to blame, it's that place.'

Even as she drove past it now, Jo could feel the negative energy seeping from the walls of the vast Victorian house above the cliffs.

Jo changed up into fourth gear again and accelerated hard, overtaking a Hillman trundling along the coast road, before hitting a small patch of black ice at the Saltdean lights and skidding slightly before righting herself. Holding her breath, she pressed down again on the accelerator, her hands shaking as she gripped the leather steering wheel tightly. Jo tried to steady her breathing; they hadn't offered her a course for driving at speed during her fifteen-week police training at the army barracks in Wiltshire, and so she was relying on her limited experience since passing her driving test four years earlier. Luckily, having grown up on a farm, and being expected to muck in with her older brother, Charlie, she had been driving farm vehicles since she was in her early teens and felt there wasn't much she couldn't handle.

Jo took a left off the coast road as she drove out towards the run-down housing estate in Telscombe, and her heart rate began to quicken. She was very familiar with Wicker Street; it was on her regular rounds, and they were often called there for domestics. Jo passed a house with a burnt-out car wreck on the front lawn where she and Constable Phillip Price had been called out, just the week before, to disarm a woman defending herself against her old man with a hammer. Phillip had been useless, standing in the corner wide-eyed, watching as she'd restrained the woman alone. Then, when Phillip had finally attempted to arrest the husband, the wife had gone ballistic at him, and refused to prosecute, because she didn't want them carting her old man off. They'd had to leave, with the hammer still wedged in the top of the chest of drawers in the bedroom. 'We should have just let them kill each other,' Phillip had grumbled as they walked away down the path, 'I'm not coming out to this estate any more, it's a waste of bloody time.' It was typical Phillip; since the day they'd met at police training, it was obvious his heart wasn't in the job. When Jo had found out that Phillip's parents, Geoff and Lorna Price, ran Morgate House, it made sense to her that he'd joined the police just to shirk his responsibilities at the children's home.

As she neared number 42, at the end of the street, she slowed, glancing briefly at the run-down front gardens, one with another burnt-out car wreck on the front lawn. 'Thirty-six . . . forty, forty-two,' she whispered to herself, as she spotted a woman standing in the street in a long dressing gown and slippers. As Jo turned off the engine, reached for her hat on the seat next to her and opened her car door, she immediately heard shouting from inside the house.

The neighbour on the street rushed towards her. 'Jim's been in the pub since lunchtime, he's in a hell of a temper,' said the woman, in a state of excitement. 'He woke my kids up as soon as he got home. The walls between our houses are paper thin, and he started shouting at Pip before he'd even got through the front door. Where have you been? I called 999 half an hour ago.'

Jo looked at the woman. 'Thank you for calling us. If you could return to your property now, Mrs . . .' She was wrapped in a towelling dressing gown, her long lacy nightie peeping from below it, her hair in old-fashioned curlers. For the two seconds Jo stared at her, something

7

about the woman's appearance jarred with her. She was dressed like an old lady, but her skin was youthful. She couldn't have been much older than twenty-five, Jo thought. But she had settled into her role for life – wife, mother, curtain twitcher – shaking her head with disapproval, while her eyes sparkled with delight at the soap opera unfolding next door.

'Brook, as in babbling brook, which my old man likes to call me,' she said, taking a deep drag with pursed lips on her Woodbine cigarette and following Jo like a wasp on a hot summer's day.

Jo moved away, rushing up the front path, past the window to the front room, where a brief glance inside told her that a man roughly six feet tall was yelling at a petite blonde woman, and that curled up in the corner together were two small children, crying.

Jo began hammering on the door as the screams and shouts from inside the house intensified.

'Police! Open up,' Jo called out, as she waited, hoping for the door to open and a chance to calm things down.

No response.

Jo rushed to the window again, watching the unfolding scene through a gap in the lace curtains as the man reached out and struck the woman, hard, with the back of his hand. She let out a cry of pain and pressed her hand to her cheek as Jo's mind raced. The world slowed down, as it always did when she first got to a job; her senses bombarded with the sounds and smells of people's lives in chaos – shouting, the waft of alcohol breath, screams of fear, the pulse of bodies surrounding her – while she tried to extract the information she needed in order to calm the situation.

'This new fella's been sniffing round here, bringing Pip food and money and whatnot.' The woman pressed on, continuing to follow her, her cigarette breath repulsing Jo. 'Someone must have mentioned it to Jim, and he's awful jealous.' The woman breathed heavily into the freezing air around her. 'Pip wouldn't sleep around. She's loyal to Jim, even though he's a pig.'

'Okay, thank you for your help, Mrs Brook. I'll take it from here, can you please go inside now!' Jo snapped as the woman glared at her, then skulked away. Jo listened for the sounds of sirens, but heard only silence, her heart hammering in her chest. She watched with horror through the lace curtains as the man, who was thickset, with a crew cut and wearing a miner's jacket, struck the woman again.

Jo winced as the woman clutched her head, letting out a piercing scream of pain as blood trickled from her mouth. Jo's eyes darted around the sparsely furnished room. The two young girls, in oversized T-shirts, screamed as their mother stumbled back and caught a floor lamp, the bulb inside it exploding and raining glass all over the threadbare rug as it came crashing down. The man watched, catching his breath, then walked over to his wife and kicked her hard in the stomach.

Jo pulled at the radio on her collar and pressed down. 'Whisky four zero one, I'm here at 42 Wicker Street. Urgent assistance required. I'm going to have to break in, he's really hurting her.'

Roger, two units on their way. Hang back – don't put yourself in danger. Repeat, hang back.

As Jo released her finger on the radio, the woman in the house reached out her hand to her children. The older one stood and rushed to her mother, throwing herself over her, trying to protect her as the father pulled her off and continued his violent assault. The woman was clinging to her children as the man continued shouting and kicking her. Jo had to find a way in, she had to get the man away from his wife before he seriously hurt her, she had no choice but to try.

Jo trained her eyes on the windows, looking for an opening, a way in, but they were locked tight. She didn't want to break a window; shards of glass everywhere would be a dangerous weapon for the man to have at his fingertips. Instead, she began running her fingers along the window-sill, looking for a weakness in the frame, piercing her finger on a large splinter of wood. Jo let out a whimper of pain as she pulled it out, but persisted, methodically, in her task.

Finally, along the third ledge, she found what she was looking for: a place where the frame had rotted away. Grabbing a rusty metal paint stripper lying discarded on the ground, she rammed it into the gap and forced the window open. *Click!* It gave way and she pushed it up with all her might.

The children stayed motionless, watching her, their dirty faces streaked with tears.

'Police! Stop that!' she shouted at the man.

He didn't even look up from his task; his eyes remained fixed on his wife and the fury he was inflicting on her body. Jo lifted her leg and climbed through the open window and onto a dark green sofa, catching something with her foot, which fell to the ground with a soft thud.

'Stop what you are doing now! Get away from her!' she

yelled, rushing over to the man and putting her arm across his chest to try to move him away. 'You need to calm down, I need to get your wife some help, you've hurt her.'

As she came between the two of them, the man's eyes, wide with rage, met hers. He heaved with anger, and glared back at her.

'She's having a fucking affair!' he shouted into her face, his saliva spraying her.

'You're scaring your children. I need you to move back,' she said, staying between them, looking at the children who had both covered their mother with their small bodies.

The man wasn't listening, he was somewhere else, his rage overwhelming him, and he wasn't done yet. Jo could hear sirens in the distance but not close enough. She was alone. The only sound in the small, damp room was the desperate whimpering from the woman and her children.

'Okay, let's move this out into the hall. You can tell me what this is about, come on,' she said, trying to push the man back.

He pushed her aside and began to kick his wife again. Jo's eyes fell on the children, and she made her way towards them, holding out her arms in the hope that they would rush to her. But they stayed deathly still, their eyes wide, one of them lifting a little hand to point at the space behind her, then opening their mouth to let out a piercing scream.

It was out of the corner of her eye that she saw a flash of light and then immediately felt a rush of heat. As she turned back to face the window she had climbed through, she saw an upturned ashtray on the floor, which she realised with horror she had knocked to the floor when she climbed into the room. In a matter of seconds, the torn net curtains had ignited, and bits of lit material were now flying like burning butterflies over the rug which was erupting in scattered balls of flame.

Jo dashed to the window and tried to pull the curtains down, but the tattered material disintegrated in her fingers, as the flames danced across the room, engulfing the sofa, which had ignited within seconds. Jo pulled frantically at the radio pinned to her collar. 'Whisky four zero one, we need the fire brigade at 42 Wicker Street urgently. Two adults and two children inside, front room on fire.' She looked desperately across the room, which was rapidly filling with smoke.

As the flames danced towards his wife's hair where she lay sprawled across the floor, the man looked up at Jo for the first time and they locked eyes.

'We need to get everyone out, now,' Jo pleaded. 'I can't put this out on my own, the fire brigade is on their way.'

The man paused for a moment, his towering frame not flinching as debris from the burning ceiling fell onto his head, glowing like sparklers in his black hair. Then slowly he appeared to soften and knelt down, lifting his unconscious wife off the floor and away from the burning rug. Jo reached for the children, pulling them towards her, as she rushed out of the room after the man, expecting him to turn left along the corridor and out of the house, ready to follow him with the children.

But, to her horror, as he reached the hall, he turned right instead, heading away from the front door and deeper into the now-burning house. He began to climb the stairs with his unconscious wife in his arms. Jo's heart stopped as she watched helplessly, clinging to the sobbing children while their father climbed higher, taking their mother away – into the heat of the fire engulfing them.

'Mum!' one of the children cried out in desperation, using all her strength to pull away from Jo and running up the stairs after her parents, as Jo heard the sirens of the police backup finally arriving.

'Holly, come back!' the smaller child cried out, as she also tried to pull away.

Quickly, Jo pulled the child back into her grasp, wrapping her arm around the little girl's chest so she couldn't escape, and reaching out to open the front door. The cold air burst in, letting some of the smoke filling up the hallway escape. She took several gasps of air, her eyes stinging from the thick black fog now engulfing the house.

Jo lifted the child in her arms and stepped outside, as two police cars, their sirens blazing, screeched up outside the house. Their car doors burst open and four officers ran towards her.

'Who's in there?' a man barked, as the others rushed in. Only Phillip Price hung back, horrified by the dense smoke pouring from the open doorway.

'There's a male and female and a child, they've gone upstairs, the front room is on fire,' Jo shouted to the first officers, realising that appearing behind them was her older brother, Charlie, who pushed past Phillip.

'Are you okay, Jo?' he asked, rushing towards the front door.

'Yes,' she said, coughing, 'but the fire has taken hold, and there's a little girl in there called Holly. Get her out of there quickly, Charlie!'

The smoke was now so thick that her brother disappeared from view almost as soon as he rushed in through the front door after his colleagues. Jo picked up the little girl who was crying, her blonde curls falling around her blue eyes. Jo clung on to her tiny frame. 'It's okay, they'll get them out.'

Phillip stood with his narrow mouth wide open in shock, not helping, rooted to the spot, complete paralysis of inaction as the smoke billowed from every downstairs window.

'Phillip, get the child some water and a blanket,' Jo shouted. 'Phil! There's water and a blanket in the boot of my car, can you get them?' she said, as Phil finally looked at her, then slowly nodded and turned to walk away.

The house let out a loud roar, as one of the ground-floor windows exploded. It was buckling from the pressure of the heat and the smoke, and Jo let out a cry of panic at the thought of everyone inside – including her beloved brother, Charlie. She put the little girl on her hip and ran round to the back of the house. Her heart raced with panic as two neighbours appeared from the darkness of the street with a ladder.

'Thank you,' Jo said. 'Can you watch the windows and see if any of them appear, then shout for me. Don't climb up it yourselves. I don't want any more casualties!' Jo rushed from window to window, desperately looking for any signs of life as the little girl looked up at the smoke escaping from the cracks in the window frames, and screamed for her sister.

'Holly!' She sobbed into Jo's neck, her hot tears leaving a trail in the black soot on her face.

'It's okay, they'll be okay,' Jo said. She could hear the sirens of the fire brigade in the distance; they were taking too long! She ran back to the front of the house, shouting her brother's name as two colleagues finally appeared at a window and opened it, letting the smoke pour out like dragon's breath.

'Round here! Bring the ladder round to the front!' Jo called out to the men, handing the little girl over to Phillip who had appeared next to her, holding a blanket. With their help, she placed the ladder next to the open window, feeling the intense heat coming through the bricks.

'Where's Charlie?!' she yelled, trying to keep the hysteria from her voice as the first two officers on the scene climbed down, and then bent over double, coughing furiously.

'I don't know, I couldn't see him,' spluttered one. 'We couldn't find the kid.'

'Charlie!' Jo screamed, looking up at the open window, beginning to cry. She had started the fire in which four people, including a young child and her own brother, were now trapped. If they didn't get out, she would never forgive herself. Her mother would never forgive her, if anything happened to her precious son.

'Charlie! Where are you?' Jo yelled, handing over the crying child on her hip to a colleague and starting to climb the ladder – desperate to do something, anything, to help. She couldn't just stand by and wait for him to die.

'Jo! What are you doing?' Phil shouted up to her. 'Come back! You can't go in there!'

'I have to find him!' Jo looked down at Phil, her body shaking with fear, as she suddenly heard her brother's voice from above her, wracked with coughing from the smoke.

'Coming down!' he said.

Jo felt a relief like she'd never known flood her body.

Her legs went weak as she looked up, her eyes stinging with tears, as Charlie appeared at the top of the ladder, carrying Holly over his right shoulder.

He began to climb down, as every window started to shatter with the intense heat, people surrounding the house ducking for cover as shards of glass fired into the night. As the fire brigade and ambulance finally pulled up outside, Jo took Holly from Charlie's arms and rushed towards the paramedics, handing her over. Jo watched as they laid the little girl on a stretcher, her face and hair black with soot, her body convulsing from coughing.

'Please, help my brother, he needs oxygen.' Jo held the little girl's hand, and pointed over at Charlie, as another paramedic grabbed an oxygen mask and rushed over to him as he vomited black bile.

The spray of water cannons and floodlights suddenly filled the night sky around them. Jo turned back to Holly, pushing her hair from her pale forehead as the little girl dropped something on the ground next to them. Holly let out a cry, as she turned on her side and vomited. Her blood-shot eyes streaming tears, she reached out for the necklace lying on the ground, the paramedic desperately trying to fix the oxygen mask over her mouth. Jo bent down and picked it up, and gently handed back the silver St Christopher on a chain.

The girl mumbled something to her, weakly, the hiss of the oxygen mask drowning her out. Jo leaned in as the girl spoke again, a tear escaping down the side of her tiny blackened face. Jo listened hard, as the girl reached up to the oxygen mask, and slowly lifted it, still clutching her mother's chain in her hand.

Her eyes fixing on Jo, she raised her voice so she could hear her, and whispered in her ear, the rush of her breath sending prickles down Jo's neck.

'It's okay,' said Jo, trying to put the mask back over Holly's mouth before she made out the words the girl was whispering to her.

'You killed her. You killed my mum.'

Chapter One

Jo

March 2015, Monday morning

'Have you seen the remains?'

'Yes, ma'am.'

'And they're definitely human?'

'Yes, there's a skull, and it looks like there's head trauma.'

'But it's otherwise intact?' DS Stanley James nodded at Superintendent Jo Hamilton.

'Forensics are on their way, so we'll know more once they've taken a look,' Stanley added. 'But, buried in a remote spot like this, I'd say we're almost certainly looking at murder.'

Jo looked over her shoulder to the area of woodland cordoned off by the first responders since the grim discovery that morning, then out at the vast expanse of English Channel which met the Telscombe Cliffs where they stood.

'Okay, let's take a look.' Jo had been sitting in her office alone, tying up the last of her caseloads for a final handover at the end of the week, when the buzz had started in the corridor. She couldn't make out what they were saying, but it always felt like electricity when something big was kicking off; people huddled around desks, whispering, the word spreading like smoke. She would wait, impatiently, for the knock on her door to tell her what it was. Finally, today, it came in the form of a phone call, from DI Fred

19

Jones. 'Ma'am, a couple of developers have dug up some human remains. At the woods near Saltdean, on the Telscombe Cliffs. Stan thinks there's an obvious skull injury.'

The relentless March rain of the last few days meant that their BMW had barely made it up the muddy track to the small area of woodland where they were now parked, next to a cluster of pickup trucks with 'ARC development' emblazoned on their flanks.

'Who found the remains?' Jo asked, her eyes fixed on the muddy tracks and the dozen trees in the clearing ahead of her. She looked over at the DS, who had only been on her team for a year but had already proved to be a valuable asset; hard-working, quick-thinking and respectful. In many ways, he reminded her of her brother, Charlie.

'Two guys digging foundations for a *Grand Designs* type project, they're turning the water tower into a residential property. They've been waiting months to get the go-ahead to start work, apparently. Good luck with that now,' he said, shaking his head. 'Kate was the first responder. She's interviewing the guys now.'

'Water tower?' Jo frowned, as Stan headed off up the track, wet mud splattering over the blue plastic coverings on his feet.

Jo glanced into the boot of Stan's car, looking for more shoe protectors, to save her new boots from getting covered in mud – or worse, confiscated as evidence. She found some and pulled them on.

'Not many people know the tower is here. It's hidden in the trees,' Stan added, as Jo caught up with him and the salty wind whipped at her skin. It was hard-going, a sea of mud, until they reached the woods, where the tangled tree roots had absorbed some of the sludge. Looking up, Jo saw it: the square concrete tower on stilts, hidden in the trees surrounding it. 'Oh, that. I haven't been up here for years,' she said. 'I didn't realise it was a water tower. I remember when it was a grain store in the eighties, some kids got trapped in it once, I was called up here to get them out.'

'The remains are just over here, ma'am,' said Stan, pointing down at a mound of earth next to a yellow JCB, cordoned off with police tape. Jo walked over slowly, not wanting to unsettle any of the waterlogged turf around Stan's feet. She stopped and looked down to see a shallow grave and the partly exposed remains in the earth by her feet. Slowly, she squatted down, squinting in the spring sunlight as she trained her eyes on the scene in front of her. A skull, a collarbone and a femur emerging from the thawing mud. A body turned on its side and curled into the foetal position.

Despite the scores of dead bodies she had seen over the course of her thirty years in Sussex Police, it was always very sad to see the evidence of a life taken away, often in its prime. Jo stood for a moment, taking in the sorry scene; human remains were something she never got used to. But a long and illustrious career meant that her mind immediately began to race with the questions the forensic pathologist would now spend the next few days trying to figure out. Whose remains were they? How did they get here? How long had they been here? How did this person die?

From experience, she knew they would be able to get DNA from the bones, but that wasn't much use if they had no idea whose skeleton it was, and therefore no clue who to match the DNA with. Once they suspected it was some-body's relative, they could test the family. But now, at this point, it fell to other ways for Jo to try and work out who it was. Namely, the fractured clues at her feet; the scraps of clothing, what looked like a bit of a woman's floral blouse – perhaps only an old sheet used to wrap the body in – and what seemed to be a piece of jewellery on a chain. Both things she would explore along with anything else forensics might find. When the pathologist gave her a likely time frame she could rake through the photographs of missing persons around that time. After that, even the tiniest detail, which she might easily miss, could be the key to working out who this was. All that information-gathering would usually take weeks – which she didn't have. Indeed, there were only five days until her retirement, when she would have to relinquish her office, status, control, and have to hand this case over to someone who probably wouldn't care as much as she did.

Somebody who wouldn't work as hard as she would. Do whatever it took to get to the truth.

And her gut was telling her these remains belonged to a girl whose disappearance had haunted her for decades. She had absolutely no proof yet, but she knew she was going to have to find a way to hang on to the case for as long as she could.

As if reading her mind, Stan turned back to her. 'If the pathologist confirms it's murder, we'll need to set up a major incident room. You're finishing soon, aren't you? Did you want me to handle it? You don't want to be taking this on in your last week.' Stan squinted in the spring sunshine and reached for the sunglasses in his coat pocket.

'Yes, I suppose you're right, I'll give it some thought,' she replied as he frowned and slid the glasses over his Roman nose. 'There's not going to be a huge amount of leg work,' Jo reflected. 'It's going to be mostly historic, sitting at my desk, going through all the old missing persons files. I'll probably make a start, check it's all set up properly, then hand it over,' she said.

'Right,' he said. 'Well, let me know if you need any help.'

Jo smiled at Stan as he lingered next to her. He was tall and fair, with a kind face, and smiling blue eyes which reminded her of her father's. Strictly speaking, he wasn't her son-in-law yet, but with his and Megan's wedding looming later in the year, it wouldn't be long before he was family. She felt his eyes on her, and the heat of self-consciousness flushed her face. He was an easy-going chap, ambitious and focused, but essentially able to switch off at the end of his shift and go home to his fiancée and eighteen-month-old daughter, Phoebe: Jo's granddaughter. She was fond of Stan, he loved Megan, and he helped to bridge the gap between them. But the fact remained that everything Jo said or did would go straight back to Megan, who would be horrified to find out that her mother might be about to embroil herself in a cold case just five days before she was due to retire. Her daughter was counting down the days until Jo finished work and could finally concentrate on her wedding; on invitations and dress fittings and table plans and wine tasting. Conversations which, Jo knew, would no doubt end in them falling out, because Megan would be able to sense her mother's grief, rather than pleasure, over the gaping hole which her retirement would undoubtedly bring.

Conscious she was being observed by her future son-in-law, Jo leaned in and gave the shallow grave her attention. It was hard to make out what was leaves and debris, and what was clothing, but it looked like there were definitely strands of material wrapped around the collarbone.

'Nobody else has been here except you and Kate?' she asked, looking up at him.

'No,' Stan said, shaking his head.

'Forensics might be able to get some clothing fragments, it looks like there's something around there,' she said, pointing below the skull. 'But I doubt there will be any fluid or blood traces on them after all this time. Hopefully, they'll be able to work out what item of clothing they might have once been.' She pointed out the scraps of muddied fabric stuck to the blackened skeleton.

'I'll come and speak to the builders with you,' Jo said, standing up. 'Obviously, no further digging here, and no one encroaching on the scene. Kate needs to stay here and arrange cover when her shift finishes, make sure there's someone on duty, day and night. And keep a log of every-one who comes and goes, I don't want anyone contaminating the scene. Have you called CID?'

'Yes, they're on their way,' said Stan, frowning over at Kate, who had yet to find out she would be babysitting the shallow grave in the freezing cold.

'It's so exposed up here. This used to be my patch, but I haven't been up to the Tye for years,' said Jo wistfully. 'Let's go and chat to the guys who found it.'

They looked towards a police car parked next to a four-by-four, its boot open, with a man in a thick bomber jacket sitting on the bumper, drinking a cup of steaming liquid.

Jo squatted down again and leaned in. 'You're right, there's a skull injury. Are we sure the guys didn't hit it with the digger?' She looked up at the teeth of the JCB towering impatiently over the area now marked off with police tape.

'Apparently not. They didn't find it when they were digging. They were clearing a large area near it yesterday and must have dislodged the earth propping up the shallow grave, then the heavy rain caused it to give way. They saw the remains when they turned up this morning.'

'Make sure you take their shoe prints and DNA, they could have contaminated the scene already,' she said, the icy wind from the sea stinging her cheeks. She had forgotten how cold it was up here; all those nights as a young WPC in the seventies, she used to pound the pavements of Rottingdean and Saltdean on her own, until she could no longer feel her feet. She knew she wouldn't be popular with Kate for requesting she stay up here, but she didn't care. She would never ask a PC to do anything she hadn't done herself in the past, and Kate knew that.

Stan looked up at the water tower. 'My guess is whoever brought the body up here was someone who knows, or knew, the area, and maybe used to hang out here. This water tower hasn't been used for fifty years. I think I came up here one summer night as a teenager, to a party. No one can hear you, the nearest house is over a mile away in Telscombe.'

'Apart from Morgate House.' Jo nodded in the direction of the children's home, the vast symmetrical Victorian red-brick building which had, for a century, towered over the Saltdean Cliffs and looked to passing ships like a doll's house. 'It's abandoned now, because it's so close to the cliff edge, but it was up and running until the nineties. Forensics will have to tell us if these remains could date that far back.'

Jo half turned and looked out towards the sea, scanning the outline of Morgate House which was due for demolition any time soon. Chunks of chalky rock were known to occasionally fall onto the undercliff walk, and the front of the house was now teetering perilously close to the edge. The council lived in fear of the cliff falling away and sections of the house crashing onto the beach below, but before they could demolish it they had faced issues raising enough money. Now, they had finally done it.

As Jo turned back to the uncovered remains, the chain next to the skull caught her eye in the winter sunlight. She leaned in closer and realised it was a necklace. 'There's something that looks like jewellery just there, look, make a note of it in your book for forensics.' Jo pulled her mobile phone from her pocket and took a photograph of the mud-covered necklace. She looked over at Stan, who was frowning at her, as she returned her mobile to her pocket. 'Write down the names of anyone coming and going. We will need to widen the crime scene; they'll want to excavate for any other evidence, like shoes, or maybe a bag belonging to the victim. I'll check if there have been any desktop surveys of the area, if anything's been found which could have belonged to them,' said Jo, referring to the historical, geological and archeological records of the site where they stood, in case anything had been found over the past thirty years which could help the investigation.

'Do you have any idea who the victim might be?' said Stan, frowning.

Jo held his gaze, then looked back down at the bones

26

ingrained with decades of mud and dirt. A small clump of grit had fallen away from the necklace, revealing a St Christopher medallion, making her heart lurch.

'No,' Jo lied, not wanting to give away the fact that her brain was whirring with possibilities. 'I'm going to go back to the office and start looking through the missing persons files.'

She walked away, towards Constable Kate Harris, who was interviewing the man sitting on the tailgate of the four-by-four. He was wearing a mud-covered jacket with 'ARC Development' on the shoulder. 'I'm Superintendent Jo Hamilton, you called this in?' Jo said to the man. 'Thank you for letting us know. The remains are definitely human, so unfortunately you can't carry on digging on the site. I suggest everyone goes home for the day.'

The man frowned, before standing up, pulling a packet of tobacco from his pocket and rolling himself a cigarette. 'Fine with me,' he said, taking a gulp of coffee, 'but the boss won't be happy. How long's this going to take? We're months behind schedule already.'

Jo nodded. 'Could be anything from a few days to three or four weeks. We'll need to check a ten-square-metre radius, to look for other bones, or evidence nearby, shoes, anything physical that could be related to the scene,' she said, pulling the hood of her coat over her head. 'If you could keep this to yourselves we'd be grateful. As soon as the forensic tents go up, the press will get wind. But we need time to excavate the site before we release a statement.'

'Sure. So do you reckon someone was murdered and buried here?' said the man, taking a drag on his roll-up.

'We have no idea at this point. As I said, your discretion

is appreciated.' Jo looked out towards the sea, and watched as two Ford Fiestas skidded their way up the tracks towards the woodland where they stood.

'Here come forensics,' said Kate as Stan appeared next to her.

'Make sure you tell them about the jewellery, and one of you should be up there now, I don't want the site left unattended at any point. Got your notebook?'

Kate nodded.

'Good, write down the names of everyone here, and everyone from forensics, anyone who shows up. Got it?'

'Yes, ma'am,' said Kate without complaint, before turning to walk back up and pulling her hood over her head to shield herself from the wind.

Jo watched Kate go. She had come a long way since she'd started straight out of sixth form five years before. Jo had tried not to be too obvious about taking Kate under her wing, but she had seen a lot of potential in her and offered her advice when she could. Kate was always the first to volunteer and had an energy about her which reminded Jo of herself when she'd started. As a girl who wore her heart on her sleeve, Kate hadn't responded too well at first to Jo's advice that, however approachable and welcoming her male colleagues appeared to be, she couldn't show her emotions to any of them or she would never be taken seriously. If she wanted their respect, she needed to be tough, get stuck in, never complain, and always fess up if she ever made a mistake. But she had taken Jo's advice on board and, as a result, Kate was popular with colleagues and had a reputation for being someone to rely on in a storm. Jo was keen to see Kate fulfil her potential and hand over the baton, and had recently recommended her for promotion to sergeant; she had been hoping to see her get it before she left.

Jo turned to Stan, who was watching the forensics team struggling to park in the mud. 'I'll head back and make a start setting this up. Call me as soon as pathology are done. Can you tell them I'll need to speak to them today about decomposition and a guesstimate for the timeline? Are you okay to brief them and keep me updated on their progress, if I take the squad car? I'll send someone to relieve Kate when I get back, and you can get a lift with her. Okay?'

Jo turned away, desperate to get down to storage at the station, find the archived missing persons files and start doing some digging. Her notebooks – which she had kept religiously from her first day on the force, in 1973 – would also be in storage and could have some memory triggers to help her.

As she walked off in the rain, away from Stan and Kate, the familiar feeling crept up her neck that she was about to be talked about. With only five days until her retirement, Stan was probably wishing, for Megan's sake, that the remains had been found just a few days later. She could imagine him pulling a beer out of the fridge after walking through the door of their terraced house in Hove, while Megan tended to their dinner, content to be a stay-at-home mum in a way that she never had been. 'How long have those remains been there?' Stan would say, as Megan raised her eyes to heaven. 'Twenty or maybe thirty years? And they turn up one week before your mum finishes. She's gonna find it hard to hand over this one.'

Jo climbed into the driver's seat and started up the

engine; it was a bright day, but the force of the wind from the coast made the landscape feel hostile. She pulled out onto the coast road, and soon found herself passing the large shadow of Morgate House. Drawn in, she indicated and turned onto Morgate Lane on a whim, bumping along the broken track which led to the padlocked gates of the now derelict children's home.

Jo pulled up, turned off the engine and slowly opened her car door. The wind was whistling in her ears as the waves broke on the pebbled beach below. As it picked up pace, it rushed through the broken windows, making a screaming sound. Jo closed her eyes, and pulled her coat around her, running her hands over the gate and the chain which rattled in the wind.

'Will they let us stay together, in the same room?' In her mind's eye, Jo looked down to see Daisy Moore crying as she clutched her sister's hand, tears leaving tracks in the dirt on her face.

The girls were a beautiful pair, both with wispy blonde hair, and grey-blue eyes. At only six years old Daisy's locks reached her shoulders, where they fell in baby curls, whereas Holly, at eight years old, had hers cut into a short bob. She was mature beyond her years, acting almost as a mother would towards her child. 'I won't let them separate us, Daisy, I promise,' she had said, pulling her sister into her.

It was forty years since the night of the fire, but leaving the girls here at Morgate House still haunted her dreams. She had watched that night when Morgate House came to life, the dull porch light flicking on, as the front door opened and a grey-haired woman appeared at the entrance. Jo had found herself moving in front of the girls instinctively, as if to stop Mrs Price taking them away, knowing that once she handed them over, their childhoods would be lost forever.

And she had been right. She hadn't seen Mrs Price again for ten years, not until one month after Jo's return from her career break, in the spring of 1985, when the station had received the call to say Holly Moore was missing. She had driven up to Morgate House, her heart filled with dread, to take a statement from Lorna Price. Holly was always running away, she'd said, sipping at her china teacup in their annex at the side of the main house, while her husband read his newspaper by the fire. She didn't want to cause the police any trouble, she'd said, but thought she'd better call to let them know Holly hadn't returned. She'd seemed irritated by Jo's concern over the fact they'd taken two days to call it in. Valuable time during which they could have been looking for the missing girl, Jo had pointed out.

Lorna Price had glared at her. 'If I called you every time one of these girls didn't come back, you'd be up here every day.'

Jo had returned to the station, full of outrage, and flagged it up with her supervisor, DI Carl Webber, who hadn't seemed a great deal more concerned than Mrs Price. Only when she had begged and pleaded, and threatened to go over his head, had he eventually agreed to put up some Missing Person posters, and sent two guys to do some door-to-door enquiries round Saltdean. But nothing had come of it, and Mr and Mrs Price were never held to account for their delay in reporting the girl missing. Gemma Smith had been right, nobody cared about the Morgate girls. Least of all Carl Webber.

Jo turned away at the painful memory and walked to the

edge of the cliff. She stared down at the beach below, her head throbbing as she watched her younger self cordon off the body of Gemma Smith in 1975. The rush of ice-cold wind in her face felt exactly as it had done that day, as she tried to hammer stakes into the pebbled beach, watched by members of the public, drawn like magnets to the bloated body of the girl with the long black hair, her dead eyes fixed on Jo.

As the memory made her dizzy, Jo stepped back, her feet unsettling a stone. It rolled over the edge of the two-hundred-foot drop and, after a long silence, cracked like a bullet onto the rocks below. Jo felt her stomach tie in knots. Finally, she had been given a chance to prove what she had always suspected about Morgate House: that the children in its care were neglected and that if the proprietors, Lorna and Geoff Price, were still alive, they needed to be questioned in more depth about the disappearances of Gemma Smith and Holly Moore.

Jo had always known in her gut that Gemma hadn't killed herself; the girl had said very little to Jo in the police car on the way back to the children's home, but she could tell she had spirit. She was angry about Morgate House but she didn't seem depressed, more indignant and ready to get away and fight her way in life. However, as a twenty-year-old female police constable, Jo's suspicions had been ignored. But if it was the body of Holly Moore on the Tye, and the dent in her skull was trauma, Jo would have the proof she needed that there had been foul play involved in Holly's disappearance, which could pave the way to open up an investigation into the death of both girls.

But time was against her, Jo would have to achieve the

impossible; move a mountain to get enough evidence to have their cases reopened, potentially as a double murder inquiry, and there was no way she could do that in a week. For forty years the death of Gemma and the disappearance of Holly had troubled her, more than anything else in her illustrious career, but she feared that they had discovered Holly's body too late. Still, she had to try.

Jo returned to her car, glancing back at the cliff edge as she started her engine. The apparently solid rock face was falling away, out of her control, soon to be lost forever – like her chance to put right some of the terrible wrongs that had consumed her all these years.

Chapter Two

Gemma

November 1975

Gemma Smith sat on the cold leather seat of the police car, watching in the rear-view mirror as the woman who'd caught her stealing food glared at her as they pulled away from Rottingdean High Street. Gemma hung her head; she could still feel the woman's long fingers digging into her shoulder like an eagle's claw, pulling her back across the shop threshold as she tried to hurry away. In a panic, she had tried to make a run for it, but the woman had clung on harder, shouting at her husband to help her, pulling at Gemma's jacket and releasing its concealed contents.

Gemma had looked up, her face burning despite the cold weather, to see a smattering of faces around her, all staring intently as her jacket gave way and four packets of biscuits fell onto the floor of the shop. She had watched them tumble in slow motion, their wrappers splitting and their contents breaking and scattering all over the ground.

Instinctively, she had bent down and started desperately picking them up. Her heart hammering hard, burying her head, knowing all the eyes were on her, and wishing the ground would swallow her up. A hand had pulled her back up, and dragged her along towards the back of the shop.

'Come with me, I'm calling the police, I'm sick of you kids raiding my shop,' the man had shouted in her face, his breath smelling of his morning coffee, as he dragged her to his smoky, dark office at the back of the grocery store.

She had sat on a wooden chair, staring at her hands, as the shopkeeper dialled the operator and asked for the local police station. Shame flooded her body as the slim man, with spectacles on a string around his neck, glared at her as he waited for the call to be put through. She couldn't look at him, she stared at his desk, covered in invoices from suppliers and a printout from the cash and carry. His calculator acted as a paperweight, and there was a petty cash tin to one side. He was a hard-working man, she thought, who got up early in the bitter cold to take deliveries and stock the shelves of a shop he had probably run all his life. She hated having to steal from him but she had no choice.

Finally, the policewoman had arrived, and taken a statement from the man, as Gemma sat listening, watching her pen scratching across her notebook at a painfully slow pace. He had known Gemma was up to something, he said, she had lingered in the shop, he knew she was one of the Morgate kids. They were always coming in and thieving stuff and he'd had enough.

'I'm giving you a warning, this time,' the policewoman – who had introduced herself as Jo – said from the front of the blue police car as she turned onto the seafront. 'The shop owner didn't want to press charges. But you might not be so lucky next time. Maybe, if you tell me a little bit about Morgate House, I can help you. Are they not feeding you?'

'Lucky?' Gemma echoed, with a scoff. She had looked out of the window at the thrashing sea. Lucky was not a word Gemma had felt applied to her very often during her young life. When she was seven years old, the police had arrived at her house after a concerned neighbour had called them. They escorted her to a children's hospital, where every bruise, burn and cut on her body was counted, measured and photographed. Various adults had asked how she had got the injuries. With her mother standing right there, she was too scared to say. But the evidence was obvious. She was taken into emergency foster care straight away. She never saw her mother or her baby brother again. Despite what her mother did to her, she missed her family terribly; she had been part of a home then, however broken; she'd felt like she belonged. She'd had a baby to look after, she was needed, loved by someone. She gave her baby brother milk, baths, and sang him to sleep. She was always very protective towards him; if she could see her mum and step-dad kicking off, she would get the baby out of the way and take the punishment herself instead.

She had then spent two weeks with a foster family who showed her that she was not the naughty child her parents always said she was. For a few precious days, she was able to play at being part of a family. It gave her an idea of what life could – should – be like for her and her brother. Having family days out, given proper meals, around a table, being asked how your day was. Simple things. She had built up hope that this family was nice, that they might keep her, that her baby brother could maybe one day join them. Then, after a fortnight, a social worker had picked her up from school instead of her foster mother, with her belongings in a bag on the back seat of the car.

'I'm taking you to Morgate House,' she'd said abruptly. 'You were too much for them.'

For the next week she had wracked her brains about what she had done or said wrong. Until she realised that she had wet her bed on the second night. They had lied to her face, pretended it didn't matter, changed the sheets and put her back to bed. They had made her feel that they liked her, that she could trust them, then pulled the rug from under her. At least her mother was honest about her dislike for her.

After that, her trust in adults evaporated. There had been dozens of them coming and going over the years: police, social workers, teachers. People claiming they would help her, if she would only trust them – before disappearing from her life forever. People like the policewoman taking her back to Morgate now.

Gemma said nothing, looking out of the window at the rain. There was no point speaking; nobody really cared, nothing ever changed.

'The owner of the shop says the Morgate House kids are in a lot, stealing from him. Do they not feed you over there?' the policewoman persisted.

Gemma watched the sea, her stomach grumbling. She felt tears sting her eyes at the thought of walking back in with no food for the little ones.

'You know, it's rude not to answer someone when they ask you a question,' the woman said, pulling up outside Morgate House.

'What's the point?' Gemma opened the door to get out, then fixed her green eyes on the woman. 'You think you care, but you don't. You'll go home to your family and forget about me. Everyone wants us to disappear. Well, maybe one day I will.' The girl had crossed her arms and glared out of the car window furiously, then stormed off towards the house when Jo opened the door to let her out.

Mrs Price was standing on the doorstep of the annex, waiting for them, glaring at Gemma as if she were something the cat dragged in.

'What on earth have you been up to now?' she spat, as Gemma walked past.

'Leave me alone,' she said, as the woman started to apologise to the policewoman for Gemma's behaviour. It was the usual empty words. 'Do come in. Can I get you a warm drink? I'm so sorry, she's completely out of control, we don't know what to do with her. We have tried everything. What? No food? Of course they have food, shall I show you the kitchen? These girls are here because they are disturbed; no foster family can cope with them because they lie and steal. It's dreadful, I feel so badly for them. But there is a limit to what we can do.'

Lorna Price dripped with charm when she wanted to. She was plump and well turned out, with a neat bob, and cashmere cardigans that smelt of fabric conditioner. She looked the picture of innocence and talked for England, in stark contrast to her husband who never spoke. Geoff Price sat permanently in his armchair reading his newspaper, with his hearing aid turned down so he didn't have to listen to his wife's wittering. He had a lazy eye, and you never knew if he was staring at his newspaper or whichever of the girls in his care was being given a dressing-down in the annex by his wife.

As Gemma crept down the hallway, she could hear the little ones scurrying about, looking out of the window at the police car. They would be hoping she had something

38

for them. Their little eyes wide with anticipation, their bellies rumbling with hunger. She couldn't face them, not yet.

She went into her bedroom and closed the door, desperate to shut the world out. She looked around the room she shared with Eve, trying to find some comfort, some feeling that she was safe now. That she was home. But there was none. Only peeling paint on the walls, sheets hanging from the curtain railing, and mattresses with no covers.

She put her music on loud, tried to drown out the panic flooding her senses. She lay on her bed, but when she closed her eyes, she saw the shopkeepers' faces, staring at her, felt the heat of the shame flooding her body again. She turned the music up louder, drowning out the voices in her head, telling her she was nothing. Nobody. As tears began to well up, she took off her top and looked at herself in the long mirror.

She wasn't showing yet, but her body felt totally different already; her breasts were swollen, she was exhausted and she had a constant burning indigestion. She ran her hands over her stomach. She hadn't felt sick for the first few weeks, but she did now. She held her tummy, willing her baby to give her strength. She had wanted a child when she had a home, and money in the bank, all the stability she craved. That time wasn't now, and she was terrified of the uncertainty that lay ahead. She just needed to stay strong, focus on the thought of her little baby brother, how much she had loved caring for him. His tiny feet and hands, giving him milk, soothing him. She would find a way to cope, give her baby the life and love she never had.

She just had to find the words to tell *him*.

But to do that, she had to find him and over the past two

weeks he had vanished. Usually he would pull up next to her in his car as she wandered around at night, and they would go for a drive. They would talk and he would give her money, and buy her food. But since she had found out she was pregnant, she hadn't seen him in her usual haunts, despite staying out late in the bitter cold. She was tired all the time, she craved warmth, but she craved him more. She desperately needed him to comfort her, to tell her it was okay.

She knew where he lived. She had been through the glovebox of his car once, when he had stopped to get some food for them, and found a payslip with his address on, which she had put in her pocket. She would have to risk going there. Maybe his patch had changed and he no longer covered her area. Maybe he had been looking for her and they'd missed each other. She couldn't think about the alternative – that he hadn't wanted to see her. That he'd found someone else. She couldn't bear that, not now.

Suddenly, the door was flung open, banging against the wall and making her jump. She was only in her bra and trousers. She grabbed her top, knowing it would be Phillip Price on the warpath.

'Mum's furious. She's had the police lecturing her that she needs to feed you all more.'

'Get out, Phillip,' she said, turning round.

He walked up to her and grabbed her by the shoulders, pressing his hand into her face, his fingers over her mouth. He backed her into her wardrobe; his body was pushing against her tummy and it was hurting her.

'You need to be careful,' he said. 'Or you'll end up getting hurt.'

'You're the one who's going to get hurt,' she said, using

all her strength to push him away. 'My boyfriend wouldn't like you putting your hands all over me.'

'What boyfriend?' he said, grabbing her wrist tight, just as her friend Eve appeared in the doorway. 'Who'd want you?' he shouted into her face.

'He's a copper, and it's getting serious, so you're going to have to show me a bit of respect from now on,' Gemma spat.

'Bullshit,' he said, glaring at her.

Gemma caught Eve's look of shock from the doorway. 'Is it bullshit, Phillip? Do you really want to take that risk? Now get out so I don't have to tell him you burst in on me getting undressed.'

'Tell who? What's his name?'

Gemma glared at Phillip as he hesitated, then turned and walked out of the room, shoving Eve out of his way and slamming the door behind him.

Chapter Three

Daisy

Daisy Moore pedalled along Brighton seafront, the cold saltwater air biting at her cheeks as a helicopter rumbled loudly overhead, hovering over Saltdean Tye for a few minutes before disappearing. However bitterly cold the day was, the thrashing sea was always a source of comfort for her. She had saved up for her aquamarine Dutch bicycle for a year and loved it more than anything she had ever owned. After having her last bike stolen, and the police not being remotely interested in looking for it, she had invested in a padlock that cost nearly as much as her new bicycle. She would fly past the drivers stuck in nose-to-tail traffic on the seafront road from Kemptown to Saltdean, propelling herself across the beautiful Sussex landscape under her own steam, the wild and exhilarating sea to her right, the rolling South Downs to her left. She could leave home in the shadow of sadness, and arrive feeling calmed, her lungs full of sea air, able to take on the highs and lows of her day as a care assistant. Only for a moment – when she passed the pitiful remains of Morgate House on the cliff edge at Saltdean – did her heart lull, the memory of the policewoman taking her there with her sister still vivid some forty years later. But she would press on, breathe deeply, pedal harder, the exertion and the biting cold forcing the past to

42

the back of her mind. She would try to push back the thought that she was torturing herself by passing the place which had caused them both so much pain, every day when she went to work. But she knew that, as long as her sister was still missing, she couldn't leave; she couldn't abandon Holly.

One day, she told herself, when she had the answers she so desperately needed, she would ride further than the coast road; she would load up a backpack, cycle down to Newhaven and take the ferry to Dieppe. One day, when she had the strength, and the money and the courage, she would leave this place behind her and cycle round Europe on an adventure. Until then, she would do her best to keep going, ignore her sadness, and give all of herself to the job she loved. Immerse herself in caring for her residents who needed her, who were lonely and scared of death, who couldn't wash, dress or feed themselves.

She spent her days giving out medications, changing catheter bags, massaging people who couldn't move, and doing exercises with people who could. She would sit down and listen when people were lonely, play bingo and dance with them when they were sad. The work was so physically demanding, she didn't have time to think; it was an escape, they loved her, and she loved them for making her feel wanted. Some of them were difficult, but most of them were as content as they could be, knowing they were at the end of their lives, and making the most of the time they had left. They saw Downside as home, and treated her like a granddaughter. Though some were bad-tempered, it was usually for good reason. Most of the residents treated her with love and made a fuss of her on her birthday and special occasions, all of which made her feel part of a family; something she desperately craved.

Daisy pulled up outside Downside Nursing Home, pushed her bike up to the sheltered railings, and clicked the padlock into place. She lived in fear of her beloved bike being stolen; it was like a friend, who gave her the freedom and peace of mind she desperately needed. She made her way up to the entrance, and punched in her PIN. The doors slid open to reveal two of her colleagues rushing past with the usual paraphernalia: bedpans, towels and sheets. They looked tired and weary. She could sense immediately that it had been a tough night. There was a tension in the air, their faces were pale and drawn, and the corridor to the staff room was quiet, meaning everyone was busy. Some mornings, the atmosphere was light, she was met with smiles and warm welcomes. But not today. They had probably had a couple of medical emergencies in the night, with the paramedics being called in – or worse, not turning up for hours – possibly even a resident passing away. She preferred the night shift, because people slept through their pain, and she had terrible trouble sleeping at home anyway, so she may as well be working. But the morning often brought problems the night had been storing up, and come 5 a.m. chaos would ensue.

'Morning!'

Daisy turned to see her colleague Amber making a cup of tea in the kitchen off the main corridor.

'Cuppa?'

Daisy was very fond of Amber; like most of the staff she was genuine, and didn't suffer fools gladly. She ran herself ragged and expected the same of everyone else. She had dyed bright-red hair worn in tight plaits, enormous bosoms and an infectious cackle.

'Sure, thanks,' said Daisy. 'How was your shift?'

'Not great, Mary had a bad night, she's got a nasty UTI and a temperature. We're waiting for the paramedics to arrive and hopefully take her to hospital. How was your date?' Amber raised her eyebrows and leaned in.

Daisy pursed her lips and shook her head.

'He wasn't Jules, eh?' said Amber, in reference to Daisy's ex. Daisy felt her eyes lingering on her, as she felt her cheeks flush. 'I saw him the other night,' Amber teased. 'He's still single and asked after you. You guys belong together.'

Daisy smiled, and bit down on her lip. 'He wants a family, and I'm too old for that,' she said, making light of an issue which had, over time, torn apart their seven-year relationship.

'Rubbish, you can always adopt. Hundreds of kids out there need a home,' Amber retorted, with no idea about Daisy's childhood spent in Morgate House Children's Home.

'Maybe,' said Daisy, who had always been afraid to commit to Jules in any real way, a feeling of panic creeping over her whenever talk of marriage or babies came up. What if they split up? she would ask him quietly. What if something happened to her? What if she ended up leaving her own child alone in the world, the way she had been left?

'How's Olive?' asked Daisy, in an attempt to change the subject.

'Olive has been very uncomfortable in the night, they had to call the paramedics out, and they suggested moving

45

her to a hospice to manage her pain, so I've called the palliative care team to come and have a chat with her.'

Daisy's stomach lurched. She cared for all her residents, but Olive was her favourite. Aged ninety, Olive had been at Downside for twelve years – for respite care, in the beginning, and more recently as a full-time resident – and was part of the reason Daisy had become a care-worker in the first place. After barely getting five O-Levels at Saltdean High School, Daisy had spent twenty miserable years doing shop and waitressing work, and getting nowhere. The hours dragged, she was bad at it, the pay was terrible, and she had ended up in despair at where her life was going. Then, when she was thirty-six, her adoptive mother, Felicity, had become so unwell she was unable to take care of her any more, and she'd gone into Downside Nursing Home. She would go in to visit Felicity, and while she slept she would chat to the other residents and the care-home staff. Daisy had immediately felt at home; she loved old people, she watched the women caring for the residents, and despite how incredibly hard it was, they seemed to love their work. She had always felt awkward with her peers, but older people she found calming to be around; they had lived their lives, they weren't trying to pretend to be anything other than who they were.

And now, she had found a real friend in Olive. She would sit and chat to her after she'd finished her shift sometimes, and as Olive didn't seem to have much family, apart from a son who visited occasionally, she seemed glad of the company. It was Olive who had suggested she apply for a job that had come up at Downside as a trainee care assistant, when she was thirty-nine.

That was seven years ago, and it had been a lifeline;

Olive knew that as soon as Daisy's adoptive mother passed away, the council would kick her out, and she would essentially be homeless. The starting wage for a care assistant wasn't much, but it was enough to rent a room in a shared house. She was at work most of the time, and they fed her at Downside as well, saving her a lot of money. In the winter months she did overtime to stay warm, meaning that if she couldn't afford to do a weekly shop and also have the heating on in her room, at least she could survive.

Daisy placed her bag in her locker, washed her hands, put on her gloves and apron and made her way straight to Olive's room. She had half an hour before her shift started, so she should be able to sit with her for a little while and hold her hand. She felt her heart racing, worrying about what she would find when she reached her friend. The word 'uncomfortable' was widely used in the nursing profession as a nod to the fact someone was in a lot of pain. Even her loveliest patients could turn on her when they were suffering, and it was something that touched a nerve and affected her deeply. Not least because she never wanted anyone to feel the way that she had felt as a child at Morgate House, lonely and afraid.

In all the years she was there, she was shown no kindness from Lorna and Geoff Price, or their son, Phillip. All the children in their care were dumped there by the police or social services and left to fend for themselves. There was a terrible lack of food, and all the children were hungry; often her sister, Holly, would steal food to feed the younger children. The house was run-down; there were no curtains, no cosy blankets, no privacy. They were never bought clothes or shoes that fitted properly, and so the children at the local school would laugh at them and tease them about being dirty and disheveled. They were outsiders at school, never invited to parties, or to people's houses, and she lived for the free hot lunch at school, which was often the only proper food she got. She dreaded the holidays, when there were no school meals, and she relied on finding bags of left-over chips or being given something Holly had stolen. The winter was the worst. Mr and Mrs Price only ever turned on the heating in their annex next to the house, and the cast-iron radiators in the children's dormitories would stay as cold as ice.

She often used Holly's coat as a blanket on cold nights, when they would cuddle up together, and talk about their mother, and the happier times. But the Prices' son, Phillip, would often lock Holly in her room at night, so she couldn't roam the streets, meaning that the younger children didn't eat at all. On those nights, Daisy would get terrible tummy ache from the pain of being separated from Holly. She and the other children would cuddle up together, and Daisy would write letters to her sister. She would post them through the cracks in the floorboards, hoping that somehow the mice under the floorboards would carry them to her. She never wanted anyone to feel as alone as she had felt on those terrible, never-ending nights; it was what made her give everything to her job.

Daisy quietly opened the door to Olive's bedroom and peered in, not wanting to disturb her. Olive's eyes were closed, but somehow, even when she was in bed, and in pain, she still managed to look effortlessly glamorous. She had a photograph by her bed of herself as a young woman, working on the farm where she grew up, sitting on a tractor, a beaming smile on her beautiful face, her long dark hair tied back with a headscarf. Long soft waves which were now cropped to her shoulders, but still tied back from her face with one of her brightly-coloured signature silk scarves.

Daisy went to walk away, anxious not to disturb her.

'Hello, dear, come in,' Olive said faintly.

Daisy turned back and smiled, slowly walking over to Olive's bed, and sitting down on the chair next to it. She took her hand and squeezed it. Olive gazed at her; she was wearing a white nightie, and her grey hair framed her pretty face.

'I think it's time to go, Daisy.'

'Don't say that, Olive. We can give you something for the pain.'

'I woke up at five o'clock and I thought I was dying, and I was happy. I just want to go now and be with Samuel.'

'Samuel?' said Daisy, starting as she realised Olive's son was standing in the doorway.

Daisy stared at him for a moment, as two figures appeared behind him.

'I had a dream that I was back at Bletchley, Glenn Miller was playing "Moonlight Serenade", do you know it?' said Olive, her brown eyes sparkling.

'Um, I'm not sure.' Daisy frowned gently.

'I can tell you, a great many people have danced and fallen in love to that song. We used to dance to it, it's so fabulous. If I close my eyes, I can still feel his arms around me.'

'Olive?'

Daisy and Olive stopped and looked over to the door, where two ladies were standing, smiling at Olive warmly.

'My name is Julia, and this is Helen, we're with the

palliative care team at the Royal Sussex Hospital. How are you feeling?'

Daisy stood up and moved aside, letting the women through so they could sit by Olive's bed. She felt herself hovering awkwardly, but couldn't bring herself to leave. It was another twenty minutes before her shift started, and she wanted to stay in case Olive needed her.

Daisy had woken up that morning with a sense of foreboding. She had been startled awake by a familiar dream that returned to her all too often: she and her sister Holly, in the bath together as children, as they often were on a Friday night, when their father was at the pub. They were happily splashing each other, with their mother singing to them quietly, feeling relaxed and knowing that their father would not be back for hours. Then, as it always did in her dream, the water started to swirl, slowly at first, then faster and faster, until it rose above their heads. She tried to grab hold of her sister, who would be sucked under as she desperately tried to hold on, before she disappeared out of sight. She would tear at the plughole until her fingers bled, then wake crying out her sister's name – as she had done that morning. She had dragged herself into the shower, trying to wash the images of her sister away, but the feeling of foreboding hadn't left her, and still hung heavily over her now.

'How are you, Olive?' said one of the women, settling herself in the chair next to Olive's bed.

Olive looked at her son. 'When the pain comes, it doesn't let up and I don't cope too well,' she said, wincing. 'I wasn't very brave this morning, I'm afraid.'

Amber appeared at the door with a jug of water which she placed on the table across Olive's bed.

'She woke up feeling very uncomfortable and anxious. She was asking for her family, so I called her son, Charlie, who arrived shortly after.'

'Can't you give her something stronger for the pain?' asked Charlie.

Daisy looked over at Olive's son, who was sitting in the armchair across from her bed. She had spoken to him a few times; he was in his late sixties, Daisy guessed, with a full head of hair still – despite his age – and blue eyes that sparkled when he spoke. He was well built, and Daisy imagined he had been very good-looking when he was younger.

'We can, but we'd need to transfer her to St Catherine's, which is the local hospice. They can put her on a morphine drip there.'

Charlie nodded. 'Is it the cancer that's causing the pain?' he asked, looking over at Amber. 'I mean, I know it's a burning pain in her chest – she says it feels like a blockage – what is it?'

'It's inflammation building up in the stomach because of the tumour,' said Amber. 'Unfortunately, the doctors can't operate because Olive has a severe aortic stenosis and she couldn't survive the anaesthetic,' she explained, turning to address the women from the palliative care team.

'The hospice will probably be a good move for now,' said Julia, turning back to Olive. 'They can support you through a bad period of time when you are in a lot of pain. They will be able to give you an infusion of pain relief, so that you're kept comfortable all the time. I'll make some calls and see when we can get you transferred, but it will hopefully be in the morning.'

'Is Jo coming?' Olive looked over at her son.

'Yes. I know something's come up at work, but she'll do her best to come today. Megan is coming in after lunch, she's just got to drop Phoebe at nursery.' Charlie stood up, moving in closer and rubbing his mother's hand. 'Daisy, are you able to sit with Mum for a bit while I make a couple of calls?'

'Of course,' she said. 'My shift starts in fifteen minutes but I'm sure they'll let me stay.'

'I'll be back by then, thanks,' he said, leaning across the bed, stroking his mother's hair. 'Won't be long, Mum.'

Olive's eyes were closed as Daisy took Julia's seat and Olive's hand.

'I'd like to see Jo,' Olive said quietly. 'I worry about her. She works too hard.'

'She'll be here, I'm sure. I think Charlie is calling her now.' Daisy sat back in her chair and her gaze fell on Olive's television which was on, in the corner of the room, with the sound turned down. *BBC Breakfast News* was showing images of a helicopter over Saltdean Tye. People in white forensics suits were walking to and from an area where a large white tent was being erected.

BBC BREAKING NEWS: Human remains found

Daisy's heart began to hammer as she read the tickertape headlines travelling across the screen.

Human remains discovered on Saltdean Tye
    Officers from Sussex Police and forensics are on the scene
    Statement expected shortly

Olive started to cough, and Daisy turned away from the television. 'Let me give you some water, Olive,' she said, trying not to look back at the news item as she felt nausea rising in her guts.

'I want to go, I want to be with Samuel.'

'Who is Samuel, Olive?' Daisy asked.

Olive turned to her as her eyes filled with tears. 'There's a book in my bedside table, in the bottom drawer, can you get it for me?' she asked.

Daisy nodded, reached down and lifted the book out, then put it on the bed next to Olive.

'Open it,' whispered Olive.

Carefully, Daisy opened the leather-bound book. It was a scrapbook filled with photographs of Olive and her children in their younger years – but also what looked to Daisy like various newspaper cuttings.

'Flip to the back,' instructed Olive.

Daisy spotted an envelope glued to the back page of the notebook, and slowly lifted the flap. Inside was a black-and-white photograph of a girl, laughing, her long hair tied back with a silk scarf, and next to her a very handsome man in a jacket with wings on the lapel, turned sideways and facing her, smiling.

'Is this you?' Daisy asked, as Olive nodded weakly.

'Yes, a long time ago now.'

Daisy slowly turned the picture over and read the inscription.

1944, Bletchley Park.

Chapter Four

Olive

Bletchley Park, January 1944

'Bletchley, next stop, Bletchley.'

The crowded train slowed as it neared the station, and Olive turned to smile at the brown-eyed, mousy-haired girl sitting on the floor next to her who had introduced herself as Lorna Sanders on the platform at Euston.

After overhearing the girl ask the guard if she was on the right platform for Bletchley, Olive had immediately felt drawn to her, suspecting she too had received a terse telegram telling her to: *Report to Station X at Bletchley Park, Buckinghamshire, on 12th January 1944.*

Olive had sidled up next to her as they both stood nervously on the packed platform in London, clutching their luggage. Olive's knees were trembling – from the cold or excitement, she didn't know which – and she had observed the other girl out of the corner of her eye as the train pulled to a stop on the tracks in front of them. She hadn't yet spoken a word to her, but she already knew they were as different as night and day.

'Hello, are you for Bletchley too?' Olive had leaned in, raising her voice so as to be heard over the cacophony of the station. For a moment Olive thought the girl hadn't heard her, until she slowly turned and stared back at her, with eyes blotchy from crying.

'Yes, I am,' the girl had said quietly, nodding.

Olive had held out her hand. 'I'm Olive, pleased to meet you.'

'Lorna,' the girl had sniffed, shaking Olive's outstretched hand.

'Shall we sit together on the train?' Olive had asked eagerly.

Lorna was smartly dressed and, unlike Olive's jitterbug feet, she stood still and firm as a chess piece. Lorna's fingernails, wrapped around the handle of her suitcase, were long and neatly painted, a pale pink colour. There was no sign of the cracked and dry skin Olive had suffered since she was a child, spending every day as she did outside, helping her father with the pigs in the wind, sleet and rain of winter – or the long, hot days of summer. Lorna's skin was pale, and as smooth as freshly rolled pastry, her cheeks and calves as plump as a prize piglet.

In contrast, Olive, named after her father's Mediterranean blood, had light brown eyes, long wavy, chestnut hair, and skin made for the sun – a shade of dark, rich Brazil nut in the summer, and still faintly tanned through the winter. Olive was made to be out in the sunshine; she loved existing in shorts and vests, spending long August evenings riding across the Sussex Downs on her boyfriend's motorbike. She hated the winter, the endless dark days, the insufferable cold and the rain. Forced to be outside cleaning out the pig pens, she was permanently cold, and however much she ate, she could never keep any fat on her bones. Though she liked her pretty name, her family never used it, and instead continued to refer to her as 'Stick' – the nickname which had plagued her since the age of three.

She still had the body of a teenage boy, something which had barely changed with the onset of puberty and loathsome periods. Not for a single day had she ever dressed as beautifully as Lorna in her pressed white blouse, long navy skirt, and soft wool cardigan, none of which would have been easy to come by in wartime. Her mousy hair tumbled over her shoulders in loose curls, which looked as if they had been set that morning, and her plump lips bore the palest pink lipstick. Olive had imagined Lorna standing in front of the mirror in her pink bedroom, trying on her travelling outfit while her mother sat on her bed, commenting encouragingly, helping her pack for her adventure.

Olive's own mother had barely spoken to her since Olive had told her she'd answered a newspaper advert for dispatch riders to help with the war effort, then received her telegram telling her to go to Bletchley Park exactly one week later. Olive had sat in her bedroom and stared down at the small slip of paper in disbelief, a feeling of excitement and nerves fluttering down her arms to her very fingertips. She had never known anything other than her village school and life on the family pig farm in Sussex. Rising at 6 a.m. for feeding time, mucking out six hundred pigs all day in the freezing cold, including at the weekends; evenings spent bagging up potatoes or sugar beet they had grown to sell to the local greengrocer. She loved the pigs, they were very affectionate, very much like a dog in their nature – and not dirty at all, as people mistakenly believed. But like her mother, she longed to get away from the harshness and relentlessness of it all.

Her mother, Sally, hated being a farmer's wife, and made no effort to hide it. They had moved from a Surrey suburb to the Sussex countryside, to pursue her father's dream of owning a farm. Her terraced home in Surbiton had been her pride and joy, along with her coffee mornings, and bridge evenings with her friends. She had been very house proud, and spent most of her life cleaning, trying to erase the smell of pigswill and urine-drenched hay from her home. As a child, if Olive came back to the house for a break from the cold and rain, she would be sent away again. Sally's desperation to keep her muddy children and husband out of her cosy and clean farmhouse was obsessive, but over the years she had slowly begun to give up – on the house, and her family – and retreat to her bedroom for hours on end, under the guise of having a migraine.

'I love your headscarf,' said Lorna, as the train rattled along. 'I've never seen anything like it. Where is it from?'

'Paris, I think. My mother gave it to me,' Olive replied, looking out of the train carriage window and remembering the dark, drab morning when her mother had called her to her bedroom.

Olive had hovered at the door nervously – nobody was allowed into her mother's room when she had one of her headaches – but for once she was beckoning Olive in.

'Come in,' she had said, her voice slow and slurred.

Olive had cautiously pushed the door open. The room smelt of perfume and cigarettes, the air was thick, all the windows were closed, and Olive coughed, her chest tightening with the contrast of being outside on the farm all day.

'Sit down,' her mother had said, patting the covers next to her.

Sheepishly, Olive had approached the bed. Her mother was smoking a cigarette and playing Louis Armstrong on the gramophone. Olive had never been invited into this space before, and her eyes darted curiously around the room.

Sally had looked up at Olive, her eyes bloodshot and matching the lipstick she had put on her narrow lips – mostly absorbed by the cigarette butts in the ashtray beside her. 'I want you to have these, Olive.' She had handed Olive a pile of colourful headscarves, all bundled up together like snakes. 'My father gave them to my mother; every time he docked somewhere he would buy her a headscarf, because she wanted to travel and see the world, but she never did . . .' Her voice had trailed away. 'She never did. Just like me. I wanted to travel, but I got tied down, Olive. I want you to have these, and every time you look at them you must think of me, and my failures, and make a promise to yourself. To live. To stay independent. Marriage is always sold to us as the ultimate prize for women. But it's not, we've been sold a pup, Olive. It only benefits men. They can still live after they are married. We cannot. Promise me you will travel, wear these every day, and go to Paris, and Milan, and Berlin. Promise me,' she had said, reaching out and squeezing Olive's hand so much it hurt.

'I promise, Mama.' As her mother held out the bundle, Olive had carefully, somewhat reluctantly, taken them. They were light as a feather, but she had immediately felt the weight of the responsibility of their possession.

Her mother hated the farm, but despite the long, hard days, and the unrewarding pay, Olive's father and brother, Michael, loved it. Father worked tirelessly; if he was poorly he wouldn't take a day off or rest, he would only work harder. He had hated life as an accountant in London, and had persuaded his wife to put their money into setting up the farm, starting out with two Swedish Landrace sows and one boar, Fred – who seemed quite satisfied with things, as her father would say. Fred knew when the sows were in heat, and that there was work in hand. They would let him into the sows' pen, just until he'd done his job, and then let him out for his dinner and a nap. 'We don't want him exhausting himself,' Michael would say, with a wink, to Olive as she giggled, turning red.

As the train drew to a juddering stop, the doors opened and their fellow passengers poured out.

'I guess this is it, then,' said Lorna, her voice trembling slightly.

Olive sprang to her feet and held out her hand, helping to pull Lorna up, which took some doing.

'Thank you, Olive,' blushed Lorna. 'Sorry, my legs have gone to sleep. I can't really move in this skirt, my mother made me wear it. I feel a bit silly.'

'Oh goodness, no, you look ever so lovely. I don't own any clothes as pretty as yours.' Olive looked down at her green khaki trousers, which had never been pressed, her thick black woollen jumper, which her father had given her, and her black working boots.

'Well, you're wearing the most beautiful silk scarf I've ever seen, and you're so pretty, you don't need to bother with dressing up. I don't think there's one boy who hasn't stared at you when they've passed us in the corridor,' Lorna said quietly.

'I don't think that's true, but thank you for saying it,' said Olive, feeling as if she already had a friend in the girl she had only known for an hour or so.

For much of the journey, they had sat on the floor, with no seats available, and chatted. Lorna had just completed her maths and further maths Higher School Certificates and had received an offer from Cambridge. But her parents had made her turn it down, for fear that any prospective husbands might find her having a career in mathematics off-putting. She had resigned herself to a humdrum life of secretarial college and administration work until she got married. Then, quite out of the blue, she had received the telegram for Bletchley. Lorna didn't know who had suggested her for the position, but she suspected it might have been her maths professor at her sixth form college who had been horrified that she had turned down her place at Cambridge.

'Of course, my parents had to let me go, the telegram was by order of the King,' she had said, taking a barley sugar from her bag and popping one in her mouth, before offering Olive one. 'But they were very displeased. They are particularly worried about where our boarding houses will be. And whether I will cross paths with any boys who might tarnish my reputation in some way.'

'Thank you,' Olive had said, taking a barley sugar from the white paper bag. 'Well, I'm pleased for you, you are obviously very clever, I'm dreadful at maths. My mother didn't want me to go either, because my brother was killed last year in France.' Olive had spoken the words quietly, her hand curled around the letter she hadn't read yet, tucked in her coat pocket – the letter her father had handed her as he waved her off at Euston.

As she had climbed into the car to take her to the station, away from her mother, for how long she didn't know, she had looked up at her mother's bedroom window, where Sally stood staring down at her daughter through the crack in her net curtains. Olive had smiled up at her mother, hoping for some recognition. But none came, her mother had just stared back, then slipped away, letting the curtain fall. She had very little in the way of pretty clothes, but she had packed her mother's headscarves, which smelt of her, and she vowed to herself she would tie one around her neck every day for luck.

'I'm sorry your mother didn't come out to say goodbye to you,' her father had said, lifting her haversack out of the car boot when they arrived at the station. 'She's struggling with you going, she's scared that after Michael . . . something will happen to you too. She's very proud of you, as am I, so take it easy on those bikes.' He had pressed the envelope into her hand then, and she could see his eyes were shining as he turned away and climbed back into the driver's seat.

'I'm sorry about your brother,' Lorna had said. 'We've lost a lot of boys from the village.'

'Mother has barely come out of her room since we found out.' Olive looked at Lorna and felt tears come. She was sharing more with this kind stranger than she had with her own family. 'I miss him terribly, I still think it's a dream. That they've made a mistake. I can still sense him on the farm, it doesn't feel like he's gone. He used to muck the pigs out every day, we'd do it together. And we'd always laugh when he put the fresh hay down for them. They love it, jump around on it like it's a mattress, he'd dive in with them, and they'd climb all over him. He found the fun in everything, even cleaning out pigs.'

She had lived for Michael's return. The days were long and tough since her brother had left to serve. Her father had been allowed to stay at home, as their pigs were now feeding a lot of the local villagers, and Olive had needed to step up and take over. It had been an unbearably hard winter; she had longed for the war to end, and for Michael to come home. Then one particularly freezing morning they had received the telegram about Michael's death in France, and the house had been like a tomb ever since.

'So where do you suppose we go now?' asked Lorna.

They had reached the entrance to the station, having half dragged, half carried their luggage along the platform. The sea of people had disappeared, leaving them alone as the light began to fade. Olive turned to see a ticket office, with an elderly gentleman sitting at the window.

'Excuse me,' said Olive, as the man lifted his head to glare at her. 'Could you kindly tell me how we get to Bletchley Park?'

He frowned at her, his grey moustache twitching slightly. 'The boundary of the Bletchley Park estate is next to the railway station,' he said, finally. 'If you walk out of the station entrance, you'll see a high fence with a narrow path next to it, follow the path, and you'll come to Bletchley.'

Olive turned back and looked at Lorna in her heels, suddenly glad she had worn her boots. 'Okay, thank you very much, sir.'

Weighed down by their luggage, they staggered up the rutted narrow path next to an eight-foot-high chain-link fence topped by a roll of barbed wire.

'So what brings you to Bletchley?' asked Lorna, out of breath, as she stopped for a moment and sat on her suitcase for a breather.

Olive turned back to look at her, and stopped, not the slightest bit tired, but not wanting to leave her new friend. 'I answered an advert in the local newspaper, for female dispatch riders.'

'You ride motorbikes?' asked Lorna, still out of breath. 'How brave! Aren't they rather frightening?'

'Absolutely!' Olive smiled. 'That's what I love. I love the freedom, I can just let go, and be me, without anyone bossing me around or telling me what to do.'

'But aren't they difficult to ride?'

'Not if you know what you're doing. Jack taught me how to ride, how to handle slippery conditions, how to lean in and take corners. Mind you, he was very nervous that I would crash. So I would drive slowly until I got all the way down the track out of our farm, then let the throttle out.'

'Who is Jack, your boyfriend?' Lorna said, her eyes sparkling.

'God, no! Shall we go?' said Olive, standing up and starting to walk again, as Lorna reluctantly followed and began dragging her suitcase behind her. 'He's a local policeman who helped us on the farm. If it weren't for him helping with mucking out in the evenings, I would've gone mad. He would do his police rounds, then arrive after his shift had ended and take over from me, then turn a blind eye while I took his Triumph Speed Twin for a spin across the Downs. Jack ignited my passion for bikes, and the freedom they gave me from my mundane, muddy, miserable existence!'

'Is he handsome?' Lorna gushed.

'Who – Jack? I suppose so, I don't know really.'

'I bet he wants to marry you.'

'I don't care if he does. I'm never getting married. My mother is utterly miserable. I want to travel and see the world.'

'Oh, I see,' said Lorna, her smile sinking.

63

'When this dreadful war is over, I'm going to ride around Europe. On the farm I feel like I'm old already, like my life is over before it's even begun. I can get so dour and depressed, I guess I take after my mother in that way. But as soon as I'm on a motorbike I know I'm alive. When I ride, even the familiar seems strange and glorious. My senses are heightened, I feel the air on my skin, I can see everything as if my eyes are taking in every detail – up, down and around. Sometimes I even hear music, whole songs I haven't heard for years and didn't realise I knew the words to. All the smells become vivid – the trees, the flowers and the grass. I find myself smiling, big, ragged, wind-swept smiles.'

'Golly,' said Lorna.

The two women struggled with their luggage through the twilight along the long, quiet path, up a gentle slope running along the fenced side of the wooded grounds until they reached the short driveway and a concrete RAF sentry post that stood on the road outside the park.

'Names, please?' The man on the gate, dressed in military uniform, held a clipboard and called out to them before they had even reached him.

'Lorna Sanders,' said Lorna, blushing slightly again.

'Olive May.' Olive felt her stomach flip as the man checked his list.

'You're expected. Go up the path, towards the main house, you'll be met there,' he said, as a second soldier in uniform unlocked the gate for them.

'Olive, look!'

It was then that they caught their first view of the mansion itself. Olive stared at its Victorian windows, Tudor gables and green Gothic roof; she thought it quite pretty, if a little asymmetrical. With the lake in front of it and the thick branches of a wellingtonia tree obscuring some of the windows, it was quite inviting. Scattered around outside the mansion, on its lawns, were single-storey wooden huts, with small chimneys belting out snakes of smoke and windows covered for the blackout. Men and women were emerging from the huts, talking, with their heads down.

The two girls, standing paralysed to the spot, suddenly jumped at the distant shrieks of train whistles. Olive turned and smiled warmly at her friend. 'Ready to do our bit?'

'I guess so,' Lorna said nervously, before they both stepped over the threshold of Bletchley Park and into their new lives.

Chapter Five

Jo

March 2015, Monday afternoon

Superintendent Jo Hamilton looked down at the 1985 missing persons file in front of her that had been kept in storage in the bowels of Saltdean Police Station for thirty years. She opened the cardboard folder, pulled out the time-worn papers – of which there were only a dozen from that year – and found Holly's near the back.

MISSING PERSON

Police are concerned for the welfare of Holly Moore, 17, from Saltdean, who was last seen on 7 March 1985.

She is described as white, 5 feet 2 inches tall, with shoulder-length blonde hair, often worn in a top knot, and has a piercing in her nose. Holly was last seen on Saltdean High Street, on the evening of 7 March, wearing a red woollen duffel coat with a hood.

If you see Holly or have any information about her, contact Sussex Police urgently on 01273 842375.

The photograph of Holly was probably a school photograph, due to the lack of any photograph albums recording treasured family holidays or birthday parties. It was a photocopied image in black and white, Holly's beautiful grey-blue eyes lost in the dull tones of the photocopier ink. Jo remembered traipsing around, taping the notices to lamp posts and shop windows – until eventually, torn and faded, they had been taken down with the passing of time.

There had been little effort expended in looking for Holly when she had gone missing in 1985; the most limited of house calls were ordered by Carl Webber, and Jo had to put up the Missing Person posters in her own time. She had asked several times if she could do some more door-to-door enquiries, to try to find out where Holly hung out and who with, but it was clear to everyone at the station that her quest to find Holly was irritating Carl Webber intensely. In the end, Charlie had told her to drop it. She would find herself out of a job otherwise, and that really would be a waste.

Gemma Smith's picture had been harder to find, as they had never launched a formal missing person's inquiry. She had been well known to the police, according to the coroner, and to DI Bart Bailey – Carl Webber's boss at the time – but according to Jo's records, there was never anything serious enough for her colleagues to charge her with. Jo had to search her own handwritten notebook – which, by law, they had to keep with them at all times and hold on to indefinitely – for the date when Gemma had been arrested at the minimarket on Saltdean High Street. It was the one time she had met Gemma Smith herself, before taking her back to Morgate House. November 1975, almost exactly ten years before Holly Moore went missing. A quick call to Saltdean High confirmed she had attended the school, sporadically, between the ages of eleven and sixteen and within a couple of hours they had emailed through a school photograph from a 1975 yearbook. After scanning it in, and playing around with the tones, Jo finally had an image to go on.

Jo stared at the pictures of Gemma Smith and Holly Moore and placed them on her desk, next to each other. Physically, they couldn't have been more different. Gemma had a heart-shaped face, and dark hair which fell in waves around her green eyes. She had only met Gemma that once, when she was arrested for stealing food, but she had been struck by her natural beauty and energy. She had seemed, to Jo, to be full of life – not broken by her experiences, as the coroner seemed to believe, when her bloated, twisted body was found on the pebbles of Saltdean Beach. The coroner's finding of suicide had never sat well with her; Gemma Smith had been a bright, spirited girl, down on her luck, yes, but it had emerged at the inquest that she was looking forward to escaping Morgate House and getting on with her life with her boyfriend.

At the time, Jo had asked her boss, DI Bart Bailey, about going up to Morgate House and speaking to the proprietors about the lack of food for the children, despite Lorna and Geoff Price being handsomely paid by the council. But he had forbidden her to meddle. 'Geoff and Lorna Price do an outstanding job of keeping a great deal of unwanted children fed, clothed and off the streets,' he had said, 'and I'm not having them scrutinised because of a mouthy troublemaker like Gemma Smith. I suggest you concentrate on your workload, WPC Hamilton, or we will have to get someone else in who can cope better.' It was as things had always been for women in the police force in the seventies: never complain, and if you don't like it, you know where the door is.

Gemma's inquest was held at the Coroner's Court on the Lewes Road; supported by her brother, Charlie, Jo had attended the last fifteen minutes in her lunch hour. She hadn't been able to attend the whole inquest, her boss wouldn't allow her the time off, but catching the tail end she had heard Lorna Price, proprietor of Morgate House, describe Gemma as a wayward troublemaker who often threatened to take her own life.

Jo had only just managed to fight back the urge to argue with her boss – she'd only met Gemma once but the picture they were painting of Gemma was not one she recognised. But inquests were mostly for the bereaved families and loved ones to attend, and Jo looked around sadly at the pitiful turnout – there were no aunties or uncles, no friends of the family. Just Jo, Charlie, DI Bart Bailey, Lorna Price and Lorna's son, Phillip Price.

She had hoped that the boyfriend Gemma had mentioned to Phillip Price might make an appearance, but there had been no sign of him. Nobody to defend Gemma's memory, and with it being an inquest and not a trial, there was no prosecution, no defence, no case to be put, just people who didn't care for Gemma, giving the coroner their accounts of who the deceased was and how they believed she had died.

'I just don't know why everyone is so sure it was suicide,'

she had told Charlie as they grabbed a cup of tea from the café opposite the Coroner's Court. 'No one is even questioning it. She didn't seem suicidal to me.'

'These kids are good at masking their pain, Jo, putting on a front. They have no one. You only met her once, but we were always picking her up. She was often violent and abusive towards us,' said Charlie, paying for them both.

'Gemma was nothing but trouble, a right pain in the arse,' Phillip Price had added, as he stood in the queue next to them and joined their conversation uninvited. 'Always running off, getting brought back. Making a nuisance of herself to my mum at Morgate. On the night she died she told Mum she'd rather die than live there any more.'

Jo had recoiled at the way he was talking about a young girl, on the day of her inquest. 'Well, that doesn't make her actually suicidal, it's just evidence she was desperate to leave Morgate. But nobody cares what I think,' she had said, watching as a stony-faced Mrs Price appeared from the ladies' toilet before Phillip rushed towards her and out into the pouring rain.

'I do,' Charlie had said, kissing her forehead before racing back to work. 'You need to keep your head down, do your time. Don't get on the wrong side of Bart Bailey over a girl like that. Troublemakers don't get promoted, remember?'

Jo turned to the picture of Holly staring back at her now. In contrast to Gemma, her wispy blonde hair was pulled back neatly into a ponytail and her grey-blue eyes were staring straight at the camera and smiling. She sat up straight, and her hands were neatly in her lap. She was a beautiful girl, with prominent cheekbones, and carried herself with pride. Jo had only met her on the one tragic occasion, the night of the fire, when Holly was not yet nine, but she could tell the little girl had a will of iron. Particularly when it came to protecting her little sister; she had wrapped her in a cloak of love as the two of them sat in the back of Jo's police car on their way to Morgate House.

Holly's little sister, Daisy Moore, who had been six in 1975, would be in her forties now. Turning forty-six to be exact, if she was still alive.

Jo turned to her computer and typed in the name Daisy Moore. No convictions, she had never been in trouble with the police, but there was a Daisy Moore on the system for a theft. On 5 June 2012, she had reported her bike stolen, from her flat in Kemptown. Her date of birth was a match, and Jo felt goosebumps prickle along her arms. Three years ago, Daisy was still in Brighton, so the chances were good that she still was, Jo just needed to see her face to know if it was her.

Jo jumped onto Facebook – which, along with all her colleagues, she regularly used as an intelligence source – and typed in *Daisy Moore, Brighton*. A few matches came up for the name, but none of the faces looked right. Eventually, she found a profile picture which was a sketch of Winnie-the-Pooh, walking away down a path with Piglet: *How lucky I am, to have something that makes saying goodbye so hard.* Jo's tummy lurched as she clicked on the profile and scrolled through. There were not many clear pictures of Daisy, but finally she found one where she had been tagged by some work colleagues in a pub, at Christmas time. She was at the end of a long table of people, with a Christmas hat on, holding up her glass and smiling at the camera. And also in a small group photo by the bar, in

71

the centre of two other friends with their arms wrapped around her waist. Jo's heart missed a beat as Daisy's face stared out at her; she looked the spitting image of her mother – the woman Jo had tried so hard to save, the night of the fire. It was a face which was etched into her mind's eye, and one which had never left her conscience.

Jo zoomed in on Daisy's expression; the smile was painted on, but it didn't reach her eyes. While those around her were clearly drunk, animated and laughing, Daisy's posture was reserved. And in the shot around the table, she sat up straight in her seat, clinging to the chair with her hand, while others drunkenly waved their arms around. Her hair was a neat blonde bob and she wore a floral shirt and cardigan, while the other women at the Christmas gathering wore glittery tops and tight skirts. Jo scrolled down to the descriptions of the photographs. One read: 'A well-earned night off at Brighton's best cocktail bar!' So Daisy worked night shifts, somewhere in Brighton. Jo let out a sign of relief; if they needed a DNA match for the remains found on the Tye, in theory, it should be fairly easy to get.

Jo started as her superior officer, Chief Superintendent Carl Webber, knocked on her door. 'Come in!' she called out, recognising the silhouette of her boss before he walked in.

'Just wondering if I could have a word about these remains which have been found?' he asked, unbuttoning the jacket of his navy suit and putting a bottle of water on the table.

'Of course, Carl, take a seat,' she said warmly, quickly minimising the picture of Daisy Moore's Facebook account.

Carl walked in and closed the door behind him.

Jo smiled gently, she had always tried her hardest to like

her boss, he was straightforward and didn't play games like a lot of her colleagues did.

The irony didn't escape Jo that despite being five years younger than her, Carl had not been hampered by sexism and taking time out for maternity leave so was now senior to her, with several years of service left.

As Carl smiled at her, Jo felt her hackles rise. Going on the history between Carl and her brother, she always felt that he was not entirely to be trusted. Being fifteen years his senior, Charlie had taken Carl under his wing when he first joined the force, and helped Carl work his way up to inspector level.

At around the age of forty, however, Carl had changed, according to her brother. He had become very secretive, stopped socialising with their group, and seemed hell bent on making it to the top. Which he did, around ten years later; just as Charlie was in his final year, Carl became his boss. And he made Charlie's last few months extremely difficult, taking him off meaty jobs, concealing information from him, not inviting him to important meetings. Charlie always felt like he'd been ghosted by Carl but remained loyal to him until his final day, when Carl failed to turn up to Charlie's leaving do. He had hoped that Carl would make a speech, and at the very least come along for the duration, but his boss never even showed and, though he hid it, Jo knew her dear brother was utterly humiliated.

Carl had it all, Charlie said – the promotion, big house, beautiful wife, perfect kids – and he didn't want Charlie around, reminding him that he'd had help getting there. However, this explanation had always niggled Jo, as not being the full picture.

He was still a handsome man, she thought, as Carl took

73

a seat: tall, broad-shouldered, with a good head of hair despite his advancing years. But there was also something about him she didn't trust, a slight shiftiness, which she couldn't really explain.

'So, I hear there have been some human remains found on Saltdean Tye? It's cordoned off, possible skull fracture, and forensics are there. Can you fill me in on where we are?' he said, leaning back and crossing his arms.

Jo cleared her throat. She'd done nothing wrong, but she still felt like she was plotting something she didn't want anyone to know about – just yet. 'Yes, as I understand it, we received a call around nine o'clock this morning, to say some human remains had been found by two builders up on Saltdean Tye, by the old water tower. I went up there with Stan, and there was no doubt there was a human skull, a femur and a collarbone, and the skull had clear trauma injury. Stan had already called CID and forensics, who arrived as we were leaving; we've sealed off the area, and I've put in place twenty-four-hour cover, to make sure nobody contaminates the scene.'

'Are you setting up a major incident room?' he asked, looking at his watch.

'I will do. Just been digging out some missing persons files from storage.'

Carl nodded, and glanced over at her screen nosily. 'Any ideas who it might be?'

Jo hesitated, not wanting to show her hand to Carl too early on. 'I'm not sure at this stage, but it could be a seventeen-year-old runaway called Holly Moore. She went missing in 1985, shortly after I re-joined. I don't know if you remember, we did a few house to house enquiries around Morgate House, the children's home where she lived. It's just opposite where the remains were found, on the other side of the coast road. The kids from there used to hang out by the water tower, it's sheltered and out of the wind. I had to go up there once to rescue some of them after they got themselves trapped inside.'

Carl stared at her intensely. 'It rings a bell. Any reason you think it's her?' he said, turning the photograph on her desk so he could look at it.

'There was a piece of jewellery I recognised. But it could be a coincidence.' She bit her lip.

'Okay, so does she have any living relatives we could get a DNA sample from?' Carl looked up at her.

Jo hesitated, she wanted to keep her suspicions about Holly to herself, but time was against her. 'Yes, a sister. Daisy Moore. According to the system, she's still in Brighton, but I'd have to find out for sure,' she said, shifting in her chair. She felt uncomfortable about the way the conversation was going, Carl had a way of making you over-share and the way he was staring at her made her nervous.

'Great, get a car to her house and get a DNA swab done,' he said matter-of-factly.

Jo felt the blood rush to her face; the last thing she wanted was Daisy finding out from anyone but her that the remains could be Holly's. She took a breath and tried to hide her panic.

'I think maybe we should wait to get the results from forensics, in case they can't get a good sample? I mean, we don't want to upset her sister unnecessarily.' Jo leaned in, wishing she hadn't overridden her instinct to keep her suspicions about Holly to herself.

'I remember you putting up missing posters for Holly Moore in your own time. Did you know her?' Carl frowned.

Jo paused, the gut-wrenching frustration of that time coming back to her as if it was yesterday. Carl had no interest in looking for Holly, it was just another Morgate girl, just another inconvenience, but she was a lowly constable, who had only just re-joined the force after taking a decade out to raise Megan, and by then, Carl was a Chief Superintendent. As Charlie reminded her at the time, if she didn't let the search for Holly go, Carl would see to it that she remained a constable her whole working life, and that wouldn't help anyone.

'I met her once as a child, but not in her teenage years when she went missing,' said Jo, her heart racing as she felt the intensity of Carl's glare. 'She was in care, she lived at Morgate House – I was just back from my career break when she vanished, but I remember the death of another girl, Gemma Smith, also from Morgate House. I'm thinking maybe they knew each other.'

Carl paused for a moment. 'Was this Gemma Smith murdered?'

Jo shook her head. 'The coroner thought it was suicide.'

'But you don't?' Carl leaned in. 'You know you only have four days to go. They're signing your leaving card out there, Jo.'

Jo smiled, trying to lighten the mood and keep him onside. She had to get to Daisy before anyone else did, she had to warn her, and she didn't trust Carl not to go behind her back.

'I'm happy to hand over the Incident Room to Stan. I know I can't oversee the whole case. But can I have your permission to look into Morgate House a bit more? I met Gemma, and I never thought she killed herself. But nobody questioned it because of her background. Those girls weren't listened to, they were written off. Phillip Price described her as "a pain in the arse" on the day of her inquest, which was nice,' Jo added.

Carl hesitated and stood up. 'You need to be taking it easy in your last week.'

'I don't want to take it easy. I've got the next twenty years to take it easy. I just want a chance to find a connection between the girls, aside from the fact they went to Morgate House. If I can't, fine. If I can, I'll hand it over to Stan. What do you say?' Jo smiled, hiding her shaking hands underneath her desk.

Carl paused, clearly reluctant to commit himself to anything. 'What's that?' he said, frowning at a file on her desk.

'It's Holly Moore's file,' she said quietly.

'And?'

'She ran away a lot, or rather stayed out after her curfew, and then would be picked up by one of our lot and brought back to Morgate. She was caught shoplifting food. Nothing serious enough for the police to press charges. I need to go through the file, but she was often picked up in Woodingdean. I think maybe she was looking for her younger sister, after Daisy was fostered and they were separated.'

Carl's stare lingered. 'Sounds like you remember her case quite well.'

Jo hesitated, 'Like I said, I met her as a child, I took her and her sister to Morgate. I was out of the force for most of the time they were there. But I kept track of her a little bit.'

Carl frowned, and Jo felt her face redden.

'I think Morgate House took a lot of problem kids off our hands,' Jo said, keen to take the attention off her and back onto Morgate. 'Bart Bailey was just grateful to have them out of the way. Even though they ran away a lot, and the place was clearly miserable,' Jo added.

'It was a children's home, in the seventies, of course it was miserable,' he said, plainly.

'Can I get Phillip Price in for an informal chat about Gemma and Daisy?' Jo's mind was already racing. 'He was a PC here when both girls went missing. But he's also the son of Geoff and Lorna Price, the couple who ran Morgate House.' She was trying not to let her desperation show.

Her boss smiled, and shook his head. 'Hold your horses, let's get a formal ID of the body first.'

The phone on Jo's desk trilled into life, and Jo reached for it. 'Hamilton,' she said, picking up the photographs of the girls and staring at them.

Constable Kate Harris's voice was faded out by the viscous wind on the Tye where she was calling from. 'Forensics have found something they want to show you, can you come back up to the site?'

'Okay, thanks, I'm on my way.' Jo finished the call, and turned to her boss. 'I need to go back up to the site, forensics may have found something.'

Jo's phone rang again, and she snatched it up. 'Hamilton.'

'Your brother's in reception.'

'Thanks,' said Jo, slamming the phone down. She felt the irritation rising in her. She hated that Carl was her senior and she wasn't just able to get on with her job to the best of her ability.

'Keep me posted, Jo, and we'll discuss Phillip Price later, don't start accusing him of anything, okay? We may well need to keep him onside to pick his brains about Morgate House. Call Stan and tell him to meet you up at the site, now.'

Jo felt her heart sink, keeping someone 'onside' was a police term for letting someone get away with breaking the law in exchange for intel. 'Stan doesn't need to come, I can fill him in when I get back,' she said, her heart lurching with the familiar feeling of a case being wrested out of her control.

'Yes, he does.' Carl's voice was clipped.

Jo nodded, her experience as a female police officer telling her not to argue in public, for fear of being labelled 'emotional'. She pulled her black woollen coat from the back of her chair. She had begun reluctantly emptying the contents of her filing cabinets and desk drawers, and there were piles of paperwork strewn across the floor. Her eyes fell on a photograph of her and her brother, smiling proudly at her police training graduation ceremony, and for some reason Phillip Price was standing on the other side of her. She could see in her own eyes that she wasn't comfortable standing near him; he had always given her the creeps, even then. She picked up the photograph, slid it into her bag; her instinct being that a photograph of Phillip around the time the girls went missing might be useful over the coming days. She paced towards her brother waiting in reception.

Carl followed her out of the door and looked down the corridor at Charlie. The two men locked eyes for a moment, but Carl chose not to acknowledge him.

'Will you just give me the nod if you're going to approach Daisy?' Jo asked, trying not to sound desperate.

'I'll do my best,' said Carl, which Jo knew meant no.

Jo tried to swallow the rising anger inside her and walked towards her brother. She was already being squeezed out of the loop, and there was nothing she could do about it.

'Hey, I brought you some late lunch, I guessed you wouldn't have eaten.' Charlie lifted a brown paper bag and a tray with two takeaway coffees up towards her and winked. Despite having just turned seventy, his bone structure and full head of hair made him look more like he was in his fifties. He had been gifted with the good looks of the family: tall, dark and handsome, with a killer smile that got him out of all kinds of trouble. He looked so like their mother, with her dark Mediterranean looks, and in temperament he took after her too. Whereas she took after their dad, with her blonde hair and blue eyes; it felt strange to her when Megan turned out to be so dark – like her mother and Charlie. She had always felt like Megan's gene pool belonged more to Charlie and Olive, the three of them seemed to understand one another – Megan seemed more at ease in their company than she ever did in Jo's.

'Thanks.' She smiled at him as he stood up. 'I'd love to chat but I'm on my way out. Walk with me?'

'Sure,' Charlie replied.

'See you, mate.' Charlie glanced back at the constable behind the counter, who had worked with him for nearly a decade. 'See you, Tom,' Charlie said, smiling in acknowledgement. Jo smiled at her brother warmly. He had always been popular and highly respected by his colleagues, and had invested himself completely in Sussex Police. She knew he missed the job, the camaraderie and people, terribly.

They headed out through the revolving doors and into the chilly spring afternoon where the light was already fading.

'I just went to see Mum,' said Charlie, as they fell into step with one another, walking along the busy street to where Jo's car was parked.

'How is she?'

'She's not well, Jo, they're moving her to palliative care. To help manage the pain.'

80

'I'll go and see her today, I promise.'

'Okay,' Charlie said. 'She's asking for you.'

'I'll go. I just have something I have to do first,' Jo said, already trying to work out how she could track down Daisy without going to her house, where she would be seen.

They walked in silence, until they reached Jo's car.

'What's going on? What's happened?' Charlie asked, frowning gently. 'I saw the forensic tents on the news.'

Jo looked up at her brother. 'I knew they'd find her one day. I just hoped it would be when I had more than five days to put it right.' Jo let out a sigh.

'Who?' Charlie stared at her, steam rising from the hot drinks. 'What's this about?' he said, as Jo looked away and shook her head. 'You're bound to feel wobbly this week. This job has been your life for the last forty years,' Charlie added.

'Forty years, and however much I achieve, it always counts for nothing because of what happened that night. I destroyed those girls' lives.'

Charlie handed Jo a coffee over the roof of her car as his younger sister let out a sigh. 'Not this again. Is it her remains they've found on the Tye?'

Jo shook her head and gazed into the distance. 'I don't know if it's her, Charlie. It probably is. If it is, I killed her a long time before she ended up on that Tye.'

'What? What on earth are you talking about?' said Charlie, staring at her incredulously.

'I started that fire, Charlie. I killed their mother. I'm the reason Holly ended up at Morgate House – and in that shallow grave.'

'Those girls lived on the Brunswick Estate, with an

alcoholic father who beat their mother. They would have ended up at Morgate House sooner or later,' he said. 'Don't do this to yourself. It's your last week, you have so much to look back on and be proud of. Don't make that fire the defining moment.'

'I can still picture them, sitting in my office, the night their mother died. I had to find someone to take them. I tried everything, Charlie. I even called Richard and asked if they could come and live with us until they were fostered. Eventually, Daisy climbed onto Holly's lap and fell asleep. She was so tired. The only place that had two beds was Morgate House,' she said quietly.

'Jo, let's go and see Mum together tonight, we don't have to stay long. She's asking for you a lot. Then you can come to dinner maybe? Sam's cooking. I hate seeing you like this.'

Jo shook her head. 'Okay. I'll call you when I'm done. I noticed the way Carl blanked you.'

Charlie shrugged. 'Water under the bridge.'

'Not for me it isn't. Forty years' service and he thinks he can just freeze you out. Well, I'm not going to let him treat me the way he treated you.'

'What do you mean?' Charlie asked.

'I mean I'm not done yet, and there's nothing he can do about it. Thanks for lunch, I'll let you know when I'm on my way to Mum's.'

'Promise you'll go and see her?'

'Promise!' Jo called out through her open window. 'I just have to go to the site first, then I'm there,' she said. Blowing her brother a kiss before turning out onto the coast road as the sun began to set over the cliffs of Saltdean.

Chapter Six

Gemma

November 1975

'Why can't I come with you?'

'Because I need to talk to my boyfriend. I can't if you're there, because I'd need to look after you.'

'I'm worried something will happen to you and you won't come back.'

Gemma looked at her friend, and smiled. 'Don't worry so much. I'm a big girl. I've got a plan, I'm going to get out of here, and I'm going to take you with me.'

Eve was only eight. She followed Gemma around like a little shadow, but she wasn't annoying like the other kids; she was gentle and cute, and she knew when to stop talking. She just wanted the reassurance of knowing Gemma was there.

'What's a copper?' Eve asked, pulling her coat tighter around her and looking at the destination on the front of the bus, which read 'Churchill Square–Woodingdean'.

Gemma smiled. 'It's someone who looks after people. So you've got nothing to worry about. Here's my bus. Now go back inside.'

'When will you be back?' Eve asked, frowning.

'I don't know, tomorrow maybe.' Gemma hugged her little friend and watched the bus pull up. 'Don't wait up.'

Gemma found herself a seat on the bus and sat down, as

Eve stood shivering at the bus stop watching her go. She couldn't help letting her imagination run away with her. Maybe he'd let her stay, maybe they'd have dinner, and spend the night together, in a bed, cuddled up together, for the first time. Like a real couple.

She had no idea how long it was going to take her to get to the address in Woodingdean, but she had a warm coat, gloves, and chocolate in her pocket to keep her going if he wasn't at home. She'd looked up his address from the payslip – 16 Downland Street, Woodingdean – and worked out her route on a map she had found in the library, drawing it out on the back of an envelope.

When the bus reached Woodingdean High Street, she got off. It was already starting to get dark, but she followed the high street down towards the garage on the corner, and then took a left.

After several wrong turns, she found it. She had no idea what to expect, what sort of house he would live in. She had always pictured him in a bachelor pad in town.

Downland Street felt remote and quiet, and number 16 was in a row of terraced houses which all looked the same to her. As she walked towards it, her heart surged with the realisation that there were lights on, and his car was in the drive. But as she got closer, her stomach slowly began to twist into a knot.

There were signs that he didn't live alone. Her heart throbbing, her chest tight, morning sickness flooding through her, she observed the evidence in disbelief.

Hanging baskets and pot plants decorated the porch and Gemma's eyes were drawn to three pairs of wellington boots lined up by the front door. She looked at the house number again: 16. And the car on the drive – she crept towards it, saw his cigarette packet and the Sting cassette he was always playing in the car when they were together. It was his, she knew it inside and out, and this home – this family home – this was definitely it. Her body flooded with panic but she kept walking towards the house, like a moth to a flame.

She walked down the pathway to the front door, although her instincts were telling her to walk away, and soon she heard a woman's voice on the other side. Quickly, she rushed round the side of the house, straining to hear so she could work out who was coming out of the door, scratching her hand on a rose bush climbing up the wall. Her heart pounded as the front door opened, followed by the thud of several pairs of feet. She stood silently, feeling bile fill her throat as she strained to listen.

'I've booked the hall, did you confirm the entertainer?' It was an adult female voice, light, happy as she pulled the door closed.

'No. We don't need an entertainer, do we, sweetie? Don't you want Daddy to do it? I can be the clown. Daddy's funny, isn't he?'

'No!' A little girl's cry.

'No?' he said as the little girl started to giggle. It was his voice in a tone she didn't recognise. He sounded happy, carefree, full of laughter as the little girl's giggle echoed through the winter afternoon.

She felt paralysed. Scared to stay, in case they saw her, but unable to run away, desperate to see more of the picture she was painting in her head. It was the sort of family she had longed for her whole life. And it was his, a family he had completely denied to her. Tears poured down her cheeks as the car started, diesel fumes spilling from the exhaust and making her feel nauseous.

As they drove away, she stepped out from her hiding place and watched them go, the shock of what she had just witnessed making her shake violently. She had recognised his voice, but he sounded nothing like the man she knew. All the nights he had picked her up, driven her around, bought her food. Told her he was lonely, given her money, made her feel special. That he had nothing, and no one, except her.

She suddenly felt the urge to get inside the house; she needed to see his world for herself. She walked up to his front door and turned the handle. It didn't budge. Undeterred, she walked round the corner of the house and opened the side gate to a small, well-kept garden with a neat fence, a trampoline and a swing. She stood staring up at the house, trying to calm her breathing. All the downstairs windows were closed, but then she noticed a small frosted window by the side gate, which was ajar. She prised it open and climbed in.

Inside it smelt clean, of fabric conditioner and air freshener, and as if someone took a great deal of time and effort over it. She stalked through the ground floor; the kitchen was spotless, and a hall table had a vase of lilies on it, and a photo of the little girl she guessed to be around four. It felt like a loving, happy home. She walked into the front room, gazed around at a sofa with scatter cushions, an arm-chair and a rug. On the centre of a glass coffee table were more flowers, and a card. She lifted it up, her hands shaking, and read: *My darling, on our tenth wedding anniversary. I'd be lost without you.*

The room spun. There were pictures of the little girl everywhere: family photographs, always the blonde child in between her doting parents. Her hair in bunches, her clothes neatly pressed. And, on the wall, a formal portrait of him in his police uniform. She knew every inch of his body, his smell, the man she thought she knew. The heating was blasting out, and there were plug-in aerosols, the floral aroma making her feel sick. She stumbled back in the hall, climbed the stairs, and at the top was faced with the little girl's bedroom. It was filled with Tiny Tears dolls, teddy bears and a dolls' house, and a soft pink lamp on her bedside table; it was the bedroom of her dreams as a child. While she rotted at Morgate House, the man who claimed to love her had been raising his own child here. All along he had been using her.

She walked over to the little girl's bed, covered in teddies, and lay down. She closed her eyes, hearing her mother's voice reading her a bedtime story; she longed for this house, this life, with every cell in her body. She ached to be loved as this little girl was, tucked into bed and read to every night.

But she wasn't, she was all alone in the world, with a baby on the way. He wasn't going to leave his family. He would deny everything. They would take her baby away, and it would end up in care, just like her. Nausea suddenly overwhelmed her and she sat up, tried to run to the bathroom, vomiting instead all over the little girl's rug. She looked at it for a while, she hadn't wanted to throw up, but she was glad now that she had. She hoped they couldn't get it out, that it would leak through to the carpet underneath, and leave the smell of her in his house forever.

As a feeling of numbness washed over her, Gemma wiped her mouth and walked into the main bedroom. She looked at a portrait of them on their wedding day; his wife was everything she wasn't, small, petite, blonde. Her hair sat in a neat bob on her shoulders. Gemma's eyes moved along to another photograph of the bride, flanked by her loving parents, who had loved her and nurtured her every day of her life. A mother and father who had helped with every aspect of family life, supported her, advised her, and had no idea who their daughter had really married.

And would probably never know.

Gemma opened the wardrobe and began sifting through his wife's clothes, her dresses and blouses. She pulled out a pair of high heels and tried them on, lifting a string of pearls from the jewellery stand on the dressing table and holding them up to her face. There were pictures of the woman everywhere, smiling, laughing. Safe, happy. Secure. Why was it that the people who are loved all their lives always get more? And the ones who aren't, those who are starved of love as children and crave it desperately, spend their lives dealing with heartbreak and rejection. *Is it because people can smell desperation?* she thought. Like a cloak you cannot shed. This man, the father of her child, who had used her, was the same man, the perfect husband in these pictures, she thought. Two sides of the same coin.

Gemma sat on the bed, imagined them making love while their baby slept, warm and cosy, in her bed next door. Did he think about her while he was screwing his wife? Did he think about his wife while he was fumbling at her school uniform, pulling down her knickers as he told her how much he loved her, how one day, when she was old enough, they would be together. Lying down on top of her in the back seat of his police car, in an empty car park in the middle of the Sussex Downs.

Lost in thought, she heard the crunch of the car pulling into the gravel driveway. She felt strangely calm, light-headed and in shock, as she walked down the stairs, towards the back door, unlocking it and then waiting. Unable to pull herself away.

Maybe she would stay, introduce herself. See his face turn ashen, listen to the excuses he made, wait until he accused her of lying. Her heart hammered as she heard the key turn in the lock. Then, slowly, the door opened.

'I'm dying for a wee,' said the woman, dashing into the downstairs toilet.

Gemma stood by the back door, staring at her. The little girl ran into the sitting room, and turned on the television. He walked into the kitchen, smiling, until his eyes made sense of who was standing there.

As soon as he saw her, his face turned to stone.

He said nothing, made no sound, as he walked up to her and opened the back door behind her. He grabbed her by the wrist as she tried to pull away, but he held her tighter, pulling her outside, before shouting to his wife.

'We need milk! Back in a sec!'

'Let go of me,' she said, starting to cry.

'Outside now!' he hissed, taking her into the garden and dragging her through the gate, before opening his car with his key.

'Get in,' he said, opening the passenger door and scanning the street to check nobody was watching them.

She felt weak from throwing up, weak from finding out

the truth, she wanted to scream at him, but her whole body was shaking.

'What the fuck are you doing in my house? Are you insane?' he barked as he drove too fast away from the house, down the back roads of Woodingdean and out onto the main road.

'You're married. You've got a kid,' she said, her throat choking up with emotion. She wiped her tears away angrily.

'So what?'

'So what? What about us? You never told me you had a family.'

He drove on in silence, she could see his eyes darting, trying to think of a way to handle her, trying to find a way out.

'I'm pregnant.'

The words hung in the air like car fumes. She had imagined her life so differently to this, dreamed that when she had a baby it would be with a lovely man. That he would give her a lovely life. And instead, history was repeating itself.

'What?' he said, pulling up outside Woodingdean Station, turning off the engine and facing her.

'I'm having your baby. What the hell did you think was going to happen?'

'I thought you were on the pill,' he said quietly.

'I'm fifteen, they won't give it you without a parent, and as you know, I don't have one.' Her voice trembled. She felt a black wall of utter devastation closing in on her.

'Are you sure?'

'Yes, I went to the nurse at the doctor's surgery, who did a test,' she said, cringing at the memory.

He stared at her. She could see his brain ticking over, trying to save himself. She had no idea how old he was but she suspected he was in his thirties. He had a whole life she wasn't part of. Why had she been so stupid as to think that a man like him would be single – and want her?

She felt too upset to be angry, but she knew she wasn't the only one in the wrong. She knew he'd get into trouble if anyone found out about them – but then maybe he wouldn't? It was her word against his. And nobody would believe her.

'Look, I'm sorry, okay. I was shocked to see you. I'll come and pick you up tomorrow night and we can talk,' he said. 'Maybe I can fix it so we can go away for a bit. Work out what to do.'

'Really?' she wiped her tears away, a tiny flash of hope swelling in her tummy. 'Shall I pack a bag then?' she said, her heart lifting.

'Sure,' he said, looking at his watch.

'I've been waiting for you, in all our usual places, but you never come round any more.'

'I know, I'm sorry, I've been really busy at work. I'll be there tomorrow at eight, my shift finishes at seven, and we can talk. I'll park over the road from Morgate and flash my headlights.'

She nodded her head. 'Okay.' She opened the car door, and went to get out before turning back. 'I don't have any money for the train. I thought you'd take me back,' she said, her voice breaking.

She hung her head in shame, she was so tired of hating herself. Of having nothing, no money, no home, no pride. He reached into his back pocket and pulled out his wallet.

He had a wedge of notes, and handed her a tenner. At least she would be able to get some chips for her and Eve on the way home, and have some change left over.

She looked at him, her eyes full of tears, then pocketed the money. 'I've got bad morning sickness. I threw up in your kid's room.'

Gemma climbed out of the passenger seat and slammed the car door, before he drove off into the night, back to his family, as she stood alone, on the cold steps of Woodingdean Station, unable to stop the tears.

Chapter Seven

Daisy

March 2015, Monday evening

'I love this picture of you, Olive, you look so happy.' Daisy stared at the image of the handsome couple. Black-and-white photographs always made people look so other-worldly, she thought, but the love Olive obviously felt for the man by her side crossed generations.

Olive let out a whimper of pain, and Daisy stood up. 'Let's see if we can make you more comfortable. I think if we sit you up it might help.'

It had been a long shift, and Daisy's whole body ached. None of her residents seemed to be getting on with the day; they had been unsettled by all the comings and goings in the night, with Olive being so poorly, and her son, Charlie, arriving in the early hours. They had all heard her cries of pain and distress. Many of them weren't eating, or taking enough fluids. They hadn't been keen to do any of the planned activities, and some of them were being very abrupt and taking out their sadness and loneliness on her. Downside was their home, and they became very attached to their friends, so the atmosphere was always heavy when someone died or was moved to respite care.

Added to which, the news had been on in the room of every resident that Daisy tended to. It seemed to be playing on repeat, like nails scratching at the blackboard of her exhausted brain. She would walk in and the radio would be on, the painful information it held seemingly on repeat, over and over: *Suspected human remains have been found near Saltdean. Police are investigating after the discovery by a member of the public.* She would deal with an unsettled, tired resident, get them comfortable, do their bed bath, change their gown, feed them their lunch. Encourage them to drink. Talk to them, try to make them smile. Then it would start all over again. Her day felt never-ending; she had started out exhausted, but now she was broken.

Normally she loved her work, however hard; the residents made it worthwhile. But on days like this, when everyone was sad, it was an uphill battle. Her nerves were frayed, her head was telling her it wasn't Holly's remains they had found, but her heart was fit to explode with angst, alongside being desperately worried about Olive.

'I want to be with him. I've loved him all my life,' Olive said quietly, as Daisy raised Olive's bed and adjusted her pillows.

'Try to drink some water.' Daisy encouraged Olive to take a small sip, before sitting down again. She turned the photograph over and read the cursive black handwriting on the back. She looked at Olive and asked, 'Where's Bletchley Park? Is that where you met? I've never heard of it.'

'Neither had I, until I got a telegram summoning me there during the war. It's an estate, north of London, where a lot of academics from Oxford and Cambridge worked to decipher intercepted messages from the Nazis. Churchill said the work we did there shortened the war by two years.'

Daisy's eyes were wide as she looked at Olive. 'And you worked there? What did you do?'

Olive coughed, and Daisy lifted her head carefully to give her some more water.

'I was a dispatch rider. I collected messages.' Olive winced in pain again. 'Encrypted messages, from radio stations all over the south coast. Then delivered them back to the mathematicians at Bletchley who cracked the codes and used the information in them to help us win the war.'

'You rode motorbikes in the war?'

Olive nodded.

'That's amazingly brave.'

Olive smiled weakly. 'It was exciting, and terrifying. We were forbidden to ever talk about it. I've never told anyone, not even my husband.' Olive started to cry. 'Do you have any idea what it's like, living with that kind of secret? Bletchley Park, and what happened there, shaped my whole life. I left, but my heart stayed there. I was never the same afterwards, a place can do that to you, Daisy.'

Olive stared at her intently as nausea began to creep into Daisy's stomach. When she closed her eyes, she could still feel Morgate House. Every single day. The cold and the sadness. Holly pulling at her arms and screaming as Geoff and Phillip Price tried to separate the two of them the last time she saw her sister. It had taken two grown men to separate her and Holly. Her foster mother had locked her in the back seat of her car as she had driven down the gravel drive away from Morgate House, away from the dark Victorian redbrick building, where the radiators were never on, and the windows were bare, where the mattresses had no warm blankets and the dining room was always closed. Where she and Holly had lived together for six lonely, cold, hungry years. The news came on again in Olive's room: *It is believed that human remains have been found on Saltdean Tye.* Daisy suddenly felt tears of fear sting her eyes; she was exhausted, but she was too scared to go home and be alone.

'Nobody understands how I feel,' Olive said.

'I do, Olive, I understand. I grew up in a children's home. I'm still stuck there,' Daisy said quietly.

Olive reached out and clenched Daisy's hand hard. 'I wish you were my daughter.'

Daisy felt her body start with the shock of Olive's words. She immediately sensed a presence next to her and looked up to see Olive's son, Charlie, standing over them both. From his crestfallen face she could tell he'd heard what Olive had said. Charlie stared at her, then at his mother.

'They've confirmed they are moving you to St Catherine's in the morning, Mum. Jo is going to come to see you there tomorrow, if she doesn't manage to pop in tonight. She's got to work late at the station, something important has come up at work,' Charlie said curtly. 'But I'll stay here for a while, and come back tomorrow to travel with you in the ambulance, when they move you. We can manage here now, thank you, Daisy. You must be tired.'

Daisy stood, stumbling awkwardly on the chair leg. She was tired – so tired, she could barely hold herself up. Olive's eyes were closed now, exhausted from waking so early and being in pain.

'Please tell Olive I'll come and visit her at St Catherine's,' Daisy said quietly, backing out of the door as Charlie nodded and closed it behind her.

Daisy stood in the hallway, not knowing where to go. She didn't want to be alone at home, but she didn't want to be with friends. It was that horrible feeling she often had as a child, that nobody wanted her, that she didn't belong anywhere. Wandering the streets, not wanting to be in her body, not wanting to be who she was. Slowly, she walked to the staff room; it was late, between shifts and she was relieved there was no one in there she had to talk to. She pulled her coat over her weary shoulders and retrieved her cycling helmet out of her locker.

She walked slowly out into the bitterly cold evening, unlocked her bicycle and clipped the helmet strap under her chin. She took a deep breath, the cold wind burning her throat and lungs, the pain of it almost comforting.

She began to pedal, trying to calm her breathing and let the rhythmic motion of the bicycle soothe her. The coast road was quiet and dark, the sea calm, the road lights faded by the fog. As she passed Saltdean Tye, her eyes were drawn to it. She tried not to look, but she couldn't help herself. She could make out the floodlights from the forensic team's tent she had seen on the news earlier. They pierced the night, sending a beam into the fog above. She imagined the men in white forensic suits, working in the cold, on a deadline, the police and journalists huddled in their cars, waiting for updates. She didn't want to go home; if she went home, someone could be waiting for her. A policeman, a journalist, a social worker. She didn't know. She didn't want to know, her whole body shook with the cold and the fear of what awaited her.

Suddenly, to her left, she glimpsed Morgate House, and instinctively turned off the main road. The light from the road lamps immediately faded, as did the traffic noise. The only sound as she pedalled towards the derelict house was her heavy breathing as bits of gravel from the broken road crackled against her wheel spokes. Slowly, she cycled towards the vast Victorian house, now cordoned off, with barbed wire topping the high fences. Daisy stopped at the gates and climbed off her bike. She took a deep breath and propped it up, feeling her heart start to race. She didn't know why she had to torture herself by coming here; Morgate House held nothing but bad memories. But she felt desperate. Anything to be near Holly. And the exact spot where she stood now, the driveway her foster mother had collected her from, and where two grown men had held Holly back as they drove away, was the last place she had ever seen her sister.

Daisy walked up to the gates, and tugged at the padlock. You would need a heavy-duty wrench to get it open, she thought to herself. The house was fenced the entire way round and very securely protected against trespassers. Looking up at the red-brick house, which was etched on her soul, she doubted anyone would want to stay long in this desolate spot. There was little of the roof left now, and the windows were mostly gone. Being at the edge of the cliff, as it was, she knew from experience how cold Morgate House was. Any drifters would freeze to death here. They would be better off in town, where they could find the shelter of a shop doorway and get change from passers-by.

Running her hand along the thick steel fences, she made her way to the side of the house, to the annex where she and Holly had been dropped off, the night of the fire. It had been an ugly house even then; she was only six years old, but she remembered looking up at the unloved building. No potted plants by the doorstep, or ivy growing up the walls. No garden for the children to play in, or trees to climb, just concrete leading to a fence to stop them straying towards the cliff edge. She had stared at her little feet, noticing the weeds pushing through the brittle driveway, the chipped doorstep, the peeling paint on the windowsill as she clutched Holly's hand tight and the policewoman had ushered them into the annex.

Daisy kept walking round now, looking for the entrance to the annex, where she and Holly had been taken that night. It was the worst night of her life, the night their mother had been killed in the fire and the last time they had a place to call home. It was a night she longed to forget, when the policewoman had pulled her out of their burning house where her mother was trapped, and then brought her and Holly here. Daisy looked up at the door of the annex, and saw that the same iron knocker was still hanging from it. She could hear the policewoman lifting it, and letting it fall, the loud clatter rattling through the black night. She closed her eyes, the night sea air rushing past her cold cheeks, just as it had done back then. She had clutched Holly's hand so tightly, as a shadowy figure on the other side of the heavy door had walked towards it, before opening it and ushering them in. She would relive the pain a thousand times over, just for the chance to hold her sister's hand again.

She had disliked Mrs Price straight away. The woman had said nothing, just nodded and smiled weakly, but it was a smile as frosty as the night. She was a small stout woman, wearing a starched shirt and grey pleated skirt. Her hair was in a bob, so greasy that it seemed moulded to her scalp. The room she ushered them into was hot, a fire

99

burned in the hearth, and there was a man sitting in the corner. Mr Price didn't look up from his crossword. He frowned and looked over at the door, then at his wife, who closed it promptly. From the moment she crossed the threshold she felt like an inconvenience. There was no kindness, no warm welcoming words for them. They had nothing, just the clothes on their backs, not even any shoes, but Mrs Price made no mention of getting them warm, giving them a bath, a hot meal, or even a blanket.

They had stood awkwardly as the policewoman talked quietly to Mrs Price. 'I'll pop to the charity shop tomorrow, and drop round some things for the girls. They lost everything in the fire.'

'There's no need. We have clothes,' Mrs Price had said abruptly, with no warmth behind her words.

Daisy had looked over at the fire. The flames were crackling, they reminded her of the flames in their house, hours before. Flames which had killed their mother.

'I'd like to help. I feel . . . it's the least I can do,' the policewoman had said hesitantly.

'As you wish,' Mrs Price had retorted.

'Can they have something to eat?' the policewoman had asked.

'Now?' she said incredulously. 'I'll try to find them something. There's no need for you to stay. Do you have their paperwork?' She frowned, glancing at the children as if she had just tasted something bitter.

The policewoman pulled a sheet of paper from her bag, then handed it over.

'We need it signed by the social worker, or we don't get the cheque,' Mrs Price had said curtly.

'I see. I'm sorry. I'll get it signed and back to you first thing in the morning. When I bring the clothes.'

Daisy had watched the policewoman's face flush red; she didn't seem like the other officers who had come to the house when her parents fought. She was much gentler, kinder. She remembered wishing the policewoman would take them to her house, and not leave them at Morgate.

'Very well. Good night, Constable. It's very late, we'd best get them to bed.' Mrs Price had walked the policewoman to the door, opened it, and ushered her out.

The officer had looked back at them. It was a look Daisy recognised. A look her mother had when her father came home from the pub in one of his rages. Panic. Helplessness. Then the door had closed and she was gone.

Mrs Price had then turned and opened an interconnecting door between the annex and the main house. Immediately, Daisy had felt the temperature change, the air in the main house was a great deal colder than the annex and not much warmer than outside. The door linking the two houses slammed shut, and Daisy had started to shake again with the cold. The warm carpets in the annex were gone, replaced with bare wooden floorboards. There were no lamps or warm drapes, only bare windows, some cracked, the paint peeling off. As they walked along the corridor, the woman's shoes were loud on the exposed floor, which was cold against their feet. Daisy had turned to look at her sister, neither of them knowing what to say, too terrified and traumatised to speak. Holly still had soot on her face from the fire; her chest hurt, she had been in there much longer than her little sister, trying to get their mother out.

Mrs Price had shuddered, wrapped her cardigan tightly

around herself and let out a heavy sigh as they followed her for what felt like forever, traipsing down two long corridors, finally reaching a large room filled with rows of beds and the outlines of bodies under blankets.

'It's so quiet,' Holly had whispered.

'Of course,' the woman had hissed, 'it's after midnight, everyone is asleep.'

'Can we have something to eat? And a wash?' Holly had asked.

'There's nothing to eat until breakfast now, I don't know why that woman didn't feed you. Make sure you're in the dining hall at seven, the other children will show you where. The bathroom's over in the corner if you want to wash your faces. Nerve of that woman, bringing you here in this state. Then get to bed, don't be making any fuss, or you'll wake the other children.'

The bathroom was basic; a toilet and a chipped enamel cast-iron bath sat on a black-and-white tiled floor, surrounded by stark grey-white walls. Daisy could feel the cold coming off them; the walls were icy to the touch. She had looked at her sister, and knew what they were both thinking: they wanted to run home, but their home and their mother were gone, there was nowhere to run to.

Daisy reached another break in the fence now, and looked down at the padlock. She was overwhelmed with the urge to get inside Morgate House somehow. She had no idea if she could pick the lock, if it was even possible, but perhaps if she could find a heavy rock she could manage to break it. The family house they had grown up in had been burnt to the ground, a new one built in its place. Morgate House was the only building still standing where she had memories with Holly. It could be that the bedrooms were still intact, that she could find the bed they had slept in together, curl up on it and disappear. She couldn't go home, she couldn't face what her instincts said would be waiting for her there.

Daisy rattled at the gate, she looked around, desperate to find something that would help her break in. She looked up at the desolate house. It was as silent as the night they had arrived. She had thought, when they first walked through the house, there should have been the buzz of children, whispering and giggling, the pitter patter of running footsteps, of doors slamming and music playing. But there had been nothing, a terrifying silence and no sign of life. Morgate House had no heart, and she'd felt it from the moment they arrived to the day she left.

Daisy walked to the edge of the driveway and looked out at the black sea. She glanced down at a rock and picked it up, groaning at its heaviness. Walking over to the padlock, she held the rock high with both hands and then smashed it down on the heavy lock with a thwack. She lifted the rock again and brought it down harder this time. It hit the padlock hard, breaking it. As the lock fell to the ground, she dropped the rock, smashing it into her shin. She let out a gasp of pain, sinking down onto the ground and pulling her trouser leg up to see blood trickling down her calf. As she clutched it, tears stung her eyes, and she looked down to see a layer of skin peeled away. Then, breathing through the pain, she heard it.

Very faintly, from the rucksack on her back, her mobile began to ring.

Shaking, Daisy looked at her watch – it was midnight.

103

Nobody called at midnight, unless something was wrong. Someone who was waiting outside her flat. She knew it in her heart. It could only be someone from the police, or a reporter who had got hold of her number. She froze, not knowing what to do, too scared to answer it. Knowing they would keep trying until she picked up. She let it ring until it stopped. Then after a few seconds it started again. Daisy hung her head and crouched down, curling up into a ball, as the wind whipped around her and whistled like a child calling out to her.

She began to cry.

Chapter Eight

Olive

Bletchley Park, January 1944

Olive and Lorna stood at the gates of Bletchley Park as the light on the first day of their new lives began to fade. In front of them stood a lake, with weeping willows like huge hands obscuring the view of the main house.

'Where do you suppose they keep the motorbikes?' asked Olive, as she began to walk along the path towards the house, craning her neck and trying to take everything in. 'Looks like there might be some stables or outhouses round the back.'

Lorna just stared, wide-eyed, taking in the hustle and bustle of the place. It was bitterly cold, but a few men and women, wrapped in coats and scarves, scurried determinedly in all directions, like ants on a mission, to and from the huts.

'Come on,' said Olive eagerly, setting off around the perimeter of the lake. 'We'd better let them know we're here, and get to our digs, it'll be dark soon.'

Lorna followed her along the path, wincing with pain from her feet, which were rubbing in her new court shoes. As they arrived at the heavy oak door of the big house, Lorna reached for the handle and walked into the grand entrance, glancing up at the stone archways opening up into a carpeted hallway. The girls stood rooted to the spot, as everyone bustled about, too busy to acknowledge them.

'New arrivals?' said a woman in a navy skirt and cardigan, clutching a pile of brown paper files to her chest.

Olive nodded. 'Yes.'

'First floor.' The woman pointed to the staircase down the hall. 'Up those stairs, ask for Commander Travis. First door on the left.' Then, as swiftly as she had arrived, she was gone.

'Who's Commander Travis?' asked Olive, as Lorna shrugged her shoulders.

'Deputy Director of Bletchley Park,' another woman said to them as she dashed past. Lorna and Olive looked at each other and grinned, you could almost reach out and feel the energy of Bletchley.

'Shall we leave our luggage here or take it up?' said Olive, frowning up at the carpeted stairs.

'I'm not leaving mine,' Lorna muttered, flushing red with the effort as she walked towards the stairs. 'It might get swept away in the hustle and bustle,' she said, watching the endless flurry of people walking past them in the hallway.

'Well, I'm not dragging mine up there. If someone wants my smalls that badly, they can have them,' Olive said, leaving her suitcase by the front door and taking two stairs at a time, heading up to the large corridor on the first floor as Lorna struggled to keep up. Olive reached the first door, as instructed, and rapped on it with her knuckles.

'Come in!' boomed a male voice.

Glancing back at a wide-eyed Lorna trying desperately to catch her up, Olive opened the heavy mahogany door to reveal a large room, overlooking the lake and the grounds beyond. There were floor-to-ceiling bookcases lining the walls and wooden filing cabinets tucked in every corner. A moon-faced, bespectacled man in a shirt and tie was sitting behind a large desk in the window, with a telephone clutched to his ear. He beckoned them both to come in. At either side of him, two women sat at their typewriters, deep in concentration, the keys clacking away as loudly as migrating geese. As the girls reached him, stepping nervously onto the patterned carpet, he abruptly slammed down the receiver and sat back in his green leather chair.

'Ah, good afternoon, ladies. Welcome to Bletchley Park. I'm Commander Travis. I trust you had a comfortable journey?'

Lorna and Olive exchanged looks, and stayed silent, the memory of being packed like sardines into the stuffy train carriage still fresh in their minds. The man stood and retrieved a suit jacket from the back of his chair and picked up a smoking pipe from the ashtray in front of him, as if readying himself to leave at any moment.

'Here, in these grounds, you will be privy to war secrets of the utmost confidentiality. Intercepted messages, coming from every German captain, military division, battleship and U-boat, have been jumbled up and transmitted by radio. These are then gathered at listening posts around the British coastline and brought to us by our dispatch riders at Bletchley Park,' he said, walking to the coat stand next to his desk. He pulled an overcoat and hat from one of the hooks and stood at the window.

'In these huts, the most powerful intellects of our generation are tasked with outwitting the Germans' ingenious Enigma machines. Compact, beautifully designed devices which are used by the German military forces to encrypt all their communications on their countless missions into different letter combinations. The Germans deem Enigma impossible to crack, but if we can unlock the secrets of Enigma, we can reach the heart of the enemy's campaign and win the war.'

Olive nodded eagerly. 'We are just grateful to have found some way of helping, sir. We want to do whatever we can do, or are allowed to do.'

'Good, well, you will need to sign the Official Secrets Act, which Patricia here will give you now,' he said.

A stern-looking woman, with glasses resting on her ample bosom, walked over to them holding two copies of a heavy document which she placed on the desk in front of the girls.

'Everyone has to sign it,' said the man, walking towards the door. 'Nothing can be talked about outside the office where you are working.'

The girls looked at one another in trepidation, as Olive reached for the ink pen being handed to them by Patricia. She leaned down and started to write her name, feeling self-conscious that her signature was not more grown up, then handed the pen to Lorna.

'You mustn't discuss anything, with anyone, not even each other. Nobody within the grounds of Bletchley, nobody you work with – and certainly not anyone outside. Not even your parents or spouse. We have organised for you to stay in a small hotel in town. Your duties will begin tomorrow morning. I will see Lorna in hut eight. And Olive in the motorbike workshop, otherwise known as the Cottage. Any questions you have, I'm sure, can be answered by Alice, who will take you to your accommodation now. Please forgive me, but I must leave you to it now until the morning. Make sure you get a good night's sleep. You will need it. Good evening, ladies.' And with that he was gone.

A blonde woman with striking blue eyes, sitting at the other desk next to the window, stood up and smiled gently at them. 'If you'd like to follow me, I'll walk you into town.' They went out into the corridor to find no sign of Commander Travis who had disappeared at lightning speed, as everyone seemed to in this building.

'It sounds glamorous but it's not,' said Alice, as they retraced their steps outside. 'The days are long, it's hard work, repetitive and intense. Nerves can get terribly frayed; the huts are stuffy and get claustrophobic. The strain does get too much sometimes.'

Olive looked over at Lorna, who was trembling with tiredness now from dragging her suitcase so far, and on the verge of tears again at the picture Alice was painting of the work she would be doing in the huts. Olive smiled kindly at her friend. 'Shall we swap?' she asked, handing Lorna her haversack.

Lorna nodded gratefully and Olive lifted the suitcase, instantly regretting it.

'How far is it to the hotel?' asked Olive, half dragging, half carrying Lorna's case which felt like it was filled with rocks. 'I'm going to be a dispatch rider, so I won't be in the huts,' Olive explained, as they made their way along the road into town.

'Marvellous!' said Alice, her blue eyes sparkling. 'Geoff Price runs the workshop for the bikes. You'll need to report for duty there at nine in the morning. It's round the side of the house, by the old stables, it's a sturdy red-brick outbuilding. You can't miss it. He's a quirky sort of chap, and he can just be a little set in his ways.'

'Are we in the village yet?' Olive asked, weary from

109

dragging Lorna's suitcase. 'It's so dark, I can barely see my hands in front of my face.'

'Yes, we are. No street lights allowed, and they have to cover all the windows, because of the blackout. It's easy to lose your way. Not long now though.'

'Are there a lot of young people at Bletchley, then?' said Lorna hopefully.

Alice nodded. 'It's mostly young people here, some straight out of sixth form. There is quite a lot of romance, everything can get rather intense. Many people have fallen in love sitting around the lake in front of the main house.'

Lorna turned to Olive and smiled for the first time since they had arrived. Olive knew from the conversations they'd had earlier that day, Lorna was excited at the prospect of husband material being on site.

'Well, I'm not interested in any of that,' said Olive. 'I just want to find some way of helping us achieve victory. I want to win this war, I'm not interested in romance.'

'Well, no one is immune to the intensity of Bletchley, but you'll find that out in your own time. Here we are,' said Alice, as they reached the door of a large Georgian building, which was plunged into darkness. Olive looked up to see a large front door, painted black, and rows of windows above her.

'You are sharing a room, it's a small hotel, about eight rooms in total, I think, but Mrs Milton will show you around, I'm sure,' Alice said, ringing the bell. 'I'll leave you to it, you must be tired. Breakfast is at eight, I believe. I look forward to seeing you around. If you both report in at nine – Lorna to hut eight and Olive to the Cottage – you will be told your duties then. Good night.'

110

The woman turned and within a few seconds Olive could see no sign of her through the blackness, there was only the sound of her footsteps clicking into the distance.

'Yes?' A thin, grey-haired lady opened the door, and glared down at them.

'Um, we're from Bletchley,' said Olive, wondering if she'd need to rush back into the darkness to get Alice, but the woman quickly ushered them in. She was in her dressing gown, with her hair in rollers, and was smoking a cigarette. 'I think you're the last in tonight so I can lock up,' she said, setting about bolting the door in a frenzy. 'Up the stairs,' she said. 'First floor. Go on, I haven't got all night.' She ushered them up the stairs as she turned and pulled two deadbolts closed with a heavy clunk.

The girls passed a front room with a small fire burning in the grate; it did little to warm the large, cold hotel, which was sparsely furnished. The carpet on the stairs was thin and worn, there were no pictures on the walls and no lampshades.

'You have to be back by ten every evening, and no male company allowed.' The landlady followed them up to the first floor. 'Breakfast is at eight, and you must be out by then for me to clean. Once a week you strip your beds, and keep the windows and shutters closed at all times. If you try and sneak anyone in, I'll know about it, and you won't be coming back here – or to Bletchley Park, either.'

The woman opened one of the doors with a key and then handed it to them. 'Keep your door locked at all times. You never know who is about.'

'Is there only one key? What if we aren't together?' Olive asked.

'You'll just have to get organised. Good night, ladies,'

she said, as Olive and Lorna stepped into the room, furnished with two beds, two lamps, a wardrobe in the corner, and little else.

'I was wondering what time dinner is?' asked Olive, as the woman walked off down the hallway.

'You've missed it. They feed you at Bletchley, I don't do food here except breakfast.'

'Not really a hotel, is it? More like a jail,' remarked Olive, under her breath, as the woman disappeared down the stairs. 'I'm sure we can get lampshades and pictures, and make it a bit more homely,' she said, turning round to see Lorna standing at the door, her face crumbling.

The room was not inviting. It had no decoration, no cushions or pictures, and only a single light bulb hanging from the ceiling. The window was a single pane and the room so cold that frost had formed on the inside. Olive rushed towards it, and pulled the curtain.

'I want to go home. I wish I'd never come here,' Lorna said, as Olive ushered her over to the bed.

'It'll be okay, you're just tired. Why don't you wash up, and I'll see what my father packed for me, I'm sure I have some sandwiches and a bit of chocolate in here. You must be ever so hungry.'

Lorna threw herself onto the bed, and began crying in earnest, as Olive rummaged in her haversack for some food. She pulled out a parcel, slipped her father's letter out of her coat pocket, and placed everything on the bedside table. Then she retrieved a sandwich, wrapped in brown paper, and an apple.

'Come on, have some of this,' she said kindly.

112

'Maybe later,' Lorna sniffed, as her cries morphed from heavy sighs and eventually into quiet snores.

Olive pulled the brown woollen blanket at the end of the bed over her new friend's body and leaned back against the headboard. She opened up one of the sandwiches her father had made for her and began to eat it, before reaching out for the parcel he had given her.

Slowly, she pulled at the brown string, until the tie gave way and the paper fanned out to reveal a beautiful leather-bound book with the word 'Notebook' in gold writing on the front. She stroked it with her hand and carefully flicked through the brand-new parchment paper, thinking of her father buying it. Carefully choosing it, on his precious time off, thinking of her going away. Finding the strength to be so kind, when he had already lost his beloved son to the war. Olive put it down on the bedside table and turned to the letter, pulling it out of the crisp cream envelope embossed with her father's beautiful writing.

My darling Olive,

I hope you arrive safely and that your journey is not too long and arduous.

I took the liberty of buying you this notebook, in the hope that you might collect some memories from this time away. I'm sure you won't be able to write about your war efforts, as they will be top secret, but perhaps you will be able to collect little drawings, passing thoughts, pressed flowers, or receipts perhaps. One day you will look back on this time as an adventure, and I find little momentos very useful in conjuring up memories and feelings. I'm sure this trip will be a rite of passage for you. I want you to be able to look back and remember it.

I know we have all suffered a great deal since the news of Michael – but mostly, probably, your mother, who has withdrawn from us completely. I am sure you have found it difficult and miss her presence. It is difficult for me to express how proud I am of the way you have coped. I know you loved Michael dearly. And I hope you know how grateful I am for all your help around the farm. We could not have coped without you. Know that we both love you very much. You must be feeling very nervous and full of suspense this evening. But I know you will be a wonderful asset.

I think it is splendid that you will have a chance to get to discover things about yourself during this time. Your mother has struggled from marrying young, and not having the chance to get to know herself well. Her passions and what she might like to do with her life, other than being a homemaker and having children. I want more for you, Olive, I want you to live, to know yourself, to be sure of what you want before you marry and settle down. It is the most important thing for a happy life. But know that, whatever that is, I will always support you.

Go easy on those bikes, and let us know how you are, if you can.

With much love and admiration,
Dad xxx

114

Olive felt a fat tear splash onto the brown paper her sandwich was wrapped in and glanced over again at Lorna, sleeping soundly now, her chest rising and falling with her heavy breathing. Olive lay down on her bed, hugging the notebook her father had given her for comfort, and pulled her blanket over her. She longed to travel forward in time, to read the pages of her notebook once it was full of the adventures that lay ahead. The anticipation and excitement of not knowing what her first day at Bletchley Park had in store soon gave way to her exhaustion, and as the January rain crackled at the window pane, she drifted off into a deep sleep.

Chapter Nine
Jo

March 2015, Monday evening

Jo walked towards the entrance of Downside Nursing Home and took a deep breath as she waited to be buzzed in. The automatic doors opened; all was quiet as she signed the visitors' book in reception. For a moment she stood, scared to walk down to her mother's room in case she found herself alone with her, not knowing what to say. Certain whatever she did say would come out wrong and upset her.

She was cold and her head was still spinning from her visit to the site to meet with the forensic pathologist.

'It's definitely a white female, fifteen to twenty-five years old, I'd say, as her bones were still growing. You can tell from where the ends of the shafts are fusing to the short bone caps. Also, the teeth were still developing,' he had added, 'but it's going to take a while to build a biological profile.'

'How long roughly would you say she's been here?' Jo had asked.

'I'd be guessing. I need to run some tests in the lab. I can see there's very little bone fluorescence, so at least two, maybe three decades, but I can hopefully give you an answer later this week.'

Jo had nodded; she could see his team packing up behind them, as the night set in. 'And any idea how she died? We noticed some head trauma earlier.'

'There are signs of trauma, but most fractures are not fatal, so I would need more time to establish if it was a fatal blow. Also, it could have been damaged by the guys excavating.'

'They're saying not,' Jo had assured him.

The pathologist had looked over Jo's shoulder at Stan; it was the briefest of glances, a tiny exchange between two men acknowledging that Jo was clearly a handful. It was a look she had grown used to. 'Still, we can't offer a cause of death at this stage. Unfortunately,' he'd added.

'Okay, you said you wanted to show me something?' Jo had asked, trying not to let the impatience creep into her voice.

He had nodded. 'Yes, indeed. When marks occur on bone and you're still alive, the bones heal and remodel. See . . . here, she had a fractured wrist.'

'Is it possible to tell if that happened at the time of death?' Jo had looked up.

'No, it didn't. If a fracture occurred at the time of death, it would be the same colour as the head trauma, but this has a darker colouration around her wrist. And you can see it's healed.' He had stood up and pulled off his gloves, indicating he was done for the day.

'So, she had broken her wrist at some point in her childhood?' Jo had asked, seeking clarification.

'Yes, I'd say shortly before she died. And it's been set, so she went to hospital.'

Jo had looked over at Stan and smiled. 'That's great. We can check Holly Moore's records with Brighton Hospital. So, how long before you can get DNA?'

'We have to fully dissolve the bone matrix to release the

DNA, which will take at least twelve hours. I'd hope to have something for you by Wednesday.'

'We'll have to hold off going to her sister before that, then. There's no point upsetting her unnecessarily,' Jo had said.

Stan had nodded, shivering and stamping his feet in the freezing cold air. Night was descending fast.

'I'll contact the hospital first thing. I may even go down there, as Holly's hospital records are going back a while, so they'll be hard to track down.'

'Okay, I'll update the boss,' Stan had offered as she half slid, half walked down the muddy bank to her car. As they were leaving, she had told Stan she was going to see her mother, and asked him to tell Megan to save her having to call her daughter and have a painful lengthy conversation about it. She was dreading it enough as it was, she didn't want to go over every detail once it was finally over.

'Megan's already there,' he had informed her. 'She's asked me to pick her up. She'll be really pleased you're going,' he added.

Jo reached into her pocket for her phone; she had texted Charlie to say she was on her way, but hadn't heard back from him. Even though she was now a sixty-year-old woman, and she had been told her mother was so frail she needed to be transferred to a hospice, she still instantly felt like a teenager again whenever she was near her. Unable to do or say anything right.

She needed Charlie here, to smooth the way, lighten the atmosphere, save her – like he always did. She would just wait in reception until he arrived, she told herself, looking around for a chair.

'Can I help you?' said a woman in a jacket with 'Downside' embroidered on the breast pocket.

'Um, yes, I'm Jo Hamilton, I'm here to see my mother, Olive,' Jo said, walking back towards her.

'Ah, yes, come this way, her granddaughter just arrived too. Her son only just left, it's lovely to see so many of you here for her.'

Jo forced a smile, her heart sinking at the prospect of Megan being there too. She looked down at her phone for any sign of a reply from Charlie, feeling her pulse throbbing in her wrist. Forty years' experience on the force, rarely fazed by drunks, thugs or hardened criminals, and yet her mother and daughter combination made her feel like her fingers were caught in a vice.

'She may be sleeping, she's had quite a lot of pain relief this evening,' said the woman, opening the door for her, which creaked, making her mother stir.

Olive lay upright on her bed, and turned towards Jo as she walked in. Her mother managed a weak smile. The room was hot and stuffy, and Jo immediately felt a tight knot in her stomach. Her mother was obsessed with fresh air, and it was a sign of how poorly she must be, to not be bothered by the lack of it in her room. Olive had grown up on a farm, and was allergic to central heating, or heating of any kind, even when it snowed. Houses needed to be well ventilated, according to her, and every day required an enormous dose of fresh air in order to sustain happiness. Fresh air was Olive's answer to any problem; she would tie her long, wavy chestnut hair back in one of her mother's silk scarves, and storm out into the wind, pelting rain and bitter cold, until her cheeks were red, and her fingers were numb.

'Shall I open the window?' said Jo. 'It's very hot in here.'

'It's okay, Mum, she gets really cold,' said Megan, in a know-it-all tone Jo was all too familiar with.

Jo felt the urge to pick her mother up, wrap her in a blanket and carry her outside to look at the stars. Olive was her mother, and she knew better than anyone what she needed.

'How are you, Mum?' whispered Megan, standing up to greet her.

Jo hugged her daughter, who smelt of baby lotion and looked like she'd been crying. Jo's eyes then fell on Stan, who was taking his coat off, having arrived just ahead of her no doubt.

'I'm well, thank you. Hi, Stan,' she said.

'Hi, Jo,' he said, smiling knowingly.

She could never get comfortable with the idea of a work colleague being engaged to her daughter. However good she knew he was for Megan. They had met at Charlie's leaving do, ten years before, and spent most of the night huddled in the corner chatting. Jo had smiled encouragingly, but alarm bells were ringing immediately, she didn't want every move she made at work going back to her family.

But Megan had been so much happier since she met Stan – she took herself and life less seriously. And when Megan was being prickly towards Jo, Stan defended her, which no one had ever done before.

But in an ideal world her daughter wouldn't be in a relationship with her colleague. Only that morning, they had been standing together on Saltdean Tye, discussing human remains. Now they were standing at the bedside of her ailing mother. It was too close for comfort.

'How are you, Mum?' Jo sat on the other side of the bed to Megan, and looked at her mother.

'My pain is getting worse. They're moving me to St Catherine's, but I don't want to leave my friends here.'

Jo took her hand. 'It'll be okay, Mum. We are all here for you.'

'I've been asking for you,' Olive said.

Jo bit down on her lip and glanced over at Megan, who was watching her. 'I'm sorry, Mum. It's been a busy day.'

'Can't they ease up on you?' Olive asked sleepily. 'It's your last week.'

Jo shifted uncomfortably in her seat, feeling Megan's eyes on her. 'I don't want them to ease up on me,' she said defensively, taking a deep breath.

'It's all such a terrible strain for Charlie, I feel such a burden.' Olive turned away from Jo.

'She's worried about the morning,' Megan added.

'What about the morning?' Jo turned to her daughter.

Megan looked over at Olive and took her hand. 'They're moving Granny tomorrow. They need someone to go in the ambulance with her, and Charlie is meeting with the solicitor about the house sale.'

Jo frowned at Megan. 'Mum's selling the house?'

'Charlie said he told you. She has to, to pay for her care. Her savings have run out,' Megan said quietly.

'I always wanted to go back there, Jo,' said Olive. 'You said this would only be temporary.'

Jo looked at her mother, and squeezed her hand tightly. 'I'm sorry, Mum. I know how hard this must be. What time are they moving her?' she added, turning to Megan.

'We don't know yet, probably first thing, but there could

be some hanging around. I'd go, obviously, but I've got Phoebe, and Stan can't take her because of the briefing.'

'What briefing?' Jo asked.

Stan frowned and looked at her. 'It's an update, on the remains, they've set up an incident room and Carl wants to talk everyone through it. He sent an email this afternoon. It must be an oversight.'

'Can we please not do this in here?' Megan whispered to Stan.

Jo tried to breathe through the rage that was swelling inside her and looked at her mother, who stared back at her.

'He probably thought you wouldn't want to go. Poor Jo, it's going to be hard to let go, it's been your life for so long,' Olive offered.

Jo felt like the kid in the playground who was last to be picked for a team match. A match that her mother would push her to take part in but would never turn up to watch. She didn't want her mother's sympathy, she didn't want anyone's sympathy. She just wanted to be allowed to do her job.

'Mum, don't worry, I'll come over in the morning and go with you,' she found herself saying. She couldn't bear the thought of no one being with her mother, she wouldn't be able to concentrate anyway because of the guilt, and there was no way she was going to a briefing she wasn't invited to. She could do some work while they waited for the ambulance, make some enquiries, while her boss was distracted.

'It's alright, Jo, Charlie will do it,' said Olive, her eyes closing.

'No, I'll be here.' Jo stood up and kissed her mother on the forehead. 'I'll see you in the morning. Stan, can I have a word outside?' she said, walking out of the door.

Stan reluctantly followed Jo out.

'Do you know anything else?'

Stan sighed. 'They're ninety-nine per cent sure it's Holly, and it's also a meeting to manage the heat from the press. They're trying to get her sister's DNA but they can't find her.'

'And who's invited to the briefing?'

'All the heads of department. Some press. I'm sure you're included, Jo. It's your case.'

'Did Carl call it?'

'Yes, but I'm sure it's just an error.'

'It's not an error. And we both know it. I appreciate the sentiment, Stan, but I'm not an idiot.'

Jo walked off down the corridor; if she had to be back here in the morning, she thought to herself, she had exactly twelve hours to find Daisy before the team did.

As Stan watched her go, Megan appeared in the hallway.

'I thought she would finally take an interest in our lives now that she's retiring.'

'Don't be too hard on her. For what it's worth, I think she's being treated badly. She's done nothing wrong, and Carl is purposely excluding her.'

'She's leaving, he can't tell her confidential information if she isn't working there any more,' Megan said curtly.

'You need to protect her, Megan, you need to persuade her to stay away. I don't trust Carl not to screw her over,' Stan said.

'What are you talking about?' Megan frowned.

'There's a lot of heat on him about this girl Holly. Why she wasn't reported missing by Morgate House for two days, why nobody even realised she was missing or looked for her in the crucial hours after she disappeared. Nobody followed up, because she was a kid in care, they just thought she'd run away again. And it wasn't even raised at the inquest. I don't know, but some of the team are saying he's going to try and pin it on Jo,' he whispered, as a nurse walked by.

'Mum had only just come back from her career break when Holly went missing. She was a lowly police constable. How can he try to blame her? That's crazy.'

'Because she went to see Lorna Price at Morgate, when Mrs Price eventually called it in.'

'And she would have done everything by the book. She would have reported it. If they didn't escalate it quickly enough that's not her fault. Who did she report it to?' asked Megan.

'Three guesses.'

'Carl. And his head is on the block, so he wants to blame her?'

'Talk to your mum, Meg, she's determined to open a can of worms with this Morgate thing, and I'm worried if she does, she'll back Carl into a corner and he'll take her down with him.'

'Why can't you talk to her? She's more likely to listen to you,' she said, sighing.

'Because it's not my place. She's my senior, and it's humiliating for her. I've got a lot of respect for her. I don't want her to know everyone has noticed the way Carl is treating her.'

'Okay, I'll try. But when she has the bit between her teeth she doesn't listen to anyone. Her mother is dying, she should be there for her. For us. I don't understand her. I really don't,' said Megan, turning and walking back into her grandmother's bedroom.

Chapter Ten

Daisy

March 2015, Monday evening

'Hello?'

'Daisy Moore?'

'Yes?'

'This is Police Constable Sarah Jones. Do you have a minute to talk?'

Daisy stood at the edge of the cliff face in front of Morgate House and looked out at the dark expanse of the English Channel lit up by the moonlight. She could smell the salty sea air, hear the roar of the waves, feel the chalk of the cliff face inches from her feet.

'Hello? Daisy, are you there?'

Daisy couldn't bring herself to reply. If she did, the woman would continue saying what she had to say, and Daisy didn't want to hear it.

'Yes, I'm here.'

'Where are you? We can come and pick you up.'

'What's this about?' she said, knowing full well but trying to slow the conversation down. The phone had rung five times in her bag – from a withheld number – before she finally answered. Her legs were shaking, feeling as if they would give way at any moment, her shin was still throbbing with pain and wet with blood.

'As you may have seen on the news today, some human

remains have been found on Saltdean Tye. We are contacting all the relatives of people who went missing between 1975 and 1985 to get DNA samples. Your sister, Holly Moore, was one of those missing people we have on record. We don't want to worry you at this stage, it is just a process of elimination. We've been waiting outside your flat for a couple of hours now. Do you know when you might be home this evening? Or we could come to you, if you're still at work?'

Tears stung Daisy's eyes. Now they wanted to speak to her, now it was too late, now they may have found Holly's body. After thirty years of ignoring her and Holly, suddenly there was a sense of urgency. Every year, on Holly's birthday, she had gone into Saltdean Police Station to ask if there had been any developments. She hated going up to the counter and asking. Who? What was the name again? Holly, Holly Moore, she would reply. It was the only thing she could do to keep Holly alive; Holly's birthday was the worst day of her year, alongside Christmas Day. Speaking Holly's name, the policeman at the counter writing it down, prompting them all to check on their system, talk about her, prick their memory and force them to recall the young girl who went missing all that time ago.

It was never the same person in charge of missing young people in Sussex; every year it was someone new, someone she didn't recognise. She would sit in reception for hours sometimes, waiting. Being ignored, while they chatted behind the perspex screen, got each other coffees, dealt with the waifs and strays coming and going. Eventually someone would appear to talk to her, their body language and tone of voice always the same. She could imagine their training: speak slowly, maintain eye contact; 'unfortunately', or 'sadly', or 'I'm sorry to say' there have been no updates, but we have your information on the system, if any leads do turn up we won't hesitate to be in touch. Before they went back to their desks, got on with their day, and her life stayed forever on hold. Thinking of the what ifs – which were bad enough on Holly's birthday, but even worse on Christmas Eve. Christmas was always a struggle, it seemed the world was awash with happy families, and she was plagued with thoughts of what life could have been like with her sister.

Holly would be turning forty-eight now, possibly a mother, making Daisy an auntie. Sometimes, on her darkest days, she would hide away under her duvet, and dream about what their life together could have been. She would pretend that Holly rented the flat below her, or the house next door, and they would never let a day go by without seeing each other. They would look after each other's children, and help each other out in any way they could. Get shopping, or pick each other up from the station when it was raining. She found Christmas and birthdays hard, but it was the tiny things she missed most. Having someone there who knew what she was thinking. And she still had their memory jar. An old jam jar they had taken from the dining room at Morgate House. Whenever they were having a bad day, they would write something down that they were going to do when they were older and had left the children's home far behind them. It was her most treasured possession, it sat above her fridge, the pieces of paper crumpled and grubby, and most of the writing faded away. When she was missing Holly, she would open one of the wishes and read it. Run her fingers over Holly's handwriting. They could have wished for anything, but the things they wrote as children made her smile every time with their modesty: a picnic, a trip in a rowing boat, a bike ride. She promised herself that, one day, when she had found Holly, and could leave Sussex, she would do them all. But at the age of forty-five, her whole life was still waiting to start.

'I'm just leaving work, I won't be long,' Daisy said to the police constable, waiting for her to reply.

'As I said, we can pick you up—'

Daisy ended the call before the woman finished speaking. She didn't want to tell them where she was, she didn't want them questioning why she was standing outside a derelict building in the middle of the night. They could wait a bit longer; she had waited long enough for them.

Once she gave them her DNA, it would be only a matter of hours before Holly was truly gone. Daisy turned back to the fence and the broken padlock lying at her feet. Slowly, she removed the chain and pushed the fence. It juddered, stuck in the dirt, buckled under the exposure of being on the seafront. She leaned against it and pressed harder. Finally, it opened up enough for her to push her way through.

She crept forward, heading towards the house; there wasn't a sound except her own heavy breathing, and the sea thrashing in the distance. As she reached the front door of the annex, she pulled her phone out of her back pocket and clicked on the torch. She reached out slowly, turned the door handle and pushed it gently – expecting it to be locked. But it creaked open and, holding her breath, she walked in.

The room was bare of furniture, but the Victorian

fireplace in the corner, which had crackled with warmth that first evening, was just as she remembered it. She could picture Mr Price sitting in his armchair, trying his best to ignore her and Holly as they came in from the cold night. She looked around the familiar room. Water dripped from what was left of the ceiling onto the exposed concrete floor – the Prices' plush carpet and oversized lamps were long gone – but Daisy's memories came rushing back all the same, the blinding panic still fresh in the pit of her stomach.

There was no sign of the interconnecting door which had separated the two vastly different sections of the house; one warm, cosy and inviting, the other cold and sparse. Slowly she walked through the archway which separated the annex and the main building. She could hear her own breath, and that of Holly's as she walked beside her. She could feel her sister's presence more acutely, along the eerily dark corridor, which dripped with freezing cold water onto her head. Goosebumps ran down her whole body. She could hear something scurrying ahead of her, she could feel the sadness of the building weighing down on her. The wind whipped through the broken windows, the sea hissed and rushed in the distance. No one would hear her if she screamed, there was no one for miles around. But she wasn't afraid, because she wasn't alone. If she reached out her hand, she would feel Holly's. She had walked along with Holly that night, hearing the scratching of mice or rats in the bowels of the crumbling building. Her whole body shook from the cold but she didn't care, she needed to feel close to Holly, nothing else mattered. At the end of the first corridor was the old dining room. The door – which had often been locked, leaving the children to fend for themselves with no means to buy food – lay on the floor in front of her.

Daisy walked into the bedroom, where rusted bed frames still lined the room. As she made her way over to the window, broken glass crackled under her feet, and she found the bed in which she and Holly had slept. Often, she would wake in the night and Holly would be gone. Her stomach would be rumbling and she would stare at the ceiling and wait for Holly to come back, terrified that something might have happened to her. She would doze off and awake to blue police lights reflecting off the ceiling and lighting up the dormitory, as a patrol car pulled up outside the house. She would watch the lights dancing above her, knowing it was Holly they were bringing back. That she had been picked up again for stealing, for trying to get money to buy them some food.

Daisy stood in the room which had been their bedroom, shining the light from her phone onto the wooden floor and up the walls. A single wardrobe stood in the corner. She reached out and slowly opened it . . . a bat flew out and darted past her face. Daisy let out a gasp of shock and staggered back, trying to catch her breath. As the wardrobe door flapped open and closed, she saw a mirror, fractured, attached to the inside door. She watched it as the door creaked back and forth to a standstill, and noticed it reflecting a dozen names carved into the back of the wardrobe. Captivated, Daisy walked over to it, her breathing still panicked, and shone the light from her phone inside. Unable to read the names clearly, she stepped into the small space, running her fingers over the letters, and spoke them out loud as if trying to bring them back to life: Anna, Sarah, Eve. Then she stopped, the realisation taking her breath away. There, in the centre, was Holly's name, and next to it was hers, surrounded by a heart. She hadn't drawn it, she would have remembered; the letters were large, dug out with what must have been a compass, and filled in with black pen. It must have been Holly.

Daisy pressed her fingers into the indentations, then turned on her camera phone and took a picture of them and the heart surrounding them. She touched it, imagined Holly standing in the exact spot where she stood now, slowly cutting out their names. Thinking of her and missing her – just as Daisy had been. Daisy stepped out, and looked back at the bed next to the window where she and Holly used to sleep. There was nothing on it but rusted metal springs, but she walked over to it, took off her coat and laid it down, just as Holly used to do for her, to make her bed more comfortable. Slowly, she climbed onto the makeshift bed and then closed her eyes.

'How was school?'

'Okay.'

'What's up, pip squeak?'

'Nothing.'

Holly had a way of knowing when she was upset, even though she would try to hide it.

'You know this coat of mine you're lying on, it makes you tell the truth. If you tell the truth, it makes you feel a million times better afterwards. But if you keep it in, it just gives you tummy ache. Have you got tummy ache?'

She had nodded. 'Nicola has asked everyone in our class to her party except me. And Peter said it's because she knows I don't have a mummy and can't afford to buy her a present.' Her voice trembled.

'Well, for starters, you do have a mum, she's with you all the time. She's watching you and taking care of you. More even than if she was alive. Mums that are alive have to leave you at the school gate, but Mum is sitting next to you, every minute of every day.'

'Really?'

'Really. And secondly, I don't know Nicola but she sounds like a horrible person, And you know horrible people end up miserable and lonely.'

'I don't care about that, I still want to go to her party.'

'Well, where is the party?'

'It's in the village hall, on Saturday, she's having an entertainer.'

'Find out the time from Peter and we'll go. I'll make sure we've got a present.'

'What if they don't let me in?'

'They will, that's the thing about mean people. They don't want everyone to know they're mean. And if you've got a big present, she definitely will.'

'But how will you buy a big present, Holly?'

'Don't you worry about that, pip squeak. Now go to sleep.'

She could feel her sister beside her now, her breath on her cheek, her arms around her, keeping her warm as the crackle of gravel under car tyres filled the room, just as they used to do when the police brought Holly back more than thirty years ago. Daisy closed her eyes again, happy in her dream.

TAP, TAP, TAP.

'Daisy? Daisy, are you here?'

Daisy started and sat up, pulling herself off the bed and looking out of the window. A car had pulled up outside. They'd got bored of waiting and had tracked her down, probably using her mobile phone signal after they'd spoken to her. She took one last look back at the wardrobe, then retraced her footsteps, heading down the long corridor, pushing open the door into the night.

'Daisy? My name is Superintendent Joanna Hamilton, could I have a word, please?'

Daisy barely looked at the plain-clothed policewoman as she rushed past her into the night.

'Please stop, Daisy, I need to talk about your sister, Holly.'

Daisy reached the gap in the fence where she'd squeezed through, leaving her bicycle propped on the far side. 'There's nothing you can tell me that I don't already know. It's your fault she's dead. You don't care, any of you.'

'That's not true, Daisy, I care very much.'

'Why didn't you care when she was still alive? When you could have found her and saved her. Nobody cared about any of us. She told you they weren't looking after us, but you were always arresting her and bringing her back to Morgate. She told you, and nobody listened. Do you know how terrifying that was for her to tell the police we weren't being fed, our clothes didn't fit, our shoes were too small? Nobody cared about us. None of you listened.'

'We did everything we could. I know how hard it must have been. I want to catch whoever did this to her. But I need your help.'

'My help? Where were you? When she went missing? When I came every year to ask if they were still looking?

134

When they wouldn't let us see each other? I didn't see her for the final four years of her life because of you. You tore us apart, and then you made sure I never saw her again.'

Jo felt a surge of injustice. 'Daisy, that's not true. I'm sorry, but I personally ensured you were given visitation rights.'

Daisy stopped and glared at her. 'What do you mean "personally"? Who are you?' Daisy's whole body shook as she stared at the woman. She was tall, with short hair, and her eyes were fixed on her. She didn't recognise her, but at the same time there was something familiar about her.

'I was the one who took you to Morgate House, the night your mother died.'

Daisy looked at her in disbelief. Her heart began to race so fast that her legs turned to jelly. 'You were the one who started the fire?'

'Daisy, it was an accident,' Jo said, her voice wavering as she walked over to her.

'Get away from me!' Daisy shouted, as the night of the fire came rushing back to her. She could still recall the sensation of the policewoman carrying her, feel the heat of the fire from their blazing house on her arms and legs. She had stared at the flames, licking up the house, like the big bonfire on the football ground on fireworks night, when their mother would give them sparklers and hot chocolate. Her father had hated fireworks night, it was the one time they were allowed out just the three of them without him and she looked forward to it all year. They had drawn their names with sparklers in the dark sky. But like so many things, the fire had ruined all that. She hated bonfires now, the flames and the heat just took her straight back.

135

'I know mistakes were made, and I want to help. I want to make it up to you,' Jo said, knowing she sounded too desperate.

'Stay away, just leave me alone,' said Daisy, shouldering her way through the fence.

'I want to get whoever did this. We care about what happened to Holly,' Jo said, knowing she was losing her.

'We don't even know it's Holly yet. You need my DNA.'

'I know it's her, Daisy.' Jo reached into her pocket and pulled out her mobile phone, the glare from its screen drawing Daisy in. Slowly, Jo handed it over to her.

Daisy took it reluctantly. 'I don't want to look,' she said, starting to cry. 'What is it?'

'It's Holly's necklace,' said Jo quietly, as the ocean roared below them.

'Her St Christopher?' Daisy asked, wiping a tear away with the back of her hand. 'Was it with the remains?'

'Yes, I'm so sorry. I wanted you to hear it from me first.'

Daisy thrust the phone back into Jo's hand and ran towards her bike. 'I'm going home, please don't follow me,' she said.

'There are reporters outside your flat, I don't think you should go home tonight, I think maybe you should stay with a friend.'

'Do you know what happened to her? Do you know how she died?' Daisy took a deep breath. 'Was she murdered?'

'We don't know that yet, Daisy.'

'If she was murdered, it's your fault. You didn't care about her. You never looked for her. Don't follow me!'

Daisy climbed on her bike as Jo called after her, and pushed herself off. She desperately wanted to get away. But she couldn't go home. She didn't want to see her friends. She didn't want to wake anyone up or talk to them. She didn't know what to do, or where to go. Instinctively, she turned right, pedalling as fast as she could, away from Morgate and Brighton and the police, and towards her workplace. There was only one person she wanted to talk to now. Only one person she could be herself with. She didn't know if she would still be awake, or if her son would still be with her.

Her hands were shaking as she unlocked the door and let herself in, locking it again behind her. She knew that the staff would be on duty doing their rounds, but she might get lucky. She walked down the corridor towards Olive's room, and opened the door without knocking. Her heart leapt when she saw she was propped up against the pillows, her eyes closed, with no sign of family. Daisy sat down next to her and started to cry.

Olive stirred. 'What is it, what's wrong, Daisy?'

'I'm sorry to wake you.'

'You didn't, I can't sleep.'

'They've found my sister's body. She's been missing for thirty years. I never knew what happened to her. The police never even tried to find out what happened to her. They don't care. There are reporters at my flat, I can't go home.'

Olive tried to sit up straighter, and Daisy helped her, easing the pillows behind her back. 'What do you think happened to her?' Olive asked.

'I think she was murdered. She would never have killed herself, or left me. For years, I've walked into every graveyard and wandered around, thinking I'll find her. Wanting to find her. I thought that anything was better than not knowing, but now that it could be her and I might finally know, I want to go back to not knowing. When there was hope.'

Olive took her hand. 'I'm so sorry, Daisy.'

Daisy felt the tears escaping but she was too consumed with anger to let go. 'It kills me that I wasn't there, at Morgate, when she went missing. I feel like I don't know anything about her. About who her friends were or what was happening at school, if she was in trouble with the police. Nothing. How am I supposed to know what happened to her if all I have is a blank page?'

'Have you spoken to the council? You should be allowed access to her social services file,' Olive suggested.

'I hadn't thought of that,' Daisy said quietly.

Olive frowned. 'It would definitely have included how she was doing at school, the staff at the children's home who dealt with her, they would have written regular progress reports. They probably made mention of who she was friends with, if they got into trouble together.'

'And you think they'd give me her file? If the police haven't got it already . . .' Daisy asked.

'Of course. You're her sister. You could also maybe track down some of the people in her year at school through Facebook, see if they know anything.'

Daisy smiled, feeling a surge of hope for the first time she could ever remember. 'I imagine you were a force to be reckoned with at Bletchley Park, Olive.' Then she frowned. 'But won't I get into trouble with the police for interfering?'

'Not if it's a man running the investigation,' muttered Olive darkly. 'Men always underestimate women; they won't see you as a threat.'

138

Olive smiled as Daisy stood up.

'Thank you. I'm going to miss seeing you every day.'

'Well, I'm not dead yet, promise me you'll come and visit me,' Olive said, winking.

'Of course I will,' said Daisy, smiling. 'You get some sleep now.'

'I will. I'm dreaming a lot about riding my motorbike,' she said. 'I haven't thought about it for years.'

'What was it like?' asked Daisy, leaning in.

'It was like meditating. It takes so much concentration, every moment you're filled with this terror that you will come off. You have to see every danger on the road ahead, anticipate anything that might run out in front of you, and in Bletchley I was in the dark, with no road signs or lights, because of the blackout. It makes you forget everything else, you have no space in your head for anything except trying not to die!'

'You're amazing, Olive, I hope you know that.'

'I wish that were true. I'd love to show you my bike one day, Daisy,' she murmured sleepily. 'I still have it stored away at my daughter's house.'

'I'd love that, Olive,' said Daisy, taking her hand.

Chapter Eleven

Jo

March 2015, Tuesday morning

'You're in early, Jo.'

The PC doing the night shift behind the counter at Saltdean Police Station smiled. A woman lying across the chairs in reception stirred in her sleep, having obviously been there all night.

'Where's my coffee?' he added, smiling cheekily.

Jo smiled weakly and walked through reception. She had hardly slept, after tracking down Daisy the night before in a complete stroke of luck after leaving her mother's care home.

She had been driving along the coast road from Saltdean, towards Brighton, wracking her brains as to where Daisy might be. There would have been no point sitting outside her flat with the press, and her colleagues from Sussex Police. Even if Daisy had come home, she wouldn't be able to talk to her without Carl being told.

As she drove past the entrance to the site it suddenly occurred to her that Daisy may try and go up there. Not with any realistic hope of seeing Holly's remains, but just to be close to her. Members of the public, and journalists, had been milling about all day, it could be that Daisy had been one of them.

Slowly she had pulled into the gravel car park, which she

had visited twice already that day. A cluster of reporters were milling around drinking tea and smoking cigarettes, a couple of them glanced over at her, then looked away with disinterest. As she was climbing out of her car, she glanced over at Morgate House and noticed something. A faint light, a flicker in the grounds, which went out again almost instantaneously.

Her instinct had told her immediately that it was Daisy. There was no reason why anyone would be at the disused site of Morgate House, there was no shelter there, it was exposed and bitterly cold. The only reason for anyone to go up there, would be to visit the past.

Pleased that she was being ignored by the rabble at the site, she had driven off again, and away from Morgate House, so as not to attract attention, then round the roundabout and back along the coast road. As she slowed to turn off the road to Morgate, she had turned off her headlights. It made it harder to see, but she couldn't risk being spotted. The night was clear, the moon bright, and she knew the road well. It was straight enough, no twists or turns, and she used the crackling, broken tarmac to guide her.

She'd had no idea if the girl would remember her – she had doubted it – but she felt strongly that she should be the one who broke the news to her about Holly. They needed to keep her onside; Jo had to make sure it was all handled sensitively. If they managed to get this opened as a murder inquiry, they were going to need a great deal of help from Daisy Moore going forward, and they needed to get off on the right foot.

Jo shuddered at the memory of their meeting. Daisy's hatred for the police was palpable and in Daisy's eyes, they were responsible for Holly's death. And when she realised who Jo was, that she had started the fire that had killed her mother, nothing Jo could do or say – even producing a picture of Holly's St. Christoper – was going to unite them in that moment.

Jo had headed home, with her notebook and Gemma and Holly's photographs, and spent her evening putting together a to-do list for the following day, including a visit to Brighton Hospital for Holly's records and a phone call to the coroner to request Gemma Smith's inquest notes. Having only caught the final few minutes of her inquest, forty years before, she needed to go through it with a fine-tooth comb for any clues it may hold to Gemma's young life prior to her death. Even as an experienced constable of two years, her gut had told her the suicide verdict had been a mistake, but it would take a great deal more than that to prove it.

Finally, unable to sleep, she had gone through her notebook, from the night of the fire, right up until Holly's disappearance, and started a timeline of her known whereabouts.

Jo walked along the corridor towards her office, and was surprised to see her light on. She heard voices as she approached the door, and checked her watch; it was only seven thirty, she thought she would have been the first in by a long way. As she reached for the handle, she saw a flutter of activity inside. Carl took his feet off her desk and hurriedly stood up when she walked in. As did Stan, who was in the seat opposite Carl.

'Morning.' Jo frowned, placing her coffee and briefcase on her desk.

The men exchanged an awkward glance and blushed

slightly, like schoolboys caught out smoking behind the bike shed.

'Morning, Jo, we thought you were heading straight to the hospital this morning. Stan was just filling me in on last night. Sounds like a good pointer with the fractured wrist, means we can ID her quicker.' Carl picked up his mug of coffee from her desk and clutched it firmly.

Jo cleared her throat. 'I've put in a call to the hospital, just waiting to hear back from them before I pick up her hospital notes. I just wanted to get Holly's file and some other bits out of the archive.'

'Don't worry, we can send Kate down,' said Stan as a knock came at the door. 'Save you the trip.'

'Where do you want these?' said the constable at the door. He was holding two large boxes, stacked one on top of the other, which he could barely see over.

'We're a bit short of space, Jo, so I've said Stan can set up in here. He's going to head up the investigation.'

Jo felt her face burn; she counted to ten, trying not to say anything she'd regret. She looked over at her soon to be son-in-law who looked at his feet shiftily.

'Can I have a word, Carl?' she said.

Carl nodded to Stan before the sergeant left the room, closing the door behind him.

'With all due respect, why do I feel pushed out here? I'm not leaving until Friday, this is still my office.'

'Of course, we know that. And we very much want you involved in setting everything up. We've got a squad car heading over to the sister now, so we will hopefully have a DNA match by the end of the day. Thanks to you,

143

everything is moving in the right direction,' he said, with a patronising smile.

'Is that why you excluded me from the briefing this morning?'

Carl glared at her. 'The story is out. We've had to release a statement this morning, it's going to be on the breakfast news,' he said, matter-of-factly. 'I wasn't excluding you, but it wasn't necessary for you to be there. It's better the press is kept updated, so they go easy on the sister.'

Jo shook her head. 'That's really your motive?' She took a breath. 'You should probably know that when I was leaving the site last night, I saw a light coming from Morgate House and it seemed strange to me, so I went over to investigate. It was Daisy Moore.' Jo was trying not to let her emotions get the better of her.

'Okay, did you tell her we need a DNA sample urgently? We've been trying to find her. She finally came home in the early hours of this morning but she refused to speak to Kate, who was waiting for her,' Carl said.

'Well, she's avoiding us, all of this furore, it's too much,' said Jo, glaring at him. 'She's very fragile. She blames the police, us, for her sister's death. This needs to be handled very sensitively if we are going to keep her onside.'

'Jo, I just think it's better if you hand this over now. There's no point you getting involved, when you've got three days left. I'll send a family liaison officer to support Daisy Moore and I'm sure she will agree to the DNA test once she realises it's the only way to get a positive ID on her sister's remains.'

'She won't,' Jo snapped.

Carl glared at her. 'Jo—'

'Don't say it! Why does everyone always tell me not to get involved when it comes to these girls? There's always some reason – it makes me think you're all hiding something from me. We both know that's what you told me when Holly first went missing.'

Carl frowned. 'I'm not sure what you mean?'

Jo sighed. 'Don't go there, Carl. Holly was missing for two days before Morgate House even reported it. They should have been pulled up for that alone, but nothing was done. You didn't even want to put any officers on the case. I had to put a gun to your head.'

'I don't think I remember it like that,' Carl said sternly. 'We followed protocol, we sent officers out door to door, and put Missing Person posters up all over Saltdean.'

'Because I forced your hand,' Jo snapped. She stormed around the desk, her heart hammering in her chest, and picked up Holly and Gemma's files. 'Morgate House have got away with murder for too long. They've never been held to account for Gemma or Holly's disappearance. I'm interviewing Phillip Price about their missing children protocol, Carl, and you can't stop me. If anyone needs me, I'll be at Brighton Hospital, trying to find out how Holly Moore broke her wrist.'

Jo walked down the corridor, towards the entrance of the police station, as a woman in her fifties walked towards her.

'Oh, Jo, just the lady. We need to finalise the menu for Thursday night. The restaurant need to know if we want starters or not. And I thought a bottle of red and white on each table, then the boys can get beer at the bar if they want it.'

'Sorry, Sue, can I call you later? I have to get into town,'

Jo called back, not waiting for a response from Sue, who had been a part of the administration team for as long as she could remember.

'Of course, no problem,' said Sue, watching Jo hurry out through reception and into the grey March day.

Jo walked through the car park, praying she wouldn't bump into anyone else, and then climbed inside her Mini and slammed the door on her world. She sat in her car, and took a few deep breaths, trying to hold back the tears as her mobile phone beeped into life. Jo picked it up, and read the message on the screen.

Hi Mum, how did it go taking Granny this morning? I got some nice bread. Phoebe excited to see you. M x

Jo let out a heavy sigh and pinched the bridge of her nose with her forefingers. She was in her daughter's good books as she'd got up at five and sat with her mother for two hours until the ambulance arrived to take her to the hospice. Olive had slept most of the time, and it had actually felt quite nice, sitting with her and not having to talk. Even though it meant she was shattered now.

She had completely forgotten that she'd agreed to go round to her daughter's house for lunch, to see her granddaughter. It was supposed to be a nice week of winding down, handing over, and reflecting on her 'long and illustrious career', as her boss put it. But ever since the discovery of the remains, she had been sucked back into 1975, utterly powerless; at sea in a male-dominated environment that managed to push her aside, regardless of the rank she had risen to.

Jo picked up her phone, and began to type.

Of course, darling, see you soon.

She loved her daughter more than words could express, but

146

their relationship had never been an easy one. Neither of them turned to each other in times of need – and if they did, they always seemed to end up upsetting each other. Feeling as she did now, she was aware of a familiar nervousness that they might have a falling out – which was the last thing she wanted. She didn't want to hurt Megan, who always sensed when work was getting to her, and found it intensely irritating.

She had fallen pregnant with Megan two years after joining Sussex Police, just around the time of the fire, when Holly and Daisy's mother had been killed. She had gone into shock when the doctor had told her; she and Richard weren't even engaged, they had been so careful. She had wanted to be a WPC her whole life, and had worked so hard to get there. She wouldn't have minded if she had never had children at all. Thanks to the 1975 Sex Discrimination Act, things were changing at work and she was just starting to be taken seriously. The seventies were not a time when you had your baby and went back to work a few months later. Child care was non-existent in Sussex in those days unless you could afford a nanny, or a relative did it, and she knew her mother's maternal instincts wouldn't have stretched that far; having a child then meant giving up work for at least a decade. And even when she had gone back, in the mid-eighties, there had been several unsolicited comments from her colleagues, concerned about who was at home with her child while she was at work.

It had been a difficult relationship with Megan from the start. Her pregnancy had been plain sailing, and she had worked until the day before she went into labour, but the birth was utterly dreadful: long, protracted and extremely painful. Megan had reflux and screamed most of the time until she was two years old. She was a very clingy child, and though Jo tried her hardest to enjoy Megan and instil confidence in her, she hated being passed to her father. She could only cope with being separated from her mother for a few minutes. Jo found motherhood suffocating and boring, and spent most of her days out and about, trying to kill the day until Richard came home and she could lock herself away and enjoy a steaming-hot bubble bath for half an hour, before Megan started screaming for her again.

Whereas Jo was blonde, Megan was dark, like her father; dark, brooding and negative. And as Jo and Richard grew apart, everything about him that grated on her, Megan seemed to echo. Richard had an innate snootiness, despite never achieving much in his life. He looked down on people – often hard-working people who contributed a great deal more to society than he did – just because they had a certain accent, or didn't dress in the right clothes. He came from a family of middle-class snobs, middle management, who thought they were better than most. Jo tried to encourage Megan to have a positive nature, but she seemed to absorb all Richard's negativity like a sponge.

As she grew, Megan continued to hate everything – playing with other children, school, clubs, sport, homework, nothing seemed to make her happy, except for being locked to her mother's side. Jo felt so suffocated, she was screaming silently for nearly ten years until she was finally able to go back to work. She had missed it so much; every day she had pined for the excitement, and the energy of the station, the variety of the work and feeling like she was making a difference, but when she came home in the evenings, she had to play down her happiness. Megan hated that her mother clearly enjoyed being away from her, and it soon became such a bone of contention that Jo couldn't even talk about work with her daughter. Or her husband, who had never supported her return to work and, alongside Megan, seethed with resentment.

Only Charlie, her brother, had got her through. Smoothed the way with Megan, who adored him, and with their mother, who seemed also to disapprove of her career ambitions. Even though Olive had been a distant mother herself and had craved a different life – something she had done her best to try to hide.

Now, thirty years after her return to the force, and with her divorce a distant memory, and Megan a settled and soon-to-be-married mother to Phoebe, their relationship still remained fragile. She knew Megan blamed her mother for her parents' divorce, and felt she hadn't been a doting enough grandmother since Phoebe was born. She was looking forward to her mother retiring, no doubt for some free childcare, and Jo felt the knot in her stomach intensify, knowing she would have to hide everything she was feeling today from her daughter – her intense fears about her retirement, her boss pushing her out, and finding Holly's remains – or it would only lead to an argument.

It was only 8 a.m., and she already felt like her insides were a box of lit fireworks, ready to explode.

As she approached the border of Kemptown it occurred to Jo that she had written down Daisy's address the day before in her notebook, when she'd looked her up on the police system. The hairs prickled on the back of her neck as she found herself taking the turning into Walpole Terrace, the main road into Kemptown, and in no time at all she

149

was pulling up next to the squad car outside Daisy's block of flats in College Terrace.

There was no sign of life; they were obviously inside now, trying again to get a DNA sample. She could only hope they were handling it sensitively, but she feared not sensitively enough. Jo looked out of her window and switched on the radio in an attempt to distract herself. She felt sick, as if she were a moth drawn to the light she knew would burn her. Repetitive songs on the radio were grating on her nerves while she sat staring at Daisy's front door. She wasn't sure why she was even there; to pry, to judge, to tell herself that she would have handled it better.

She hadn't realised that a news bulletin had started, until she heard Holly's name.

'Human remains have been found in Brighton in the search for a seventeen-year-old girl who vanished without trace thirty years ago.

'Sussex Police officers discovered the remains on the Tye near Saltdean in East Sussex. It is believed that the remains could be those of Holly Moore, of Morgate House children's home, who was last seen in Rottingdean. Formal forensic identification of the remains has not yet taken place, but they appear to have been there for some time and tests are being carried out to identify the victim and establish the cause of death.

'Detective Chief Inspector Carl Webber said his team and forensic experts will remain at the site in the coming days to complete their examinations, and he thanked local people for their patience.

'He said, "The discovery of human remains by my colleagues searching the area is both shocking and deeply disturbing for everyone concerned. We will be gathering DNA samples from

the relatives of those who went missing around that time.
Their families will be supported by specialist officers."'

There was suddenly a loud bang as a woman rushed out of the front door and slammed it behind her. She was crying as she hurried towards a blue bike chained to a wrought-iron fence at the front of the flat. She struggled with the padlock, muttering under her breath.

Within seconds the family liaison officer came after her, swiftly followed by PC Sarah Jenkins.

'Daisy, I think it's probably best if you don't go to work today,' she called out. 'There could be reporters keen to talk to you, and we can't protect you there.'

'You've never protected me – or Holly – why would you start now?'

Jo watched as Daisy put her helmet on her head.

'Well, we are very sorry you feel that way, and we want to put it right.'

'You've got what you came for. You've got my DNA, now leave me alone. I need to get to work, people are relying on me. Please can you move out of the way?'

Daisy wheeled her bike to the kerb as a tall young man, with short dark hair, bounded over.

'Hi, Daisy, my name's Mike, I'm from the *Sussex News*, can I have a word?'

'Not really, I'm in a hurry,' Daisy said, trying to push off on her bike.

'Can I give you my card? I know this must be a difficult time, but if you ever need someone to talk to about your sister Holly, please give me a call. Sometimes it helps to talk to a stranger.'

Daisy looked down at the card, then reluctantly took it.

'Sir, please step back,' said PC Sarah Jenkins.

As Jo watched Daisy secure her helmet and jump onto her bike, her mobile came to life again,

'Megan mob' flashed on the screen. Jo picked it up, her eyes still on Daisy.

'Hi, Mum, can you get some milk?'

'Yes, of course,' Jo said, watching Daisy as she turned out of the end of her road.

'Are you okay?'

'Yes, darling, I'm fine. Just tired,' said Jo, starting her car engine as she watched the PCs walk back to their vehicle.

'You don't have to come if you don't want to,' Megan said quietly.

It was a familiar passive-aggressive question; Jo hadn't even got to her daughter's house, and already Megan had picked up that something was wrong.

'Of course I want to come,' Jo lied.

'Well, just so you know, you can do what you want. I don't mind,' Megan added.

'I'll be there at one, with the milk, I can't wait to see you both,' said Jo, as cheerfully as she could muster.

As she pulled away and started to make her way along the seafront towards Rottingdean, she could see Daisy's bike up ahead, weaving skilfully out of the path of a car pulling out, and then speeding off through an amber light. Every muscle in her body wanted to follow her, to check if she was okay. To tell her she was sorry.

She pictured Gemma in the squad car, forty years before, holding her hands in her lap. She remembered trying to get the young girl to talk to her. Gemma had opened the car door, as if to go, then turned back.

'What is the point?' Gemma had fixed her green eyes on her. 'You think you care, but you don't. You'll go home to your family and forget about me, in a day or two. Everyone wants us to disappear. Well, maybe one day I will.'

Jo looked down at Gemma's picture in the file next to her. She was a superintendent, she had worked her way up, over the course of thirty years, given up everything. Yet at this moment in time, she felt as powerless as the day she had started in the police; there was a lot more going on in Carl's team than they were ever going to share with her.

She needed to go back to 1975, to find out what had really happened. Back to when she had cordoned off the body of Gemma Smith, lying twisted on the rocks below Morgate House. Back to the day of Gemma's inquest; an inquest she had attended as a twenty-year-old, with no experience. Where Constable Phillip Price, the son of the owners of Morgate House children's home – who Gemma herself had described as a creep – had called Gemma 'a pain in the arse'.

She needed to look at the inquest's findings with fresh eyes, with eyes that had now been in Sussex Police for forty years. She was on her own, but she wasn't out yet, she still had three days.

If Carl wasn't going to do any digging into Morgate House, then it was down to her to find out the truth.

Chapter Twelve

Gemma

November 1975

Gemma looked at her watch – which told her it was half past eight – and then back down at Eve who had fallen asleep listening to her reading *Snow White*, which she had bought from the local charity shop. So far that night she had read the story to Eve, and the other children, four times. Looking up every other minute, to see if his head-lights had appeared on the other side of the road. He was half an hour late. Would he come? If not, what would she do? If she went back to the house to confront him, would he deny her existence, say she was lying? He'd had time to work out a plan by now. She wondered how he had explained away the vomit on the rug. Presumably he would have blamed his little girl. What was his wife thinking? Did she suspect anything? Her head felt like a wasp nest.

She had no idea what the night held. She still couldn't believe he had suggested going away. She had packed a bag, but she felt stupid, stuffing her pitiful wardrobe into her torn rucksack; she had imagined his wife packing for a trip, with drawers full of lovely clothes, perfume and make-up. The thought of going away with him made her ecstatically happy, maybe he would decide he wanted to be with her.

She daren't get her hopes up, but if she never came back here, there was only one thing she would miss – Eve.

As Eve's little chest rose and fell in her sleep, Gemma slid the poem under her pillow; she had written it when Eve was watching cartoons, before bed. She didn't know how to find the words to tell an eight-year-old that she was going away. Gemma knew that once she was out of Morgate House, even for a night, there was no way she could come back. Even if he didn't want her, he would have to give her money to get her set up, then in time she would stand on her own two feet. She had hovered over the page for so long, not knowing what to write. She didn't want to give a little girl promises she couldn't keep. She wanted to do everything she could to come back for Eve, but she may not be able to. She was having a baby. Life was going to be very hard.

Dear Eve,

I'm sorry I had to leave you.
It is nothing you have done.
You are a perfect little girl
Whose life has just begun.

In time I hope you'll understand.
I had to go away.
I will always be looking out for you,
Making sure that you're okay.

Work hard at school, bright Eve,
It's the only way out of this life.
Tell Mr Haig I'm sorry
For all the trouble and strife.

I'll see you in the next life.
We will live together as we have dreamed,
in a pretty flat on the seafront,
decorated in blue and cream.

I love you like a sister.
I hate to go away.
I know you'll have a family one day
And your happiness will come to stay.

Gemma x

Gemma slid the poem under Eve's pillow and stroked her face as the tears began to flow. She felt even more nauseous now than she already had from her unrelenting morning sickness, her emotions from the past twenty-four hours veering from anger to sadness. Every time she closed her eyes she saw his wife. A woman she had no clue even existed until yesterday. Someone she knew nothing about, apart from her relaxed voice as she called out to her husband while Gemma hid by the back door. And the photographs dotted around the house. A woman so different from her in every way: tall, blonde and elegant. She looked at the camera with confidence and ease, as if she hadn't a care in the world. From the moment she had discovered her existence, Gemma had immediately felt an obsessive need to know more about her.

She had woken at six that morning in a state of frenzy; her shock from the night before had faded and evolved into something more complex. An urgent desire to go back to the home of the man she was deeply in love with, and spend the day finding out everything she could about his life.

Everything he had told her had been a lie. She knew he was on the early shift today; he would finish at seven in the evening, he had told her.

He had given her ten pounds so she could go back to the children's home. She wasn't going to school today, she had decided; she would go back to Woodingdean, wait for him to leave for work, then try to follow his wife and their little girl.

The bus up to his house had been slow, people getting on and off on their way to work, going to college; she thought she might throw up several times but managed to breathe through it. She had found the house straight away this time, his car was gone from the drive, and she walked past, glancing in the living-room window, holding her breath. Her heart had stopped as she saw his wife, standing by the window, with a phone receiver to her ear. She had tried not to stare but failed, tears stinging her eyes as the woman threw her head back and laughed at something the person on the other end of the line was saying.

She had scuttled off, walking to the end of the road. It was a bitterly cold day, so there were not many people around to notice her, except an elderly man with a shopping trolley, who smiled cheerfully. Gemma had stood at the end of the road as a woman glanced at her from her kitchen window. She couldn't stay there, she'd decided, but it was a cul de sac, with only one way out. If the wife was going out, she would have to walk or drive up to the main road, so Gemma could wait it out there and would see her if she left. Wrapping her coat tightly around her, she sat on the hard plastic bench at the bus stop; after an hour, it felt like a block of ice as she lost all feeling in her hands and face.

Only three cars went out of Downland Street as she sat

there. She had begun to worry that it was getting dangerous for the baby inside her to sit there any longer, shaking
uncontrollably from the cold, when his wife walked past,
pushing their little girl in a pushchair. In a panic, she had
turned away, scared that the woman would see her. Then,
as she watched them walk up towards Woodingdean High
Street, she had started to follow. The woman was wearing
a long black coat and sturdy boots, and her stride was quite
fast so that Gemma had to struggle to keep up. She had no
idea where the woman was headed, but she had watched as
she turned into the library, and disappeared inside. Gemma
hadn't felt safe following her in – she had no idea if he had
said anything to his wife – but she watched through the
glass door as the woman smiled at the librarian at the
entrance. As she got her little girl out of the pushchair,
taking off her mittens carefully, one by one, she didn't look
like a woman who had just been told that her husband was
leaving her. She looked happy and carefree.

Unable to bear the cold any longer, Gemma had gone
into a coffee shop opposite and bought a cup of tea with
sugar in it. She couldn't eat but she needed some sort of
energy, to get her through the day. She had sat in the window, close to tears, imagining them enjoying the warmth
of the library, reading books together, curled up happily.
After an hour, the woman in the coffee shop had asked her
if she wanted anything else. Everywhere had its shelf life,
she thought. You were only welcome anywhere for so long,
until they asked you to move on.

Stepping outside, Gemma had seen a BMW pull up
across the road, and a woman she suspected to be in her
seventies climbed out. As she walked up the steps to the

library, his wife had appeared at the door and the three had greeted each other. Drawn to the scene despite her fears, Gemma had crossed the road, walking slowly past as the two women chatted.

Gemma wasn't able to catch much, but their body language said it all, as the older, beautifully turned-out woman held on to the little girl, playing with her, talking to her while the wife put the pushchair in the boot. They obviously spent a lot of time together. The little girl was completely at ease with her grandmother.

'Well, I can have her Friday if that makes life easier?' she'd said as Gemma walked past them with her head down. 'Would you like to have the day with Granny? We can plant some sunflowers in the garden.'

'Thanks, Mum.'

She had stood not five feet away, a ticking bomb; just a few words from her would end their world. But instead she had walked past, as they helped the little girl in, showered her with kisses, and then drove away together. Just as he had done. Leaving her cold and alone on the pavement.

Why had he done it? Why had he strayed from his beautiful family? He had everything. Why had he made her believe they had a future together? They had nothing. She was nothing to him, and he would never leave them.

With the heaviest of hearts she had gone back to Morgate House. The minutes until seven o'clock had dragged all day; she ached to see him. When she was with him, despite her anger, she would feel elated, time would fly. She dreaded already how fast the minutes would go. Slipping through her fingers.

Then, suddenly, he would be gone. And the countdown would begin again to the time she next saw him. Perhaps, this time, it would be different. Perhaps, this time, he would say they were going to be together. But seeing his family today, she knew, deep down in the pit of her stomach, he wouldn't. From the way he had looked at her when he found her in his house, she knew it was over between them. All he would care about now was covering his tracks – and to do that, he would need to persuade her to get rid of their baby.

He would try to convince her it was for the best. That her life would be over. That she was only fifteen, she couldn't have a child on her own. And for most people he may have been right, but not for her. Everything had changed. For the first time in her short life, she had a family. She had a child growing inside her who would look like her. Someone who would be a link to her parents and who she could belong to. Her morning sickness was taking over as she felt her body adjust to the changes taking place inside it. She was already a mother. She had been terrified, at first. Paralysed with fear.

But slowly, the baby growing inside her was giving her strength. She had been reading all week about how much of the baby had formed by eight weeks. How its tiny features were growing a little bit every day, the lips, nose and eyelids were forming, and even its features taking shape. All her senses were heightened, the world smelt and tasted completely different; she felt like she had a superpower growing inside of her.

Every minute he kept her waiting, her anger had started to overtake her fear. He had a nice home, a nice car, that little girl of his wanted for nothing. Even if he didn't want

160

her, he could support this baby growing inside her. It was giving her strength. Even if she hated herself, this baby – which she was convinced was a girl – was not going to grow up as she had. She was going to have a happy childhood, unrecognisable from her own. She was going to matter and, in turn, Gemma would matter, because she was her mummy.

Gemma looked down at Eve, as the little girl stirred. She looked up to see car headlights flashing, and her heart stopped for a moment. Then she kissed Eve, picked up her coat, opened the window and climbed out.

'Where are you going?' the little girl asked sleepily.

'Just for a walk, I'll be back soon, don't worry.'

'With him?' Eve murmured.

Gemma nodded, slid the window back down and started to walk towards his car.

'Where do you think you're off to, young lady?'

Gemma looked back to see Mrs Price standing at the entrance to her annex, her arms crossed. She had nothing to say to the woman, who looked up to see his headlights flashing again at them.

'Who is that? Come back inside now.'

'I'd rather kill myself than spend another night in this dump.'

'I'll call the police.'

Gemma laughed and shook her head. 'No need, they're already here,' she said, walking away as Mrs Price watched her go, scowling at the man as he climbed out of the car.

All her life she had felt out of control. Being passed around, with no one ever asking her what she wanted for herself or her life. Now, as she saw him, she felt a tiny bit of control creeping back. A feeling in her belly. His headlights were on full beam as the rain danced in front of them. A motorbike roared past her on the dual carriageway, then the road was quiet again.

It was dark as she went to cross, and he called out to her, 'Wait there, I'll come over.'

Gemma looked back at Mrs Price, who was watching them, before closing the door to the cosy annex behind her. Gemma noticed torchlight in the window she had climbed out of. Eve was awake, maybe watching them through her window.

Gemma pulled her flimsy coat around her as her heart sank. 'Let's walk,' she called out, knowing in that moment that he didn't care. If he wanted the baby, he wouldn't want her walking around in the rain. He would want to protect her. Take her somewhere warm. Keep her safe. As he reached her, and they started to walk, she felt angry for the first time. She had never really cared about how he treated her before, but now there were two of them. Her standards were higher. Much higher.

Would she want her daughter to get pregnant by a man in his car, sending her back to a children's home while he went home to his wife? Would she want her daughter to be with someone who let her walk around in the freezing cold while she was pregnant?

No. But he was here. A faint hope still burned in her that he would do the right thing. She felt brave for her baby, but she was shaking with the cold and fear. They walked silently, side by side, their breathing in time. Soon, too soon, he would leave her. He would be gone and she would blame herself, as she always did. If she had said the right thing, done the right thing, acted the right way, he would have stayed.

If she was more like her. Like his wife.

'How are you feeling?' he said finally, as they hovered around a bench on the cliff edge.

She'd walked on these cliffs a thousand times, the view and the sea air had saved her on countless occasions, they had always made her feel better – but not now. She had spent the day following his wife and daughter; she was bubbling over with rage. And yet now she was near him, she was just elated to see him. She knew she was pathetic. But she had missed him so much, she was pregnant and young, a sea of hormones. She just needed him to tell her that it would all be okay. That she wouldn't be left high and dry.

Gemma felt her heart racing in her chest, she tried to steady her breathing as the sea crashed against the rocks below. 'I want to keep it. I want to be with you.'

'It won't work, I have a family already. You need to get rid of it. You're just a kid yourself,' he said, his voice hard and cold.

'Why does this child matter less than your little girl? Why do you want to murder this baby, and cherish that one?'

He glared at her, he had never looked at her that way before. All his words, his false promises.

'You should have more faith in people,' he said, his tone changing, soothing her. 'I want to help, you aren't alone Gemma, you've got me. I just can't have another child.'

She felt rage building inside her, and the cold night did nothing to cool her down; she felt hot, so hot. Despite the freezing temperature, she was only wearing a thin coat;

she held her bag in her arms, to hide her shaking hands and to protect her stomach from the cold. She had a radiator inside her, giving her strength to speak up, not to give way to him.

'I want to have this baby, with or without your support.'

'I know this is a difficult time, but you're so young. I don't want to see you throw your life away.'

'I'm going to go to college and get a degree, and I'm going to do everything right that my mother did wrong. I'm not throwing my life away, this is the start of the life I always wanted but didn't think I was worthy of. My baby's life is beautiful and worth living. I'm already picturing her first steps, her first day of school. I'm having her. And you need to accept that.'

'You need to get rid of it,' he said, his soothing words forgotten. 'You're being naive, Gemma.' He walked over and clutched her arm. 'You don't have a job, any money, you live in a children's home. They'll probably take the baby away.'

Gemma pulled away. 'No. I'll get a job, I'll find a way. It's my body, I have the final say. I'm not trying to make problems, but you will need to tell your wife about us. I'm keeping this baby, and I'm going to be part of your life, so you need to accept that. If you love me, like you said, you would love my unborn child too.'

He scoffed and walked away, looking out at the moon over the sea. 'I'm not telling my wife anything. It would kill her.'

Gemma felt her voice break. 'I can only hope that, in time, you come round. You need to take responsibility and –' Gemma paused, trying to stop her voice from shaking, 'if you don't tell your wife, I will.'

'Look, okay, let's just calm this down. I'll lose my job, I'll lose everything – you're fifteen, for God's sake. I can give you some money, but you can't tell a soul.'

'No. She needs to know who you really are,' Gemma said, turning back towards Morgate House. It was so cold, she needed to get inside to stop herself from putting her baby in danger.

She didn't hear the footsteps behind her, the sea was too loud, and the wind too strong. When he first grabbed her arm, she actually felt her heart soar. It had worked. He had changed his mind. She had been strong, walked away, and now he wanted her back.

But as she looked up at his face, she knew something had shifted. His eyes had turned to stone, fixed not on her but on the cliff edge. As she faced him, he grabbed her other arm and began walking her backwards. Whereas the wind had been strong before, now it took her legs from underneath her, whipping and lashing at her arms and face. She had never been this close to the cliff edge before; the wind became frantic, as if it would peel the skin from her face. For a second or two her brain froze, and she struggled to comprehend what was happening. He lifted her up by her arms, and she struggled awkwardly to free herself, his fingers digging in so deep that she cried out for him to stop. But there was nobody to hear her. She looked around, the only lights coming from the cars on the road, and Morgate House in the distance; the windows of the annex were like eyes watching her.

He was walking her towards the edge, towards the two-hundred-foot drop. She opened her mouth to scream but he released one arm and hit her hard with the back of his hand across her cheek. In the few seconds it took for him to drag her further, her feet digging into the grassy ridge, her brain stumbled to take in the fact that she was about to die. She desperately thought of who would miss her when she was gone, and there was nobody. She thought of Eve, asleep in her bed, with her letter saying goodbye under her pillow. And of Mr and Mrs Price, sitting in the cosy annex, watching television, without a care in the world. There were no parents to mourn her, no sisters or brothers to miss her or look for her, nobody to notice she was gone. The only person who would truly love her unconditionally was growing inside her, and would die with her.

As he grabbed her arm, dug his fingers in deep, and pulled her towards the edge, she fought hard, for her baby's life and her own. She kicked his legs and scratched at his face. She hated herself for being so stupid as to come out here, into the pitch blackness, to this place from which there was no escape from him, for not thinking that this might happen. There was no comfort for her anywhere, no way of outrunning this huge man with an iron grip on her. She had felt powerless for most of her life, but never so much as she did now, with the sea drowning out her shouts.

They reached the edge and the wind was like a sledge-hammer. She bit down hard on his hand, and for a moment he let go. She was shaking with fear, her legs were weak, but she ran as hard as she had ever done in her life. Within seconds he reached her and pulled her over, dragging her along the grass as she clawed desperately at the soil. She knew she was fighting for her life, she knew what was going to happen.

He dragged her up by her hair, the pain shooting through her head and neck, and carried her towards the edge. She screamed and thrashed, but he only tightened his iron grip, then with one final groan of effort, he shoved her towards the edge, where she stumbled helplessly. As the wind fell silent, all of a sudden, she lost her footing and fell, the wind rushing over her body, whistling in her ears, and she hurtled the two hundred feet to the rocks below.

Chapter Thirteen

Daisy

March 2015, Tuesday morning

Daisy dashed out of the front door of her flat, ignoring the reporters trying to talk to her and the police car parked outside, and cycled off in the direction of Downside. Glancing back several times to check she wasn't being followed, she took a left off the seafront and headed back in the direction of town. She didn't want anyone to know where she was going, even though she wasn't doing anything wrong – yet. If the police had done any research at all, they'd have known it was her day off. Olive was right, she could probably do quite a lot of digging and no one would notice. It was also a blessing, keeping busy; there was no point in sitting at home, driving herself mad thinking about whether or not it was Holly lying in that shallow grave, in a spot she had cycled past every day for ten years. She needed to keep calm and stay focused.

Daisy cycled through the North Laine towards Brighton Town Hall – which she had found out, the night before, was home to Brighton Council. Despite the council being her guardian for ten years of her life, she knew very little about its workings. She had never been inside the Grade II listed building, which she often passed, and whose vast columns made it look more like a Greek palace than an office building in Sussex. Daisy pulled up outside and padlocked her bike to the cycle rack.

She took a deep breath, walked into the high-ceilinged hall and followed the signs to reception.

'Can I help you?' asked a bespectacled woman behind a counter.

'I hope so. I used to live with my sister at Morgate House, a children's residential home in Saltdean, and I'm wanting to get hold of my sister's social services file. Do you know how I might get it?'

The woman peered back at her, over her glasses. 'Saltdean is Lewes Council, I'm afraid. But you'd need to write to them – rather than turn up in person. You'll need some form of identification, to prove you're a relative, and as much detail as you can supply about your sister, so that they can find her file. You may not be allowed access to all the information they have about her, though.'

'Why?' Daisy said, leaning in.

'If any of its contents would prejudice a legal inquiry, or to protect anyone else who may be mentioned in it.'

Daisy felt herself flush red with anger. So anything useful Holly's file might contain, she wouldn't be allowed to see.

'Is there anything I can do, if they don't let me have it?'

'You can go through a judicial process, but obviously that's expensive and timely, with no guarantee of success, but it's your right. Would you like Lewes Council's address?'

Daisy felt her heart sink. 'Yes, please. What about *my* file? Presumably they have to give me that?'

'Not necessarily, for the same reasons. But by all means try, I don't want to put you off, and you may get lucky.'

Lucky? To get her hands on her own file, with all the details of her life. Daisy stepped back, conscious there was a line of people behind her, as the woman scribbled down the address of the relevant department at Lewes Council. Daisy stood staring at the piece of paper in her hands. A man behind her cleared his throat.

'Do you know what school she went to?' the woman added, as the man stepped forward and let out a sigh of frustration.

Daisy shook her head. 'I'm not sure.'

'Most likely Saltdean High. It might be worth seeing if they have anything – reports or records. They'd probably be more likely to hand them over to you. Good luck.'

'Thank you,' said Daisy, walking back out into the cold spring air, the woman's words coming back to her: anything that would 'prejudice a legal inquiry'. Anything that made the police or Morgate House look bad, Daisy thought to herself.

She unlocked her bike and looked down at the piece of paper with the address for Lewes Council. Even if she did write to the council to ask for Holly's file, it would probably take weeks for them to reply, by which time the police would have got wind of her interest and taken anything out she might be able to use. She put the address in her rucksack and began pedalling back towards the seafront.

She couldn't remember which school Holly had gone to, but she could picture the school uniform. A navy-blue skirt, white shirt and blue blazer with a light blue trim and some sort of bird on the blazer pocket, an eagle maybe. She remembered it clearly because it was paid for by social services and the only new items of clothing she had ever owned. Holly had brought the uniform home and modelled it for her. Pouting and posing, as Daisy sat watching her, giggling.

'I'm going to do well at school, Daisy,' Holly had promised her. 'I'm going to get a good job, and buy us a house. You'll see, this isn't our life, Daisy, just hold on, we're getting out of here.'

Since the day her foster mother had taken her away from Holly and Morgate House, she had asked about Holly every day. The pain of being separated was so bad she was physically sick most mornings after she woke up. Her foster mother kept telling her she would arrange a meeting, but it never happened. In the end, the pain had got so bad that she ran away one night, in a bid to get back to Morgate. She had waited until her foster mother had gone to bed, then wrapped herself up in her coat and scarf and started walking in the direction of the seafront. She knew Morgate House was by the sea, and she had decided that if she just kept walking, she would eventually get to it. She hadn't got far, before a police car picked her up and took her home.

'What if you'd been killed?' her foster mother had said, after the police left.

'I don't care. I'd rather die than not see Holly again. And if you don't let me see her, I'll go back to Morgate until you do. You can't keep us apart.'

'She's not there,' her mother had said. 'She's been adopted too. She's happily living with another family.'

After that, a few weeks had gone by; she hadn't been able to eat at all and would cry herself to sleep every night. Her

171

foster mother had taken her to the doctor, and they had put her on some tablets to help her sleep.

Then suddenly, out of the blue, a letter from Holly had arrived. A letter which dropped through the letter box, just as she was walking down the hall, so that her foster mother couldn't hide it from her. A letter which she scuttled up to her room and read. A letter she still had today, folded up tightly in her jewellery box.

February 1985
My darling Daisy,

I miss you. They are saying I can't see you at the moment as it will be too upsetting for us both to then be parted again. I don't agree with them, but sadly, I don't have a say for now as I am too young. But that will change.

It hasn't stopped me looking for you. They won't give me your address but I have a new friend who knows your address and is forwarding my letters, so I will be sending more. I know you aren't far away, though. I found a letter from the council saying you are in Coldean. Me and my friend Eve catch the bus there sometimes, and walk around looking for you. But the police always pick us up and bring us back.

I know the past years since Mum died have been hard, but you are in a loving home now. I am happy knowing you are safe and warm and well fed, away from Morgate. You must be strong until I come and find you. And I will find you. Have faith.

I am seventeen now, and you are fifteen, soon I will be eighteen and I will be allowed to apply for you to come and live with me, but first I need a home for us. I am trying hard at school. I've chosen my A levels, I love English, my teacher is really kind to me. Next year I am going to start working in an estate agent in Brighton. I have been to several already and one has said they will give me an interview for a job. I am going to show people around houses and if they buy them, I get a commission, which is a lot of money! One day I will have saved up enough to buy our own house, and I will come and find you. We will finally be together, in a house that is ours – one they can't take away from us.

I have always wanted to give you everything in life. For now we have to just pretend we are together – you are always in my dreams. No one can come between us unless we allow them to. We have faced so many hard things together; we can survive this time apart. Be brave. I have locked my heart away so it doesn't hurt so much, and you must learn to do the same. We will always find a way back to each other. Look after yourself until I come for you.

All my love,
Holly xxx

Daisy had read the letter so many times she knew it off by heart. Soon after she received it, she had written a calendar on her wall, and crossed off the days until Holly was eighteen, when she would come for her. Ever since that day, she had been waiting. The pain of waiting had become almost all-consuming. Holly's eighteenth birthday came and went; she started feeling so anxious, waiting for Holly to come, she wasn't able to eat or sleep. Her foster mother had taken her to the doctor, to give her something to settle her stomach. Then one day, in town, she had passed a lamp post with Holly's picture on it. She had stopped in her tracks to read the poster.

'**MISSING PERSON**', the text stated in bold, emblazoned next to the Sussex Police emblem.

The photograph was a photocopied image in black and white, Holly's beautiful grey-blue eyes lost in the dull tones of the photocopier ink. Daisy had stood there, staring in disbelief at the picture of the sister she hadn't seen for four years, taped to the lamp post in the middle of the street, where she had promptly vomited onto the new trainers her foster mother had just bought her.

Her life was still on hold even now. She had not moved on a single day since she received the letter from her sister. Her life had become an endless chart of crossing off the days, but she didn't know what she was waiting for. For them to find Holly's body. For Holly to finally come and get her. To be free, and for her life to begin.

Daisy reached Ovingdean, where she stopped and googled Saltdean High on her phone. It was a vast cream rectangular building, which looked like a Lego house, on three floors. She tapped on images and scrolled down until she reached one of the school uniform; it was exactly as she had remembered it, with the navy-blue blazer and light blue trim.

'Me and my friend Eve walk around looking for you,'

Daisy muttered to herself, recalling the words in her sister's letter.

She looked up Saltdean High on Google Maps, then climbed back onto her bicycle, and headed up towards the South Downs. It didn't take long to find the campus; a huge concrete jungle squatting on the landscape, and she cycled through the gates, passing a group of teenagers hovering at the entrance.

'Can I help you?' said the slightly frazzled-looking woman behind the sliding glass window at Saltdean High reception. She had a pencil behind one ear and another in her hair, keeping it partially off her face.

'I'm not sure,' said Daisy, trying to sound confident. 'I'm trying to organise a surprise reunion for my sister, and I was wondering if you have any records of the names of the people who were in her year?'

'I think that might be a question for the volunteers who run our community association. I can give you their email address, but they are only part-time so you could be in for a wait,' the receptionist said, smiling and turning away.

'Um, actually, her birthday is next week. I don't mean to be a pain, but you wouldn't have a list on your system, would you? Or any records I could root through. I don't mind doing it myself, I can see how busy you are.'

Daisy flushed red as the woman glared back at her. The phones in the office were ringing constantly, and there were two girls waiting behind her.

The woman let out a heavy sigh. 'What year was it?'

'Well, I think she would have been here between 1978 and 1985. So any of those, I guess,' Daisy said sheepishly. Pushiness didn't come naturally to her.

'Hold on.' The woman turned round and walked over to her colleague. 'Are you sure you want the whole year?' she called out. 'It's a ten-form entry per year. Do you not know her class?'

'Sorry, I can't remember – and I don't want to ask her, as then she'll know what I'm up to.' Daisy smiled, trying to lift the moment, as the woman scowled back at her.

The girls in the queue behind her sighed. Daisy looked over her shoulder and apologised. One of them was scrolling through her phone and reading the news. Daisy saw her click on the article with the words 'Human Remains found on Saltdean Tye'.

Finally, the woman reappeared at the window.

'I don't have any lists that go back that far, but we had a thought: there are all the old yearbooks in the library. They go back to the seventies, I think. But you can't go down there without a DBS check.'

'I have a DBS, I'm a carer at Downside Nursing Home.'

'Are you?' said the girl behind her. 'My nan goes there, my dad got sick of her living with them and talked my mum into it. He says the girls that work there are saints!'

'Oh, that's nice to hear. What's her name?' Daisy asked.

'Shirley Reed.'

Daisy beamed back. 'I know Shirley, she's lovely,' she lied. Shirley was notoriously grumpy and demanding, and most of the girls did anything to avoid having her on their shift.

'Well, you can't just go down to the library, I'm afraid,

you'd have to be accompanied,' the receptionist said. 'You'll have to make an appointment for next week sometime.'

'It really needs to be today. It's her birthday next week, and I need to get the invites out.'

'I can take her, I'm going down anyway, I'm on a free period,' the girl said, popping a mouthful of bubblegum which stuck to her lips.

'That's so kind . Thank you so much.' Daisy beamed, a flutter of hope in her tummy.

'Yeah, no worries. Sam, can you get this signed for me? I'll see you later.'

After signing in, Daisy followed the girl down the endlessly long corridor, packed full of teenagers rushing past them, until they reached the relative quiet of the library.

'What are you after?' said the girl, her green eyes peering out from behind a long fringe.

'Yearbooks, from 1978 to 1985. I need the people in my sister's class.'

'That'll be in the archives,' she said, ignoring the librarian scowling at them for talking.

Daisy followed the girl to the back of the long room, passing high windows and scattered long wooden tables, until they reached a high bookcase packed with multi-coloured A4 hardback books, stretching the width of the room.

'There you go, the eighties is at the top, there's a stool down there, and a photocopier you'll need change for is at the front,' the girl said. 'I'll be over there if you need me. I'll have to take you back, I'll be here about an hour.'

'Thanks,' said Daisy, as the girl walked off.

She turned to the vast expanse of books in front of her.

After scanning the shelves for a minute or two she found the right years, and carefully pulled them out. They were thick and heavy, and no doubt packed with information that wasn't relevant to her. She looked at the clock, and took a deep breath, then sat down at one of the tables, lifting the first of the seven large yearbooks towards her, and began to turn the pages.

Chapter Fourteen
Olive

Bletchley Park, January 1944

'Hello?'

Olive stood at the entrance to the motorcycle workshop, and looked around for some sign of life. It was a large open space, with brick walls painted grey and a corrugated iron roof. Motorbikes in various states of repair were dotted around, and in the corner was a workshop with the word 'Motorbikes' in shiny brass lettering above the door. A man in grey overalls was standing in the workshop with his back to her.

'Mr Price?' said Olive, from the other side of the workshop, not knowing if she was allowed to walk into the Cottage, as it was called, without permission.

Tentatively, she stepped in, looking around her.

The bikes looked to her to be mostly Norton 500s and Triumph 350s. Some had smashed headlights, or the back wheels taken off, presumably to fix punctures or brakes – the most common problems she knew of with motorbikes. The open space smelt of petrol and oil and reminded her of her father's workshop on the farm – although the levels of tidiness were very different. Her father was not an organised man; paint lids would always be left open, oil cans tipped over, drill heads and spanners left out to rust in the rain. The scene in the Cottage was very different; no tools or oily rags had been left out, the floor was pristine, the bikes were clean, their headlights shining, and bikes were clearly being worked on systematically, one by one. On neatly stacked shelves to the side of the workshop were goggles, helmets, neatly folded overalls and gloves.

Olive glanced around, and saw through the small window of the workshop that the man was now on the telephone and deep in conversation. Olive walked slightly nearer and glanced at the tools on the wooden workbench: a wrench, two spanners, an oil can and an oil tank for topping up the bikes. She was comforted to see it was the usual paraphernalia, all of which she knew how to use.

'Right, I understand, will do. Thank you,' the man said, his voice deep and slow, before returning the receiver to its cradle and slowly turning round to face her. He stared, saying nothing.

Olive stared back, stunned for a moment by his slightly unnerving appearance. He was heavily built, with pale skin and thinning hair, and his left eye, which was staring at her intently, had what appeared to be a defect; the lid of his eye was swollen, so much so that he looked as if he could barely see out of it. Perhaps, thought Olive, the reason why he hadn't been called up for national service. There was an awkward silence, as he continued to stare and say nothing: no welcoming words, no instructions as to what her duties for the day might be.

Olive smiled broadly, in an attempt to break the silence, and reached out her hand. 'Olive May, pleased to meet you.'

He stared down at her hand for an uncomfortably long time. At last, the man reached for a rag hanging from the brown tool belt around his waist, wiped his hands on it and took hers.

'Geoff Price,' he said slowly, gripping her hand so tightly that it was slightly hard for her to pull it away.

Finally she did, stepping back as her heart fluttered uncomfortably. 'What a splendid workshop. You keep it very tidy, I must say,' she blurted, feeling herself flushing. 'It must be a wonderful place to work, if a little cold.'

She smiled broadly, convinced he could sense her discomfort and her attempt to act more mature and worldly than she was.

'Ah good! You're here already!' came a voice from behind her.

Olive turned, with huge relief, to see Commander Travis bustling towards her.

'I see you've met Geoff already. Geoff runs a tight ship here, we'd be lost without him. I'm sure the two of you will get on splendidly,' he said, nodding at Geoff.

The man continued to stare wordlessly at Olive.

'I'll let you get back to your work, Geoff,' he said, steering Olive away. 'I trust you slept well and are settled into your accommodation? I've just seen your friend Lorna, who is starting her training in hut eight. I've heard great things about her mathematical talent, and I'm sure we shall see wonderful things from her. And you, Olive. Here at Bletchley a different kind of war is being fought to the one we have seen across the country and Europe – this is a secret war. We are racing against time to break "unbreakable" enemy codes and ciphers and turn the tide in the Allies' favour. Codes which, without our dispatch riders to bring them to us, we would be utterly helpless to crack.'

Olive nodded eagerly at Commander Travis as Geoff returned to his workshop and closed the door. She tried to shake off the nerves she had felt around him and focused on Commander Travis, who was walking her towards the bikes.

'The main role of a dispatch rider, young Olive, is to collect enemy signals from the radio stations across the south of England and bring them back to us. I warn you, it's a hard and dangerous job. You will have to travel backwards and forwards from the intercept stations at all times of the day and night, and in all weathers. And there are stringent security precautions expected of you.' Olive listened intently, fearful she would miss something in Commander Travis's tirade of information. 'There are seventy dispatch riders at Bletchley. We divide you into three shifts: midnight to eight, eight to four and four to midnight. You rotate shifts every six days. At the start of your shift you must report to me and I will give you an envelope with an address on it. You are to have zero curiosity about what you are carrying, except for the destination and any priority on the dispatch envelope.

'There must be no stopping between Bletchley Park and the designated destinations, unless in an emergency. If you see another dispatch rider in trouble you are not permitted to stop and help them. It could be a trap. You must take all necessary action to ensure dispatches are delivered safely and on time. You mustn't stop for any reason. And above all that, you are strictly forbidden to discuss any aspect of the operation with anyone outside Bletchley Park, at any time. I cannot stress this enough.'

'Yes, sir,' said Olive.

'You will be riding through all weather conditions, including snow, sleet, wind and heavy rain – which is obviously the most dangerous for the bikes. Are you used to riding in adverse weather conditions?'

'Yes, sir, I'm a good rider,' said Olive, nodding earnestly.

'They are heavy, these bikes. There's not a lot to you, is there? We need to fatten you up,' he said, frowning at her, as if the size of her waist were a code that needed cracking.

'I grew up on a farm, sir, I'm tougher than I look,' Olive said, as confidently as she could muster.

'I'm sure you are. The young ladies at Bletchley never cease to amaze me with their strength and stamina. But what I will say is that this is a very intense environment, no one is immune to it. And you will become close and trust the people you work with implicitly. But careless talk costs lives, the walls have ears. Never talk about anything you are doing, or anywhere you are going, outside the Cottage. Not even to Lorna and other friends. And they will be instructed to do the same.'

'Yes, sir.' Olive stared at the man and began to feel quite dizzy. She had barely slept or eaten much breakfast, and the tsunami of information was proving overwhelming. She had never done well at school, she found concentrating hard, and her ability to take in a lot of information all at once was not good.

It was one of the reasons she loved motorbikes so much. At school she felt trapped, the classroom felt like a prison. Her brain was busy trying to cope with taking in too much information. It took all her concentration just to sit still in her chair at her desk, so she had no capacity left to listen to what was going on at the front of the classroom. She was

183

forever in trouble; her school reports talked endlessly of her being in another world, how she never listened to any of the teachers and would amount to nothing. To her, school felt like a narrow cell, from which she was desperate to escape, and every minute felt like an hour.

On her bike, it was the opposite: she felt alive. She was on her own, and she had to rely on herself entirely if something went wrong, there was no one there to help. She had acquired a basic grasp of mechanics. She wanted to understand how the bike worked, how her body moved with the engine, and controlled it, like she was part of an animal. It was both terrifying and strangely calming at the same time. Knowing that if she stopped concentrating for a moment, she could take a corner wrong, ride through diesel on the road, go over some black ice, and the back wheels could slip out, sending her skidding along the road under her bike.

Even if going at a relatively low speed, a 30mph crash in a car was an annoyance, but on a motorbike it was a severe injury; she knew she was taking her life in her hands every time she climbed on, and it suited her personality. It was strangely calming, because she was concentrating so much – assessing the angle, the cornering speed, what was coming up, what was beside her – it was like meditating. It centred her so completely, her busy brain had to focus entirely on not coming off the bike.

Olive began to feel herself panicking as Commander Travis continued and her brain began to overload and crash. She could cope with the physical hardship, the mechanics and the skill of riding motorbikes, but taking on huge amounts of information was not her strong point.

'Don't worry,' said Commander Travis, as if reading her mind, 'it is a lot to take in at first, but it will all become second nature. And Geoff is here at all times, to help with any queries you may have. The man doesn't sleep.'

Olive smiled warily at the prospect of having to turn to Geoff, a man who barely spoke, for all her queries.

In her peripheral vision, she saw two men walking into the Cottage. She glanced over briefly; both were tall and wearing green overalls, and one walked up to the workshop and tapped on the window.

'And of course you will have your fellow dispatch riders who can help fill you in,' continued Commander Travis. 'Olive, this is Samuel . . . and James. Samuel, this is Olive, who is starting with us today.'

'Welcome to Bletchley,' said Samuel, smiling warmly at her.

Geoff appeared from the workshop, scowling at the new arrivals.

'Ah, there you are, good chap,' said Samuel, slapping Geoff on the shoulder. 'How are my brakes coming along this morning?'

'Samuel is with us from Canada. He is a pilot and also rode motorbikes in Canada in a professional capacity, so we are very lucky to have him,' Commander Travis said proudly.

'I don't think Geoff thinks he's lucky to have me, do you, Geoff? Can't wait for me to go home, I'd say,' said Samuel, laughing and winking.

Olive felt her stomach do an involuntary flip.

Geoff muttered something to himself and walked over to Samuel's bike as the two began immersing themselves in

185

the task in hand. Olive felt instantly comforted that Geoff was obviously a quiet sort of fellow with everyone, and she would not be alone if she struggled with him. She couldn't help noticing that Samuel was extremely good-looking, tall and blond, with freckles on his nose. He had a leather jacket on, and a scarf draped casually around his neck. He reminded her of a poster she had once seen in a diner in Brighton, with a man sitting in an American fighter jet, and the tag line: *You don't stop flying when you get old. You get old when you stop flying.* Olive tore her eyes away from Samuel and dug her nails into her skin to get her attention back to where it needed to be – a trick she had developed at school. Sometimes she would tear at the skin around her fingernails so much that they bled.

'As you may or may not know,' Commander Travis confided, 'we have removed all the road signs, railway station hoardings, town, village and place names across the British countryside. Essentially anything that could identify or indicate locations. The purpose of this is to confuse the enemy upon invasion. Obviously, it makes your job all the more challenging. I'd advise you not to use the same route twice, as a precaution, in case you are being followed. Therefore, you will rely very heavily on your map.'

The commander walked over to a row of canvas panniers, neatly lined up next to the helmets and goggles.

'Here is your map case,' he said, reaching into a pannier, 'which is a standard part of your equipment. It's essential you carry a map with you at all times, even on planned routes, as your intended course may not be available. Roads are often closed, due to bomb damage or debris, and you will quickly have to find an alternative that will keep you as close to the designated track as possible, to avoid delays. How are you with map reading?'

'Good, I think,' said Olive, nerves rising in her again. She had never so much as left her village before, and maps were something that belonged in geography lessons, at which she had failed dismally.

'You are also required to carry a standard gas mask at all times,' Travis instructed. 'They are heavy and cumbersome, and some riders choose to take the risk of not having one. That choice is yours, of course, but I advise that you do. As I said, you will work in shifts. At the start of your shift, you report for duty at the house. You will be given an envelope with an address on it. You must use your map to go to the address specified on the envelope as quickly as you can. They, in turn, will give you a message to return to us.'

'Can I ask, how many deliveries will I do in a day?' Olive asked, slightly nervously.

'That's a good question and depends on where you are sent. Usually, we don't send you further than one tank of fuel can take you, for obvious reasons – we don't want you breaking down. However, Royal Signals Dispatch Riders are required to wear a band around each arm at all times.' He reached into a pannier and retrieved two blue and white armbands, pulling one onto his upper arm, to demonstrate. 'All the riders wear them, and they confirm that in an emergency you have the right to stop any army vehicle and ask for petrol. They also mean that you are not to be held up or delayed at road blocks by police or the military, and you can seek assistance and shelter at an army camp or barracks if on duty. Dispatch riders are responsible for the delivery of up to three thousand messages per day from the various intercept stations. Riders are based all over the country, not just here, but we have a number of riders permanently on standby at the park, of which you are now one.'

Olive nodded, as Commander Travis reached up and pointed at the shelves. 'Every morning or evening, depending on your shift, before you report for duty, you will need to come here and take everything you require from these shelves. Geoff will remind you of everything you need, but you'll soon get the hang of it. You'll also need goggles, of course. You get no end of stuff in your eyes – dirt and flies – and one chap collided with a pigeon the other day at fifty miles an hour and it would have taken his eye out. Aside from the rain making the road slippery, and causing your back wheels to slip out, the biggest hazard is wild animals crossing the road – deer and foxes. If you hit one of those, it's either you or the bike that will come off worse. So goggles and helmet are essential. And now,' finished the commander, 'I will give you a tour of the site.'

He led her away from the garage as Olive glanced back at Samuel, who looked up at her and smiled.

'You come in along Back Lane, where there is an entrance with a metal gate, controlled by a guard in a sentry box. This reduces the noise of the motorbikes, of which there are a great number, as there are so many of you. And the occupants of the huts need to apply their utmost concentration at all times.'

'Is there a uniform? I mean, what do we wear?'

'Everything you own! You will be colder than you've ever felt in your entire life,' Samuel called out.

'You should try cleaning out a pigsty in the snow at six o'clock in the morning,' Olive called back to him.

Samuel laughed as Commander Travis continued, 'Right, after you, young lady. Do you know how to shoot while riding your bike?'

'Well, I used to shoot rabbits at night in the back of my brother's pickup while he tore around our fields, so I'm a pretty good shot.'

Commander Travis laughed. 'She's a little firecracker, this one, Samuel.'

'I can see that,' the Canadian joked.

As Samuel laughed, behind him Geoff stood, stony-faced, before turning and walking back into his workshop and closing the door behind him.

Chapter Fifteen

Jo

March 2015, Tuesday morning

Jo walked through the vast sliding glass doors of The Keep, off the Lewes Road, and up to the man sitting behind the desk frantically tapping away at his computer.

'Hello,' she said, as he glanced up briefly. 'I've had an email to say that the inquest notes I've ordered are ready.'

He looked up at her, then the clock, clearly in the midst of a busy day. 'Can you sign in here, and do you have a membership card?'

'No, sorry, I don't,' Jo said.

The man let out a sigh, and nodded his head. 'I'm afraid you'll have to wait until after lunch now; we close in fifteen minutes and I'm already helping someone.'

Jo reached into her bag, pulled out her police ID, and laid it on the counter. 'I'm Superintendent Hamilton, I'm not sure if I need a membership card. I'm just collecting some inquest notes – I have an email here from the coroner, approving it.'

Despite working in Sussex Police for more than thirty years, she had never got used to the change in people's demeanour when they realised she was a police officer. While she was in uniform, it was never an issue, but as she'd gradually worked her way up, and was dressed in plain clothes, it became more noticeable. Quite often, their eyes would widen and they would sit up straight, as if she were a headmistress about to discipline them. Unlike some colleagues, she never used it to get special treatment, but in situations such as this – when she needed clearance in order to get the inquest notes – it usually led to a dramatic change in attitude.

Jo felt her phone vibrate in her pocket and pulled it out; it was Constable Kate Harris. Jo took a deep breath and answered it.

'The DNA results are back – it's 99.7 per cent certain it's Holly Moore,' said Kate.

Even though she knew they were Holly's remains lying up there on the Tye, an overwhelming wave of sadness engulfed her and she found it desperately hard to remain composed. 'Thanks for letting me know,' said Jo, struggling to keep her voice steady. 'Did Carl tell you to call me, Kate?'

There was a long pause. 'No, I just thought you should know.'

'I see. Well, thank you. I appreciate it.'

'For what it's worth, I don't approve of the way you're being treated,' Kate said quietly. 'Nobody does. I owe you a lot, and I'd be prepared to stick my neck out for you, even if it means me losing out on this promotion. I don't want to work for a force that treats women like you badly.'

Jo held her breath and fought back tears; everyone at the station was talking about her being excluded from the briefing. 'I'm sure Carl has his reasons. I wouldn't want you to miss out on anything, Kate. Your support means a lot.'

She put her mobile back in her bag as she heard footsteps coming along the hallway towards her.

'Please leave your bag and coat in one of the lockers, and go through the sliding door on the right. There should be someone behind the desk who can bring out your file.'

'Perfect, thank you.' Jo looked around the room at the rows of lockers and picked one.

It had been a long time since she'd been to The Keep. Normally, she would have sent one of her team down, but she was in no rush to get back to the station. She barely had an office left, after Stan had moved his stuff in while her seat was still warm, so she didn't even know if she'd have somewhere to work – and that was alongside the humiliation of Carl and his cronies clearly hiding aspects of the case from her. So she had decided to retreat to The Keep to gather her thoughts and read Gemma's inquest notes in peace.

Jo walked through more sliding doors, and was directed to the reading room at the back of the building, containing huge tables, where anyone could access the archives, documents and historical records of the whole of East Sussex, some of which dated back to the 1700s. Only inquest notes under seventy-five years old were restricted – to blood relatives of the deceased and to the police, who were allowed access to them with the coroner's consent.

Jo sat down at one of the tables, trying to breathe through the panic and slow her anxiety down after the events of the past twenty-four hours. Before five minutes had passed, a lady in a blue cashmere jumper, with tortoiseshell-framed glasses on the end of her nose, walked over and gently placed a file in front of her. Jo looked down at the black lettering and felt her heart stir at the sight of a small envelope clipped to the front. Quite often, a suicide note was attached to the front of a file, but for some reason it startled her to be facing it so abruptly, as if she were looking into a shallow grave. She put it to one side, and began to read the inquest notes in front of her.

The first thing that struck her was how flimsy the file was. Forty years ago, in 1975, she had managed to rush to the Coroner's Court, and grab the tail end of the inquest in her lunchtime. Her boss at the time, Bart Bailey, hadn't allowed her the time off to attend the whole inquest. She had presumed that a great deal of evidence had been given prior to her arrival, that there would have been a thorough report from the pathologist who had carried out the post-mortem on Gemma's body, details of the police inquiry into the days leading up to her death, accounts from the people who knew her – teachers perhaps, or a friend from Morgate.

But there was nothing other than a one-paragraph statement by the police constable who had found her corpse on Saltdean beach, saying that he had answered a call on his radio, responding to reports of a body on the beach, and that it was a popular suicide spot. On the next page, there was a short summary of the post-mortem findings.

The deceased was admitted to the mortuary at the Royal Sussex County Hospital at 11.45 a.m. on Thursday 20th November 1975, having been brought there by the police. She was examined by the pathologist and was found to have a scalp wound, clinical evidence of fracture of the pelvis, and a fracture of the skull which was not confirmed by X-ray. There were altogether five fractures of bones. Death was due to shock following multiple injuries.

Jo flicked backwards through the pages several times, looking for the rest of the report. But after that brief paragraph, there were just the testimonies she had herself witnessed after she arrived. She had heard DI Bart Bailey talking about Gemma, which was written in full in the back page of the document in her hands. She read it carefully and it was just as she had remembered; a scathing attack on Gemma's personality, describing her as a runaway, troublesome, a delinquent, with no mention of any other side to her. Lorna Price, the head of Morgate House, had also stood up, and had pretended to care for Gemma. Goosebumps flushed up Jo's arms now, to see Lorna's signature, like a ghost from the past bringing back to life the complex feelings Jo had experienced that day. There was no doubt in Jo's mind that Lorna Price had neglected her duties at Morgate House, failed to clothe and feed and care for the children she was paid to look after. Gemma had died in her care, and yet Lorna Price had cleverly laid all the blame at Gemma's door. Carefully carved out a picture of a troubled girl she had tried in vain to help. Who had talked to her of hating the world, of having no one, of running away and nobody noticing she'd gone; a wild animal she couldn't tame – however hard she'd tried.

Jo had looked around the Coroner's Court then, with no family members to defend Gemma, and felt like her heart

194

would break for the girl. She hadn't known it at the time, but her instinct had told her, even then, what thirty-plus years' experience told her now: the success of an inquest, and the ability to get justice for your loved one, was always – *always* – down to the deceased's family and how hard they pushed.

Every time she attended an inquest, families were the ones who put forward the requests for further evidence, information or statements. Requests that were always met defensively, and pushed aside, for fear of blame. Sometimes, the same arguments were put forward, again and again, by bereaved relatives, often in a state of shock and with no knowledge of the process – but their distress, the fire in their bellies, and wanting justice for their loved ones, spurred them on.

The four pages Jo held in her hand now, in The Keep, were evidence that nobody had cared for Gemma. Nobody had been there to fight for answers, to push for tiny scraps of disclosure, and to get to the truth.

Most shocking of all, there were no 'Actions to be taken', no 'Lessons to be learned', no 'Coroner's concerns', no 'Recommendations'. No accountability for either Morgate House or Sussex Police.

Jo's eyes fell again on the envelope pinned to the front of the file. She suspected that it held Gemma's suicide note, and slowly began to open it. She pulled out the single piece of paper that Gemma had written on. To her surprise it contained, not a note, but a poem, addressed to 'Dear Eve'. As she read the lines, clearly addressed to someone Gemma cared for deeply, Jo's eyes misted over.

When she reached the end, Jo put down the poem, and

wiped away her tears that were brimming over. It was hard to tell from Gemma's words, if she was going away. Or if she was intending to take her own life. 'You are a perfect little girl, whose life has just begun.' It sounded as if Eve was much younger than Gemma. Who Eve was, and whether she had been questioned by the police, were not questions that had come up at the inquest. It could be that Eve knew nothing at the time that could have helped the investigation, but there was also a small chance she might now remember something that would be relevant.

It should be easy enough to track her down from the Morgate House records and meet up with her. If she was younger than Gemma, there was also a chance that she had still been there when Holly and Daisy arrived.

Jo sat back in her chair, and reread the poem; it still sounded to her like more of a goodbye than a suicide note. As if Gemma had to leave for some reason. It didn't sound to her as if the girl was planning to take her own life.

Jo scanned the lines again, her eyes snagging on one of the verses.

Work hard at Saltdean High,
It's the only way out of this life.
Tell Mr Haig I'm sorry
For all the trouble and strife.

Jo looked at her watch: eleven thirty. It was a long shot, but she could fire off an email to the school office at Salt-dean High, and try to find out if Mr Haig was still alive, and would be willing to talk to her. If he was, she could possibly pay him a visit the following day. There was a chance he'd remember Gemma. Jo reached for her phone, and googled the school office email. She composed a brief message, with her Sussex Police signature, and pressed send. If he had been Gemma's English teacher in 1975, there was a chance he wasn't still alive – and even if he was, he would be of the age where he probably wasn't on email. It might be some time before she got a response.

Jo started to pack up her things, and looked at the clock. She needed to get back to the station before the lunchtime briefing, and try to get hold of Holly and Daisy's case notes – which would no doubt be buried in the bowels of Brighton Council's offices.

Jo took a photograph of Gemma's poem with her mobile phone and slid the piece of paper back into the envelope, before attaching it to the front of the inquest notes. As she left, she handed the file back to the lady behind the counter.

She climbed back into her car and sat for a moment trying to fight back images of the night of the fire. Forty years later and the fear that she remembered in Daisy's eyes was still there. She started up the engine and headed back to the station along the seafront. She knew she should go home, but she didn't want to be alone. She didn't want to think about her mother, and how she needed to be with her. But she didn't have time to sit by her mother's bed – and besides, Olive didn't want her there any more than Jo wanted to be there. They always upset each other, even without meaning to. There was plenty of time still. Now, she had to focus on the fact that she only had a few more hours before she would be taken off the case completely.

Pulling into the station car park, Jo's mobile began to ring. Glancing at the screen, she saw it was an unknown number. She pulled into her space, facing the entrance, turned off her engine and answered the phone.

'Hello, Joanna speaking,' she said, letting out a small sigh.

'Hello? Can I speak to Superintendent Jo Hamilton, please.' The voice on the other end of the line was faint.

Jo pressed her phone harder to her ear. 'Speaking,' said Jo, frowning.

'Ah yes. My name is Professor Edward Haig. I have just received an email from Saltdean High School, which they forwarded to me. I believe you are looking for Gemma Smith's English teacher?'

Jo's heart rate began to quicken as she looked up to the steps of the station, from where Carl was emerging.

'Yes, I am indeed.' Jo kept her eyes on Carl as he lit a cigarette and looked back at the doors to the station, as if waiting for someone.

'Well, you're speaking to him,' the man said, clearing his throat. 'I remember young Gemma very well.'

Jo felt her breath catch. 'Thank you so much for getting back to me so quickly.'

'I think the Saltdean Police signature on your email probably meant you skipped the queue. They forwarded it on straight away, and I've been at my desk this morning catching up on paperwork.'

Jo leaned forward, as if to close the distance between them.

'Gemma's passing still saddens me to this day, she was such a bright spark. I was very fond of her,' he said, as a dog barked in the background. 'I never felt she was the type to take her own life. I mean, you can never tell. But it never sat well with me.'

Jo took a deep breath, unable to share anything; she had to choose her words carefully. 'We are just doing some enquiries about Morgate House at the moment, where Gemma was in residence.'

'Yes, terrible place, as far as I could tell. I felt sorry for the children there, they were all very wayward and hard to work with – apart from Gemma, who very much wanted to learn. I was actually helping her with a sixth form college application when she died.'

Jo looked up at the entrance of the police station. A second person was emerging, a man, tall, with dark hair and a narrow face, wearing a black bomber jacket. She recognised him immediately as Phillip Price, her ex-colleague and the son of Lorna and Geoff Price, managers of Morgate House. Jo felt her face flush with rage as Carl pulled a packet of cigarettes out of his pocket and offered Phillip one.

'Of course, I told all this to the police officer who came to see me. I wanted to attend the inquest, to speak up for Gemma. But nothing ever came of it. I never heard anything back.'

Jo felt panic begin to flood her system as she watched Carl light Phillip's cigarette. The two men shared a joke, leaning in, laughing, their eyes locked, as one.

'Police officer? Which police officer?' Jo asked, suspecting already, but still having to go through the motions.

'Well, I got in touch with the police to say I'd like to speak at the inquest, when I heard there was going to be one. And an officer came to see me. I told him about

Gemma's college application. I was at the inquest, I tried to speak to the coroner, but when I pressed the issue, I was asked to leave.'

Jo's mind raced back to the day; she remembered Phillip Price referring to a troublemaker at the inquest. Jo watched as Carl and Phillip continued to chat happily on the station steps, like old pals. It made her feel sick just to look at them. Her eyes fell on the photograph of Phillip standing uncomfortably close to her at her graduation; it was peeping out of her bag on the seat next to her.

'Professor Haig, if I email you a photograph now, could you tell me if it's the man who came to see you?' said Jo, pulling the picture out.

'Of course, I'd be delighted to help in any way I can,' he said, before reeling off his email address. 'It has always troubled me,' he added.

Jo put the picture on her seat and snapped it with her phone camera, then attached it to an email and sent the image off to him.

'While that's coming through, I was just wondering if you also knew of someone called Eve. Gemma mentions her in a poem the coroner interpreted as a suicide note. I think she was quite a bit younger than Gemma, but I presume she would have also ended up at Saltdean High.'

'No, I can't say the name is familiar, but she could have been in another class. I remember another girl very well, who was also at Morgate – Holly Moore.'

Jo's heart skipped a beat. 'Holly Moore? The girl who went missing in 1985?'

'Absolutely. In fact, I was going to mention it, as I kept a letter of hers she gave me one of the last times I saw her. I always hoped I might be able to give it to her sister, as she wrote it for her.'

'Her sister? Daisy?' Jo asked.

'Daisy, yes. They were separated, I believe. It hurt Holly a lot, that she didn't know where Daisy was. I believe they said her sister was fostered and they weren't allowed to stay in touch. She tried desperately to find her, and gave me a letter for her, in case Daisy turned up in my class one day. But she never did, sadly.'

'Would I be able to see the letter?' Jo said, her heart soaring at the chance of a way in. 'We're hoping to speak to Daisy later today, and it would be lovely to have it.'

'By all means, I've got your email here now. I'll dig out the letter, scan it in and send it over. It may take a little while, I'm not terribly savvy with these things. Let me just open this attachment you've sent me now. Hopefully, it will let me. Ah . . . yes, here we go.'

Jo watched as Carl and Phillip stubbed out their cigarettes, and Carl shook Phillip's hand. Jo felt the rage inside her consume her before Professor Haig had a chance to confirm what she already knew. Carl looked up and his expression froze for a minute, as he saw her watching them.

'Yes, that's him. That's definitely the chap who came to see me,' he said, with conviction.

Jo felt her adrenaline soar; Phillip Price had been to see Gemma's teacher and had actively stopped him attending Gemma's inquest. 'Okay, thank you so much, you have been very helpful. I look forward to receiving Holly's letter when you have a chance. Goodbye, Professor.'

'Goodbye, Superintendent,' he said. 'Don't hesitate to contact me again if I can be of service.'

201

Jo finished the call and watched Phillip Price turn back and walk through the revolving doors of Saltdean Police Station behind Chief Superintendent Carl Webber. Slowly, he turned back and stared at her with the lazy, self-satisfied Cheshire Cat grin that had always turned her stomach.

Chapter Sixteen

Holly

January 1985

'It's cold this afternoon,' said Eve, linking her arm through Holly's as their feet fell in time, walking along the frost-covered pavement. 'Did you want to try the local schools, see if any of them have Daisy on their records?'

It was only four o'clock but the sun was already going down on the short winter day. They had bunked off school at lunchtime and decided to get the bus to Coldean and pound the residential streets and parks, looking for Holly's sister, as they had done several times in the past weeks. Ever since the day Holly had snuck into the office at Morgate House, and found a letter from Brighton Council about her sister, Daisy Moore, her obsession with finding her had reached new heights. She had held the piece of paper in her hand, its print faded from years of being locked away in the filing cabinet, as she read the words telling her that her sister – who she grieved for every day, as if she had died – was settling in well with her foster parents in Coldean, and that they had applied to adopt her. And as a result, Daisy would not be returning to Morgate House.

Despite the fear of being discovered, she had rooted through the rest of Daisy's file in a state of complete panic and found nothing but her birth certificate, a number of cards she had written to her sister – which hadn't been sent – and a very old letter, a shade of yellowy brown, on Saltdean Police headed paper. Signed by someone called Constable Joanna Hamilton. It stated that following the 'unexpected death of their mother' on 14 December 1975, Daisy and Holly Moore were now in the care of Lewes Council.

It was at that moment – looking down at the cards to her sister which had taken her hours to write, and which she had begged and pleaded with Mrs Price to send to Daisy – that she had realised she was entirely on her own. Nobody was going to help her find Daisy: not the police, not Mr and Mrs Price, not her social worker, who changed with every visit and fobbed her off with all their non-committal, neutral talk. 'We want to help', 'We are here to listen', 'If there is anything you want or need you can always ask, and we will do our best to get it for you.' She had tried so many times, asked everyone she could think of for help with finding Daisy. But it was always the same; she would wait for weeks, then a different social worker would turn up, with no news of Daisy, only the same infuriatingly spine-less language. In the end she had given up. Shut down, and stopped speaking. Now they wrote things in her notes like 'difficult', 'uncommunicative', 'untrusting', 'closed off'.

If she had any hope of ever seeing her sister again, she had to track her down all by herself.

'I don't know. Even if we find the school she's enrolled at, they probably won't tell me and will just contact her fos-ter parents and have the police visit me at Morgate to tell me to stay away. I don't seem to have any rights at all to see my sister. They didn't even let us say goodbye.'

'I know,' said Eve, squeezing her friend's arm as they walked along. 'You'll find her. I know you will.'

'I don't understand why siblings in care that are separated aren't allowed to see each other. It's just cruel,' she said quietly.

'You've never really told me about Daisy,' said Eve. 'I mean, I knew her a bit, but you and me weren't really friends until she left. You two didn't really talk to anyone else. You were inseparable.'

Holly looked over at Eve. Since losing Daisy she had found it hard to get close to anyone. Friends in care become your siblings. But you never knew when you were going to be ripped apart, moved on to a foster family, or to another children's home. You could never feel safe and secure.

When Daisy was taken away, Holly had quickly learned to rely only on herself. She was fond of Eve, but she no longer trusted relationships – especially not with adults, who would always let you down – and believed that no matter how good something appeared, it never lasted for very long. She could be moved without notice at any time. Without anyone ever asking her what she wanted. She felt isolated and alone. She cared for Eve but she kept her at a distance. It wasn't Eve's fault, but she couldn't afford to get too close to anyone.

Holly missed Daisy more than anything, and not a day went by when she didn't think of her. The rawness of her mother's death had come back with a vengeance. When she'd had Daisy by her side, she could cope with her grief. But without Daisy to look after, feelings of isolation and mistrust overwhelmed her, and she was left feeling utterly alone in the world. She longed for the days when her father's temper had been her only fear. When she had a home, and a mother and a sister. She'd take a beating every day to be back there.

'I can't remember a time without Daisy,' said Holly, as they walked along, their feet tapping in time on the pavement. 'I was two when she was born, and I already knew that my dad was a scary man. But I didn't know how to deal with it until Daisy came along. She gave me something to focus on. Someone to protect. And she was the opposite of me. I'm selfish and I have a temper, I lie and I steal to get what I need to survive. But Daisy is good, she was born good.'

'Maybe that's because you protected her, she didn't need to lie and steal and do all the things you had to do to survive,' Eve said, shuddering in the cold.

'I don't know. She had this huge sense of right and wrong. She would look at me wide-eyed, if I went to steal some change from Dad's trousers, or some food from the shop for us to eat. She would start to cry, saying it was wrong. She would rather starve than steal. And she would defend people, like my dad, who didn't deserve defending, and give people the benefit of the doubt. She was so kind. She *is* so kind. I hate that I talk about her in the past tense.'

The day they had come to take Daisy away, with no warning, Mrs Price had walked into the dormitory, smiled and asked Daisy to follow her, telling her that there was 'someone here to see her'. Holly had looked at her sister, her heart racing, knowing something wasn't right. She had followed them along the corridor, despite Mrs Price telling her to go back to her room. Fear had rushed through her body, as Daisy smiled at her excitedly. Mrs Price never smiled, they never had any visitors, and just the fact that she was even in the main house – which she never visited – made Holly sick with worry. It had happened in a second, her nerves making her hang back slightly. Mrs Price had led Daisy into the annex, then in a flash slammed the door, shutting and locking it behind them. Holly had stared at the heavy oak door in shock for a moment, trying to take in what was happening. As if her sister had suddenly been sucked into another time and place. Though only a door separated her, there was no way through. She knew, as her heart thudded in her chest, that Daisy was gone. She had banged on the door of the annex until her fists hurt, then rushed back down the corridor, climbing out of the dormitory window to see Daisy being led away from Morgate House by a woman with a neat blonde bob who she had never seen before.

'What are you doing?' she had said, running up to the stranger. 'Where are you going with my sister?'

'Holly, please calm down. Daisy is just going for a day visit.' Mrs Price was flushed, and smiled as she spoke, trying to appease her.

Holly knew she was lying. 'What's a day visit? Where is she going? Who is that woman?' she spat, lunging forward to grab her sister's arm, as Daisy started to cry.

'Holly, get a hold of yourself,' Mrs Price had said, prising her fingers away, one by one.

'No, I don't trust you. I want to go with her. How do I know you'll bring her back?' Holly was feeling terror like she'd never known. Like the night her mother died, when she had been powerless to keep hold of her hand as her father took her upstairs. Her little sister's face had crumbled as the realisation of what was happening began to take hold.

'I don't want to go!' Daisy had shouted. It was then that Mrs Price had rushed into the house and called her husband – a tall man, with a lazy eye – who Holly had no chance of overpowering. He had charged out of the house, and wrapped his arms around Holly while the woman in the blue suit pulled Daisy away. Holly had made one last lunge at her sister, grabbing her hand, but Daisy had gradually lost her grip, her fingers slipping agonisingly out of her sister's grasp. As the two girls screamed for one another, the Prices' son had rushed towards them, helping the woman force Daisy into the car. Pushing her tiny body into the back seat, shouting at her as she cried for Holly. Holly could still hear her sister's cries in her dreams as the woman started up the engine of the blue VW Beetle before being driven away. She had bitten down on Mr Price's hand, and he had cried out in pain. As he finally released her, she ran frantically down the drive towards the main road.

'I knew I wasn't ever going to see her again. I knew it, because I couldn't breathe.'

'You will see her again, you will find her, Holly,' said Eve.

As the girls turned onto the main road, they saw him, sitting in a Ford Sierra police car, waiting, with his engine off, on the other side of the street. It was dark, but he was parked under a street light. The silhouette of the man looked like a cartoon character; he sat motionless apart from dragging on a glowing cigarette. Holly's stomach flipped with a familiar panic. Mrs Price must have been told that they had bunked off school, and the police were out looking for them already.

'Shit, do you think Mrs Price reported us missing?' said Eve. 'I really don't want another police report with my name on it. They'll kick me out of school,' she said.

He seemed to be watching them as they stopped in their tracks.

'Let's try the park,' said Holly nervously, as the two girls looked at the man, then turned off the main road and retraced their steps.

The girls clung to each other tightly as they walked towards the deserted park, the swings squeakily blowing in the icy wind. Holly turned back, to see that the car had moved to the other side of the road and the man was now climbing out of the driver's seat.

'Should we make a run for it across the park?' Eve said anxiously, breaking into a fast walk.

'I guess so. If we get separated, I'll meet you back at the bus stop,' said Holly, as the two broke into a run.

As Holly stumbled down the path, she felt sure that the man was following her. When she glanced back, she could see him standing at the entrance to the park. Eve had already disappeared; they should have stayed together, she thought, feeling suddenly alone. Her breathing quickened in a panic, knowing the school had called Mrs Price, who, in turn, had called the police. She reached the other side of the playground, but there was no way out, as it backed onto houses.

'Holly! This way!' Eve shouted.

She looked around desperately, following Eve's voice, until she spotted her climbing over the top of a wooden fence, before dropping down into someone's garden.

'That's private property. We'll get in trouble,' Holly hissed, her whole body shaking with adrenaline. She looked back to see him walking towards her. Her legs burning, she started to climb, her feet slipping as she tried to get a grip on the wooden slats. Her arms weren't strong enough and the fence was too high. Eve was taller and stronger than her, she kept trying desperately to pull herself up, as Eve shouted at her from the other side to hurry. Her arms shaking with the strain, she managed to find a foothold but her fingers began to slip and suddenly she lost her grip.

When she fell, she had nearly made it to the top and knew it was going to hurt. She put her arm out first, and as she hit the ground the pain exploded, shooting through her wrist. She heard the bone snap as she crashed onto the concrete below. Holly clutched her wrist, the pain too severe to cry out, as she took fast intakes of breath. She could hear his footsteps, and tried to get up, but she couldn't.

Holly started to cry out from the agony, sobbing as he appeared next to her. He walked around her where she lay gasping from the pain climbing up her arm. Moonlight poured through the clouds as he reached her, turning the silhouette of his long black coat into a cape.

'Are you alright?' he said.

'I've hurt my arm,' she said, unable to stop the tears.

'Let me help you up,' he said, putting his arm under her and taking her weight as she cried out with pain. 'I think we need to take you to hospital.'

As they walked, he wrapped his arm around her waist. Every step she took caused a stab of pain to rocket through her. It felt like an hour, but finally they reached the car. He opened the passenger door for her and eased her in. When he put her belt on for her, he knocked her arm and she let out a gasp of pain. She looked down; her wrist was already swollen to twice its size, and every tiny movement and bump was agony.

'Why were you following us?' she said.

'Why did you run away?' he retorted, getting into the driver's seat.

'Because I was scared,' she said, shaking from the shock. At least it was warm inside the car, the heater was on. 'We can't leave Eve out there, it's freezing.'

'Where is your friend?' he said, peering through the windscreen.

'At the bus stop. At the top of the road.' She was trying not to cry any more. She took deep gulps of air and clung to her elbow with her good hand in an effort to stop the excruciating pain whenever she moved.

He started the engine, put the car into gear, and cruised slowly up the road. Eve was waiting at the bus stop, shaking from the cold. He pulled up and she climbed in to the back seat.

'I think I've broken my wrist,' said Holly.

The two of them locked eyes in the rear-view mirror.

'So what are you kids doing roaming the streets of Coldean in the dark?' the man said.

Holly sat back in her seat, the pain in her arm was too bad to talk.

'We were looking for Holly's sister,' Eve said quietly.

'Does your mum know you're out here in the dark?' he asked.

'My mum's dead,' Holly said quietly.

'Why were you following us?' asked Eve.

'I wasn't. Until you started acting suspiciously. Are you girls in from Morgate House?'

Holly nodded. They drove along in silence. It seemed strange to her that she was sitting in the front; police officers always put them in the back.

'What happened to your sister, she run away?'

'Some woman came and took her away. The old witch won't tell me where she is.'

'Ahh . . . Mrs Price. You know, I might be able to help you find your sister. I have some contacts at social services,' he said, turning and smiling warmly.

Holly's heart lurched for a moment before her defences crept in. 'Why would you want to help me?' She winced from the pain as they went over one of the new speed bumps.

'That's my job, isn't it? We're not all bad, you know. You should have a little more faith in people.'

They drove through the streets of Coldean in silence, down to the seafront, and along to the Royal Sussex County Hospital Accident and Emergency entrance.

The man opened the passenger door, and helped Holly out, then turned back to Eve. 'I'll just take her in and then I'll drop you back to Morgate. Do you want something from the vending machine?'

'Okay,' said Eve, looking at him as he stood next to the car. There was something about him that made her nervous, but she had no idea what it was. Everyone made her nervous, she thought to herself. She never trusted anyone,

212

so why should he be any different just because he was a police officer? 'We'll get in trouble for being picked up by the police again,' she said.

'Don't worry, I'll talk to Mrs Price. It will be okay,' he said, walking away as the sliding doors to Accident and Emergency closed behind them.

Chapter Seventeen

Jo

Spring 2015, Tuesday afternoon

Jo walked up the path of her daughter's small terrace on Hove seafront, clutching a bag of freshly baked rolls, a frog cupcake for Phoebe, and the milk her daughter had asked her to get. She reached out for the brass knocker on the powder-blue front door and fixed a smile on her face, knowing that her daughter was already needling for an argument she didn't have the strength to engage in. Jo waited, a tight knot forming in her stomach. She longed for an easy relationship with Megan, her only child, and watched other women with their daughters, shopping, talking and laughing – wondering how much of the void between them was her fault.

They were so different, not least because a lifetime in the police force, seeing the worst of people, day in, day out, had left her with a dark sense of humour Megan didn't share; it had been her way of coping with bearing witness to so many violent incidents on the job. But Meg didn't appreciate her making light of the tragedies that had littered her daily life. There was nothing funny, she said, about picking up the helmet of a motorcycle rider half a mile up the road from their body, with their head still in it. Or being called out to an old lady who had made herself a cup of tea and promptly died in front of the television, where she had stayed for a year without anyone noticing.

214

Meg was a highly sensitive person who took offence easily and spent her life on marches, or starting petitions against the latest thing to have caused her outrage. If Jo dared to make a flippant comment about anything Megan was sensitive about, she would pull Jo up on it immediately. As someone who had spent her life on the front line, defending the defenceless and helping those in trouble, Jo found Megan's unforgiving attitude hard. She felt they were both coming from the same place, they both cared deeply, they just had different ways of showing it. Theirs was a relationship that had all the ingredients to work, they just viewed life from different perspectives.

Until Meg met Stan, it seemed to Jo that Meg had a particular aversion to the police. She rarely asked her mother how work was, or showed any interest in her life at the station. She quickly changed the subject if Jo had had a bad day, and needed someone to talk to. And while Jo understood that Megan probably didn't want to have those terrible images in her head that plagued her mother – and worried about Jo getting hurt in the line of duty, particularly when she was young – it upset her that Megan couldn't find it in her heart to support her the way she did Stan.

Megan had always had a will of iron, for as long as Jo could remember. Her daughter held grudges hard and fast. She could recall events that had happened to her when she was four or five years old; the tiniest of mishaps sometimes, which she seemingly could not let go of. Jo tried to understand, and to sympathise; her daughter was very sensitive and couldn't help what hurt her. But it made Jo feel on edge, worrying what she was going to do wrong next to upset her. Jo had forgiven people her whole life – strangers who had hit her, bosses who made her life impossible – yet Megan, her own daughter, could not forgive Jo her imperfections, of which she knew she had many.

But Megan was also capable of huge surges of love and affection. She would surprise Jo with the most thoughtful gifts, spend money she didn't have on her favourite food, hand out enormous hugs which almost always caught Jo off guard. Jo had grown accustomed to not being able to be tactile with people; she had to keep her emotions steady and not show her vulnerability. She couldn't hug colleagues, or show affection to any of the children she found in the most dreadful circumstances imaginable. She knew she had become out of practice at being tactile, and found it hard to reciprocate when Megan threw her arms around her. Not least because it sometimes came shortly after a cutting dig about her work, or a rant about something which had upset her daughter; she never knew, from one day to the next, which side of Megan's personality she was going to get that day. But she knew that if she was in trouble, Megan would do everything she could to help her – she would drive through the night to be by her side, if Jo asked her to.

Jo heard voices on the other side of the front door and felt her stomach lurch. Did Megan have a visitor she didn't know about? Or had Megan told her that her dad was popping in, and she'd forgotten, like last time? She hated seeing her ex-husband, not least because Megan and her dad were much easier with each other than she and Megan were, and, though she knew it was churlish, it made her jealous. Richard and Megan saw the world in a very similar way, and she suspected Megan's dislike of the police stemmed from him. Richard had blamed Jo's work for the breakdown of their marriage, but while it had been a contributing factor, Jo felt the main reason was more likely to have been that she wasn't a very good wife, and Richard was an unsupportive narcissist.

Of course, working in the police had undoubtedly affected their marriage; Jo had been told countless times that if your husband isn't a police officer he won't understand the crazy life that you lead. Richard had wanted her home at a set time, expected dinner on the table, and if her annual leave got cancelled because she had to work a double shift, or she had to miss a family wedding because she had to go to court, he was, understandably, furious. Work colleagues were not understanding about her having a child, particularly in the eighties, and she remembered sitting in her interview prior to her return to Sussex Police and being told by her sergeant that having a child was her problem, not theirs. He had crossed his legs, leaned back in his chair, and growled, 'I hope you aren't expecting any special treatment, because you won't get it.' If Richard had loved her, and believed in what she was doing, he could have made it work for them all. But he had chosen not to. And yet, as she climbed the ranks and earned more, Richard had been able to cut back on his work as a supply teacher. He could easily have taken the driving seat, looking after Megan and supporting Jo's dream of making it to superintendent, but he made her feel as bad as he could if she ever missed an assembly or a sports day. It wasn't Megan's fault that, over time, she absorbed her father's negativity; Richard was a strong character, and Meg adored him. But Jo had hoped that, as the years passed, her daughter would have grown up and made up her own mind about her mother's career.

She knew Megan was going to mention her grandmother, but she couldn't handle that drama now on top of everything else. Olive was a different person for Megan and Charlie, and they always made Jo feel bad for not seeing her mother more often.

Their childhood, on a farm in the Sussex countryside, had been fairly idyllic, if a little feral. She had been aware of her mother's sadness since a very young age, but thought that everyone's mother locked herself away for days at a time, had headaches every Saturday, and started drinking at lunchtime. Their father had, mostly, raised her and Charlie, and Jo spent most of her young years following the boys in her life around as they mended fences, tinkered with tractors, and fed the farm animals. She was a daddy's girl, so she didn't really miss her mother's presence in her life. She was happy, mucking in with everything, and occasionally going to school – when her father remembered to take her.

So it wasn't until after her father's death, when Olive moved in with them, and Jo was consumed with grief over her dad, that she realised for the first time how distant they really were. Her dad had been taken from her too young, he had only been in his sixties when early onset dementia kicked in, and she had been so wrapped up in caring for him, that it had taken the spotlight off the relationship with her mother – and what a dysfunctional relationship they had. Coinciding with her return to work, her fellow police officers had commented on how lovely it must be to have her mother at home to help with cooking and childcare. And Jo would just smile and say nothing, as her mother did little to help her and continued to lock herself away, making snide comments about how Jo ran her home and what a shame that she was missing so much of Megan's childhood. She had wanted to scream that she was very present, and missed very little; that having a mother at home all the time didn't automatically make her attentive – stay-at-home mothers were often unfulfilled and miserable, as Olive had been – but Jo didn't have the strength to fall out with her mother and her husband at the same time.

Of course, Richard had loved having someone to back him up, and between them they had tried to break her resolve and make her quit. And she nearly had, after one double night shift, drained of all emotion – after long hours without food, a hot drink, or even access to a toilet, and in a state of intense stress, having been up all night shutting down an acid house party at a disused warehouse in Shoreham. She had come home to the three of them eating breakfast at the kitchen table together. Catching her in a weak moment, Olive and Richard had made her write her resignation letter, there and then, and she was about to hand it in the following day, when she was called out to a traffic pile-up on the coast road. Jo had been the first on the scene as one of the cars was catching fire, and had smashed the window and managed to drag a young mother and her baby to safety. The emotion and exhaustion of the past months had got the better of her, and she had broken down on her brother's shoulder when Charlie had turned up shortly afterwards in a squad car. He had taken her to her favourite café for a cup of tea and listened intently – as only he ever did – and convinced her not to quit. That day she had, instead, asked Richard for a divorce – and told her mother to move out.

Jo had wanted to take Megan out for lunch today – they got on better in neutral territory – but Megan always wanted to stay at home. As the clicking of footsteps reached the front door, her nerves began to build, the lack of sleep, and the emotion of finding Holly's remains, bubbling over inside her. She didn't want to fall out with her daughter, but it felt inevitable. As the door opened, she found herself taking a steadying breath. To her intense surprise and relief, there standing in front of her was not her daughter Megan, but her brother Charlie.

'Hey, Bear,' said Charlie, a shortening of Pooh Bear, a nickname he had given her for as long as she could remember.

She felt her whole body relax, like it always did around her older brother, as he stepped back and fully opened the door onto Megan's black-and-white checked hallway.

'What are you doing here?' said Jo, crossing the threshold and giving Charlie a big hug. He always smelt the same, of the outdoors, and sunshine, whatever the weather. She stepped forward and looked at him, his blue eyes crinkling when he smiled, his wind-kissed cheeks sporting a faint line of lipstick where she'd kissed him.

'Oh nothing, just went to see Mum at the hospice and thought I'd drop in on my favourite ladies,' he said. As Phoebe came waddling down the corridor towards him, Charlie swept her up in his arms.

'Hey, Mum,' said Megan, from behind him, drying a mug with a tea towel. 'Kettle's on, did you get milk?'

'Hi, darling,' she said. 'I did, and some other treats.'

'Oh, Nana's got treats!' Charlie tickled Phoebe and

pulled a face. Megan laughed as Charlie turned and walked back towards the kitchen.

'Thanks for sitting with Granny this morning.' Megan's smile was genuine, it reached her beautiful blue eyes, she looked relaxed, there was no tension between them now that Jo had been at Olive's bedside, and behaved in her daughter's eyes and done what was expected of her – rather than gallivanting around trying to keep criminals off the street. More often than not, she felt as if she were the child, and Megan the parent.

Jo closed the front door behind her, and watched her brother walk away. Charlie's presence had lifted the atmosphere, as it always did, and she felt like crying with relief.

'How's my best girl?' said Jo, as Phoebe grinned back at her and they reached Megan's small cosy kitchen. 'I got her a cupcake, I hope that's okay?'

Megan took a deep breath, inhaling the smell of the freshly baked bread, and then smiled, taking her mother's coat from her. Jo felt her nerves immediately evaporate as she eased herself down into one of the chairs at the kitchen table. Charlie took the frog cupcake out of the bag and began pretending to eat it as Phoebe giggled and snatched at it.

'How did it go with Granny this morning?' Megan asked.

'It was fine, I just sat with her; she was very sleepy, I don't think she even knew I was there,' said Jo.

'She definitely did,' Megan said, smiling at her uncle as he played with her daughter.

Megan loved Charlie, almost as much as Jo did. On the worst days, after Richard had moved out, he would appear, like a rainbow after the rain. He would wash up the dirty dishes, put laundry in the machine, hoover, then sit and play with Megan while Jo slept. It was the only time she slept deeply, knowing he was there in the next room, like he had been when they were little. He had been born with a kind heart; some people were just good, to their bones, and it used to infuriate Jo sometimes, how easily it came to him. He had a way about him – of being generous to people without them knowing.

As a teenager, he had worked in the local grocery store in their village for years, and he got to know two families who struggled terribly to make ends meet. At the end of every day, there was bread, a little stale but fine to toast, fruit slightly past its best but still good enough to make jam, cheese a little hard to sell, but delicious to melt in a frying pan. Once a week, he would gather it all up, ask his boss if he could take it home for the pigs on the farm, and instead leave a hamper on the doorstep for each family, then walk away so as not to embarrass them.

Charlie had a charm that melted even the hardest of hearts. It had served him well as a police officer. His height, his broad shoulders, wide smile and his floppy, dark brown hair made him an unmissable presence, physically and emotionally. He always managed to bring out everyone's softer side. Jo had learned so much from him: about how to defuse a situation with humour, and about how always speaking to people with respect, regardless of how abusive they are being to you, can have shockingly positive results. He had been hugely respected on the force until Carl took over, and began pushing him out. Just as he was doing now with Jo. She didn't know what Carl had against their family, all they had ever offered was decades of loyal service.

While their mother never showed much of an interest in her career, she was openly bursting with pride over Charlie's. It had been obvious to Jo, all her life, that Charlie was her mother's favourite, and Olive did little to hide it. But somehow Jo hadn't minded. Her father had doted on her in equal measure, and acted as the glue to make the family unit work, surprisingly harmoniously. It wasn't until he died, and everything collapsed like a game of Jenga, that Jo realised how much he had hidden.

'So how's things with my favourite girl?' said Charlie. 'She started nursery this week, didn't she?'

Jo felt a stab in her stomach – her daughter hadn't mentioned anything to her about Phoebe starting nursery – but she forced a smile.

'Did she, Meg? That's great news.'

'Not really, I felt terrible leaving her.' Meg bit down on her lip.

'I'm sure she will have a lovely time.' Jo stopped herself from saying more. Meg hated her commenting on things that upset her, and often said she was being flippant. Jo looked down at her hands, wanting to say that there had been no childcare at all for her generation, apart from unreliable, homesick au pairs who needed mothering themselves. That young women today didn't know they were born, with childminders and nurseries, where they could leave their children to be played with, fed, cared for, all day long. It would have transformed her life completely. But of course she said nothing of the sort.

Meg nodded. 'I know.'

'She'll love it, it'll be good for her to be with other kids,' Charlie added, pouring the tea.

'I know all that, but I still wish I didn't have to leave her.' Meg handed out the plates and placed a board of bread and crackers on the table.

'Are you looking forward to getting back to work?' asked Charlie, as Meg sipped at her tea.

'Not really, but we can't live on Stan's income. It's not like the old days, when houses were cheap and you could survive on one police salary. Society bullies mothers into working now, we aren't allowed to stay at home. I just don't want to leave Phoebe. They won't watch her the way I do.'

'It'll be good for you both, you'll enjoy work once you're there,' said Charlie, winking at her.

Jo felt her face flush, waiting for Megan to object, but because Charlie had said it, she just smiled.

'So how's things with you, Jo?' Charlie asked, setting Phoebe down in her high chair as Megan held out the cup-cake. 'You seemed pretty upset yesterday at the station.'

Megan looked over at her mother.

'I'm alright, thank you for asking.'

Charlie stared at her expectantly. She looked back at Megan, she didn't want to talk about work, and she certainly didn't want to bring up the fact that Stan, her soon to be son-in-law, was now heading up the investigation into Holly's death.

'Carl is freezing me out because I'm leaving, just like he did with you. It hurts.'

'No, he respects you, they just can't tell you much because you won't be around much longer. Besides, it's a big deal finding a body, especially a young girl. The press are all over it, so he will be under a lot of pressure to keep

224

any developments quiet. Have they identified who it is yet?' asked Charlie, taking a slurp of his tea.

Megan stood up and began slamming around with cutlery in the sink, which Jo felt she was doing on purpose to drown out their conversation.

'Yes, it's Holly Moore,' Jo said quietly. 'I'm just worried they won't want to open the can of worms that is Morgate House, because too many of them ignored what went on there. It would be like shining a torch on themselves.'

'What do you mean, what went on there?' asked Charlie.

'I don't know, that's what I need to find out.' Jo sighed, rubbing her temple.

'Mum, you're leaving,' said Meg, coming back to the table. 'Aren't you looking forward to spending more time with me and Phoebe? I'm going back to work, I'm going to need you. And then there's the wedding.'

'Of course I am, darling,' Jo said, nervous of the prickliness in Megan's tone. 'It's just I've always blamed myself for those girls ending up at Morgate.'

'It's best you let it go, Mum,' Meg said quietly. 'You've always had a thing about those girls from the fire. It wasn't your fault, they aren't your responsibility. And Morgate House closed years ago!'

'I just can't help feeling it's fate; they have played on my mind for forty years, and now Holly comes back from the dead. Days before I leave. They sent a FLO over to see her sister, Daisy, and she wouldn't talk to them. There's a connection with me – I met Holly when she was alive, there's history there. I know she wouldn't talk to me when I spoke to her last night—'

'You spoke to her?' Charlie echoed, frowning.

225

'Yes, I found her, up at Morgate, she was wandering round the grounds in the dark.'

'Did she recognise you?'

'No. When I told her who I was, she got very upset. But I'm sure, given time, I can get Daisy to talk to us. She's the key to whatever happened to her sister, can't they see that?'

Charlie and Megan exchanged a look as Megan filled the kettle up to make more tea.

'They *can* see that, Jo. That's why they've assigned a Family Liaison Officer. They'll get her to talk, that's what they're trained to do, you need to have a little faith and try and let go,' Charlie said gently. 'Time just isn't on your side with this one.'

'There were so many girls from Morgate House at our school; even if her sister won't talk, there will be others who will have known her. They can't be hard to track down. Now the press are interested in the case, Carl will finally be following all that up – thirty years too late,' Megan added.

'I didn't know you were at school with anyone from Morgate House,' Jo said, turning to Megan.

'Of course I was, everyone from the area went there. The teachers called them "Morgates". They were all the same, nobody wanted them in their class because they were so badly behaved.'

Jo frowned, and sat back in her chair. 'You would have missed Holly, but you may have crossed paths with Daisy. She's seven years older than you, I reckon, so she might have been in sixth form when you started in year seven.'

'If she lasted that long . . . most of them dropped out,' Megan said, wiping the icing off Phoebe's hands, before lifting her out of the highchair.

226

'You never told me any of this.' Jo frowned.

'You never asked,' Megan quipped.

Charlie took Phoebe, who was on Megan's hip, and sat down on the floor with her, taking out some of her toys and playing with her. 'I thought we could go for a walk,' he said cheerfully, changing the subject.

'We could maybe drive over to the hospice, visit Granny,' Megan said, her smile returning to her lips. 'We should try and be there as much as we can—'

Jo's mobile buzzed in her pocket, notifying her that she had an email from Professor Haig, which had an attachment. It must be Holly's letter, she thought, she needed to read it urgently.

'I'm sorry. I'd love to, but I've got to follow up Gemma's inquest notes which I got at The Keep this morning,' Jo said, her heart rate quickening.

'It sounds like you should just leave them to it today, Mum. Why don't you come with us to the hospice? Granny doesn't have time on her side.'

'I'm sorry, Meg, I'll go tomorrow. I can't go again today, I've got too much to do. And I don't want to leave them to it. I did that thirty years ago, and two girls – and that's just the ones I know of – ended up dead.' Jo's legs trembled as she stood up and kissed her granddaughter. 'I'm sorry if you feel that I'm letting you down. But I don't want murderers walking the same streets as you and Phoebe.'

'Mum, please, let it go,' Meg said quietly.

Jo turned to see her daughter's eyes fill with tears. 'It's just a few more days, Meg. Trust me. Then it'll all be over. I just have to know I tried everything.'

'No, it won't,' said Meg, reaching out and clinging to her mother's hand. 'It will never be over.'

'I'll let myself out,' said Jo, walking away, desperate to get to Holly's letter.

She climbed into her car, taking several deep breaths, and frantically opened the email from Professor Haig. *As discussed, please find attached.* Her fingers trembling, she clicked on the attachment.

Dear Daisy,

I hope this letter finds you. I miss you so much, but I know that if you are reading this then you will hopefully be comforted knowing I have never given up the search for you.

I dream of being reunited with you. I dream of what could have been if it weren't for that fire. I daydream obsessively about the happy times with Mum – when Dad was at work or the pub. When we played Knock Down Ginger and the lady next door came after us with her broom. When we played hopscotch with all the other kids in the street until Mum called us in for dinner. When we lay on the grass in the park and spotted animals in the clouds.

I think of the night of the fire, I blame myself for not getting the bedroom door open. I was only eight, but I still think it's my fault she's dead. How different life would have been if that policewoman hadn't started the fire. Or if it had only been Dad who was killed.

If only. If only. I go round and round. If I still had you, I could cope. But they took you away, and they won't let me see you.

Sometimes I think my insomnia is a gift. I don't want to dream about you and Mum, it's too painful. I often dream we are in a bath together, like at Wicker Street, when Mum used to wash our hair and sing to us. Please know that I have tried so hard to find you, I have walked the streets most nights looking for you. I just want to know that you are happy – I can bear not seeing you again if I know you are okay.

I wish nothing but the best for you, my beautiful Daisy Boo. If anything ever happens to me, please live your life for the both of us. I'm sorry I broke my promise to never be separated from you. I will never get over the pain of them taking you away. I tried everything to track you down, but they said your foster mother wanted to keep me away from you.

I hope she is kind to you. I hope you finish school. I hope that you can find a way to recover from all you have been through, and to be truly happy. That is my greatest wish. I love you, Daisy, more than anything or anyone in the whole world.

Your loving sister,
Holly xxx

She had it! She had a way in with Daisy.

Slowly, she began to breathe more steadily and calm herself down. She knew that she should trust in Carl and his team that they would handle the case well. But a burning feeling of injustice at the way Carl was treating her made her very nervous – she suspected he was spending most of his energy trying to cover up his own colleagues' mistakes and negligence at the time of Holly's disappearance. He didn't want her around, pointing out what they failed to do at the time Holly was first reported missing. All of Carl's energy would be expended trying to cover up his team's mistakes and keep things from the press. Trying to protect Phillip Price from the spotlight, in case it made him look bad. She had no faith at all in them trying to focus on who killed Holly.

Jo looked at her watch; if she went back to the station now, she might get lucky. Maybe Carl would be out and about dealing with the press, or on site, and she could ask around, and get some intel on Holly and Daisy so she was fully up to date before she approached Daisy with the letter.

Her body shook with adrenaline. This letter from Holly was her one chance, and she wasn't going to blow it.

Chapter Eighteen

Olive

Bletchley Park, March 1944

Olive slowed round the last bend of her hour-long ride as she approached the town of Bletchley. It had been an endlessly long night, starting her shift at four in the afternoon, and making three trips during the past eight hours, the last one down the A5 to the War Office in London and back.

It was now nearing midnight, and she was so exhausted she felt that her eyes might start bleeding if she didn't stop riding soon and get some sleep. Her head hurt intensely from concentrating so hard, and she had got lost twice in the country lanes. All the road names and signposts had been taken down in case of a German invasion and she had only a map, a small torch and a smattering of landmarks to help her get her bearings. When she did reach a village it was of little help; all the windows and doors were covered, to prevent the escape of any glimmer of light that might aid enemy aircraft. Street lights were all switched off, and essential lights such as traffic lights and vehicle headlights were all fitted with slotted covers, as was her bike, to deflect their beams downwards to the ground.

The pressure was always on her to move as fast as she could, but with no light, the roads had become a dangerous place and the restrictions had greatly increased the dangers of night driving. She had read in the newspapers that fatalities on the roads had increased as a result, and it all added to her fear of getting lost in the pitch-black English countryside. The first time, she had managed to turn back quite quickly and get back on track. But on this last journey, she had completely lost her way after taking a wrong turn and had become so panicked that she'd had to stop and try to calm herself, with her motorbike engine still running – despite having been told by Commander Travis that they were forbidden to stop for any reason.

Directed to one of the huts by Commander Travis, as she always was at the start of her shift, she had been handed her envelope, given her destination, a map, and told she must under no circumstances stop, speak with anyone or do anything to jeopardise her mission. She would be delivering messages, she had been told, to the intercept stations, written in code that had taken the work of some of the country's best mathematicians to crack, and it was her primary role to get swiftly to her destination. She had been handed a large envelope, stamped 'On His Majesty's Service', and, as always, had been reminded that there was to be no stopping between Bletchley Park and the designated destination, except in an emergency. She was to have zero curiosity about what she was carrying, except for the destination on the envelope and any priority status written on it, and she was to take all necessary action to ensure her dispatch was delivered safely and on time. Above all, she was forbidden to discuss any aspect of the operation with anyone outside the park at any time.

Since her brother's death, she had wanted nothing more than to help with the war effort, and she had craved the adventure and opportunity that Bletchley brought, but every day left her frantic with stress and worry, under the constant pressure of finding her way in the dark against the clock. Added to which, she was never allowed to take the same route twice, in case she was being followed. But few had any sympathy for her, it was tough for everyone, they were all here to do a job, to play their part. And as Geoff, the manager of the bike workshop, pointed out, the mathematicians got all the glory, but it was the ordinary folk – the dispatch riders and the staff keeping everyone fed, watered and housed – who were the unsung heroes of Bletchley. 'And besides,' he had added one day when she arrived back at base, covered head to toe in snow, as she had not been allowed to stop even to brush it off, 'a layer of snow actually can sometimes help to keep you warm on a bike.'

Olive had been at Bletchley for two months now, and though she had tried her hardest to warm to Geoff, he was still exceptionally cool towards her and hard to get to know. He had an unnerving way of staring at her a little too intensely when she talked and waiting an uncomfortably long time to reply. He ran his garage with military precision and had a sharp tongue for anyone who didn't return a bike, or a piece of kit, exactly as it had been given to them – at least, without a very good reason. He would mumble to himself, and slam the door of his workshop whenever something or someone displeased him, and only Samuel, the Canadian she had met on her first day, had the confidence to tease him about his organisational skills and precision. Geoff was an Olympic champion at sulking, Samuel said. Olive knew she was usually good at charming boys, and she could keep up with the best of them in any given pursuit, but Geoff was exceptionally frosty. However, she had noticed over the past weeks, given that she worked hard, did everything she could to keep him onside, and played by the rules, he was starting to warm to her a little, lending her the more comfortable helmets and gloves, giving her the bikes that were less prone to breaking down. And even, on occasion, lending her his own torch, which was a great deal brighter than the others, and meant she could actually see the map. And heaven knows she needed all the help she could get.

Dispatch riders had been chosen for the job of delivering coded messages because of their speed, but that brought with it a tremendous pressure, and what felt like a ticking bomb echoing inside her head. She had grown up in a small community, knowing only life on the farm and at her village school – and she had never travelled any further than London. She had no real experience of map reading and of being under pressure, and as she rode on in the relentless blackness, every hedgerow rushing past her looking the same, every junction she reached seeming to resemble nothing on the map, the pressure would slowly get to her. She had often felt like she was going round in a circle, with no train tracks or village signs to guide her, the envelope with the big red 'On His Majesty's Service' stamp burning a hole in her bag.

For the first time that night, panic had started to take hold of her completely, getting under her skin like the cold, affecting her ability to judge distance, to stay focused, to keep calm and press on. She had started to hear her brother's voice inside her head, laughing at her happily, as he used to do when she got stuck climbing trees as a child. But as exhaustion and disorientation got the better of her, his laugh had become distorted and twisted like a clown's. As she started to lose her bearings entirely a police motorbike on patrol had suddenly appeared, coming towards her from the other direction. She had waved him down in desperation and the man had stopped, and looked at her navy and white armbands, which told him she was a dispatch rider. His bright blue eyes were just like Michael's and as he had pointed her in the right direction, she had felt such an all-consuming sense of relief she had almost cried. It felt like she had seen her brother's ghost, as if he had come back to help her.

Olive bit down hard on her lip until she drew blood, to keep herself focused. She had been riding in temperatures close to freezing all night, and she felt like her entire body was seizing up from the onset of hypothermia. She couldn't stop shivering, her breathing was shallow, and when she had left the War Office in London for the last trip back to Bletchley, she felt like her speech was starting to slur. Her arms were so cold, they felt as if they might snap like icicles if she moved them. She knew she would have no strength in them when she finally arrived, and would have to drive round in circles at Bletchley until someone was able to take the bike for her. Hopefully, Geoff would be at the workshop, she didn't have the strength to hold the bike up herself to get off.

She pressed on, changing down into second gear so as not to make too much noise as she rode through the village. Though it had been dark for hours, it was a relief to feel the presence of the houses, and people inside them, after hours weaving through the country lanes with nothing but the noise of her engine for company. All the houses had blacked-out windows, so she could barely make them out, but she knew they were there, and she knew she was close to Bletchley Park. All the Bletchley bikes had silencers on their exhausts, in addition to the narrow slats covering their headlights, so as not to disturb the villagers or draw attention, but still she slowed herself down slightly so as not to wake – or run into – anyone in the darkness. As she accelerated away from the village towards the gates of Bletchley, she remembered the walk she and Lorna had done from the station that first day. Dragging their luggage behind them, feeling a mixture of terror and excitement at the prospect of what lay ahead.

Passing the Travellers' Inn on the outskirts of Bletchley, where she and Lorna were billeted, she pictured Lorna getting up for her shift. Lorna had been on the dreaded night shift all week, from midnight until 8 a.m. She would have slept all afternoon and evening, and would now be getting dressed in to her skirt and cardigan, pulling on her thick tights. She suffered terribly from the cold and had trouble sleeping at strange times because of the shift work – and then could barely stay awake until morning. She had tummy ache a lot of the time, and complained of her stomach being upset. 'When you wake up in the morning, normally you have breakfast. But you get off a night shift in the morning, go to bed, and when you get up again, at five or six, it's the evening meal that's laid on. So you're having an evening meal for breakfast!' Most people suffered slightly bumpy tummies, but Lorna's body couldn't cope at all.

Lorna came from a small town, with a doting mother whose prewar domestic life had been very orderly; she'd served up three regular meals, always had the fire lit in every room, and tucked her daughter up at night with warm milk. Lorna wasn't used to the intense discomforts that Bletchley brought. The cold rooms, the swallows nesting in the house and flying in and out of the broken windows. Often, mice turned up in their bedroom – some dead, brought in by the landlady's cat, some alive and scuttling around the floor under their beds. Growing up on the farm, it was all very familiar to Olive, and she hardly noticed the discomforts and relative lack of freedom. She took huge satisfaction in the knowledge that she was finally doing her bit and helping to fight the people who had killed her brother.

For Lorna it was different, she was an urban girl, and was struggling to adjust to life at Bletchley. She had been suffering a great deal in the two months since they had arrived. She was deeply homesick, and the work in the huts was tough, stressful and monotonous. While Olive felt terrified most of the time, at least she was outside, in the fresh air, her own boss, and she was happy to be away from the farm. Lorna repeatedly complained of the stuffiness of the huts. The young recruits, like Lorna, squared up as well as they could to their extraordinarily complex, gruelling, grinding tasks. The nature of the work, according to Lorna, often had very little to do with mathematics and everything to do with patience and concentration. When they were on the same shifts, Olive would often listen to Lorna crying herself to sleep. She would try to comfort her, but there was nothing she could say.

Olive approached the side gate, where all the bikes came in and out at night, to avoid disturbing anyone working in the huts, and was waved through by the guard on duty who knew her well by now. She could hear music, the sound of a live band, and she remembered suddenly that tonight was the dance in the ballroom. Lorna had been talking about it

237

all week; there was to be a band, with a trumpet, a saxophone, a double bass. As she neared Bletchley House, it was so loud she could hear it through her helmet.

Her stomach was rumbling, and she knew she'd be forced to go down to the canteen after she delivered her envelope to hut eight. The food this late at night was indescribably awful, catering for so many people, particularly in wartime. But she was weak with hunger, and watery cabbage and some form of boiled chops would at least help to warm her up. Olive revved the engine gently to stop herself from stalling and looked towards the Cottage for any signs of life. She needed to drop off her bike, and get to hut eight, but her limbs were so cold she knew she didn't have the strength to hold the bike up while she climbed off. Gently she rumbled over to the workshop, mindful that she needed to get her envelope to hut eight in the next minute or two. She was shaking so hard from the cold she couldn't think straight, there were no lights on at the workshop and she couldn't see any sign of Geoff anywhere. Normally she would just prop the bike up herself, but she couldn't risk it coming crashing down and damaging it.

'Good evening,' came a voice out of the darkness. It was one she recognised, a Canadian accent.

Olive stopped and turned in the direction of the man appearing from the shadows.

'Do you need any help?' he said, smiling at her, his blue eyes shining in the dark. He was dressed inappropriately for the cold weather, wearing a thin scarf around his neck and a black T-shirt.

'Aren't you cold?' she said, her voice trembling.

'No, I've got my whisky jacket on,' he said, putting a

small hip flask into his back pocket. 'I haven't been out here long, I saw you from the window at the house and thought I'd give you a hand.' He smiled at her. 'Here, let me take your bike so you can get off.'

'Thanks, I'm so cold I'm worried my legs aren't going to hold me up. I thought I was going to have to drive around for a while looking for someone, the place is deserted.'

'There's a dance in the ballroom,' he said. 'Put your weight on me. I've got you,' he reassured her.

She managed to ease herself off the bike, and leaned into him; he smelt of whisky and cigarettes and women's perfume.

'I got lost, I thought I'd never get here,' she said, her voice shaking. 'It just seemed to get darker and darker.'

'You're fine. Take your delivery over to the hut, and I'll take your bike back,' he said, starting to walk away.

'Thank you,' she said, with a sigh of relief.

'Do you fancy coming along for a drink?' he asked.

'No, thanks, I think I'll head back for some sleep. I don't feel too good,' she said, staggering slightly, before steadying herself on a bench.

'Do you want me to take your delivery for you?' Samuel called back to her.

'No, I might get into trouble. I can take it. I just need a second,' Olive said, crouching down and taking a few deep breaths.

'Everything alright?'

Olive turned round to see Commander Travis appearing from hut eight with a colleague.

Olive stood up. 'Sir, I'm sorry, I was just making my way over to you.' She reached into her bag and handed over the envelope with the words 'Commander Travis, Hut 8' etched in bold writing on the front.

'Thank you. No need to apologise. You've made excellent time, Olive, as always. Well done,' he said, handing the envelope to his colleague who headed back towards the hut. 'We need to get you into the warm. Come and have a drink.'

'I'd really rather get some food and get home, sir. I don't feel terribly well, it's very cold tonight,' Olive said, trying to force a smile.

'See if you can borrow one of the vehicles from the Cottage, Samuel, when you drop her bike off. Drive Olive back to her digs, will you?'

'Be right back,' said Samuel, starting up Olive's bike and hopping on.

Olive watched Samuel disappear into the night, towards the garage, and then turned back to Commander Travis who was heading towards the main house.

'Come into the house, Olive, while we wait for Samuel,' he said. 'There's a fire lit in the hall.'

'I'm fine really,' said Olive nervously, at pains not to get a reputation for being weak. 'I just need to eat something.' She stood on shaky legs, praying they wouldn't give way underneath her. She started to follow him, feeling as if the distance of fifty yards went on forever.

Finally, she reached the entrance to the main house, where she reported to Travis at the start of every shift. 'Okay, I'll see if there are any leftover sandwiches in the hall. You wait here,' he said, as music wafted out from the ballroom.

'Thank you, sir, that's very kind.' She felt nauseous, and weaker than she ever had in her life before. He legs were shaking violently as she found a chair in the corner of the imposing entrance. Needles stabbed at her face as her frozen skin started to thaw in the warm air from the hallway. She felt as if she were in a fog as people rushed by her, smiling and laughing. The sudden contrast of the freezing night and the heat of the main house made her skin burn and she frantically began to remove the layers of coats and jumpers she had been wearing to protect her from the cold. As she put her head between her knees, she became aware of the presence of someone standing over her. She looked up, presuming it was Commander Travis or Samuel.

Geoff was staring down at her. She felt her stomach churn nervously, as it always did when she was with him. She didn't have the strength to pretend she liked him, and to be polite.

'What's wrong?' he asked her bluntly.

'Nothing, I just got a bit lost and very cold. I'm fine,' she said, wishing he'd go away.

Commander Travis appeared with a plate of sandwiches, and put them down on the table next to her. She sat back and began to eat one, the heat from the fire warming her through.

The music sounded wonderful, they were playing Glenn Miller's 'Moonlight Serenade', and two girls passed her, dressed in full skirts and silk blouses, with their hair rolled up and pinned in French pleats.

'Olive, are you alright?'

Olive looked up to see Lorna walking towards her. It was good to see her. She looked pretty in a long skirt and fitted cotton blouse. Samuel was following close behind.

'She's fine,' said Samuel, before she could answer. 'I

think we should have a dance before I take you home. Here,' he said, passing her his hip flask.

'She doesn't look fine,' said Lorna, frowning. 'You're shaking. She needs to go back to the room. Geoff, take her will you? My shift starts soon so I can't leave now.'

'I got very cold riding, but I'm okay. I just need to warm up a bit,' said Olive, taking a sip, as Lorna looked at them both disapprovingly. 'What rotten luck working tonight, Lorna.' Olive smiled up at Samuel as the whiskey began to take effect.

'That girl you were dancing with just now is looking for you,' Geoff said, glaring at Samuel.

Olive took another sip of Samuel's whisky and began to feel better. The fire was warming her, and the whisky and the sound of the band were lifting her mood. 'I wish I was dressed for the ball.'

Samuel looked down at her and smiled. 'You're the prettiest girl in the room, I'd say it doesn't matter a jot. What do you say, Lorna?' he asked, winking as Lorna frowned back at him.

Olive lay back in her seat, and giggled. Samuel took a packet of cigarettes out of the arm of his T-shirt and lit one with a Zippo.

'Come on, let's dance,' he said, taking her hand, and pulling her along the corridor, towards the intoxicating music and warmth of the ballroom.

In the mirror in the hallway, Olive glanced and looked at her glowing reflection. She had been brought completely back to life by Samuel's charisma; as he held her hand it felt like a lightning bolt recharging her body. She could see her friend, standing next to Geoff at the mouth of Bletchley

House. Both of them were staring at her, fixed with a look of utter distain which brought her momentarily back down to earth, just as Samuel pulled her away into an embrace so tight she could feel his heart beating along with hers as the music engulfed them as they began to dance.

Chapter Nineteen

Daisy

March 2015, Tuesday afternoon

Daisy sat on her bedroom floor, which was entirely covered with photocopies from the pages of Saltdean High yearbooks, and let out a frustrated sigh. During a frantic hour in the high school library, she had skim-read as much as she could of the annuals, running from 1978 to 1985, looking for any sign of her sister Holly and – she had desperately hoped – any group photographs of Holly with girlfriends she might have a chance of tracking down now.

Holly had clearly not been a star at school; there were no pictures of her in any of the school plays, or on school trips, and no mention of her in any of the lists of prefects, or in the photographs of sports days or matches. In each yearbook, the only picture of her sister had been in the head shots, which were in neat rows at the back of every book. Hundreds of them, listed one after the other. One of the pictures of Holly she had seen before; it had been used for the police Missing Person poster, the one which had ended Daisy's world when she first saw it on a lamp post, thirty years ago. But there was another photograph of Holly and, although it was small, soulless and provided her with no useful information, it still sent a volt of electricity through her. For a brief second, as Holly stared back at Daisy from the pages of the yearbook, her blue eyes wide, a closed-mouth smile on her beautiful face, she was alive again.

In the last two annuals Holly was completely missing, even from the head shots in the back pages. Obviously absent from school for the school photographer's visit in the year leading up to her disappearance – for reasons Daisy could only guess at – there was no mention of her at all. Daisy took a sip from the mug of tea on her bedside table and scanned the faces alongside Holly's, and once again her eyes settled on Eve Taylor's photograph. After seeing Eve's name carved into the back of the wardrobe at Morgate, she had been ecstatic to find her in the yearbook. It felt to her like the only lifeline connecting her to Holly's past.

It had taken no time at all to find Eve's picture, as there was only one Eve in Holly's year. Like the others, the picture was small, and it was hard to get a sense of her personality, but she had a pretty face, a dark bob, and she was smiling widely at the camera. She had a kind expression and a warm smile, and Daisy could imagine her and Holly being friends.

For an hour or two after finding Eve's picture, she had been elated. She had Eve's full name; and the girl had been in the same year as Holly, making her forty-eight now. Eve Taylor: she had written the name down, underlined it excitedly in her notebook, ready to investigate as soon as she got home from Saltdean High.

The police and reporters had been waiting for her; forensics had her DNA now, so within hours they would know for definite the remains were Holly's. She had locked up her bike outside the flat and made a dash for the steps, not answering any of their requests to talk to them about Holly.

She hadn't eaten all day but she was feeling sick, and strangely disconnected from her body, knowing that it was Holly's remains up on the Tye. Eager to begin, she had rushed up to her small one-bedroom flat at the top of the tall Victorian building, which had a sea view from her bedroom at the back.

Daisy stood up now and stretched her cramped limbs. She heated up some soup, which she hadn't been able to face earlier, and set about trying to find Eve Taylor on Facebook. She clicked on each one systematically, looking at the picture on her laptop, then back at the photograph from the yearbook, then again at the picture. With each one that was clearly not her, Daisy's heart began to sink into a black hole. None of them looked anything like the girl in the school photograph – even taking account of the fact that thirty years had passed. She was probably married now, Daisy thought, and not even Eve Taylor any more. After two hours willing one of them to be Holly's Eve, she sat back, taking a break from the screen and massaging her tired eyes. If Eve wasn't on Facebook, what chance did she have of finding her? If the council weren't going to give out her own sister's notes, they were hardly going to hand her any information about a stranger. There was no guarantee Eve was even on social media; she could be long gone and live in another country entirely. Panic started to rise inside Daisy's guts; she had been elated when she found Eve's full name so easily, but she was being an idiot. Was she going to message every single Eve Taylor? And what would she say? Even if she did find the right one, it could take days for her to see the message and reply. And even then, the chances that she had any idea what had happened to Holly was one in a million.

Daisy stood up, walked over to the window and peered through her blind at the reporter from this morning, sitting on the steps, illuminated by the outside light. He was sipping from a polystyrene cup and talking to a girl with a ponytail, presumably another reporter. He had been outside all day, waiting for her. He must know something she didn't. She looked at the police car parked outside her front door and watched as the policewoman from earlier climbed out and started pacing, with a mobile phone clamped to her ear. Was this the call that would change her life forever? Would this policewoman, who hadn't even been born when Holly went missing, be the one to tell her? Even though the policewoman on Monday night had told her it was definitely Holly, there was still a sliver of hope that she was wrong. Maybe it was someone else's necklace. She knew it was stupid to hope, but hope was all she had.

Would they knock on her door, or call her? Would they do it as soon as they knew, or wait until morning? She couldn't face another night on her own, she felt like she would die of loneliness. Even though it was the start of spring, it was barely six o'clock and the sun was already sinking. The nights seemed endless, she couldn't sleep, and when she did she had nightmares about Holly standing on the cliff edge at Saltdean while it crumbled away below her feet and she screamed out her name. Daisy looked at her phone; she longed to talk to someone, but she didn't know who. She didn't want to risk dragging anyone she cared about into this mess. The person she really wanted to be with was Jules. But they had split up only six weeks before, and it wasn't fair to drag him into her mess while they were both still heartbroken. Besides, it was too raw, it would lead to too many questions about Holly and their childhood, which she wasn't in any state to discuss. But still, she pictured him sitting there with her, leaning forward on the sofa, staring at her attentively with his big brown eyes. He had unlimited patience – it drove her mad sometimes how patient he was with her. He always looked at her expectantly when they woke up in the morning, waiting for her to say the words he wanted to hear: that she was healed and she could commit to him. It was a pressure that, in the end, she just couldn't bear.

Momentarily, her work friend Amber sprang to mind. But if she went to Amber's house, the reporters might follow her, and that would be selfish. Added to which, she never felt more lonely than when she was in other people's homes. Amber had a huge family; Daisy was always drawn to the family photographs, screaming out the void between their lives and hers. Pictures of Amber with her parents, on family holidays, at graduation ceremonies and birthdays, all propped up on the bookshelves or on the living-room wall. Precious moments taken for granted, accompanied by peppered conversation highlighting the fact that they lived in another world Daisy could only imagine in her dreams: 'My dad is popping over later to look at my car', 'My mum's making me dinner tonight so I've got a good meal in me before my exam tomorrow', 'My sister's getting married next summer, and she's driving us all mad already.' It would never be said with malice, and quite often Daisy would be invited along as a guest to the celebrations, but nothing stoked the furnace of her intense loneliness like being carry-on luggage in other people's lives.

Besides, she didn't feel ready to talk about Holly, she was

still processing the idea that they could have finally found her. And if they had, she was never coming back. She had always thought she wanted answers, but now they were on the horizon, all she wanted to do was run from them. She never talked to anyone about Holly, it was too upsetting, too hard to know what to say, or where to start. None of her friends knew that she had a sister. Holly was a name she never spoke without crying, and so she had simply stopped speaking it and kept her sister's memory locked deep inside.

Daisy turned her attention away from the window, back to the photocopies scattered across the floor. She scanned the rows and rows of faces, and tears began to spring to her eyes. Who did she think she was fooling, playing detective? Was she more likely than the police, with all their resources, to come up with an answer to what happened to her sister? She closed her eyes and tried to calm herself down, but the panic inside was rising, squeezing her lungs, and she couldn't catch her breath. She walked to the kitchen and ran the cold tap, splashing cold water over her face, and opening the window as the loud roar of police sirens rushed along the seafront. Was that connected to her sister, whatever was happening? She wanted to know and didn't want to know in equal measure. She couldn't bear to turn on the news again; she didn't want to hear that they were Holly's remains, from the television, on her own, with no one to comfort her. She tried to breathe but her chest was heavy, and she sat down on the floor, her chest so tight it was as if someone was sitting on it. She closed her eyes, but all she could see was her sister in that shallow grave on Saltdean Tye, alone. Her beautiful Holly. Had someone murdered her, then dug a hole in the ground and thrown her body

249

into it, like a rag doll? Kicked mud in her face, until she was obliterated, and left her in the cold and the dark? All alone.

Suddenly, the buzzer in her hall sprang to life. It sounded to Daisy as if it was at the end of a long tunnel. She stood rooted to the spot, staring at the floor, as her whole body began to shake. The buzzer went again, trilling through the silence of her flat, making it impossible to ignore. Slowly, she turned and walked towards it, her short hallway feeling like a walk along death row. She tried to tell herself that it could be a friend, or the reporter again, but her instincts screamed otherwise. Daisy stopped at the other side of the door as the buzzer went for a third time.

Her hand shaking, she reached out and pressed the intercom. 'Yes?'

'Daisy? My name is Superintendent Jo Hamilton, we spoke last night at Morgate House. Can I please come in and talk to you?'

'What do you want to talk to me about?'

'I'd rather not say over the intercom.' The woman paused, Daisy could hear the hesitation in her voice. 'It's about your sister Holly. Could you let me in, please?'

Superintendent Jo Hamilton, she was the one they had sent. The one who had started the fire. She was the one who would end Daisy's world – for a second time. Immediately, Daisy felt her legs go from under her and she sank to the floor. She knew, without the woman saying a word, they had the DNA results. It was over, Holly was gone, and she was never coming back. Daisy was all alone in the world now. She felt a tide of grief rush over her, and a

250

sprinkling of images filled her mind's eye. Little moments: Holly stroking her hair, Holly cuddling her, Holly making her laugh, Holly playing with her. She felt them all being sucked away down a tunnel, gone forever.

The buzzer went again; her legs had no strength, she couldn't cope with the avalanche of despair she was feeling. She didn't want to open the door to a stranger, a police-woman who had started the fire which had killed her mother, hear her fake words of comfort, when it was her fault. Holly was dead. She didn't want the woman in her house; she knew what they had come to tell her, and she didn't need to know any more. She needed to get outside so she could breathe. Quickly, she grabbed her keys, stuffed a coat into her rucksack, and opened her front door, rushing down the stairs towards the ground-floor entrance. She could still hear the intercom buzzing upstairs in her flat.

As she opened the door and hurtled down the steps, the cold evening air hit her. A familiar figure, with short blonde hair, wearing a blue fitted jacket and white shirt, walked towards her.

'Daisy? My name is Superintendent Joanna Hamilton, could I have a word, please?'

Daisy could feel the woman next to her as she walked over to her bike and undid the padlock. She turned back to see her standing over her, and hovering closely behind were the two reporters.

'Daisy, is it possible for us to go inside and talk? It's important,' the woman repeated, turning irritably to the journalists behind her.

Daisy said nothing, grabbing the handlebars of her bike and wheeling it to the kerb.

'Daisy, please stop, we need to talk about your sister Holly.'

'Why? So you can tell me our DNA is a match, that it's her up there on the Tye?' Daisy watched the woman's face, waiting for any sign of denial as she felt tears stinging her eyes. 'Well, now I know, so can you please leave me alone?'

Daisy could see the pair scribbling into their notebooks frantically as she climbed onto her bike and prepared to pedal away.

'Can you confirm that Holly Moore is the name of the victim?' The reporter who had been waiting outside her flat all day stepped forward, eager for news.

'Victim?' said Daisy, glaring back at them. 'So she was murdered?'

'We don't know that. Daisy, wait, there are details I need to discuss with you. And I have something to show you. It's very important we talk,' the policewoman shouted after her as Daisy turned away.

Daisy pulled hard on her brakes and looked back. 'There's nothing you can tell me that I don't already know.'

'Daisy, please can we go inside and talk? I have some details I'd really like to share with you.'

'Will the police be releasing a statement this evening, Superintendent Hamilton?' said the reporter, glancing up at her with his eyes wide.

The woman turned red and snapped back at him. 'If you don't give us some privacy, I'll be cautioning you.'

'That's what you do, isn't it?' blurted Daisy. 'Shut people up. Do you not want them to hear what I've got to say? Do you want to keep everything secret? How you let my sister die up there.'

Daisy looked around as she became encircled, more reporters pushing their recording devices under her nose. The policewomen from the parked squad car tried to push them back, and the superintendent put her arm around Daisy.

'Get away from me!' Daisy yelled, pushing Jo away. The reporter behind them was gleefully making notes. 'Don't follow me!' she roared, pedalling off.

Daisy pulled out in front of the traffic as rain began to spatter on her face. The tears were streaming down her cheeks, mingling with the rain, until she was completely soaked through. She had nowhere to go, she couldn't go home.

Olive wouldn't be at Downside any more, they had moved her to the hospice. But she knew where it was. She had sat in ambulances there in the past, with patients who had no family. It was only a short ride down the seafront to Rottingdean. She just had to hope that Olive was well enough to see her.

She pulled up outside St Catherine's and propped her bicycle up, before pulling her coat from her rucksack and wrapping it around herself in an attempt to hide her dishevelled state.

The woman on reception smiled gently at her and Daisy introduced herself as Olive's granddaughter.

'Take a seat and I'll see if she's up,' said the woman, disappearing off.

She was completely soaked through, and she left a track of sodden footprints in her wake as she made her way to the seat in the reception area. Several people came and went, smiling and cheerful. It always amazed her what a happy place the hospice was, a place which cherished life, every last day that you had left. It was a privilege to work there, a nurse had said to her once, sharing the last days of someone's life was an honour.

'You can go through, she's awake,' said the woman, smiling. 'Room four, down on the left.'

Finally, she reached Olive's room and a wave of relief swept over her. She crept in, still panting and out of breath from stress and exhaustion. She slowly lowered herself into the chair beside Olive's bed. A soft bedside lamp was on and there was a comforting glow about the room.

'Hello, young Daisy, what are you doing here?'

'I just wanted to see you. You look better.'

'Yes, the painkillers are working a treat. I'm feeling better, my daughter was with me this morning, and my granddaughter this afternoon.'

'You're lucky to have a family that loves you so much,' Daisy said, starting to cry.

'What is it, Daisy, what's wrong?' Olive said, taking Daisy's hand.

'I'm sorry, I didn't know where else to go. The police have confirmed it's Holly's body.'

'I'm so sorry, darling,' Olive said quietly. Her breathing was very laboured, but the room was calming.

Daisy laid her head down next to Olive's outstretched hand and began to sob. 'I feel so guilty.'

'Why?'

'Because I feel relieved. I feel relieved that she's at peace but I hate whoever did this to her.'

Daisy cried, tears dripping onto Olive's bedspread, as Olive gently lifted her hand and stroked her head.

254

'Did you manage to get hold of Holly's social services file?'

'No, but I went to Morgate House, and found a name there, next to Holly's. Someone called Eve. I've been looking for an Eve Taylor, who went to Saltdean High with Holly, but it's impossible, she's not on Facebook. There were so many people in Holly's year. I can't possibly go through every single person and try to contact them.'

'Yes, you can,' Olive said calmly, pausing to catch her breath. 'Start with the boys, because their surnames don't change when they marry. You need to be organised and systematic. My friend Lorna worked in the huts at Bletchley, codebreaking is a marathon. It was long, and boring and monotonous. You need to take the day off from work, set yourself up somewhere with no distractions, start early and work until it gets dark. Take one name at a time until you find someone who knows her.'

'But won't the police be doing that? How am I supposed to find out anything they won't?'

'It sounds to me like none of the kids at Morgate liked the police much. If you can find this Eve, I suspect she would have a lot to say about your sister. You just need to decide you're not going to give up. Then you can't fail. If you can find someone, get them to agree to meet you in person. Face to face is better than the telephone. When you speak to someone directly, both of you are less likely to get distracted. They are more likely to remember something useful than if they are at home, with kids in the background, the television on.'

Daisy lifted her head and wiped her nose with the back of her hand. 'Okay,' she said quietly.

'I know it's hard, but you just need to keep your emotions out of it.'

255

'Thanks, Olive,' said Daisy, squeezing her hand. 'Do you mind if I sit here for a bit? I don't want to go home.'

'No, I'd like that,' said Olive dozily, as Daisy looked down at the photograph in Olive's hand.

'Did you ever try to find Samuel?' she asked Olive.

'I thought about it, but the world was a much bigger place then, and I had nothing to go on. Plus I had a baby, a husband and a home. I couldn't go to Canada. The pain was so bad at one point that I nearly left them both, but I loved my son too much, so I stayed.'

'I'm sorry, Olive,' said Daisy, stroking Olive's hair. 'He looks very like your son Charlie. Is he Samuel's child?' she asked gently.

'Yes, but Charlie doesn't know that. He'd be devastated,' Olive said, starting to cry as Daisy took her hand.

'Did Samuel know that you were pregnant?'

'No, they wouldn't let me see him.'

'Who wouldn't let you see him?'

'Geoff Price,' Olive said quietly. 'The creep who ran the motorbike workshop. He wasn't allowed to fight because of his lazy eye, so he ended up at Bletchley Park.'

'Geoff Price?' Daisy repeated, frowning. She shook her head, and spoke the name out loud again. Geoff Price. It was a name she knew well. Geoff Price was the man who had run Morgate House, who had sat in an armchair in the warm cosy living room, while the children in his care froze and starved. She didn't know why she hadn't thought of them before. Lorna and Geoff Price and their creepy son, Phillip, who used to walk in on the older girls like Holly when they were changing.

Phillip who signed up for the police. She remembered

now, Holly telling her the police ignored her because of Phillip. He would accuse her of lying about the conditions at Morgate; he was the reason they always got away with it. Phillip Price was the reason why Holly hated the police so much.

Daisy curled up in the chair next to Olive and held her hand. She was on nights the next day, so tomorrow morning she would get up early and she would start hunting down all the boys who had been at school with Holly and Eve.

And she wouldn't stop until she found someone who was willing to talk to her.

Chapter Twenty

Holly

February 1985

'Lots of salt and vinegar, just how you like them,' said Holly, smiling at her friend. 'I got some extra to take back with us too.'

'Thanks,' said Eve. 'So, what does he want for this money he gives you?'

Holly smiled. 'Nothing! He just wants to help.'

'And you believe that?' Eve asked.

Holly shrugged. 'Well, he said he sees a lot of kids ending up in the prison system, just because they grew up in care and had nobody looking out for them. He said a little kindness goes a long way. You've got Damian. Why shouldn't I have someone?'

'It's a bit different, I'm at school with Damian. This guy is like forty years old and in the police.'

Holly hugged the bag of chips in her hands, grateful for the warmth. 'Don't worry, I'm not going to do anything stupid. If he wants to give me some money so I can buy us some food, who cares? I don't see you complaining.'

Eve nodded, and silence fell as they ate. 'Has he said anything else about Daisy?'

'No, he's got a contact who works in social services, he's going to see if he can find anything out. See, I'm using him really.' Holly smiled at her friend. 'I don't care what he wants, if he leads me to Daisy, I'd do anything.'

Eve looked at her friend nervously. 'Do you think maybe he'll play on that?'

Holly shrugged and went back to her food as Eve looked up to see car headlights flashing across the road. Eve frowned at the car, lost in thought.

'Are you okay?' asked Holly.

'I don't know, I'm worried you won't come back,' Eve said quietly.

'Don't be silly.' Holly looked up excitedly, putting the extra bag of chips on the wall where they were sitting. 'Here, give these out to the little ones. I'll see you back at Morgate later. Don't worry so much, I'm a big girl,' she said with a grin.

Holly glanced down the road before crossing over to where his car was parked. It wasn't the police vehicle he had first picked them up in, so she presumed it must be his own car. He was off duty, she thought, which meant he was seeing her in his own time.

An unfamiliar feeling washed over her as she walked towards him. For the first time she could ever remember, she felt safe, as if someone was looking out for her. She had no illusions; she knew it wasn't real, that it wasn't going to last. But she didn't care, she could enjoy the distraction. He had insisted he wanted nothing from her but to help, and if that changed she could walk away. She was used to putting up a wall. And it gave her a feeling of hope for the future, that he might be able to help her find Daisy.

Holly reached the car and opened the passenger door.

'Hey, kid,' he said from inside, as she climbed in.

The car smelt of aftershave – expensive, not the type the boys at school used. The interior was clean and warm.

'How you doing?'

'Good, you just bought me some dinner.'

'Wanna go for a drive along the seafront?' he asked, smiling.

'Sure,' she said, looking out of the window as Eve watched them go.

Eve stared at her intently as they drove away.

'I can't be long, as Mrs Price is locking up at ten. She said she's sick of us all roaming the streets.'

'She's right. We need to keep you girls safe. How have you been? How's school? I hope you've been going.'

'It's fine.' Holly looked at the lights of the pier flashing past as they drove along, people walking around huddled up together. A brief trip into the cold, out for a drink, before returning to their warm and cosy homes. She thought of Eve walking home on her own; she had tried to brush aside her friend's concern, but it was bothering her. 'My friend Eve doesn't approve of you. She doesn't know what you want from me.'

'Well, she's right to be concerned for her friend, you should look out for each other. But I don't want anything from you. In fact, I came to let you know I've got some news about your sister.'

Holly felt a surge of electricity course through her. All these years of grief, of missing her, of pounding pavements, and writing letters that were never sent, and after a week of knowing this man, he had news. She daren't reply, or even breathe.

'You've gone very quiet,' he said, leaning forward.

'I'm too scared to say anything.' Holly looked down at her hands, which were shaking.

'So I've found her case worker, she's not prepared to give out her address, but if you give me a letter for her, I'll make sure she gets it.'

Holly felt her whole body collapse, and she started to cry. 'Thank you so much,' she said, her voice shaking.

'It's okay, kid. I'm sure we can arrange for the two of you to see each other again, in time,' he said, turning to her.

She didn't know this man well, but his voice was so calming. She didn't know how old he was, but she guessed he was around forty. He was very handsome, in a Tom Selleck kind of way, and he was tall and heavily built, like a bear, his shoulders and hands were large, and he had a presence about him that made her feel safe. She felt so at ease with him, like she had always known him. She ached for him to be her father or her big brother, to have had someone like him looking out for her, her whole life.

But at least he was here now, and this felt like a chance. A new start for her, and Daisy.

'Did they say why I'm not allowed to see her?' Holly asked.

'Her foster mother thought it would be too upsetting for her to have you visiting her and then leaving again.'

'But she's safe? She's okay?' Holly asked. She couldn't stop the tears. She was only two years older than Daisy but she had always looked after her. She could barely cope with the separation, so she couldn't even imagine what it had done to her little sister. They had never even been apart for a night since the day she was born.

261

'Yes,' he said. 'She's living locally, I don't know where, but in this catchment area.'

'Is she happy, do you know? Is her foster mother nice to her?' Holly said, as he handed her a tissue.

'I don't know. But I've agreed to act as a middle man, and once you've exchanged a few letters backwards and forwards, and they can see you are both calm and able to handle it, maybe I can persuade them that you two can meet,' he said, smiling warmly at her, his blue eyes sparkling.

'I can't believe it,' Holly said, whispering through her tears. 'Thank you so much.'

'You're welcome,' he said, pulling over at the West Pier, but keeping the engine running so they were warm. 'I'll take you back in a minute, I don't want you getting into trouble because of me.'

'I don't care,' she said, lunging forward and kissing his cheek. She needed to feel close to him, it had been so long since anyone had helped her, done anything for her. He had appeared out of nowhere, like a guardian angel, and she didn't know how to express what she was feeling.

He smelt so good, not like the boys at school, with their pimples, and their bum fluff, fumbling around under her shirt, while she wished she was anywhere else but there. He moved slowly, curling his hand around the back of her neck, and gently kissed her forehead, then her cheek where her tears were still falling. His touch felt so good. His shirt was unbuttoned slightly, and his tie loosened. She looked at him, and he smiled gently at her, and then she leaned forward and kissed him. It was like nothing she had ever experienced, he was so gentle, she felt his hand move down to her waist; she always wanted the boys at school to stop,

262

but she was terrified he would pull away and stop touching her, her whole body was shaking. Everything she needed to know about what he would be like as a lover was in that kiss. She wanted him to do anything he wanted with her, anything at all, but she knew he wouldn't do anything – because he was a gentleman.

'We'd better get you back,' he said, finally pulling away.

She leaned back into her seat, and tried to catch her breath. She felt more turned on with that kiss than she had ever felt before with anyone. She didn't know who this man was, or what he wanted, but just having someone there, to talk to, to help her, to kiss her, was all she had ever wanted or needed.

They drove back in silence, and although she was willing him to move his hand over onto her leg and touch her, he never did. He turned several times and smiled at her, clutching the steering wheel, driving fast but in control. When they pulled up outside Morgate House he kissed her again before she climbed out of the car.

'I'll see you soon. Bring that letter next time,' he said, winking at her.

'I will,' she promised, as she prepared to cross the main road. She saw Mrs Price's curtains twitching at her window as she turned and watched him drive away.

It was only quarter to ten so the side door was still unlocked. She opened it, feeling like she was floating along the corridor to her bedroom. She had done it, she had found Daisy, she was going to write a letter to her sister that would actually end up in her hands. *Maybe I can persuade them that you two can meet.* He had said it like it was nothing.

As she opened her bedroom door, Eve was waiting for her, sitting on the bed, with a brown envelope in her hands.

'Hi, hun, how are you?' said Holly, walking over to the wardrobe and hanging up her coat.

'I'm okay. How was it?' Eve asked.

'Amazing, he's going to get a letter to Daisy, and he thinks he might be able to arrange for us to meet.' Holly turned to her friend as her voice broke. 'But please don't tell anyone. If Phillip the Prick gets wind of it, he will do everything he can to put a spanner in the works.'

'I won't say anything,' said Eve quietly. 'Holly, can we talk?'

Holly frowned over at her friend. 'Sure, what is it? What's wrong?'

'I don't know how to say this,' Eve said, fumbling with the envelope in her hands nervously.

'Just say it. What's happened? Did someone hurt you?'

'Not me, but my friend, Gemma, when I was eight years old. She used to live here, at Morgate,' Eve said, looking up at Holly.

Holly slowly sat on the bed next to Eve, as Eve reached into the envelope she was holding and pulled out a picture of a girl with dark shoulder-length hair, in a denim jacket, laughing.

'She used to look after me,' Eve said. 'Then one night, she just disappeared. She never came back. I was so upset, I didn't know what had happened to her. Over time, I was told she had killed herself, I didn't even know what that meant. They had found her body on the rocks, here, below Morgate House.'

264

'That's terrible, Eve, I'm so sorry.'

Eve nodded, wiping away a tear as she looked at Gemma's picture. 'She was so kind to me, she looked after me. A part of me died when she died. I never let myself care about anyone again, until I met you.'

Holly took Eve's hand, and squeezed it.

'The thing is, I don't think she killed herself. A few years ago, I tried to find out a bit more about what happened to her. There were newspaper cuttings I found at the library about it,' she said. 'They photocopied them for me. There was something called an inquest. They said that she was suicidal. That she was always getting into trouble. But it's not true. She was happy.'

'You were very young, though, you couldn't have known.'

'No, the night she died she said she was just going out for a walk and would be back soon. She was planning to leave Morgate, and take me with her. We were going to make a new start.'

'People who are depressed say things sometimes to make themselves feel better.'

'No! No, Holly. It was real. She was real.'

'Okay. I believe you.'

'The thing is, she had a boyfriend, he was a copper. He flashed his headlights at her, the night she disappeared, just the way your guy does.'

Holly felt her heart plummet. She stared at Eve, not knowing if she was playing games with her. 'Eve, that doesn't mean anything,' Holly said, sitting back. 'Why are you saying all this. You don't want me to find Daisy, is that it? You don't want to lose me?'

'No, that's not it. I promise. I'm just scared for you. He

used to take her out, give her money so she could buy food. She was really in love with him.' Eve started to cry. 'She didn't kill herself, I know she didn't.'

Holly looked down at the newspaper cutting. *Body of missing runaway teenager found on Saltdean Beach* shouted the headline. Holly's hands started to shake as her eyes scanned the rest of the article and settled on Gemma's smiling face.

'That was ten years ago, it's probably not the same guy. And even if it is, we don't know he did anything to this girl Gemma.'

'I found this, in her things, after she died,' Eve said, pulling out a Saltdean Police payslip, wiping away the tears with the back of her hand.

Holly looked down at it, fear flooding through her.

'It's got his name and address on,' Eve said quietly, her lip trembling as she handed it over.

Holly looked at it, she was too scared to open it. Her first thought was not for herself but for Daisy. If it was him, it would mean that he had lied about Daisy. And that all her elation and excitement was for nothing, she was no closer to knowing where her sister was, or to being reunited with her. If it was him, he had done this before. She was one of many vulnerable girls to fall in love with him.

Her hands shook, as she carefully unfolded the slip of paper and slowly read the name printed at the top.

Chapter Twenty-One
Olive

Bletchley Park, April 1944

Olive woke with a start as the spring sunshine poured onto her pillow. She looked at the alarm clock beside her bed, telling her it was seven o'clock in the morning. She had made it to bed by midnight, but it had been another gruelling shift and she felt as tired as if she hadn't slept a wink. She lay back and stared at the ceiling, the familiar sickly feeling rising up in her stomach from drinking too much of Samuel's beloved whisky to warm them up, the night before. She turned and looked over at Lorna's bed, which was empty, and then inhaled the aftershave from Samuel's scarf, which he had wrapped around her on the walk home and then used to reel her in for a kiss.

She had never been scared in her life, but she was scared now. Her heart felt like she was standing on a cliff edge, and being pulled back at the last second before she fell. Her feelings were too strong for the three months that she had known him. She suspected that he liked her, but she knew the only reason she was holding his interest was that she was hiding how she really felt.

She had seen what the other girls were like around Samuel, they tried to hide it but they failed miserably. The night it all began had been a dream. He had led her onto the dance floor of the ballroom, just as the music began to slow. She felt like all eyes were on her; in contrast to all their pretty outfits, she had been wearing her jodhpurs and knee-high leather boots, and after taking off all her thick layers of coats, jumpers and gloves, was left with just a white blouse. She had taken her mother's pink headscarf from around her head and wrapped it around her neck in an effort to dress up her outfit, and let her long dark curls hang down her back. Every other girl in the room was full-skirted, with fitted bodices, dainty sandals, and flowers tied to their wrists and hair.

All eyes were on her, as Samuel pulled her into him. He smelt so good, she knew she was one of many that evening, and her cheeks had flushed red with embarrassment.

'Don't worry about them,' he had said, as if reading her mind.

'I don't care what anyone thinks. But I don't exactly look the part.'

'I love that you came in here. You're the bravest girl I've ever met.'

'Because I'm not wearing a dress?'

'Because you're fearless,' he had said, as she leaned into him and closed her eyes. 'You're not scared of anything.'

In that moment you would never have known there was a war on. The Glenn Miller songs took her back to hot summer nights on the farm, when her mother would listen to them on her gramophone, locked away in her room with the window open.

'My mother loves this song,' he had said, as if reading her mind. 'Can you imagine how many people have danced and fallen in love with this playing?'

'Quite a few with you, I should imagine, but I doubt the

feeling is reciprocated,' she had said, as he looked down at her and laughed.

'Don't ever lose your spirit, Olive, I've never known a girl like you before. You must come to Canada, and see me. Promise you will. You'd love it there. It's hot in the summer, we swim in the lakes and go hiking, and it snows in the winter. I'll teach you to ski. You'd be wonderful at it.'

He had lifted up her chin then, and kissed her. She knew every girl in the room was staring at her, that Lorna would be glaring with disapproval, but she didn't care. She knew how to play Samuel, she thought, as her mind spun with the whisky and the band and his smell.

Unlike them.

They stared too much at him as he walked around the Bletchley Park campus, smiled too widely as he nodded hello, laughed too hard at a throwaway comment he made as he passed. They lingered too long in the hope that he would walk into the dining hall or ballroom. They would save their rations up and give him cigarettes or whisky, to try to buy his affection. They would hold out for a dance with him and turn down the other boys in the hope he would choose them. Drink too much to give them confidence and then make fools of themselves fawning all over him.

Olive did none of those things. She would purposely turn up late if they had an arrangement to meet, flirt with other men when she was with him, change the conversation if it turned to talk of emotions or love in any way. If they had a chance to be alone, she would turn him down, and opt instead to go for a picnic by the lake at Bletchley or a walk in a group into town, and link arms with one of the other boys as she chatted to them. Above all, she refused to go to bed with him. Her mother hadn't taught her anything practical about life – Olive couldn't cook, she couldn't clean, she couldn't darn, she couldn't sew – but she had taught her about love, as if it were something to be managed. On nights when her mother emerged from her bedroom, in a fog of wine and sleep, she would tell her daughter that the only way to a happy life was to marry well. She had married for love, she said, so she had married beneath her. 'Never fall for a man who can't provide well for you,' she would say, as Olive's poor father pretended not to listen, 'the sex fades, everything fades, even the most passionate love, but money doesn't fade. If you can get a man who is kind, and who you are fond of, and who earns a good wage, to marry you, mark my words, you will respect him and grow to love him, and you will be happy for the rest of your life. It is the weariness of life that wears you down, the penny-pinching and the worrying about where the next pay packet is coming from.'

Olive's heart would ache for her father as he stared at his newspaper, as the fire crackled on the other side of their cold farmhouse. He would pretend to be absorbed but every word would cut him deeply. It was what her mother wanted; she wanted to punish him, for taking her to the countryside, away from her friends, from town life, from everything she loved. To the smell of pig shit, and flies and dirt, and scraping by on a farmer's wage.

'And when you find him, he will want to think he has done well to catch you. Be fun, be friendly, be smiley, be good-natured, but be slightly unavailable and aloof.' She pressed on, her voice slurring. 'Be a little late, never pay for anything, never buy him a birthday present or make any mention of the anniversary of your first kiss, or dance, or meeting. Never cook or clean for him, never buy him thoughtful presents. Flirt gently around other men. Be elusive, make them laugh. Talk of travels you yearn for and of interests you hold, read the newspaper, have adventures. Be organised and neat and well turned out – men don't ask chaotic girls to be their wives – but be cool, be unavailable, don't let him think he's got under your skin. And don't ever go to bed with him until a ring is on your finger.'

The latch to the bedroom door clacked, making Olive jump. For once she and Lorna were on the same shift, starting at eight, so they didn't have to creep around trying not to wake the other one up. Lorna came rushing into the room, still in her white nightie, and began dressing, pulling her thick tights up under her nightdress. Olive looked at Lorna longingly; she was always well turned out, her hair looked soft and newly washed, her skin looked freshly moisturised, her nails were polished and unchipped – even when she finished a twelve-hour shift, or when she got up first thing in the morning.

'God, it's so cold, it's nearly May, when is spring going to start?' moaned Lorna. 'I hate that outdoor toilet, it's a block of ice. I always think the skin on my bottom is going to stick to it when I stand up.'

Olive smiled at her friend as she dragged herself out of bed and started to dress in the ample layers of clothing she needed to stay warm on her bike.

'Goodness, I'm tired. I don't know how you find it so easy to cope when they change your shifts every week,

271

from day watch to night watch. I just about adjust and then they change it back again,' Lorna said, buttoning up her blouse, then brushing her hair in the cracked mirror on the wall.

'I think it's harder for you. You have to sit in those stuffy huts and concentrate for hours on end, no wonder you get sleepy. I can't exactly fall asleep whizzing round those country lanes in the dark. Commander Travis has been singing your praises to me, saying you're a rising star.'

'I don't feel like one. They don't need me to use my mathematics, it's just tedious and stressful. I'm translating German decrypts for hours and hours; they want me to do it quickly, and they need one hundred per cent accuracy. One of the girls couldn't stop crying yesterday, so they've signed her off sick and sent her home. I was so jealous she was getting to see her family.'

Lorna had experienced a difficult few months, settling into a life that was so different to the comforts of home. She had cried herself to sleep every night, telephoning home and writing at every opportunity. But it seemed that Geoff taking an interest in her had helped her turn a corner, as was often the case with homesick girls. Contrary to worrying about romances taking place at Bletchley, the superiors seemed to actively encourage it, saying it was much better that any affairs went on in-house rather than off campus, where the consequences of an indiscreet comment about Bletchley to an outsider could be catastrophic. Lorna had dug deep, risen above the discomforts of the outdoor toilet, and the mice and the broken windows, and focused on Geoff and her work in the huts.

'I'll never love this place like you do, Olive. I'm counting the days until I can go home, however long that may be.'

'I just love not having to go to school any more, or clean out the pigs, to feel useful. I don't ever want to go back to that,' said Olive, pulling on her third jumper before stepping into her overalls and doing up her belt.

'How do you manage to eat so much and stay so slim, you're thinner than me even with all those layers on,' said Lorna, as the two of them made their way to the door.

'I think the cold is making me burn fat I don't have, I'm so hungry all the time. I wish they would feed us more. There was a new chap serving up dinner in the dining hall and I put on Samuel's dark glasses last night and tried to get second helpings but he turned me away.'

Lorna laughed. 'Well, I wouldn't bank on Samuel taking you back to Canada when the war is over, if that's what you're hoping.' Lorna opened the door for Olive and they stepped out. 'I warn you, the landlady's on the warpath. She saw you and Samuel kissing last night, she followed me and stood outside the lavatory door saying she's going to report you. You need to be careful.'

'Of what? I haven't done anything wrong. He didn't come in. We just had a kiss in the doorway. Not that he didn't try every trick in the book,' she said, smiling to herself at the memory.

'I don't know why you're bothering with him. You'll only get hurt. I don't know why you'd want to do that to yourself, every girl he's ever spoken to ends up sobbing all over campus.'

Olive felt herself flushing red. 'Well, I'm not like every

girl. Anyway, why shouldn't I like someone? You're seeing Geoff, don't you worry he will hurt you?'

'Maybe, but I'm not going out of my way to get hurt. Heartache can ruin your life, you know, you shouldn't go looking for it,' said Lorna as the two rushed down the hall to avoid their landlady.

'I thought mathematics was your field, not love,' Olive said quietly.

Lorna flushed and then shrugged. 'Well, Geoff says Samuel is a cad. He's reckless, he doesn't look after his bike. He doesn't care if it breaks down and causes an accident. He's selfish.'

'Well, Samuel says Geoff is a bore about the bikes. It's his job, goodness knows we all work hard enough. Why can't he just get on and do his job without moaning, like everyone else has to?'

'That's not fair, he works harder than anyone,' Lorna snapped.

Olive felt tears sting her eyes, and fought them back. 'Please, let's not quarrel. I'm happy for you and Geoff. Can't you just give Samuel a chance? I'd love it if we could all perhaps go out together.'

'Maybe,' Lorna said dismissively. 'I care about you, Olive. I'm worried for you.'

'Well, has anyone ever thought to maybe be worried for Samuel? Why is it always the girls who have to be hurt? Maybe I'll hurt him.' Olive winked, trying to convince Lorna, and herself.

'Because we're the ones who have the babies,' Lorna said simply.

'Well, that's not going to happen, because I'm not going to bed with him.'

'Good, you keep it that way and you've got nothing to worry about.' Lorna linked arms with her friend as they walked through the village towards the gates of Bletchley.

Olive felt sick from the whisky Samuel had given her the night before. The bile started to rise in her throat and she couldn't keep it down. She rushed over to the side of the road, unable to stop it, and vomited.

'Oh goodness, Olive, are you alright?' Lorna said, walking over and rubbing her back.

'I'm fine. It's just these shifts play havoc with my stomach. And Samuel's whisky doesn't help,' said Olive, as a feeling of unease began to creep through her. She was never sick.

'You're not pregnant, are you?'

'Course not. I'm not that sort of girl,' she said, mindful that anything she said would get back to Geoff.

She wasn't a virgin, but she wasn't about to tell Lorna that. She'd probably never speak to her again. It was well known that people who lived in small communities in the English countryside were more relaxed about matters such as premarital sex than their town counterparts. It had only happened once, with Jack, and wasn't exactly the experience that she had read about in her mother's Mills & Boon novels. He had produced a rubber johnny, and it had all been over rather quickly, after a bit of fumbling around in the haystack at the back of the farm. It was when they were walking back to the house that Jack had told her of his intention to marry her, something that had horrified her so much she had only managed a brief laugh before disappearing into the house.

'You'll feel better after some breakfast,' Lorna said, walking towards the dining hall.

'You go ahead,' said Olive, feeling her stomach churn again. 'I'll grab some bread in a minute.'

As the Cottage came into sight the two girls looked over to see Samuel and Geoff talking animatedly. Samuel was on his bike and looked like he was shouting at Geoff over the noise of the engine. Geoff was red in the face and gesticulating. Olive and Lorna exchanged a concerned look before Geoff suddenly pushed Samuel, causing him to lose his balance.

'You bloody idiot!' Samuel shouted, before revving the engine and turning to look at Olive as she walked towards him. He glared at her for a moment, his blue eyes flashing with fury as he kicked the bike into gear, gunned the engine and pulled away.

'He hasn't even got his helmet, he's intolerable!' Geoff bellowed, as he stormed past them both.

'Samuel's left early,' Olive said, walking over to Geoff. 'Everything okay?'

Geoff glared at her, not replying.

'Geoff, what happened?' said Olive, going after him.

Lorna gently held Olive's arm back, to stop her, then followed Geoff into the workshop and closed the door. Olive walked over to her bike and began packing her gear, a feeling of deep unease adding to the nausea in her stomach. She tried not to stare, but she could see Lorna and Geoff talking in the workshop. Geoff was shouting and Lorna was trying to calm him down.

'Olive, I need this delivered immediately to the War Office.'

Olive turned to see Commander Travis standing at the entrance to the workshop.

'Can you go now?' he said, handing her an envelope with 'His Majesty's Service' stamped on the front.

'Yes, sir,' she said. 'I just need to do my checks.'

'Geoff's done them for you, I believe, I spoke to him half an hour ago in light of this being urgent, and he confirmed it's all done. I know I can trust you to get there quickly. I'm assured he has checked your tyre pressures, brake cables, oil level, spark plugs and battery. Your tool kit is also fully stocked, and your map is in your saddle bag.'

'Right, yes, sir, okay, thank you,' said Olive, turning the petrol on, setting the ignition and closing the air lever, before she opened the throttle and kicked down hard, as the engine roared into life.

'Report back to me as soon as you get back. I'll be waiting in my office,' he said.

Olive squinted through the window of the workshop, wanting to know what had happened between Samuel and Geoff. But Commander Travis was glaring at her expectantly, as she pulled on her helmet, gloves and goggles and buttoned up her jacket.

Leaving the park, the road was wet from the night before. She had been woken twice by the sound of the rain pelting at their broken window. She could hear the familiar sound of water coming in through the roof, but there was nothing she could do, except worry about the state of the roads the next day.

She lifted her leg and changed into third gear, she had sensed the urgency in Commander Travis's voice, he usually liked to chat, but today had been different. She knew the lanes around Bletchley well, and in the daylight, her anxiety was much lower than at night. The risk of wild-life running out in front of her, or skidding on a patch of oil on the road she couldn't see was much reduced in the day. She swallowed her nerves and kicked down into fourth gear, watching the speedometer move slowly up to fifty.

It was then that she saw him. It was a farm track she knew, one she often saw the army use for military training exercises. She had no idea why he had turned off, but obviously he had been in some kind of trouble; perhaps Geoff hadn't refuelled Samuel's bike or topped up the oil, and he'd been hoping the army truck she could see at the far end of the track might be able to help. Travelling as fast as she was, she only glimpsed the scene along the track for two seconds, but she knew immediately that it was Samuel, that his bike was on its side on top of him, and that he was unconscious.

In the time it took to make the decision to turn off the road, onto the farm track – away from her mission, and the ticking clock – in order to help him, she knew the consequences of her decision would be dire and that her career as a dispatch rider was over. She had been told countless times to never stop, even to help a fellow rider. That the only priority was to deliver her message. As she turned in, her eyes locked on the army vehicle a hundred yards up the track, she could see movement, a man in uniform jumping out from the back, and a plan began to form in her mind.

She would raise the alarm and then immediately be on her way. She would not attend to Samuel herself, and when she arrived at her destination she would be completely open and honest about what she had done. She would probably still be dismissed but there was a faint hope, if the hold-up was less than five minutes, they would chastise her but give her a second chance. She had to do something, she couldn't just leave him to die. She couldn't live with herself.

Olive finished the turn, and pulled the throttle to straighten up, but the back wheel kept going. A pile of mud from the army truck had been left on the road, and though she tried to straighten up, she couldn't stop herself from hurtling round the bend. This was why Samuel was down, she thought, as the back wheel spun out. The slippery mud had taken Samuel's bike out, and now it was going to take hers. Her senses slowed down, as she heard the groan of the engine, the squeal of the spinning tyre, the burning of the exhaust, the spattering of mud. She lost control and her bike began to lean to the left. Instinctively, she put out her left arm to break her fall. It couldn't have been more than five seconds, but in that time the same thought ran through her mind, over and over: this is going to hurt. This is going to hurt.

She held her breath as she fell, and as her hand hit the ground she remembered her father telling her that it takes a great deal of energy to snap a bone, the pressure as it bends and flexes, then eventually shatters. A sharp, intense pain suddenly rushed up her arm as she crashed down. The motorbike groaned and fell like a shot boar, landing on top of her.

Olive lay on the ground, trying to deal with the pain, taking deep breaths, lying on her back and crying out from the agony, staring up at the grey sky, her shattered arm twisted underneath her.

Slowly, she lifted her head, and looked up the track to see the army vehicle's engine starting up, the exhaust fumes puffing out, men's voices shouting, the vehicle juddering before it pulled away.

Then silence.

Olive looked over at Samuel; he was white, and unconscious. He had not moved since she had fallen, and blood was trickling from his nose. He wasn't wearing a helmet. She called out his name and got no response, his eyes shut tight. Olive stared at his torso, praying she would see some movement, his breath rising and falling. She spat away the tears and blood and closed her eyes, swallowing down the agony in her arm. She had to get up, get back to Bletchley and get help.

It couldn't have been more than a minute since she had turned into the track and come off her bike, but in an instant the intense feelings of the past weeks at Bletchley vanished and she was a child again, trapped, helpless, grief-stricken. It had all been a game, she was the girl she had always been, and she was utterly alone, the bravado gone in an instant. The message she had been entrusted to deliver was still in her satchel, lying spattered with mud at her feet. And it was all her doing.

She lay in the mud, her brain taking it all in. Everything slowed down. She looked up and saw every cloud, every piece of dirt on her arms, every little fleeting thought clear, as if she were writing it down for an exam. She could feel her heart thudding, the adrenaline pumping, her focus intensifying, developing tunnel vision as she stared at Samuel. She could see everything so clearly.

Her left arm screamed with pain as she looked at it and

then looked away. It was limp, broken in several places, she thought. There was a risk she could go into shock. She was on her own, the army truck was gone, there was no one coming. She needed to push herself up with her other arm and somehow get back on her bike.

Olive closed her eyes and gathered her strength. She would have to ignore the pain; she and Samuel could be lying here for hours if she didn't. Pushing with her elbow, yelling from the agony, she managed to twist, and wriggle and fight her way out from under the bike. She stood for a moment, panting with the pain and the exertion of finally getting out. She looked over at Samuel lying in the mud, not knowing whether to try to help him. She couldn't attempt to resuscitate him with a broken arm. He was already lying on his side, in the recovery position, so there was nothing more she could do for him now, she just needed to focus on getting help. Olive stood over her bike, convinced she didn't have the strength to lift it, but knowing she didn't have a choice. Her left arm hung down, every slight movement causing a shooting pain to travel up her whole body, which made her cry out. She took several breaths, then gripped the handlebars tightly with her right hand. Letting out a loud, primal groan, she succeeded in pulling the bike up with her right hand. Gasping for air, she managed to get her body under the bike and pushed her leg against the tank to stop it falling back down. Again she took several breaths, letting out a cry of pain when she caught her wrist, then worked her body further under the bike and pushed it upright. Her left arm screamed with a searing pain, she tried to hold it still, but it was impossible.

281

She had to ignore it, she had to get back on the bike and ride until she found help.

Olive sat on the bike, and vomited for the second time that morning. She leaned over to her left, taking all the weight of the bike on her left leg. She took a deep breath and lifted her right leg, easing it down and onto the kick starter. She opened the throttle, and then leaned in; holding her broken wrist up in the air, she pressed the valve meter with her left elbow, and kicked down hard on the starter. The bike rumbled into life. For a moment she gathered herself, then paddled forward, pushing the bike with her legs until it was rolling along the track, before she put it into second gear.

She could get back to Bletchley in second gear, she thought to herself, she could ride with one hand. She guessed the distance was about seven miles. As she pulled out onto the road, it started to rain again, and she focused on the feeling of the cold rain on her face, trickling down her cheeks alongside her tears. She counted in her head, to ten, over and over, on repeat, as the bike's engine grumbled.

She just had to get there before Samuel stopped breathing. Before she passed out from the pain. She could do it. She had no choice.

Chapter Twenty-Two

Jo

March 2015, Tuesday night

Jo Hamilton sat outside Saltdean Police Station, looking at the entrance and hoping that Chief Superintendent Carl Webber would leave so she could get inside and speak to the team. She had been waiting for nearly an hour, and it was getting dark. As she sipped on her cold tea, she looked at her watch, and let out a heavy sigh just as the revolving doors turned and a figure emerged. It was difficult to make out his features in the fading light as he walked down the steps, but she knew the walk, and her heart began to hammer.

She knew she wasn't allowed to speak to him and accuse him of anything; she knew that Carl and Stan were now in charge of the investigation, that it had been taken from her. And that he wanted her off the case. But she couldn't help it, rage was consuming her. Jo stepped out of her car, locked the door and waited as Phillip Price walked towards her. As he neared her, his face fell, and he tried to carry on as if she weren't standing in his way. Jo looked up at the revolving doors of the police station to make sure Carl was nowhere in sight.

'Phillip, can I have a word?' she said, standing in his path as he stopped in his tracks and glared at her.

'I've been told not to talk to you,' he said, trying to edge past Jo in the car park, his dark beady eyes fixing on her, as they did with every woman he met.

'By whom? Carl?' Jo asked, immediately regretting letting him know she cared. It may not even be true, Jo reflected; Phillip's mind games had always been his forte.

She glanced up at the police station to double-check Carl hadn't appeared. The thought of being kept at arm's length by her own team made her feel sick, but she pressed on. 'You know the remains we've found are those of Holly Moore. Do you remember her? She lived with your parents at Morgate House for most of her life, before she vanished in 1985.'

'Sure, we looked for her for weeks. I'm surprised you remember, though, you were at home raising your kid then, weren't you?' Phillip said, walking off as she followed behind him, keeping in step.

'No, I had re-joined the force, so I was very much around when Holly went missing.'

'Whatever,' he said, dismissively.

'Did you know her sister, Daisy, was fostered? Even though I asked for them to be kept together?' Jo tried to keep her voice steady.

'Maybe. There were so many girls, I can't remember.' Phillip reached his car and pressed his fob to unlock it. 'I'm not supposed to talk to you, Jo. Can you move out of the way, please?'

His black hair was much thinner than it had been when they'd graduated from police training forty years ago, but he still had the same slicked-back look. He always used too much gel in his hair, too much aftershave, too much moisturiser on his skin. It all worked in harmony to make him glisten like a slug.

284

'Don't play games with me, Phil. Why were the sisters stopped from seeing each other?' Jo stood her ground, blocking his way.

'It was standard for foster parents to cut all ties, it helped the kids settle.' Phillip kicked a stone at his feet. 'Mum never turned away a potential foster parent. Why would you want her to leave Daisy at Morgate when she had the chance of a proper home?'

Jo flinched, slightly unnerved by Phillip's reasonable answer. 'Because she was separated from her sister. It must have been utterly devastating. Why weren't they allowed to see each other?'

'It's just how things were then. Foster parents wanted a fresh start. They didn't want siblings hanging around, making visits, everyone getting upset, having to say good-bye. They thought it set the kids back. Things were handled differently then. People didn't think about the kids.'

'People like your parents, you mean?' Jo quipped.

Phillip frowned. 'Holly was trouble, and Mum would have told Daisy's foster parents that.'

'Trouble? How was she trouble?' Jo felt her voice waver.

Phillip let out a sarcastic snort. 'Do you think those girls were saints? Do you think we were cruel? You wouldn't have lasted one night . . . there were so many do-gooders like you, telling us how to run the place, then pissing off back to their comfortable lives. If you cared so much, why didn't you foster them both?'

Jo stared at Phillip with hatred as the heat rushed into her cheeks. 'How did Holly break her arm?' she persisted. 'Did something happen to her at Morgate? You took her to A&E, didn't you? I'm waiting to hear from the hospital now, I'll know from the records who her chaperone was, so don't lie to me.'

Phillip opened the car door and climbed in. 'Jo, Carl is trying to protect you. You need to listen to him and stay away from this case.'

Jo felt rage hurtling through her veins and put her leg in the way of Phillip closing the car door. 'He's not trying to protect me, he's trying to protect you and himself, and the unit. I might not be able to prove who killed Holly, but I can prove that you interfered with Gemma Smith's inquest. It's a criminal offence to interfere with a witness, Phillip, and you also tampered with evidence. You made it look like suicide, and stopped there being an investigation into Gemma's death.'

'I've got no idea what you're talking about, Jo, but I'm going to report this conversation.' Phillip slammed the car door shut and reversed at speed, forcing Jo back.

She looked up to the third floor of the police station, where Chief Superintendent Carl Webber was standing at the window of her office, staring down at her.

Jo charged towards the entrance, held her ID up to the door access pad, and the red light flashed. She stared at it in disbelief, then tried again, pushing against the door in frustration as it stayed firmly shut. She glanced up at the PC manning the reception desk, who was busy with a ranting member of the public, and pulled her mobile out of her bag. She scrolled through her contacts, found Kate's number and dialled it.

'Hi, Kate, it's Jo, could you pop down to reception? I just need to run something past you.'

'Sure, glad to help,' Kate said cheerfully.

286

Jo's heart raced. She would wait until Kate opened the door and then go through with her. She wouldn't tell her she was locked out, and that Kate had let her through, as it could get her into trouble.

'Hi,' said Kate brightly.

'Sorry,' said Jo, holding the door, 'I just wanted to know if Carl was here before I went up to collect the last of my things. It doesn't matter if he is, but I thought you might know where he is, so I can try to avoid him.'

'He is, he's at a meeting in the incident room,' said Kate.

'Great, thanks,' said Jo as they walked through reception together. 'I appreciated your call earlier, Kate. You are a very loyal person, and you'll make a great superintendent one day.'

Kate smiled at Jo as they took the stairs two at a time. 'Everyone has noticed what's happening. We're all with you, Jo. You've got a lot of friends here.'

Her training, followed by more than thirty years of hard-earned experience, had taught Jo not to feel – that to react with emotion, when you walk into a situation where you are faced with the worst of humanity, helps no one. Anger shows you are out of control, that people can take advantage of you because you are weak. Rage, she had been told endlessly, erodes the sense of community between police officers, breaking it down into one of competition and suspicion. She had been trained to keep her feelings inside all her adult life, being pushed into passivity against her will for the greater good. And she had done it willingly, because she believed she was valued, that they were all working together in the service of a common cause. Being in the police was her life, and she had sacrificed everything

287

for it. Now, with only days to go, a horrific realisation was dawning. She was tasting life as an outsider, seeing what others, like Daisy Moore and Gemma Smith, had seen, and what she had previously been blind to. She had been used, and now she was being tossed aside, in full view of everyone.

Jo reached the top of the stairs and told Kate to wait a few seconds in the corridor so she wasn't seen with her. She took a deep breath and charged through the double doors of her department.

She looked around and the hub of activity took her breath away. From where she stood in the central corridor, she could see that the main meeting room had been set up as an incident room, with at least six of her team huddled around a board. As she approached the window, she could see it was adorned with a timeline and a dozen photos of Holly Moore; last known location, last sighting, witness statements, these were all points of reference she was familiar with. Two members of staff were dashing around with clipboards, no doubt pursuing further lines of enquiry. As she reached the window, she could see Carl Webber talking through the board with the officers huddled around him.

In the next room were half a dozen telephone operators taking calls on the incident line. They were typing frantically on their keyboards as the lines flashed continuously. She walked in and overheard their conversations, asking how the caller knew Holly, when they had last seen her, taking down their details. Most of the calls would be pranks, but one or two would be genuine, and it was up to the call handlers to decipher which.

She walked back along the corridor; people were rushing

about, there was a huge energy, phones were ringing, people talking animatedly on their mobiles. As she looked up, she saw Carl staring at her. Her office door was open, so she walked in.

Carl wound up the briefing, followed her and closed the door behind him. 'Before you say anything, Jo, I'm putting you on gardening leave, as of this moment.'

'Why are you doing this?'

'Because I don't want you working on this case any longer.'

'Why not?'

'Because it's too personal to you.'

'Why? Because I cared about Holly before she was on the news, before you had a gun to your head to crack this case? I don't know why you're pushing me out, but you did it to Charlie too. I can't let you do this, you won't get justice for these girls.'

'Jo, you need to trust me. You need to go home.'

'No. I've just had an ex-teacher telling me that Phillip forged evidence for Gemma Smith's inquest. The teacher's seen a photograph, and he's confirmed that Phillip went to visit him.'

'You shouldn't have done that. It isn't your place. Jo, I respect you hugely, but you have to trust me on this. I don't want you discussing this case with Phillip Price. He's helping us with our lines of enquiry. He's giving us a lot of valuable information about the girls at Morgate House.'

'What valuable information?' Jo snapped.

'I can't share that with you at this point,' Carl said quietly.

'Phillip Price is implicated, I know it. Tell me what's

going on, Carl! I've given my life to this place, you owe me that much.'

'I can't share that with you at the moment. Trust me, it's better that you don't know.'

'Are any of the Morgate girls talking to you? Is Daisy?'

'No, not yet. But they will.'

'No, they won't, because they don't trust us. And who can blame them? When we're crawling into bed with the likes of Phillip Price who, at best, treated them with complete disdain – and, at worst, may have been involved in the death of their friend.'

'To be honest, Jo, it doesn't matter if they speak to us or not. We can proceed without them.'

Jo stared at him, incredulous. 'So still, even now, their voices don't matter?'

'Go home, Jo. I know this is a difficult time for you, but you need to let go.'

'What does that mean?' Jo scowled.

'It means you've done forty years of service, you are a credit to us all, but when it comes to this, you need to be kept away.' He had the emotionless voice those in authority have when the chips are down.

'I'm not going to let you bully me into silence, like you bullied those girls, Carl,' Jo said calmly.

'I strongly advise you to go home, or I will have to take further action. As your boss, and a friend, I am imploring you to stop. Or I will have to make you.'

'You're not my friend. You screwed my brother, and now you're screwing me. I don't know what you and Phillip are up to, but I don't trust you. And I'm not afraid to go over your head on this. Don't push me, Carl.' Jo stared into Carl's eyes, and shook her head. 'I've wanted to be a police officer since I was ten years old and watched my brother take his declaration. I'm proud to be a police officer, Carl, it's more than a job to me. I took the same declaration when I was nineteen: that I will to the best of my power keep the peace and prevent all offences. And unless you are going to fire me now, I will continue to faithfully uphold all my duties until I retire from my role as superintendent on Friday.'

Carl stood silently, his gaze dropping to the floor, as Jo turned and stormed out past Stan, who had been listening at the door, and the office manager, who smiled brightly. 'Oh hi, Jo! Everything is confirmed for your leaving do on Thursday night. Did you want to meet for a drink first before dinner?'

She couldn't trust herself to answer, but she knew there would be no leaving do now, and she would never again return to this office to which she had dedicated most of her life. She had managed to keep the tears back as she spoke with Carl, but now they came as she dashed down the stairs and hurtled through the revolving doors to the safety of her car. Jo started the engine, trying to calming herself with deep breaths so she could drive. She had no hesitation in deciding her destination. Turning out onto the coast road, she passed the site of Morgate House before reaching Kemptown and Daisy's road, where several people were now parked outside.

Jo turned the radio on, frantically searching for a news station with her trembling fingers.

The remains found on Saltdean Tye have now been confirmed as those of Holly Moore, a seventeen-year-old girl who went missing from Saltdean in 1985. Despite an extensive

search, no trace of Miss Moore had been found until yesterday.
Relatives have been told and are being comforted by police.

Jo looked over at the two police vehicles outside the building; she recognised the FLO as Sam Scott, who was still sitting in her car. Daisy still hadn't let her in, and there were now half a dozen reporters milling around outside. Jo needed to work fast; she knew that Carl would probably be in touch with all of the team, including Sam, telling her to keep Jo away from Daisy.

She opened the car door and walked over to Sam's unit vehicle.

'Hi, Sam,' she said, as lightly as she could muster. 'No joy, then?'

'Nope, she doesn't appear to be at home, and she's not returning my calls.'

'Do you have a landline number for her, by any chance, in case she's turned her mobile off? It might be worth me trying. I met both the girls once, when they were young.'

Sam frowned, her professional experience making her hesitate. 'Um, okay. Do I need to clear it?'

Jo frowned. 'With whom? I'm in charge of the case, but feel free to check in, if you want.'

'Sorry, yes, of course, I'll write it down for you.'

Jo waited, looking around in order to seem casual, then slowly took the piece of paper from Sam. 'I'll let you know if I get anywhere.'

Jo took a breath, then picked up her mobile. She daren't risk texting, in case they used it against her somehow.

It rang for a tortuously long time, then eventually went to answerphone.

After leaving a message urging Daisy to contact her, Jo

sat staring up at the flat, wondering where Daisy was, and willing her to get in touch. Her fingers played across the phone screen as she reread Holly's letter sent over by Professor Haig.

Dear Daisy,

I hope this letter finds you. I miss you so much, but I know that if you are reading this then you will hopefully be comforted knowing I have never given up the search for you.

I dream of being reunited with you. I dream of what could have been if it weren't for that fire. I daydream obsessively about the happy times with Mum - when Dad was at work or the pub. When we played Knock Down Ginger and the lady next door came after us with her broom. When we played hopscotch with all the other kids in the street until Mum called us in for dinner. When we lay on the grass in the park and spotted animals in the clouds.

I think of the night of the fire, I blame myself for not getting the bedroom door open. I was only eight, but I still think it's my fault she's dead. How different life would have been if that policewoman hadn't started the fire. Or if it had only been Dad who was killed. If only. If only. I go round and round. If I still had you, I could cope. But they took you away, and they won't let me see you.

293

Sometimes I think my insomnia is a gift. I don't want to dream about you and Mum, it's too painful. I often dream we are in a bath together, like at Wicker Street, when Mum used to wash our hair and sing to us. Please know that I have tried so hard to find you, I have walked the streets most nights looking for you. I just want to know that you are happy – I can bear not seeing you again if I know you are okay.

I wish nothing but the best for you, my beautiful Daisy Boo. If anything ever happens to me, please live your life for the both of us. I'm sorry I broke my promise to never be separated from you. I will never get over the pain of them taking you away. I tried everything to track you down, but they said your foster mother wanted to keep me away from you.

I hope she is kind to you. I hope you finish school. I hope that you can find a way to recover from all you have been through, and to be truly happy. That is my greatest wish. I love you, Daisy, more than anything or anyone in the whole world.

Your loving sister,
Holly xxx

Jo looked up at Daisy's front door, which was now plunged in darkness. There was no point looking at

Morgate, she wouldn't have gone back there. The press would already be door-stepping all her friends. If the press knew where she was, the FLO would have got a tip-off.

Nobody knew where Daisy Moore had gone. She had vanished into the night.

Chapter Twenty-Three

Holly

March 1985

'Where are you going?' said Eve, as Holly walked along the corridor of Morgate House, towards the back door.

'Just for a walk. I haven't been anywhere other than school for a fortnight, I'm going crazy,' said Holly, smiling at her friend.

'Have you seen him?' asked Eve, standing at the door of her bedroom with her dressing gown on.

'No, of course not, I haven't left here.'

'What are you going to do?'

'I don't know. What can I do? I don't even know what to think, I don't have anyone I can talk to about this. Obviously I can't go to the police,' Holly said quietly. Her heart felt heavy; since her conversation with Eve she felt like she was losing Daisy all over again.

Holly had experienced utter elation for the first time, a sense of hope and excitement. Finally, she was going to have some contact with her sister. She had someone in her life who could actually help her, root for her, fight for her, and be her rock.

She'd had no idea how badly she wanted these things until she felt them for the first time in his car on the seafront. She had felt alone for so long, so desperately alone. Like she had failed her mother, her sister and herself, for not being able to claw her way out and help them.

Then, as suddenly as she had found someone to help her, the prospect had been ripped away. She didn't know if Eve was right. If he'd had anything to do with Gemma's death. She didn't know what to believe, or think. But what she did know for sure was that he had done this before. Preyed on girls like her. And she couldn't now trust that he was going to find Daisy for her. She couldn't trust anything he said.

And yet she had still written the letter to Daisy that he told her to. It had taken her a week to write, and she walked around with it everywhere. She was scared to see him, in case she said something about Gemma, and it made him angry. But at the same time, she was desperate to see him and give him the letter. She felt like her mind was going to split in two from the pressure.

Holly headed for the door.

'Do you want me to come with you?' asked Eve.

'No, I'm fine,' said Holly. 'I won't be long, I just need to be near the sea.'

Holly walked out of the front door of Morgate and made her way to the entrance of the under-cliff walk and began making her way along the seafront towards Rottingdean. It was a clear sunny day, but already the light was going. The beach was beautiful, the air clear and crisp. As she walked she slowly started to feel her strength return.

She needed to try to breathe, try to stay calm. Eve was probably letting her imagination run away with her. Life at Morgate was incredibly hard and it was more than likely that this girl, Gemma, had fallen in love with him and possibly taken her own life as a result. But that didn't mean he'd killed her. The way she felt about him, in that one

297

kiss, she knew how easy it would be to fall madly in love with him – she had started to herself. She took a deep breath of air, inhaling through her nose, and looked out at the ocean. It was flat calm, and the low clouds were hovering over the surface of the water like seagulls looking for fish. The sea looked so welcoming, despite the cold, and she paused to look out at it, listening to the water crackling over the pebbles by her boots.

In some ways she could see this as a blessing, she thought. She was lucky really, she had no doubt that he was in a position to help her find Daisy. And now she'd been warned that she wasn't the first girl he'd befriended from Morgate, she could stop herself falling in love with him. Nothing had really changed, he still wanted to help her, she had just been given a sign to keep her heart safe, which she should have done anyway.

Holly let out a big sigh; her heart was slowly lifting from the pit of despair she had felt over the past few days. Slowly. There was still so much to be excited about, this was still a chance to find her sister, more realistic than any before. She could use him, maybe she'd be the one to break his heart. Why did everyone always think it had to be the girl who had her heart broken?

Before she knew it, she was at Rottingdean. She walked up the slope, away from the beach, as the light was fading, and realised she had some change rattling around in the pocket of her jeans. She would get some food from the chip shop and walk back.

As she crossed the road, she saw him.

Sitting in the car park on the other side of the pelican crossing. Her heart missed a beat. He was smoking a cigarette and reading the paper, and she tried not to stare but couldn't help herself. All her talking to herself for the past hour seemed to evaporate as she stood there, paralysed, her heart hammering in her chest. As if knowing she was watching him, he looked up, and stared directly at her. In the space of three seconds, she knew she had given herself away. His smile turned into a slight frown and he beckoned to her to come over.

She felt painfully self-conscious, he was a police officer, she couldn't play him, he would know immediately that something was up. She felt nauseous, and scared, trying to take deep breaths.

'Hey, kid,' he said as she reached the car. 'Haven't seen you around for a while. Wanna go for a drive?'

'I can't today, I have to get back,' she said, her voice trembling.

He cleared his throat, frowning back at her. 'It's cold, kid. Get in the car, I'll drop you,' he said, starting the engine.

She nodded. What could she do? He could think of any number of ways to get her into his car, and come up with any number of excuses. If she just went along with it, maybe it would be okay. She felt her whole body shaking violently. The picture of that girl, Gemma, was imprinted on her mind, smiling back at her.

She walked round and got into the passenger seat as he scanned the area, presumably to check no one was watching. She had barely closed the passenger door before he was pulling away. She didn't want to be in the car with him, she didn't want to be anywhere near him, she felt scared. Mostly scared of herself, and the way she was reacting. She felt panic overwhelming her. She couldn't fool him, he would know immediately something was wrong, the way she was acting.

'Are you okay, kid?' he asked casually. 'You write that letter we talked about?'

'Yeah,' she said, desperate to say the right thing, to pretend, to look at him as she had done before, so he wouldn't suspect, but she could only look out of the window. She clasped her hands together in her lap, so he couldn't see how much they were shaking. As they pulled onto the coast road, blind panic began to take over.

'Give it here, then,' he said irritably, his voice clipped, as she handed it over. 'I thought you'd be out every night looking for me, with that letter burning a hole in your pocket. Where have you been?'

'Nowhere.' She'd had no idea before if what Eve had claimed was true, but the way he was acting, the change in him, was scaring her. He was completely in control and she, as was the story of her life, could do nothing. She could only sit in his car, trapped, watching her life run away from her.

'What's up?' he said, clutching the steering wheel tightly. His knuckles were white from the strain. He was agitated about possibility that she might know something about him. His reaction to her fear was fuelling it tenfold.

She shrugged, scared to say anything, she had no idea where they were going, but the atmosphere in the car was already different. His bear-like frame, so comforting before, felt threatening. The car, previously a warm, safe haven, was now stuffy and cell-like.

'Let's go up onto the Tye and watch the sun go down,' he said.

'Sure,' she said, trying to sound relaxed, wishing she hadn't gone out, wishing she was anywhere but here.

As he pulled onto the track, she felt her whole body prickle with goosebumps. She sat back in her seat and looked out of the window, thinking of an article she had read once about a woman who was raped. 'Why didn't you cry out, why didn't you run away?' the reporter had asked her. 'I just wanted it to be over, I thought if I let him do what he wanted, it would be over quickly and he wouldn't kill me.'

They turned off the main road and into a car park, just as the last of the light faded. The ground was uneven and they bobbed about as he navigated through to the other side and drove on up a track. She looked at the speedometer, he was only doing five miles an hour. She could jump out and try to get away, but he would just run after her. He would catch her in seconds, and then he would know she was hiding something. Her head throbbed with the stress, and she couldn't breathe.

'Come on, let's go for a walk,' he said finally, as they reached a second car park at the top of the track.

The place was deserted. He got out of the car, walked round the front and opened the passenger door for her.

She looked back down the track, her legs throbbing with adrenaline, desperate to make a run for it, but what was the point? There was no way she could outrun him. His manner was different now, he seemed jumpy and defensive. She was shaking. She couldn't fool him.

'You seem different,' he said. 'What's up?' He lit a cigarette and they walked up towards the woods.

'Nothing. I've just got a lot on my mind,' she said, starting to cry.

'Why are you crying?' he asked, frowning at her again.

'I'm not,' she said. 'Please, can you take me back to Morgate? Mrs Price wants us back early,' she added feebly, putting one foot in front of the other, making herself walk in one direction when she desperately wanted to run in another.

He said nothing, taking a drag of his cigarette. She glanced over at him, as a tear dropped from the end of her nose. His face was hard, empty.

'Are you going to tell me what's going on?' he said. 'Because you're kind of annoying me. I offered to help you, I'm willing to stick my neck out for you, and you won't be honest with me.'

'I'm scared to say anything in case it makes you angry,' she said, her voice shaking.

'Okay,' he said. 'Why would you make me angry? I've never been angry with you. What's happened to make you think that?'

She had to tell him, she couldn't lie, but she didn't need to tell him all of it. She could still save herself, if she just found the right words.

'Did you know a girl called Gemma, from Morgate House?' she said, so quietly he had to bend forward to hear her.

'No,' he said, after a long pause.

She nodded her head, knowing he did, and that by denying Gemma's existence he was hiding something.

'Why?' he asked.

'Someone told me she loved you so much that she killed herself.' Holly started to cry. 'I just felt like I could imagine loving you like that. It made me feel vulnerable.'

302

'Is that right? Who is this someone? Why do they think I knew Gemma?' His voice was cold. He stopped walking and stared at her.

'I don't know,' Holly said, starting to cry again.

He pulled her hair, hard, so that she let out a scream. It made her lose her balance and she fell down onto her knees.

'Who is this someone? Tell me her name, is she at Morgate?' he said, pulling her head back even harder so that she felt her neck would snap.

'Hannah, her name is Hannah,' she said, as he glared at her with his blue eyes. 'Please, let me go,' she said, panting from the pain.

'Does she live at Morgate?' he said.

She knew there was no one at Morgate called Hannah, but he knew Eve. Eve had been in his car. He would talk to her, he would ask her if she was the one who said he knew Gemma. She had to get away, she had to warn Eve. She had to try, she had to find the strength.

As soon as he let go of her, she started to run. She ran harder and faster than she ever had in her life, she didn't look back, she just kept pushing forward, as hard as she could, trying harder than she could ever have imagined. All the time knowing he would catch her. The ground was hard and solid from the cold, as she hurled herself down the hill. She heard him coming after her, the crunch of the gravel under his shoes; he didn't shout or call out her name, but she could feel his footsteps getting closer. He kicked her legs when he caught up with her and she stumbled, tripped, and came crashing down. She put her arms out, but her wrist was still not fully healed and pain ripped

303

through her as she hit her head hard on the rocky ground. She immediately felt the blood trickle down her face. As the pain seared through her head, she looked down at the lower car park, where another car was pulling in. She reached out, dragging her nails along the ground, as he picked her up and her vision began to blur.

Her head screamed with pain as she felt him lifting her and carrying her. When she next came round he was laying her down, and she felt that she was in water. She reached out with her hands, pushing his face away, fighting her hardest, desperate to see Daisy again. He placed his hand on her collarbone at the base of neck and she tried to sit up, but he held her down, and wouldn't let her up. She looked around desperately, she was lying at the bottom of the water tower, and he was standing over her. She was wet, the water was dirty, and brown, and there was a cloying stench.

She screamed as he pushed her under. Angry with herself for not taking in a breath before he pushed her back down. She closed her eyes, thinking of all the times she and Daisy had played training games in the bath at their house; trying to hold her breath while Daisy timed her. Whiling away the hours, with nothing else to do through the hot summer months, and no money to go out, she would run them a cold bath. She lay there for a while, knowing she couldn't hold her breath for much longer, but painfully aware she mustn't inhale the dirty brown water into her lungs.

Holly gathered her strength, tried to push his hands away; she managed to turn and pull herself up, gasping for breath, but he pulled her back under again. She tried pushing against his hand with both of hers, summoning all of her strength . . . she was so small compared to him. She tried to feel around in the water, desperate for something to grab hold of that she could pull herself up with, to get a second of air. Knowing she wasn't going to last much longer. Once more she managed to break free, take a gulp of air, then he forced her under again. Splashing. Struggling. Her air was running out.

The last thing she registered after the struggle was the sensation of him turning her over, being held down by the base of her neck and her ankles. She was trying so hard to push herself up.

Then the point came when she stopped struggling. She didn't have enough air to keep going, and in a last desperate attempt to appease him she thought maybe he wasn't letting her up because he was punishing her for struggling.

Like her dad. Always being punished for something. She could never do anything right.

She fought the crushing feeling in her lungs . . . when her body was pleading for her to inhale. She fought it for Daisy, the thought of never seeing her again, of her being all alone in the world, making her fight long after she wanted to give up.

But she got to the point where she couldn't fight it any more. Inhaling water was a relief for half a second, before the water weighed into her lungs. She gasped, three inhalations of water before they were completely full. The water felt cold in her lungs even though it felt lukewarm on her skin.

I don't know how I'm going to survive this, she thought . . . I don't know how long it will be before I am able to breathe in air again.

It hurt so badly, her chest burning, her lungs in a vice.

Holly opened her eyes and stared through the murky water. As the blackness crawled in through the sides of her eyes, like spiders, she saw Daisy underneath the water, swimming up towards her, her arms open wide.

And finally, she let go.

Chapter Twenty-Four
Daisy

March 2015, Wednesday morning

'Daisy?'

Daisy opened her eyes to see Olive's son, Charlie, smiling down at her, clutching a cup of steaming coffee in his hand.

'I think you might need this more than I do.'

'What time is it?'

'Six o'clock in the morning. What are you doing here?'

'I came to see Olive last night, I must have fallen asleep. Sorry. I'll go now, I don't want to wake her. Send her my love, tell her I'll visit her tomorrow.'

'No need to be sorry. It's lovely that you care. See you later,' he said cheerfully, as he lowered himself down into the armchair she had just vacated.

Daisy walked outside. It was still dark and she set off back to the flat with her bicycle light on. The air was salty and clear, and she took deep breaths of it, drawing it down into her lungs, as she cycled fast along the seafront. She had slept in the chair next to Olive's bed, but it had been the best night's sleep she could remember, and she hadn't stirred. She hadn't let Superintendent Joanna Hamilton tell her any details about Holly, because she hadn't felt ready to hear them, but the fact was that at last she knew where Holly was, and that she was at peace. Her neck hurt from where she had slept, hunched slightly awkwardly in the armchair, but she felt free and full of purpose. As she passed Saltdean Tye she felt an overwhelming sadness at the thought of Holly's remains lying in the earth for all those years, not knowing what had happened to her. But it was swiftly followed by a clear-headed determination that she had never felt in her life before. For the first time, she felt a sense of purpose, she knew what she needed to do: she was going to find Eve Taylor, and work out what had happened to Holly – and why.

To her surprise, when she reached the flat, nobody was waiting for her – perhaps they had not expected her to reappear in the early hours – so she locked up her bike and dashed into the building, up the stairs and into the safety of her flat. She took a hot shower, made some strong coffee, and then immediately turned to the photocopies laid out all over her floor. She fired up her laptop and opened up a spreadsheet; she was going to list everyone's name alphabetically, and, as Olive had suggested, she would start with the boys first.

She began by scouring Facebook for photographs of anyone who still looked like their school head shot, and then sent a generic message.

My name is Daisy Moore. My sister, Holly Moore, was at Saltdean High with you, in your year. I'm trying to track down a girl named Eve Taylor, who was good friends with my sister at school. If you know how I might be able to reach Eve, please PM me. Thank you in advance, Daisy x

The first two hours, she must have cut and pasted the same message a hundred times. She figured it didn't matter if the person she was messaging on Facebook only looked vaguely like the person in the Saltdean High School year-book; she needed to spread her net as wide as she could and pray she got a catch.

By lunchtime she was starting to flag, she could see from all the blue ticks that nearly all of the people she had contacted had read her note, but only a couple had replied, to say they were sorry but they hadn't known either Holly or Eve. But most hadn't replied at all. The determination she had felt earlier in the day was fading into sadness again, but she made herself keep going, throwing open the window, despite the freezing temperature outside.

Her hand hovered over the TV remote, desperate to watch the lunchtime news but knowing that if they mentioned Holly it could send her into a spiral of depression, which would only distract her from her task. Her eyes fell on the picture of Holly, and she pulled it towards her and stroked her sister's face. Her laptop pinged and she looked up to see a new message.

Hi Daisy, thanks for your message. I didn't know Holly well, because I only started at Saltdean the year she went missing – which was something everyone talked about a lot. I hope you and your family are doing okay now. Eve Taylor was actually in my form, 9NS, I wasn't friends with her, so I can't tell you much, other than that she used to play the guitar. I remember because my mate fancied her and called her Guitar Girl. I think maybe he took her out for a drink once. It might be worth messaging him actually, Damian Connors, in case he remembers something else. He's on Facebook, he lives in Tunbridge Wells now, good luck with it. Mike.

At last, a lead. She scanned the head shots for Damian Connors. She remembered she hadn't messaged him because his picture had looked nothing like the one person on Facebook with the same name, but she found him, based in Tunbridge Wells, and sent off a message.

She stretched, to ease her aching shoulders, and her glance fell on the answerphone, sitting next to the TV remote. The light was flashing, indicating someone had left her a message. How had she not noticed it before? She walked over to it and pressed 'play'.

'Hello, Daisy, it's Superintendent Jo Hamilton, we met at Morgate on Monday night.'

Daisy reached out her hand to cut the message short, then stopped and let it continue. 'I have a letter here for you from your sister Holly.' Daisy instinctively put her hand up to her mouth, as the room started to spin. 'I spoke to Holly's English teacher at Saltdean High today. Holly left a letter with him in the hope that one day you'd go to the same school and he'd be able to give it to you.'

Daisy reached out for a chair and pulled it towards her, sinking into it before her legs gave way. 'She never stopped looking for you. I would really love that chance to talk with you. Please call me,' said Jo, before reading out her number, then ending the call.

Daisy sat for a moment, staring into space in disbelief. She stood and began to pace her small living room; a letter from Holly, waiting, unread all this time. She sat down and put her head in her hands, it was all too much. She didn't want to see Superintendent Hamilton, but at the same time she didn't want to read the letter alone. She needed some air but there was a group of reporters camped on her doorstep now, as well as two police cars, and she didn't have a hope of getting out unscathed. The thought of reading Holly's letter was too much to resist so, with shaking hands, she fired off a text to the number Superintendent Hamilton had left.

Come over.

The presence of reporters downstairs meant the police had obviously released the news that they were Holly's remains. Daisy looked over at the TV remote again, then at her watch; the lunchtime news would be starting shortly. Slowly, she crossed the room and picked up the remote, then realised her hands were shaking violently. She didn't want to see images of the site where they had found Holly's remains – it would be too much to bear, she would never be able to get them out of her head. Instead, she walked over to her laptop and clicked on the BBC News website.

Human remains found on Saltdean Tye identified as teenager who disappeared thirty years ago.

Holly Moore, 17, from East Sussex, was last seen on Saltdean High Street, on the evening of 7th March 1985, wearing a red woollen duffel coat with a hood.

An extensive missing person investigation was launched at the time but she was never found. Today Sussex Police said the remains have been identified as hers.

Police were called to an area on Saltdean Tye just before 9 a.m. on Monday, following reports that bones had been discovered. An investigation is now ongoing to determine the cause of death. Holly's family are being supported by specialist officers.

Chief Superintendent Carl Webber of Sussex Police said, 'Our thoughts go out to Holly's family and friends at this incredibly difficult time. At the time of Holly's disappearance an extensive missing person investigation was launched, with a number of searches carried out, as well as CCTV and door-to-door enquiries.

'Sadly, this is not the news that many will have hoped for. However, our investigation will continue to establish the full circumstances and provide the answers Holly's family deserve.'

Anyone with any information is asked to contact Sussex Police.

Suddenly, her mobile beeped, making her jump and she reached out for it and read the screen. *Daisy, it's Jo. Thank you for your text. I'm at the fire exit at the back entrance to your building, can you let me in please.* Daisy frowned at the message. She never used the fire escape; Jo was obviously trying to avoid the pack outside her flat for some reason. She looked over at the printouts covering the floor

312

and then turned and began to gather them up. Superintendent Hamilton had wasted no time in reacting to her invitation.

Daisy knew she was being stupid, running from a woman with all the inside knowledge about the case – and it was possible that she may give away something useful. If this woman wanted to talk to her so badly, maybe it was time to let her. She had absolutely nothing to lose at the moment. And knowing there was a letter from Holly was just too much to resist.

Slowly she walked down her hallway to the fire escape door which backed onto her kitchen, and opened it, calling out to Jo to come up. As Jo began the climb, her boots clattering on the wrought iron steps, Daisy looked out over Brighton, and to Saltdean Tye beyond. She had spent many nights up here, smoking, thinking about Holly, wondering where she was, and as it turned out, she could see the place where she was buried in a shallow grave the whole time.

'Hi,' Jo puffed, tired from the climb.

'Hi,' Daisy replied, stepping back from the door and letting her through.

For a moment they stood staring at one another, the weight of Holly's presence bearing down on them both.

The woman looked tired; she was wearing the same blue fitted jacket she had worn the day before, and looked as if she hadn't been to bed.

'How are you feeling?' Jo asked.

'Numb,' said Daisy, walking back with her into the safety of her flat.

'I'm so sorry about Holly.'

'Why do you need to sneak in like that?'

Jo stared at her. 'Because I've been taken off the case.'

'Why?' Daisy glared. 'And don't lie.'

'Because I'm determined to find the truth, and there are a lot of people who wanted it to stay buried. I should have done more when your sister went missing, and I'm ashamed of that, but I'm determined not to let them silence me now.'

Daisy sat down, feeling tears coming and swallowing them back. 'Can I see her letter?'

'Of course,' the woman said, putting her bag on the table and pulling out two sheets of paper with Holly's slanting black handwriting on them.

Daisy recognised her sister's writing straight away, and she started to cry.

'I'm deeply sorry you weren't allowed to see each other,' the policewoman said. 'I'm putting in an official complaint, I intend to get you some compensation and an official apology. I had temporarily left the force, I had no idea you'd been separated.'

Daisy started to cry again. 'Am I allowed to have Holly's necklace?'

'As soon as we find the person who did this to Holly, it's yours. But we may need it for evidence. It was how I knew it was Holly, she was clutching it the night of the fire,' the woman said.

'How did she die?' Daisy said, looking up at her.

'We aren't sure yet, but we think it was a head injury,' she said quietly.

Daisy sank down onto the chair next to her. 'Who did it?'

'We don't know. But I promise you, I'm going to find out.'

Daisy stared at the woman, wanting to believe her, but past experience not letting her. Daisy lifted Holly's letter, and started to read. Before the second line she was crying so much she had to stop. It was too much. 'I remembered something that might be useful,' she continued, as the woman found her a tissue in the kitchen and returned with it. 'Phillip Price, he was the son of the people who ran Morgate House, Geoff and Lorna Price. He was a creep. He was always walking into Holly's bedroom when she was getting changed. He was a police officer. He would talk to any of his colleagues who brought Holly home, and make sure she was never believed. Are his parents still alive?'

The woman nodded. 'Lorna Price is still alive, Geoff died.'

'Where is she?' said Daisy, suddenly thinking of Olive. If she failed to find out anything about Holly's last days, she could at least try to find Lorna, and possibly discover something about Samuel to comfort Olive.

'Lorna's in a nursing home, I believe. But I'm not allowed to tell you which one.'

Daisy bit down hard on her lip. 'I think I'd like to be alone now. Can I keep Holly's letter?'

'Of course, it's yours, I've scanned it in case we need it. I hope that's alright.'

Daisy heard her laptop ping. She desperately wanted the policewoman to leave so that she could check her messages, and digest Holly's letter.

'If you think of anything else about Phillip Price that might help us, any details at all, however insignificant they might seem, please let me know.'

Daisy nodded as the policewoman turned to go. She

315

followed as she walked along the hallway and stepped over the threshold.

'I really appreciate you talking with me today, Daisy. I hope we can continue to work together.'

Daisy just wanted her to go. She felt a twang of guilt that she had used Joanna Hamilton to extract information. She had no intention of working with her, any more than the policewoman would consider doing her any favours. It was all an act, pretending to be her friend when she needed her.

Daisy closed the door behind Jo, and rushed to her laptop. To her intense relief there was a message from Damian.

Hi Daisy, good to hear from you. I remember Eve well, we went out for a while, she upped and left and moved to London, suddenly, when we were about seventeen. I was pretty gutted, I was mad about her. Anyway, I went to our school reunion about five years ago and she was there. She said she'd always thought about me, but she had no choice but to skip town and disappear for a while. I was married by then, as was she – not very happily though, I don't think. Her name is Eve Slade now, it was on her name badge. I remember because of the band. I never looked her up though. Hope that helps.

'Eve Slade,' Daisy said out loud.

She fired up her laptop, and typed the name into Facebook. Immediately there was a match. Her heart racing, she looked at the photographs on Facebook, then at the ones in the Saltdean yearbook. Eve had obviously changed

316

a lot in thirty years, but it was definitely her. Daisy sent off a message, asking Eve to contact her about her sister Holly, asap, then picked up her mobile phone and dialled.

She was no good at lying, particularly when it was someone she worked with, but she had no choice. Jo had told her that Lorna Price was in a nursing home, and if she was going to confront the woman, she had to do it face to face.

'Hi, Sarah, it's Daisy, yeah, I'm good, how are you? I was wondering if you could help me out with something. I've had a referral for a patient and I need to arrange transport, but they didn't say which home she is currently at. Her name is Lorna Price.' Daisy waited, her heart hammering in her chest. 'Lakeview, in Hassocks? Great, thanks a million.'

Daisy looked at her watch; it was still only two, and her shift didn't start until seven. She googled Lakeview Residential Home and was relieved to see it was only a short ride from Hassocks station. If she left now from Brighton, she could get the train to Hassocks and be back in time for work.

Her heart began to race. She had no idea if she would even be allowed in to visit Lorna Price when she got there, or what state of health she would be in. But she decided that, for Olive's sake, and the chance of finding out a bit more about Samuel, it would be worth the risk.

Besides, Lorna Price would have been one of the last people to see Holly alive, and if nobody else was going to ask her about the night her sister disappeared, then she had no choice.

Daisy had been absolutely terrified of the woman from the day she went to Morgate House until the day she left. But she knew that confronting her about the way she had treated her and Holly, and all the children in her care, was something that she had to do – if she was ever going to find any sort of peace.

Chapter Twenty-Five
Olive

Bletchley Park, May 1944

'Unfortunately, your arm needs breaking again and resetting, Miss May, as it's not healing as well as we would like it to. The problem we have is that we can't give you a general anaesthetic.'

Olive looked up at the doctor, sitting in the seat next to her. He was a tall man, nearing his sixties, she guessed, with kind eyes, and a moustache that twitched when he spoke. It had been a nurse who had set her arm in a plaster cast on the day of the accident, but there had been a problem. An X-ray two weeks after that day, when the pain was unrelenting, had shown it was broken in several places and that it wasn't healing properly. So she had been referred to a specialist, a consultant, in whose office she sat now, on her third trip to Stoke Mandeville Hospital.

Since the morning of the accident, she had endured two weeks of sitting in her bedroom above the pub alone – with no visitors other than Lorna. The pain in her arm had been getting worse by the hour, and after fainting for the second time she had been taken to Stoke Mandeville hospital by Geoff, where they had taken a second X-ray of her arm and some urine and bloods to check her kidneys and heart. Despite Olive's repeated attempts, she hadn't been told anything by Geoff or Lorna about the consequences of failing to complete her mission to help Samuel. She asked countless times what had become of him, but Lorna kept saying only that she knew he was alive, and in the hospital. That she hadn't been told what state he was currently in, and would try to find out. Olive knew her friend was lying to her; she didn't know why, but she suspected that Geoff had something to do with it.

'Obviously, we can't do this kind of surgery with just a local anaesthetic, so we may have to delay, depending on how you feel. However, every day we leave it, the bone is obviously growing in a way it's not supposed to, which could lead to much more extensive problems in the future.'

Olive looked out to the hospital corridor behind him, to the signposts she had passed on her way in. She knew Samuel had been taken to Stoke Mandeville but she had no idea which ward he was on. If he was here, she was determined to find out today. Her arm had been agony, she couldn't sleep or eat, and the pain made her feel constantly sick. The car journey to the hospital had been excruciating, in more ways than one, every bump and pothole sending the pain shooting up her arm again. She also knew Geoff had information he wasn't sharing with her, and she had tried – and failed – to get it from him. She was more lovesick than she imagined a person ever could be. She could see no fault in Samuel; he had been badly injured, so there was a good reason why he had not been able to contact her, or show any gratitude for what she had done for him. Most likely, it was some intervention of Geoff's. She thought about Samuel constantly, day and night; she obsessed to such a degree that she would start sweating and shaking when she thought about never seeing him again. She couldn't hold down food, and she would vomit regularly from the pain and stress. Lorna had listened at first, comforted her and mopped up her tears, but in the end she had begun to avoid her, coming back to the room late at night, and refusing to talk about Samuel with her any more.

Olive obsessively ran through every single scenario in her mind as to why Samuel hadn't been able to get word to her. She worried that he was as desperate as she was. She wrote him endless letters, but with no address to send them to, and Lorna and Geoff refusing to deliver them, they sat by her bed staring back at her. She thought of nothing else but him, went over in her mind every minute they'd ever spent together, and obsessed over whether she would ever be reunited. She berated herself endlessly for pretending to be cool with Samuel. What if that were the reason he was staying away, what if he thought she didn't care? She was a stupid child who had thought she could play with love. All the girls who had shown their true feelings, they were the clever ones, not her; perhaps he was thinking about one of them now. She had laughed at them for being foolish, but she was the fool. Thinking she was better than them all.

Olive looked at the doctor; the prospect of being admitted to the hospital where she knew Samuel was made her heart soar. Geoff would have to leave her here, overnight, and she would find her way to him. She didn't care about the pain in her wrist, at times it was a welcome distraction from the heartache she felt, and right now she was glad of it for bringing her closer to him.

Eventually, when she had broken down in the car on the way here, and begged him, Geoff had said that Samuel was in hospital with a broken collarbone, leg and punctured lung, but that he was on the mend and would be discharged soon. She had saved his life, he'd said, and he didn't deserve it. After that, he said he didn't want to speak of the man again, he'd endangered his own life, and hers, and caused both of them to fail on their missions. He was, quite rightly, being sent home in disgrace.

His answers had only served to make her panic more. She asked, again, if he would give Samuel a letter from her, but he refused to even consider it. When was he being sent home? How long did she have left to try to make contact with him? When he returned to Canada she knew there would be no hope of ever finding him again.

On top of her anxieties about Samuel, four weeks had passed and Commander Travis had yet to speak to her, or give any indication of what his intentions were regarding her position as a dispatch rider at Bletchley Park. It was obvious to her that with a badly broken wrist, she couldn't ride at the moment, but surely after a period of bed rest – at worst, a trip home to recover – she could come back? She missed her job so intensely, the possibility that she might not be allowed to ride again adding to her angst exponentially. She had heard of people being chastised by MI5 for indiscretions, and making mistakes, but surely she wouldn't be sent home for saving the life of a fellow dispatch rider?

'Miss May, are you listening to me?' the doctor asked, peering at her over his spectacles, as he clutched her notes in his hand.

'Yes, you said I need an operation on my arm. Does that mean I'll be staying overnight? I have a friend here, a colleague, and I was hoping I might be able to see him. If possible,' she said, her lip starting to tremble.

'Miss May, I'm not sure you're taking in what I'm telling you. Perhaps we can discuss your colleague later when we've talked about you. As I've tried to explain, when you broke your arm, it broke in several places, which must have been extremely painful for you.'

She looked at him intently for the first time; in the weeks since the accident, the memory of coming off her bike still haunted her. Of driving along the lanes with a broken wrist, seven miles in second gear, holding on with one hand, feeling every bump in the road, as if a red-hot poker were being stabbed into her arm. She had finally reached the gates of the park, and yelled at the guard that there was a driver down at Plumpton Farm who needed help . . . and from then on she had no memory.

Vague flashes haunted her dreams, blurred memories of being taken to the infirmary by Geoff, of sitting in the hospital waiting room, her arm swollen and limp, every throb of the blood pulsing through it making the pain so bad she had been sick again on the floor at his feet. The nurse had put her arm in a sling, which made her scream with pain, and she had asked repeatedly about Samuel and whether he was alive. She remembered vividly the smell of TCP from the child in the cubicle next door, crying out from having stitches in his head, the sight of his blood on the floor, X-ray machines, doctors and nurses leaning over her, giving her pills, then finally an injection to help her sleep – after which she woke, the following day, in her bedroom above the pub with Lorna.

If she was having an operation then she would be admitted overnight, which meant that this man, this helpful doctor, might be able to tell her where Samuel was. If she could just see him for herself and speak to him, she could

322

maybe get a hold of herself, calm herself down from this hysterical state she found herself in. Olive felt her heart lift for the first time in weeks at the thought of her plan.

'So when can I have this operation?' Olive said, smiling gently, hope sweeping through her.

'You can't, Miss May. That's what I'm saying. You can't have an operation because we can't give you a general anaesthetic.'

'Why not?' she said, focusing on his expression. This was her chance to see Samuel again, and the doctor was giving it to her with one hand and immediately taking it away with the other.

'Because we did some blood tests when you were last in, and because you were fainting I thought it wise to check before we operate . . .' He hesitated. 'You're pregnant, Miss May.' He paused for a moment, then cleared his throat. 'I take it from your reaction you weren't aware of your condition?'

Olive looked at him and felt herself starting to shake violently. His words were causing a reaction in her body that her mind could not keep up with. Frantically she searched for an explanation, her mind turning to Lorna's talk of her work in the huts; of searching for clues, for patterns, for a way through the maze.

Pregnant. She scrolled back through the timeline of her relationship with Samuel in her mind, like a ticker tape of dates, reaching back to March, to the night of her near hypothermia, when Samuel had taken her home, when she was violently ill. When she had sensed that he had stayed, when she had felt him there but thought that she was dreaming, when she had felt him on top of her, and she had

323

felt sore the next day. She had dismissed it, she felt sore and bruised in every cell of her body, she told herself. And he was nowhere to be seen when she woke, so she must have imagined him being there in the night. And how could she ask him such a thing? She couldn't. It would make her look like a tramp to even mention it, she would have to know about such things to even think it. Asking a man if he'd had his way with her without her consent, it was a dreadful accusation. He would never have spoken to her again. It wasn't possible, he wouldn't do such a thing.

But he had. And she knew that was why their landlady was so furious whenever he came near. She had said to Olive once that she knew he had stayed the night, and Olive had denied it vehemently. But her landlady was right; she knew now that on one occasion he had. She cringed at the thought of the girl in her thinking she was clever, thinking she was grown up, worldly wise.

'Miss May? I take it from the lack of a wedding ring that you aren't married. May I ask if the child's father is aware of your condition?'

Olive began tearing at the skin on her nails. Her mind spiralled as it had always done as she sat in class; while the teachers tapped their nails on the blackboard she would visit places in her head, take herself away in order to cope. She would make up stories, travel, run away from the seat in which she was forced to sit. She would go away, across the ocean, to the other side of the world.

Suddenly, she heard her mother's voice, slurred and sleepy. 'Don't go to bed with them until you have a ring on your finger.' She was pregnant, with Samuel's child. But there was a chance he loved her. She would tell Samuel, and maybe he would marry her. Slowly, a smile caught the edges of her lips, and the news which had taken her breath away with horror, only moments earlier, slowly began to evolve into hope as a possible way of tricking them into letting her see Samuel.

She smiled. 'He doesn't yet, but you see, the colleague I spoke of earlier, he's actually my fiancé. And I believe, because our engagement isn't official, the hospital hasn't let me see him. But I think in light of this development, I would really like to tell him myself, if possible.'

The doctor looked at her intently. 'Yes, well, of course. I can understand that. Perhaps if you let me have his name, I can see if I can find him for you.' He turned to go, as her heart surged, thudding in her chest like a child on Christmas morning.

'Yes, it's Samuel. Samuel Williams,' she said, unable to keep her smile from spreading. 'He was brought in a few weeks ago, after a motorbike accident. He works at Bletchley Park. He broke his collarbone and his leg. We have spoken,' she lied, 'but, as I said, we haven't been able to see one another yet.' She spoke confidently, smiling broadly, the pain in her arm vanishing from the effect of adrenaline.

'Right, I'll see what I can do. So just going back to you, Miss May, we will need to decide what to do about your wrist. General anaesthetic is a risk to the baby, so you will have to wait until you have given birth to have the surgery. As I mentioned earlier, we can't break your arm again and reset it under a local anaesthetic.'

'Yes, that's fine, I'll wait,' she said. 'My fiancé is Canadian, so it's possible I would have the surgery there, when we go back.'

'I see. Well, I realise you are in a lot of pain, but we can help you manage that. It will be hard to cope with a broken arm once the baby is born, but hopefully you have family – and Mr Williams, I'm sure, will be able to help. I know that young men these days are much more hands on than I was.'

'I'm sure he will,' she said, beaming as the doctor nodded.

'I'll speak to Matron, see what I can find out, and then she can show you up to him.'

'Thank you, Dr Miller.'

Left alone, Olive sat on the chair trying to take it all in. She was having Samuel's baby, and once he knew, she was hopeful he would want to marry her. She had no idea what had happened that night, she had no memory of it, perhaps she had consented and forgotten. Perhaps it had been magical and he was hurt she had made no mention of it. It didn't matter, what mattered was that they were going to be together. And at last this unrelenting pain and obsession would end.

Olive looked at the clock on the wall. The small hand turned painfully slowly, like it did in the classroom at school during an exam, when she felt she saw it curve backwards at times.

Finally, just as she was beginning to give up hope that he would ever return, the door swung open, and Dr Miller came back into the room.

'Unfortunately, the gentleman in question has already been discharged.'

Olive immediately stood, pain shooting up her arm, which made tears prick her eyes. 'I don't understand. What do you mean, he's been discharged?' she demanded, panic soaring through her, her fantasies of the past ten minutes evaporating suddenly.

'He has left the hospital, and he won't be returning, Miss May,' the doctor said, returning to his notes and scribbling on them frantically, before pushing them into a brown envelope.

'Well, where has he gone?' she snapped.

'I'm not at liberty to share that information with you, Miss May,' he said, opening the door and holding it for her.

'Did you tell him about the baby?' Olive felt her voice waver.

Dr Miller looked out to the corridor, where a man was standing, and blushed slightly.

'I believe you are returning home to Sussex; we can send your notes on to the Royal Sussex, and they will be able to take over from here.'

'What do you mean, returning home? I'm not going home, I want to talk to Samuel, where is he?' Olive followed the doctor's eyeline and looked over to see Geoff standing at the door.

'That man told you we weren't engaged, didn't he? He's got nothing to do with me, or Samuel. Please don't believe him, ask Samuel yourself.'

'We will be in touch, Miss May. Please take care of yourself, you will need to go and see your GP when you get home, to talk about your options.' Dr Miller looked over at a nurse in the hall, gestured for her to take his notes and then turned away, the consultation closed.

Olive rounded furiously on Geoff. 'What did you say to him? I want to see Samuel. Why are you doing this? This has nothing to do with you. We're having a baby, do you know that? Samuel needs to know.'

'He knows,' Geoff said quietly, looking at the floor.

'You're lying,' she said, backing away from him.

'Doctor Miller just told him, as he was leaving.'

'It's not true,' she said, turning towards the doctor. 'Samuel is leaving now?' she asked.

Olive ran through the double doors, towards the stairs, taking them two at a time, until she reached the hospital entrance. Frantically she looked around, and saw Samuel on the far side of the car park, climbing into a taxi.

'Samuel!' she called out.

Slowly he turned and looked at her. He didn't reply and his face was emotionless as he climbed into the back seat of the taxi just before it pulled away.

Olive stood and watched him go, knowing she would never see him again. She could feel her heart shatter, and knew that even though she was only twenty years old, she would never recover from this feeling.

She started to cry, wanting to escape, to be anywhere but here, where she felt so exposed and utterly alone. She felt the presence of someone creeping up behind her and, knowing who it was, she started to walk away. She had to get away from Bletchley, she felt humiliated that Geoff knew about the baby, and soon Lorna would too, and probably Commander Travis, and all the girls she had watched Samuel flirting with.

It had nothing to do with any of them, the only person it concerned was Samuel, and Geoff had made sure he was out of her life. She had never understood why Geoff had interfered so much, why he was so determined to destroy any chance that she and Samuel may have had. Why he had been the one to take her to hospital and have any say in what she was told about Samuel's condition, and whether she could or couldn't see or contact the father of her child.

As she walked away, she heard Geoff's voice behind her. 'I'll drive you back to your lodgings and you can pack.'

Olive turned and glared at him, daring him to come any closer. She wanted any excuse to lash out, to vent all the rage and fury she felt on him. 'I pity you,' she said as he looked down in shame, hiding his lazy eye behind his long, greasy fringe. 'The only reason Lorna is with you, is because she is desperate to get away from her parents. She doesn't love you and you don't love her. You have been jealous of Samuel from the start, because I wanted him, and not you. As if I'd ever be interested in a sad, creepy, cruel sorry excuse for a man like you. I'd rather have my heart smashed into a million pieces, than settle for what you and Lorna have.

'You are hateful. Just stay the hell away from me!'

Chapter Twenty-Six

Jo

March 2015, Wednesday afternoon

Jo paced her flat, listening to the infuriating Royal Sussex Hospital hold music and staring out at the grey sky hovering over Brighton seafront.

It was already Wednesday afternoon, time was running out, it was her leaving party the following evening – if it was even happening, given her latest run-in with Carl – and after that, the chances of making any progress on Holly's murder would be near impossible. While she was at the dinner, they would probably take her mobile off her, and her ID. All the while smiling, making light of her inability to let go, hoping she didn't mention Gemma and Holly's case, and giving speeches about her incredible contribution over her forty years on the force.

As it was, her options were already extremely limited. Chief Superintendent Carl Webber had officially put her on gardening leave, so she had no access to her office, to forensics, or to the Sussex Police computer system – and she would probably not be allowed back to the crime scene. By now, everyone in the team, including the family liaison officers, would have been told not to speak with her about the case. The walls were closing in.

All she had was Gemma's and Holly's files – which she had taken out of the building with her, and which they probably wanted back – and her name. Which meant that when she called up places like Brighton Hospital, the fact that she was a superintendent meant at least some fast-tracking.

'Hello?' a female voice finally said on the end of the line.

'Yes,' Jo said, trying not to snap.

'Sorry to keep you waiting. As it's so far back, I don't have any notes on my system for Holly Moore or Gemma Smith, just their dates of birth. Do you want those?'

Jo's heart sank. 'Sure,' she said, writing them down. 'Well, is there any other way of finding them? Are old hospital records stored somewhere?' she asked desperately.

'We only keep them for six years after the last entry, but GPs keep them for longer. It might be worth trying there. I've got them both listed as being registered to St Luke's Surgery, in Saltdean.'

'Okay, thank you for your help.'

Jo looked at her watch. It was already three; if she went all the way to Saltdean, there was a chance they wouldn't have anything and it would be a waste of an afternoon. And it was unlikely Phillip Price would have accompanied the girls to any doctor's appointments. She needed to know who had been with Holly when she broke her arm, so that she could find out what had happened.

She googled the number and dialled it, but as with every doctor's surgery in the country, she got a busy line. She tried again, twice, until eventually she gave up, and looked on their website for an email address. She quickly bashed out an email entitled 'Sussex Police: URGENT', and made a request for any notes they had on Gemma Smith and Holly Moore, being sure to attach their dates of birth and her full title. Hopefully, by the time she got there, they would have at least read it and started to search their records. She grabbed her car keys, hurtled down the stairs into the hall of her terraced house and pulled open the front door.

It was also weighing on her mind that she needed to find the girl called Eve to whom Gemma had written her good-bye poem. But that could take days, if not weeks. She needed the Morgate House records to get hold of Eve's surname, and any forwarding addresses. But she had no idea if she would still have access to them. Even then, so many kids in care just disappeared – there was every chance she would never be able to track Eve down.

Grabbing her bag from the hall stand, with Holly's and Gemma's files in, she climbed into the car and pulled out onto the seafront. It had been forty years since the night of the fire, since she had driven this exact route along the coast road and received the radio message to attend a violent domestic which had changed her life forever. Her mobile began to ring , pulling her back to the present. She looked down, saw 'Charlie' on the display, and answered it, putting it on loud speaker.

'Hey,' she said, opening the window to let in some sea air.

'Hi, can you talk?'

'Sure. What's up?'

'I've just been to see Mum again, she's really not well.'

Jo's heart sank. 'Please don't make me feel bad. I was there Monday night, and yesterday morning. I've only got a couple more days, Charlie, then I'm out, and I'll have all the time in the world for her.'

'She may not have a couple more days. I'm not trying to make you feel bad, I just don't want you to say you didn't realise how little time she has. And she keeps asking for

332

you. She can't understand why you won't just see her for an hour. And to be honest, I can't either,' he said abruptly.

'Okay,' she said, sighing. 'I'm just going to Saltdean surgery and then I'll come over. Where are you?'

'At the hospice. Why are you going to the surgery, are you okay?'

Jo sighed. 'It's not for me. According to forensics, Holly Moore broke her arm before she died. I need to find out who her chaperone was, but the hospital records don't go back that far.'

Jo glanced to her left; she was approaching Wicker Street, where Holly and Daisy's family home had been before it burned down, the address to which she had been called on that fateful night in December 1975. When she had been a brand-new constable, working her beat. Goosebumps crept up her arms at the memory of it.

She let out another sigh. 'You know, if I'd been busy on another call, I never would have gone to Wicker Street that night. I wouldn't have started that fire, the girls' parents would be alive, they would never have gone to Morgate House, and Holly wouldn't have been murdered. None of this would have happened.'

'Jo!' Charlie snapped. 'I'm trying to be patient here, but it's wearing thin. I know you don't like the woman very much but could you stop using that dead girl as a reason not to visit your dying mother? Just sit here, and hold her hand. You don't have to say anything. Holly Moore has been dead for thirty years, what difference is two more days going to make? Your mother, the woman who gave birth to you, is dying right *now*.'

Charlie ended the call. He had never spoken to her like

that before. The shock of it made tears sting her eyes and she pulled into Wicker Street to catch her breath. The fact was, he was right, she was avoiding going to see her mother. She couldn't handle dealing with her feelings over her death. They'd had a strained relationship all her life, her mother had not been there for her during her toughest years and seemed to always take her ex husband and Megan's side. It felt like at every opportunity she'd let Jo know she was disappointed in her.

Charlie, on the other hand, could do no wrong. She adored him. It was easy for him to be with her, he had a lot to be grateful for. Whereas Jo, well, she didn't know how to feel – or what to think, or say.

Once she started to cry she couldn't stop. She buried her head in her hands, trying to force away the memory of the girls' screams that night as she dragged them from the fire. It was too late, Charlie was right, she couldn't solve this whole case in two days. It was hopeless, she was soon to be retired, with no career to distract her, no husband, no parents, and only a strained relationship with her daughter to show for it. She had let Holly and Daisy down all over again. Slowly, her tears began to subside until she was left with just a throbbing headache. She turned her head, and looked at the street sign next to her. Wicker Street. She could still hear the crackling of her police radio, the voice coming in from the station.

Any unit to attend 42 Wicker Street, Saltdean. Report of a violent domestic by the neighbour . . .

What was the woman's name? She could see her now, scurrying out of her house.

'Jim's been in the pub since lunchtime, he's in a hell of a

temper,' the woman had said, in a state of excitement. 'He woke my kids up as soon as he got home. The walls between our houses are paper thin, and he started shouting at Pippa before he'd even got through the front door.'

Jo had looked at the woman, wrapped in a towelling dressing gown, her long lacy nightie peeping from below it, her hair in old-fashioned curlers.

Jo remembered her now, it was coming back. The woman had been dressed like an old lady, but her skin was youthful and she couldn't have been much older than twenty-five. Maybe she was still there, Jo thought, looking down the road, which she hadn't driven down since that night.

Brook . . . Mrs Brook, that was her name – 'babbling brook' she had said her husband called her.

Jo started the engine and pulled away, desperately trying to drag back fragments of the conversation she'd had with Mrs Brook all that time ago. Something about a new fella sniffing around . . . and the husband had got wind of it.

Was that why the girls' parents had been fighting that night? It was something she had never even thought about since. Someone had been bringing Holly and Gemma's mother food and money, Mrs Brook said. But who?

Jo's heart started beating faster as she reached the site of the old house. The road was entirely different now. Over time, the council houses had gone from run-down squalid shells to well-kept private properties, thanks to Thatcher's Right to Buy scheme. The front gardens, no longer home to bonfires and burnt-out cars, now boasted neatly manicured lawns and flower beds.

Jo stopped the car and stepped out, taking Holly's file with her. She opened it and flicked through, looking at the letter she'd written herself, handing over custody for the girls to Brighton Council that night. Holly and Daisy Moore of 42 Wicker Street. This was definitely the right place.

Where Holly and Daisy's house used to be was now a modern, new-build home. She walked up to get a closer look, and then slowly turned to the house next door, which she recognised immediately. A curtain twitched and fell back into place as soon as she started walking towards it.

The likelihood of Mrs Brook still being here after all this time was pretty slim, but then again, people did stay in houses for a lifetime. Her mother had. Also, Jo felt she was due a bit of luck. So far, since finding Holly's remains, it felt like she had been swimming against a rip tide.

Jo walked up to the front door, reached out and pressed the button, and before it had stopped buzzing, she heard footsteps.

Tapping footsteps, someone in heels. Someone house-proud.

Slowly, the front door opened and a face peered round.

'Yes?' the woman said.

Jo recognised her immediately; bar a few wrinkles, and much less bleach in her hair, she hadn't changed over the years. Jo's heart surged with anticipation.

'Hello, my name is Superintendent Joanna Hamilton, I'm sure you don't remember me but—'

'Oh, you're wrong. I do, I remember you. You were here the night of the fire. Won't you come in?' Mrs Brook said, opening the door wider.

Jo nodded her thanks and stepped over the threshold.

Chapter Twenty-Seven

Daisy

March 2015, Wednesday afternoon

Daisy climbed off her bicycle, which she had ridden from Hassocks station to Lakeview Residential Home, and padlocked it to the bike rack. She took a glug of water, and a few deep breaths, before walking towards reception. She was clutching a bunch of lilies she had picked up en route, and she beamed at the girl warmly.

'Hello, I'm here to see Mrs Lorna Price,' Daisy said purposefully.

'Is she expecting you?' asked the receptionist.

'Not exactly, but I lived in the children's home that she ran, so she knows me. My name is Daisy Moore, I was just passing and wanted to say hello,' Daisy said, as innocently as she could.

'Okay, I'll call up to her room. Take a seat.'

Daisy smiled again, trying not to relay her nerves as the girl picked up the phone. If Mrs Price wouldn't see her now, she wouldn't get another chance to talk to her about Samuel before Olive died.

'She's just about to have her nap, but if you're happy to stay for just a short time, that's fine,' said the girl.

Daisy nodded.

'She's in Room 14, second floor. Stairs are just along the corridor on the left. I'll order you up some tea.'

'Thank you so much,' said Daisy, as her nerves began to creep in. Lakeview was much smarter than the care home where she worked. Mr and Mrs Price had obviously stacked up quite a generous pension from running Morgate House; they certainly hadn't spent any of their income on the children, so it had to have gone somewhere.

As she reached the second floor, her heart began to race. She had no idea what she was going to say. Or how she was going to broach the subject of Olive and Samuel. She hadn't seen Mrs Price since the day she was taken away from Holly at Morgate House, and she realised, from the way she was trembling, that the trauma from that day was still bubbling close to the surface. Daisy walked along the corridor, counting down the numbers to herself, 'Twelve, thirteen, fourteen.'

Finally, she reached Mrs Price's room. Taking a deep breath, she lifted her hand to the door and knocked twice.

'Come in,' said a voice, faintly, from the other side.

Daisy opened the door, peering in to see a woman sitting by the window in an armchair, looking out over the ample grounds. She didn't turn to look at her as Daisy crept into the room. The closer she got, she felt her body tense up. She had a growing sense of panic that she was doing something wrong, and that she was about to get scolded for it, as she always had been as a child whenever Mrs Price came into the main house. There were no warm memories of Morgate to draw on; no kindness had ever been show to Daisy by the woman sitting in the chair by the window. A woman whose job it had been to take care of her and Holly.

Daisy shook her hands out, as if to get rid of the unhappy memories, and forced herself forward. Mrs Price was the one who had failed, she was the one who should be ashamed, and yet, standing here, looking at the back of Mrs Price's head, seeing her distinctive bob – now grey instead of brown – it was Daisy who felt utterly wretched.

'Who is it?' said Mrs Price.

Breathing slowly, Daisy walked over to the window and stood facing the woman as she slowly looked up at her, squinting slightly in the winter sunlight coming in through the glass. Her face was just as it had been back then: spherical, and bloated, her fringe cut too sharply, and a scowl settling on her thin eyebrows.

'I'm Daisy Moore,' she said, looking around for somewhere to sit.

'Daisy?'

'Yes, I'm Holly's sister. We both came to Morgate House after our parents were killed in a fire.'

The woman looked accusingly at her. 'I hope you haven't come bearing grudges,' she said. 'We did our best, Geoff and I. And it wasn't always easy.'

'Actually, I've come to pick your brains. About an old friend of yours. Olive May, you were together at Bletchley Park, I believe,' Daisy said, trying to hide the tremble in her voice.

Mrs Price hadn't invited her to sit down, so Daisy hovered awkwardly next to her chair. She had a way of making you feel uncomfortable, thought Daisy, even in her old age.

'Yes, that's going a long way back,' said Mrs Price. 'I'd say more an acquaintance than a friend.'

Daisy nodded. 'I see. Well, I'm Olive's carer, and in the last couple of days she has been moved to respite care. She doesn't have long, and she has been thinking a lot about a man called Samuel, who I believe she met at Bletchley.'

Mrs Price snorted, and shook her head disapprovingly. 'Well, he did have that effect on all the girls, but it's a pity for her that she never moved on. I did warn her to stay away at the time, but she thought she knew better.'

There was a knock on the door, and a girl in a blue pinafore came in with a tray of tea. 'Here you are, Lorna. I've got a couple of packets of biscuits for you too, and some water for your visitor. You need to keep your fluids up today so it's nice you have a guest. Make sure she drinks plenty of tea,' the girl said merrily to Daisy, as she scurried around happily, laying the tea out.

She probably works her fingers to the bone for Lorna Price, thought Daisy, staying late to make sure she was happy. Just as Daisy did for all her patients. With no clue as to what Mrs Price was really like, and all the suffering she had caused in her lifetime.

'She has always desperately wanted to reach out to Samuel, and try to find him.' Daisy pressed on, as Mrs Price eyed the biscuits. 'And to tell him that he and Olive have a son. I mean, really it's her dying wish. She always felt, if Samuel had known, he would have married her and her life would have been very different.'

Mrs Price let out a loud snort, shaking her head. 'Samuel did know.' She bit into a biscuit greedily, as the crumbs fell from her lips. 'Geoff told him.'

'Why did Geoff tell Samuel that Olive was pregnant? What business was it of his?' Daisy asked, feeling herself burning with anger on behalf of her friend. 'It sounds to me like he was a little too involved – perhaps he had a crush on her?'

Mrs Price's eyes flashed with rage; it was the first time Daisy had ever seen the woman show any emotion. 'Quite the contrary. I suggested he do it. I knew it would be the best way to get rid of him. He was a philanderer and a coward.'

'Some men change when they meet the right woman. That wasn't your decision to make, it wasn't your place to tell him,' Daisy protested.

Mrs Price scoffed again. 'Geoff urged Samuel to do the right thing and marry her. But Samuel wasn't having any of it. And we found out later why – he had a family of his own waiting back in Canada. He was already married. I warned Olive he was a cad, but she went ahead regardless.'

'I see.' Daisy felt her defences rise on Olive's behalf. She was her friend, she was dying, and this cruel, heartless woman was berating Olive for falling in love when she was twenty years old. 'Well, not all of us can cut off our emotions like you, Mrs Price,' snapped Daisy.

Mrs Price turned to Daisy and glared, before finishing her biscuit and continuing. 'Of course she blamed Geoff. She thought that he'd deliberately sent Samuel away without telling him. Because that narrative suited her fragile ego best, I suppose. Less painful than someone not wanting to know you're having their baby. Of course, I always saw him for what he was. He was not a nice man, seducing young girls, abusing his power over them. Clearly, it's in the genes. Like father, like son,' she added, pouring tea into her cup and not offering Daisy any.

Daisy frowned. 'What do you mean, like father, like son? Are you talking about Olive's son, Charlie?'

Lorna shook her head. 'All I know is, if she'd have listened to me, she wouldn't have got herself in trouble. It's very easy to blame the men, but you young girls aren't always the victims you make yourselves out to be. If you showed some restraint and stopped being such temptresses, it would solve a great deal of society's problems.'

Daisy felt her face flush, and she glared at Mrs Price. 'Do you know they've found my sister's remains on the Tye, opposite Morgate? They think she was murdered.'

Mrs Price stopped munching for a second, and froze, staring out of the window at the sunset.

'Do you think she deserved it? That she was a temptress?'

'I told you not to come bearing grudges,' Mrs Price spat.

'Am I not the first, then? Who else has been up here? There were enough of us,' Daisy said, finding the strength from somewhere to continue, the tremble in her voice fading. 'Why did you agree to see me, if you thought I might bear a grudge?'

Daisy frowned, staring at the woman, sitting all alone in her chair.

Slowly, it dawned on her: she had let Daisy up because she had no one. Because she was a lonely old woman, whose husband had died. A woman who hadn't had daughters of her own, and never received any visitors. She was willing to risk a visitor filled with hurt and pain, rather than no visitors at all.

Daisy turned to walk away. 'I won't tell Olive what you told me about Samuel, because I care about her. She's my friend. Something you know nothing about. You and your husband are the reason Holly was walking the streets at night. You are the reason someone was able to pick her up. She was hungry and lonely. I hated that place. We all hated it. It was your job to look after us, and you failed. I'm sorry that you are obviously a very lonely, sad old lady, but quite honestly, Mrs Price, you deserve to be.'

Daisy walked out of the room, down the hallway. She felt the tears coming, but as she rushed outside and gulped in the winter air, she realised that, more than anything, they were tears of relief. She had faced Mrs Price, and the woman no longer had any power over her. There was nothing she could do to hurt her – or Holly – any more.

The train journey back to Brighton passed in a blur, as Daisy sat back in her seat and thought about Holly. For thirty years her every waking moment had been clouded by worry for Holly. She had felt unable to rest, unable to sleep, thinking the worst. That her sister was trapped somewhere, that she was unhappy, that she was trying to find her and couldn't. A sadness that she would never see her sister again still engulfed her, but there had been a shift. The helplessness and frustration were easing; the heavy, crushing weight on her chest was lifting. Older, comforting memories were beginning to creep in; she was starting to remember happier times, in their home, playing with the hose in their front garden, eating sandwiches in the park, watching the sunset at the kitchen window. Holly's smile.

Daisy cycled down to the seafront and looked at her watch. She still had an hour before her shift started, and Olive was weighing heavily on her mind. She knew St Catherine's well – she had been there several times, visiting old patients.

The light was going as she turned left at Rottingdean and cycled along the narrow road through the village, panting hard as it wound uphill. She was grateful for the sea air pumping through her tired legs. On the other side of Rottingdean village she cycled through the gates of St Catherine's and parked her bike outside the main entrance.

343

The receptionist recognised Daisy and waved her through to Olive's room.

Daisy walked in quietly; Olive was asleep and all the blinds were closed. Although she knew it was coming, the change in Olive still startled her, and she felt a stab of emotion. She had an oxygen tube in her nose, and a hospital gown on. The oxygen was hissing quietly as Daisy sat down by the bed and took her hand.

Olive stirred and opened her eyes.

'Hi, Olive, it's Daisy.'

The old lady smiled and tried to say something.

Daisy leaned in.

'I told Charlie that Samuel is his father. He didn't take it well,' Olive said slowly. 'He did everything to try and please my husband, Jack, he followed him into the police. But they never got on. Charlie said he wished he'd known. That Jo was always Jack's favourite. And now he knows why.'

'It's okay, Olive,' Daisy said, stroking her hand. 'You did your best. Charlie will be okay. You need to rest now.' She looked very pale and weak, thought Daisy, in the twelve hours since she had last seen her, the light in her eyes had gone out. Daisy sat for a while, holding Olive's hand. Thinking about Samuel, wishing she had better news. The comment Mrs Price had made about Samuel came back to her suddenly: 'Seducing young girls, abusing his power over them.' And then she'd added, 'Like father, like son.' How did Mrs Price know Olive's son? It made no sense. Perhaps she had been confused. Olive doted on Charlie, and Daisy had seen nothing but kindness from him.

'I don't think I ever did really love Samuel.' Olive turned her head away and began breathing heavily again. 'I think

344

I was just in love with the idea of him. He represented freedom, escape, travel abroad. I think he knew about the baby.
I was just in denial, he wasn't a good person, he wouldn't
have loved me like Jack did. Jack asked me to marry him
before I went to Bletchley, and he still wanted me when I
came back pregnant. I didn't deserve him. I used him as an
excuse, for not having the courage to live my own life. And
Charlie looked so like him. So like him – it made it impossible to forget Samuel.' Olive's voice trembled.

Daisy took Olive's hand. 'You did have courage, Olive.
It must have been so hard to leave Bletchley, after all that
excitement and adventure, and go back to your real life.
You mustn't be too hard on yourself. What you did, everything you achieved, it was extraordinary.'

Olive smiled weakly at her friend. 'Daisy, what happened
to that nice man who used to pick you up from work? Julian?'

Daisy looked up at Olive, taken aback by the question,
tears stinging her eyes. 'We broke up.'

'Why? He was so lovely, he adored you, I could tell. The
way he waited so patiently when you had to work late,
the way he sat and chatted to me when he could have stayed
in the waiting room.'

'He is a lovely man. I miss him. But he wanted a family,
and I've always been scared of becoming a mother.'

'But you'd be the most wonderful mother, look at how
you are with all of us.'

'What if something happened to me, or worse, the baby?
What if they were left all alone in the world? Like I was.'
Daisy bit down on her lip, trying not to cry.

From the depths of her bag, Daisy's mobile phone began
to buzz.

Olive clutched her hand. 'You're not alone. And Holly would hate to think of you putting your life on hold like this.'

Daisy stared at Olive, and wiped away her tears with the back of her hand. The fact was, since she had found out about Holly, the one person she had wanted to run to had been Jules. She had wanted to share her jumbled thoughts with him, her feelings of guilt about the sense of relief, knowing Holly was at peace. But she was scared of where it would lead, of hurting him again.

Daisy's phone persisted and she reached into her bag. She pulled out her mobile. 'Sorry, Olive, I need to answer this.'

The display showed an unknown number and Daisy walked over to the window to answer it.

'Hello?' she said cautiously.

'Hello, is this Daisy?'

'Yes.'

'Oh, hi, my name is Eve. Eve Slade, you left a message for me on Facebook, about your sister Holly.'

'Eve, hi!' said Daisy, her heart lifting as she turned to Olive, who had started to doze off again. 'Thank you so much for calling. It's great to hear from you.'

'No problem. It was good to get your message. I really cared about Holly. I saw on the news last night they may have found her. I'm sorry, this must be a very hard time for you.'

'Yes,' said Daisy quietly. 'It was a bit of a shock, after all these years. They're saying she was murdered,' she added.

'Well, I'm sorry to say I don't find that hard to believe.'

'Really, why?' Daisy asked, walking further away from Olive's bed, so as not to disturb her. She opened the window slightly to let some air in; despite the freezing

346

temperature, the spike of adrenaline from talking to Eve was heating her up from the inside out.

'Holly was seeing someone. He used to prey on girls at Morgate House, girls who were vulnerable. He would buy them food, give them money, and make them fall in love with him so he could use them. Holly was seeing him when she disappeared, but she wasn't the first . . .' Eve paused.

'Are you okay?' asked Daisy, frowning.

'Yes, it's strange talking about this. I just ran away when Holly went missing, I was scared he would come after me. It was the same man who killed Gemma.'

'Gemma?'

'Yes, my friend Gemma Smith, she took me under her wing and looked after me. I went to Morgate very young. They said she killed herself, but she didn't. She was meeting him, and I know it's the same man who Holly was seeing because Gemma had his payslip in her things, and Holly said it was him.'

'It wasn't Phillip Price, then?' Daisy asked.

'God, no, he was a creep, Gemma and Holly both hated him. He knew both girls were seeing this guy and I suspect he helped to cover it up. And I think Mrs Price did too. I think they wanted Gemma's death to look like suicide, because otherwise there would have been a shitstorm and it might have closed Morgate House.'

'So do you remember his name?' asked Daisy, realising her hands were shaking.

'Yes, hold on. I've still got the payslip here somewhere. I kept it just in case one day I needed proof.'

As Eve went quiet on the other end of the line, the door to Olive's room opened, startling Daisy. As she looked over,

347

still holding the phone to her ear, Olive's son walked into the room. He saw her immediately, standing by the window.

'Hello, Charlie,' Daisy said immediately. 'I just wanted to see how Olive was, I won't stay.' He looked downcast, thought Daisy, as he put his bag on the floor next to his mother's bed and frowned at her.

'Hello, are you still there?' Eve said.

'Yes, I'm here,' said Daisy, smiling awkwardly at Charlie, who was placing grapes and a bottle of water on the table in front of his mother.

'I've got it here. The payslip.'

Daisy flushed red, slightly distracted, embarrassed that she was in Charlie's mother's room, on her phone, making herself at home.

'His name is Charlie.'

'Sorry, what?' asked Daisy, as the line cut out for a moment.

Suddenly, Olive's monitor burst into life, and an alarm went off by her bed. Daisy moved out of the way, and put one finger in her ear so that she could hear better.

'The man, the policeman who was seeing Gemma and Holly when they disappeared. His name was Charlie. Charlie Hamilton,' said Eve.

Daisy frowned in confusion, then looked up and stared over at Charlie, who was staring right back at her.

Daisy froze. She felt her whole face burn as he locked eyes with her. She was paralysed, her mind thrown into a complete spin. Finally she spoke. 'Okay, Eve, thank you for calling. I'll call you back in a bit if that's okay.' Her whole body started to shake as two nurses rushed into the room and began desperately working to save Olive's life.

Chapter Twenty-Eight

Jo

March 2015, Wednesday afternoon

Jo looked round Mrs Brook's living room, and smiled up at her as she brought in a tray of tea.

'This is very kind of you, you didn't need to go to so much trouble.'

'It's no trouble. All my babies have up and left, they're very good to their old mum, but it's nice to have company,' she said, taking the fine bone-china teacups off the tray, and pouring Jo a cup from the pot. 'Sugar?' she asked, peering at Jo eagerly as she held a sugar cube in silver tongs over Jo's cup.

'No, thank you,' said Jo quietly, scanning the room.

The woman was pouring tea from a teapot in the shape of a thatched cottage, and there were several others like it in a display cabinet on the wall. The room was very busy, with lots of flowery cushions, throws and vases, as well as countless gold-framed pictures of school-aged children posing for the camera.

'I've thought of you often,' Mrs Brook added, perching on the edge of an armchair, with her legs crossed. 'That fire stayed with me for a long time, it was so dreadful, Pip dying like that. What happened – I mean, how did the fire start? I presume it was that pig she was married to.'

Jo hesitated, she had never really spoken to anyone about

that night. The police didn't have any kind of counselling service in those days, and so it had just been buried, presumed forgotten.

'No, it's wasn't the husband, it was me,' said Jo. 'It was an accident, I knocked over an ashtray trying to get in.'

Mrs Brook glared at her, eyes wide. She looked like a woman who took a great deal of pride in her appearance, Jo thought. She hadn't known Jo was coming, and yet she was fully made up, her hair was styled. And her house was immaculate and smelt of air freshener, masking a faint hint of cigarette smoke.

'That must have been terrible for you to live with,' she said. 'I know you were trying to save those girls. What happened to them?'

'I had to place them at Morgate House children's home. I didn't want to,' Jo said quietly, 'but there was no one else who could take them. I even considered taking them in myself at the time, but we didn't have the room and I was pregnant, although I didn't know it then.'

'You mustn't blame yourself. I always said he'd kill her one day. They would have ended up at Morgate, sooner or later. I saw about Holly on the news. It's dreadful. How's Daisy doing?'

'She's had a rough time,' said Jo, sipping gratefully at her tea. 'She doesn't trust the police, so she's struggling to open up to us, but we will get there.'

'I'm not surprised, I was always having to call the police out when her parents were fighting. He'd come back in a terrible rage and start on her.'

'I was wondering what it was they were arguing about, the night of the fire. It's so many years ago now, but I remembered you saying something about the husband being jealous. About another man, bringing round food and money?' Jo prompted.

'Yes, it was that policeman who started coming round. He'd bring her stuff, I suppose to try and help. But it just made things worse, because whenever Jim found out he got so jealous. But Pip was never unfaithful, she was very loyal.'

'Policeman? How do you know it was a policeman?'

'Because he was one of the response units that turned up one night. He came back the next day, with two bags of groceries, and some toys for the girls. Pip actually made him take most of them away again, because she said her husband would be suspicious.'

'I see,' said Jo, reaching for her bag and pulling out her file. If she could get this woman to ID Phillip Price, Carl wouldn't be able to ignore it.

'Do you mind if I smoke?' said the woman, lighting up before Jo could answer. 'It got to the point where she was very stressed if he was coming round. She kept asking him not to come, because Jim always seemed to know. But he was very persistent, he started making her promises that he could protect her and the girls, so she gave in. She desperately wanted a new life for them.'

Jo pulled out the file on Daisy and Holly and placed it on the table next to her bag. The woman reached over for her ashtray, tipping Jo's bag off and spilling its contents.

'I'm so sorry,' said Mrs Brook, helping to pick up Jo's belongings, and lifting up the picture of Jo at her graduation ceremony.

Mrs Brook stared at the photograph as Jo took it off her and handed her one of Phillip Price.

'I know it's been a while. But do you think that could have been the policeman you mentioned?' Jo laid the other pictures down on the coffee table.

Mrs Brook took the photograph of Phillip and stared at it, taking a deep drag of her cigarette. 'No, that's not him. He was a big fella, broad shoulders, dark floppy hair, blue eyes. I remember his piercing eyes.'

Jo looked at her, and felt her heart rate quicken. She watched, as if in slow motion, as Mrs Brook reached out her hand and pointed at one of the photographs on the table. 'That's him, that's the fella.'

Jo suddenly felt a bolt of fear flood through her. Almost scared to look, she slowly turned her head towards where the woman was pointing. There, as clear as day, was a picture of her and Charlie at Jo's graduation ceremony.

'I don't understand, what do you mean?' asked Jo, her mind scrambling, unable to take in what the woman was saying.

Mrs Brook pointed at Charlie again, at a photo of him with his arms around Jo, smiling proudly. 'That's him, the guy who was bothering her. I remember, because he was so good-looking.'

Jo looked at her, the room was suddenly very stuffy, all the flowery furniture and air freshener not so quaint any longer. 'You must be mistaken,' she said abruptly.

The woman's face fell. 'If you don't want to listen to me, why are you here? You police are all the same, you always stick together.'

'I'm sorry, it's just . . . it's such a long time ago, are you sure?'

The woman nodded, picking up the photograph and then placing it back down again.

Jo's head started to spin as she tried to stand up. 'Can I use your bathroom, please?'

'Yes, by the front door, on your right,' said Mrs Brook, rather taken aback.

Jo rushed down the hall and stood over the sink, turning on the cold tap and splashing her face with water. There must be some mistake, there would be an explanation. She would talk to Charlie, and he would have a reason. Jo stood, staring at her face in the mirror. Why would Charlie have been hassling Daisy and Holly's mother? He was completely professional, he always had been. It made no sense.

Jo sat on the toilet, trying to calm herself down as she heard her mobile phone ringing in her pocket. She lifted it out and looked at it; it was a withheld number.

She put the phone to her ear. 'Hello,' she said quietly.

'Is that Superintendent Joanna Hamilton?'

'Yes.'

'It's Jane here, from St Luke's Surgery. We got your email. We are pretty busy here today,' she quipped, 'but we've managed to find some records for both girls. Did you want to collect them?'

'Um, yes, I will. Is there much in them?' Jo could hear Mrs Brook crashing around the kitchen, clearing up the tea things.

'No, the last entry for Gemma Smith was in October 1975. She came in for a pregnancy test, which was positive. Other than that, there's nothing except some antibiotics for an ear infection.'

Jo felt the bile rising in her throat at the news of Gemma's pregnancy. 'I see. And Holly?'

'Holly, I'm afraid we don't have any doctor's records, but we were able to find her hospital notes, as it was ten years later.'

Jo was shaking so much she could hardly hold her phone. 'Are they signed by anyone, a chaperone? She would have been accompanied, as she was only seventeen.'

'Um, let me see.' Jo held her breath, suddenly dreading what the woman was about to find. 'Yes, it looks like a . . . C. Hamilton,' said the receptionist, 'but do come and get them. We close soon, though, so maybe in the morning.'

Jo couldn't speak to finish the call, the room started to spin and she put her hand on the wall to stop it. Images of Charlie over the last forty-eight hours flashed in her head. Turning up at the station to talk to her about the body on the Tye, asking her questions, dissuading her endlessly from pursuing the case. Is this why Carl had tried to keep her at arm's length? Was it true what Phillip Price was saying, that he was trying to protect her? Did everyone know? She couldn't take it in, it was too much, her body was shaking so violently that her stomach started to heave, she lifted up the toilet seat and threw up into the bowl.

Charlie? Charlie killed Holly and Gemma. It couldn't be true. It was impossible. She sank to the floor and buried her head in her hands, still wretching from the spasms in her gut.

She couldn't cry, she couldn't feel anything, she tried to stand but she couldn't move. Her legs had completely given way. Mrs Brook started frantically knocking on the door.

'Are you okay in there?' Mrs Brook said, knocking harder. Jo willed her to go away, to take back what she had

354

just told her about Charlie. To go back in time and not have come to this house.

Using the sink to pull herself up, she stared at herself in the mirror. She looked terrible. She wiped her mouth and rinsed it with cold water, then flushed the toilet again. Finally, she opened the door, to Mrs Brook looking very alarmed.

'Thank you so much for your help. I'm sorry, I have to go, but I really appreciate your time,' said Jo, rushing past her to get her bag.

'Were you sick in there?' said Mrs Brook, outraged. 'What's the matter with you? Are you ill?' She followed Jo out onto the street.

'I'm fine, Mrs Brook, thank you for your help,' she said, wishing the woman would go away and leave her alone.

'Charming!' the woman said finally, before turning around and slamming the front door behind her.

Jo's thoughts immediately turned to the photograph she had sent to Mr Haig, Gemma's teacher, the day before. She couldn't just rely on Mrs Brook, maybe this was all a huge mistake. Just because Charlie had been in Holly and Daisy's house the night of the fire, didn't mean he was a killer. She frantically scrolled through her phone until she found the number of Holly's teacher from the previous day.

'Hello?'

'Hello, Mr Haig, I'm so sorry to call again.' Jo's voice was weak and shaking. 'That photograph I sent you earlier. There were two men in it. Which one came to visit you, about Gemma? Was it the smaller one, with black hair?' Jo said hopefully.

'No,' he said firmly, 'it was definitely the taller one. Why?'

355

Jo rushed away from the house, she needed to talk to Charlie. She needed to give her beloved brother a chance to defend himself. Her hands shaking, she began frantically scrolling through her phone until she found her brother's number. She had no idea what she was going to say, but she needed to know where he was. She needed to see him, to speak to him. It rang and rang, until eventually it cut out.

Almost immediately, her thoughts turned to Daisy. Where was she? Was she in danger? She tried Daisy's number – no answer. Jo left a message.

She dashed to her car and started the engine as Mrs Brook peeked through the lace curtain at her. Scrolling through the contacts on her phone, she found Chief Superintendent Carl Webber's number and called him.

'Carl, it's Jo.' She took a deep breath. 'I think my brother was involved with these girls.'

There was a long silence before he spoke.

'We know, Jo. I've regarded your brother as a suspect for some time,' Carl said. 'That's why we were trying to protect you from the investigation. But we're struggling to prove it,' he added.

'For God's sake, Carl! You should have told me! You've put Holly's sister Daisy in danger. If anything happens to her, I'll never forgive you.'

'We couldn't tell anyone, we had no proof, Jo,' said Carl.

'Well, I have proof. And it's not me who needs protecting,' snapped Jo. 'I can't get hold of Charlie – or Daisy. We need to find her, now. Can you track her phone?'

'I'll do everything I can,' said Carl. 'I'll call you straight back.'

Jo ended the call and slammed the gear stick into first.

356

She needed to get to Daisy – she couldn't let Holly's little sister die. As she drove towards the seafront, her mobile rang again.

'Yes?' said Jo, answering on speaker phone.

'Is that Joanna Hamilton?'

'Yes. Who's calling?'

'It's St Catherine's Hospice, in Rottingdean. I'm sorry to say that we think your mother has had a stroke. Would it be possible for you to get here in the next hour?'

'Oh God, please not now,' Jo said, slamming her fist on the steering wheel. 'Thank you for letting me know. I'm on my way. Is my brother Charlie there?'

'Yes, I believe so. And she has another visitor with her, a Daisy Moore.'

'What?! Why is Daisy Moore there?'

'Because she's your mother's former carer, I believe.'

'Jesus Christ!' exclaimed Jo. 'Can you ask Daisy to ring me urgently? I can't get hold of her. I need to speak to her now. Please tell her I'm on my way,' Jo said before ending the call.

'No, no, no, no,' shouted Jo, turning right onto the seafront, and pressing down hard on the accelerator.

Chapter Twenty-Nine

Daisy

March 2015, Wednesday evening

Daisy stood at the window of Olive's room as the nurses rushed round her, administering oxygen and a sedative, until her breathing slowly began to stabilise.

'I don't understand, she was okay. It's not her time yet.'

'We think she's had a stroke, Daisy, they can often happen very suddenly. The doctor is on his way.'

Daisy looked over at Olive tearfully. She had seen this so many times before. Olive's body was giving up; her heart couldn't fight any more, she was getting ready to leave this world.

Daisy looked at the floor, her breath quickening. She was still reeling from the conversation with Eve, she couldn't take it in. Charlie Hamilton. The name of the man who was seeing her sister was Charlie Hamilton.

She daren't look at Charlie, but she knew he was watching her. Silently.

There was an urgent knock on the door, making her jump, and the receptionist walked in. 'Daisy, we've spoken to Olive's daughter. She's on her way. She's asked if you can call her urgently, on her mobile.'

'Olive's daughter?' said Daisy. 'I've never met her. I don't know her number.' She frowned over at Charlie, feeling herself flushing red.

'I think you do,' he said. 'She's heading up the investigation into your sister's death.'

Daisy stared back at him, her heart hammering in her chest. Jo was Olive's daughter?

Daisy clutched her phone tight in her hand, and looked up to see Charlie watching her with a look on his face she had never seen before. He didn't move or blink; his eyes had turned to stone. Waiting for her next move. Slowly, she bent down and picked her rucksack up from the floor and put it over her shoulder. She hung her head, desperate to disappear, to be at home, to be at the police station. To be anywhere but here, in this room, with the man who had killed her sister.

She glanced up, barely able to breathe. He was ignoring the nurses, ignoring his mother as the nurses settled her, staring fixedly at Daisy as she crossed the room, with her phone in her hand.

Daisy said nothing to him as she passed the end of Olive's bed. The sounds of the room were overwhelming, the heat from the radiator, the beeping machines, too many people crowding round Olive's bed, fighting to keep Olive alive. She was suffocating under the pressure. He stood in her way as she tried to reach the door.

'Excuse me,' she said, her hands shaking as her phone began to ring. She looked down. 'Jo Police' flashed on the display.

Charlie could see her phone screen, he read the display, glaring at her before slowly moving aside. Daisy watched as he walked over to his mother and kissed her on the forehead. Daisy fumbled with the handle and opened the door, walking out into the corridor.

'Mr Hamilton, your mother doesn't have long, I'm

afraid, her heart is not pumping strongly enough to get the oxygen she needs to her brain.'

Daisy heard the nurse's words as she dashed down the corridor, looking behind her to check Charlie wasn't following her. She walked through the sliding doors and out into the night, before finally answering her ringing mobile and pressing it to her ear.

'Daisy, it's Jo—'

'I think your brother might have something to do with Holly's death,' Daisy said, panicked.

'I know,' Jo said. 'We're on our way to pick him up now. I'm so sorry to have put you in this situation. I had no idea you were looking after my mother. I had no idea about my brother. Stay where you are. I'll be there in five minutes, I'm on my way to the hospice.'

'Olive's dying,' said Daisy, shaking violently and starting to cry. 'You have to come and see her.'

'I know, I'm coming. Just stay inside, where people can see you. I'm on the coast road, I'll be there in five minutes. There's a unit on its way to you.'

'Okay,' said Daisy, looking back at the hospice as she ended the call.

All her instincts were telling her not to go back in. Her whole body was shaking violently. All this time she had been sharing a room with the man who had killed her sister. She couldn't see him, she would be sick.

Daisy clutched her phone, starting to pace. 'Come on, come on,' she said, looking out at the road. There was no one sitting at the reception desk. It was after six o'clock, and the receptionist had probably gone home for the day. It was dark now and quiet. She was alone.

Everyone was tending to Olive. She wanted desperately to be there with her, to hold her hand, and she couldn't. She couldn't bear to be close to him, she felt physically sick. Her head was filled with images of all the times when she had sat in a room next to him, plagued with thoughts of her sister's death. Frantically she rummaged in her bag for the keys to her bicycle lock. She needed to get away from here. She needed to get away as fast as she could.

Suddenly, Charlie appeared in the corridor, walking towards her purposefully. She looked at him, her body flooding with adrenaline. She glanced out to the main road, walking over to her bicycle for comfort. Jo would be here any second; if she cycled to the main road she would meet her. She started to cry, fear and panic intertwined like rope. Daisy undid her lock as Charlie got closer.

'Stay away from me!' she shouted, her voice breaking with stress.

Charlie said nothing, but his eyes locked on her as he got into his car.

Daisy climbed on her bike and began pedalling furiously towards the road. She was nearly there, she thought. *Jo will be here any second, just hang on, just hang on.*

For a few seconds, all was silent. All she could hear was her panicked breathing as she pounded desperately on the pedals.

Then, out of nowhere, he was there, in his black BMW, accelerating past her, around the front of her bicycle, and then suddenly turning in, and slamming on his brakes.

As though in slow motion, she hit his bonnet, and her body was propelled over the front of his car, slamming into the road beyond. For a moment, she lay motionless; she hadn't had time to put her helmet on, her neck was scream-ing with pain, and she could feel liquid pouring into one eye. She tried to get up, heard the sounds of him moving, the car door opening, his footsteps on the ground next to her. She felt herself being pulled up, dragged towards the back of his car; her body was in shock, she was paralysed from the force of the crash; he was strong, like a bear, and compared to him she was small. It was nothing for him to lift her, throw her into the back of his car. She hit the cold leather seat with a thud, and the pain shot through her neck, head and legs.

She tried to kick him, tried to move, tried to sit up, but she was dizzy, disoriented, and he was fast. *Surely Jo will see him when he drives away, please see us. Please be here.* She was pleading out loud as she heard his shoes tapping, the door slamming and the engine revving.

Then they were moving. There was a crunch as he drove over her bicycle and screeched out onto the main raid.

Her whole body screamed in pain. She could feel blood trickling down the side of her face. She didn't know where they were going. 'Please, please,' she said, over and over. She wanted to live, she wanted to live so badly, for her and Holly. She couldn't let this man take her life too, she couldn't. She thought of Holly, of how scared she must have been. How alone she must have felt. Where were they going? Was he taking her up to the Tye, was he going to bury her in a shallow grave too? Daisy started to cry. She was feeling what Holly had felt before her death.

Suddenly, they turned off the road. Daisy felt the ground change, as the car struggled along bumpy terrain, pebbles spat up, hitting the side of the car. She knew instantly where they were; he was taking her to Morgate.

The car stopped, and he jumped out, opening the boot and rummaging around. *You have to get out, you have to move. Now!* The words exploded inside her head, as she pulled at the door locks that wouldn't open. She kicked the door, but she knew it was futile. She had hurt one of her legs in the crash, pain was splintering up her knee, she didn't even know if she could walk.

'Get out!' he ordered, opening the back door of his car.

She half fell out, and he pulled her up. She was dizzy, the pain in her head was excruciating, and nausea overtook her. She bent over, vomit and bile pouring out of her mouth onto his black polished shoes.

'Walk!' he shouted into her face.

'Fuck you!' she screamed as she dug her nails into his arm. But his fingers only gripped tighter, bruising her wrist, as he dragged her along the path towards Morgate. Every step, the pain screamed through her legs, her back, her arms. She tried to lash out, tried to pull away, tried to scream. But he was so strong, so much bigger than her. Every second, she thought of Holly, how her sister had been through this. How she couldn't let this monster win.

They reached the metal gates in the fence surrounding Morgate, and he reached out his foot and kicked the spot where she had broken the padlock, only days earlier, flinging the gate open.

'Let me go!' she yelled.

They were inside now, the walls as cold and hostile as they had always been. Her legs gave way as he dragged her through the corridor she had walked a thousand times as a child, broken splinters of wood digging into her injured legs. Then he stopped, panting, taking the rope which was hanging over his shoulder and stooping to tie her hands together.

'Stop! No!' She lashed out, kicking him hard under his chin so that for a second he lost his balance and fell backwards.

Desperately, she tried to get up. Her legs were red now from the blood pouring from her gashed knees where she had fallen. The pain shot through her as she limped agonisingly back down the corridor, and he came running after her, dragging her back by her hair and slapping her face. He pulled her backwards, harder now, forcing her to the ground, where she cowered against the door frame of the dormitory.

Daisy buried her head in her knees and cried, 'I hate you! You killed my sister. You took everything from me!'

'No! She took everything from me!' he boomed, shouting into her face. 'I wanted to help her. Just like I wanted to help your mother, and Gemma. But it wasn't good enough. Holly had to go digging around in the past. Why can't people ever show any loyalty? I was never enough for my father, I was never enough for my wife.'

Daisy stared up at him, every piece of her skin burned, and her head was spinning. She looked around for a way out but she was too broken to run. He would just catch her and pull her back.

'I didn't want to kill Gemma, I never planned it, but she pushed me too far. I would have given her money, I would have supported her, but she had to talk about telling my wife,' he said, glaring at Daisy. 'And then your sister found out. I never wanted to hurt her, but she forced my hand. If I hadn't rescued your sister from the fire that night, none of this would ever have happened. We should never have got out, we should all have died.'

Charlie stood her up, and dragged her into the dormitory, pushing her forward so she collapsed in agony on the bare stone floor. Every cell in her body hurt from the crash. There was nothing she could do. Nobody would find them here before it was too late. She sobbed, begging for her life, as the blood from her head wound continued to pour.

For a moment, it was silent, the only sound her own terrified breathing.

As she cried, she heard the roaring of the ocean outside as it started to rain. And then she smelt it. The strong pungent stench of petrol.

She looked around desperately in the dark, realising she was all alone. Realising he was gone. And then, from behind her, she saw a flicker of light from the corner of the room, and as she turned in horror towards it, she felt the heat.

Chapter Thirty

Jo

March 2015, Wednesday evening

Jo screeched up to the entrance of St Catherine's Hospice and climbed out of her Mini, running towards the sliding doors.

'Daisy!' Jo called out, looking around her desperately. She ran down the corridor, calling out Daisy's name.

Finally a nurse came out. 'Can I help you?' she said, frowning at Jo.

'My name is Superintendent Jo Hamilton,' said Jo, pulling out her badge. 'I'm looking for Charlie Hamilton, he was here with my mother, Olive, and a woman called Daisy Moore.'

'Your mother is here, she's in Room Five, shall I take you down?' asked the nurse.

'No, I need to find Daisy as a matter of urgency, the woman who was with my mother. Is she here?'

'No, your brother and Daisy left, not long ago.'

'Do you know where they went?'

'I'm sorry, they didn't say. I don't understand, do you not want to see your mother?' said the nurse, staring at her in bafflement.

Jo rushed back into reception, and out into the night. 'Daisy? Daisy!' she called out, running around the car park, looking for Charlie's car.

She looked out onto the main road, and jogged towards it, retracing Daisy's steps, all the while calling out her name.

She looked around desperately. Daisy had vanished, everywhere was cloaked in darkness. Then something glimmered in the moonlight, a silver handlebar, thrown aside. She rushed over to it, and looked down at Daisy's mangled bicycle lying on the ground.

'Oh, Charlie, no,' Jo mumbled to herself, pulling her mobile from her pocket and calling Carl.

His phone rang endlessly, then finally he answered.

'He's got her, Carl, he's got Daisy. Have you tracked her mobile?'

'Not yet, we're working on it.'

'Jesus Christ, hurry!' Jo shouted, ending the call. She rushed back to her car and started the engine, slamming it into gear and pulling out onto the seafront. 'Where are you, Daisy, where are you?'

As she overtook several cars on the coast road, Morgate House came into sight, and then suddenly she saw it. A flicker of light on the ground floor. Jo slammed on her brakes, as the car behind her sounded its horn in protest, and she turned into the driveway. The car rolled across the uneven ground and narrowly avoided the fence running around the perimeter of the house.

The smoke was clear to see now, drifting out from the front of the house. Jo looked over to see Charlie's car, parked not ten feet away, with all the doors open. She rushed over to it. 'Daisy? Daisy!' she called, popping the boot and checking inside, before looking over to the house in horror.

She pulled out her mobile and called the fire brigade as

she ran frantically round the perimeter, looking for a gap in the fence. She stared up at the house in the moonlight, a mere shell of the one she had dropped the girls at, that fateful night. It was raining now, but the smell of smoke was undeniable.

'Daisy,' she cried out in desperation, putting her fingers through the mesh of the fence and shaking it with frustration. 'Hold on, I'm coming.'

There was no sign of Charlie anywhere, they must both be inside together.

It was dark as she tried desperately to find the gap in the fence Daisy had made only days before. She kicked at it frantically, making her way round the bolted-together sections, until one finally gave way. She looked down at the ground to see a broken padlock and enough space to push her body through.

'Daisy, hold on, I'm coming,' she cried out, running towards the house and launching herself through what was left of the annex door.

Despite the lack of glass in the windows, and the holes in the roof, the house was already filling with smoke. Her body throbbing with fear, Jo began to cough, as the smoke crept up the walls and along the floor like coiling serpents. The night of the fire at Holly and Daisy's house came flooding back to her in vivid flashes of memory, the panic of being trapped, the feeling of being enveloped by something that was unstoppable. It had spread so fast, within seconds, she had been surrounded.

Jo pulled off her shirt and wrapped it round her head, pushing on down the long corridor, yelling out Daisy's name.

'Daisy, where are you?' she shouted helplessly.

Had Charlie killed her already? Where was she?

Jo looked behind her. The smoke had completely filled the hallway now, there was no way out.

'I'm in here!' Daisy's voice was faint.

Jo stumbled on. She was starting to get dizzy from the smoke. The corridor was endless, with scores of rooms and doors leading off it, any one of which might hold Daisy.

'Daisy!' Her voice was cracking, the smoke invading her lungs.

'I'm in here!' Daisy's voice was louder now, clearer.

'Daisy, follow my voice, we have to get out of here right now!'

Jo could see the lights from the fire engine through the thick smoke, and hear the sound of men's voices as they rushed around outside. The heat was starting to intensify; she felt like she was at a fireworks display on a cold November night, too near the bonfire. She was frozen with fear as a huge piece of timber crashed down in front of her, splintering into pieces which dug into her leg like scalding shrapnel, sending shockwaves of pain up her whole body.

'Daisy, hurry!' Jo croaked, trying to raise her voice.

'I'm here, please help me,' came the hoarse reply.

Jo reached out her arms, desperately feeling her way in the darkness. The smoke was getting thicker, making it harder for her to see. She was coughing so much it was hurting her lungs. She touched the brick wall next to her, and could feel the building warming up from the heat.

'Daisy, where are you—' she shouted, her words cut off by a spasm of coughing. Once she started, she couldn't stop. She knew she was going to lose consciousness soon. She had seconds to get them out, before it was too late for both of them. Suddenly, she felt a hand, and she grabbed it, pulling at Daisy's arm, dragging her back into the corridor, groping for a way out.

'Where is he?' Daisy said weakly.

'I don't know. We need to move now. I've got you, I'm going to get you out.'

Jo coughed, pulling Daisy along the hallway. She was finding it hard to walk, the lack of oxygen draining her body of its ability to function. She tried to hold Daisy up, but her arms were weak.

'Daisy, can you walk?' Daisy's body slumped into her, as Jo frantically tried to keep her upright, coughing violently. Daisy's body was too heavy, the smoke was too strong, she could barely drag herself, let alone another human being.

She fought so hard for air, but there was none, and she could no longer see – there was no way out. She got down on the floor, she couldn't breathe, she couldn't move.

As she began to lose consciousness, she sensed someone's arms around her torso, felt her body being lifted and dragged back along the corridor. The smoke began to lessen as they reached fresh air, and she looked up to see a window. As she gulped in the air, she held her face up towards the cold night sky and felt the spray from the water hoses raining down on her.

'Charlie,' said Jo, reaching out for his arm. And in the darkness she felt his hand, reaching out for hers. 'Charlie, please get Daisy out.' Her voice was hoarse from the smoke. 'This isn't her fault. I wasn't a good enough sister to you. I should have seen how much pain you were in. I've let you down,' she said, starting to cry. Clutching his hand, tighter and tighter, until she felt herself being lifted up again, sensing her brother's bear-like grip around her. Memories flooded her foggy mind of them as kids, him lifting her up into trees so she could climb higher with him, holding her hand as they laid tracks with sticks in the wood. Pushing her small frame behind his to protect her from the school bully.

'I love you,' she said quietly, as he lowered her onto the wet grass outside Morgate.

'I'm sorry,' Jo mumbled as she lay in the grass and looked up at the sky as two firemen rushed over to her, and began lifting her up. She put her arms around their shoulders, barely able to move her feet as they lifted her and walked her away from Morgate House.

'There's someone else in there.' Jo began to cry as the smell of burning increased with the sound of timbers exploding behind her. Slowly, they lifted her onto a trolley and put a mask over her face.

'There's a woman inside,' she said through her mask as she felt a needle go into her arm. Her eyes were stinging, her lungs felt as if they were burning. She tried to pull the mask off, to tell the firefighters to get Daisy and Charlie out. But her arms were too weak. Slowly, she turned her head towards Morgate, to see two firemen walking away from the burning building holding Daisy's unconscious body.

'It's okay, she's out. They've got her,' the paramedic reassured her, as Jo took deep gulps of the oxygen.

'Charlie,' she said quietly, watching the flames lick up every surface of the derelict house. Her brother, her champion, her friend, her mentor – was inside Morgate House as it burned.

Chapter Thirty-One
Megan & Jo

March 2015, Thursday morning

Jo walked in through the doors of St Catherine's Hospice and smiled at the girl behind reception. She still hurt everywhere; her lungs ached from breathing in so much smoke and the hospital had wanted to keep her in overnight for observation, but she needed to be here. She needed to say goodbye.

'I'm here to see my mother, Olive May,' she said, as the girl looked down the list on her desk.

'Of course, she's in Room Five, just along the corridor. Her granddaughter is in there already.'

'Thank you,' said Jo, looking up ahead of her and summoning up the energy to push herself forward. The news that Daisy was doing well, and was out of ICU, had been more of a relief than she had ever felt in her life.

But she still couldn't take in the enormity of what had happened in the last twelve hours, and the fact that Charlie was dead. It had been her life's mission, for as long as she could remember, to know what had happened to Gemma Smith and Holly Moore, and now she knew, she would give anything to un-know.

Jo reached Room Five, and took a deep breath. She had already spoken to her mother's doctor, an hour before, who had told her that her mother didn't have long – hours, he suspected.

Olive's heartbeat and circulation had slowed down, so that her brain and organs were receiving less oxygen and were slowly shutting down. The doctor said she was losing control of her breathing, but that she was calm and had nothing to be frightened of. She wasn't in pain, she was on a morphine drip, which was constantly topping her system up, ensuring she didn't suffer at all.

Jo knocked gently on the door and entered. The room was dark, and her mother lay on the bed, asleep. She had an oxygen tube coming out of her nose, and a cannula in her hand. Other than that, she just looked like she was sleeping. A nurse stood on the far side of the bed, taking her mother's blood pressure, which made her mother stir.

Megan sat by her grandmother's bed; she looked like she had been crying all night. She adored Charlie as much as Jo. She stood up and walked over to Jo and flung herself into her arms. It had been a long time since her daughter had sought her comfort, and, strangely, it felt good to be needed by her.

'Hello,' said Jo quietly to the nurse tending to her mother.

'Hello,' said the nurse cheerfully.

Jo always admired people who worked in places like this; they were always so positive and happy, saying that it was an honour to care for people in their last days, and that hospices were places that celebrated life. But standing at the door of her mother's room, Jo wished she could be any-where but there.

'I'm done,' the nurse said, as Jo let go of Megan's hand and walked over to her mother's bedside. 'She's just dozing.'

'Oh, right, thank you,' said Jo, lowering herself down gently into the chair next to her mother's bed as Megan hovered nearby. She looked up at Olive's face, her grey hair was down, flowing around her shoulders. She looked peaceful, happy almost. Jo felt a stab of sadness suddenly. They'd had such a difficult relationship. Why hadn't they tried harder?

On the bed next to Olive was a leather-bound notebook she had never seen before. Jo reached out and opened the first page; inside was a black-and-white photograph of her mother as a young girl, in khakis and her trademark silk scarf, standing next to a tall handsome man in a flying jacket. Jo stared hard at the man, who looked so much like Charlie that it made her stomach flip. She turned the photograph over and looked at the back: 'Bletchley Park – 1944'.

Jo felt the book slipping and tried to grab it as it fell, scattering its contents everywhere. A dozen newspaper cuttings littered the floor and Jo reached out to pick one of them up, realising it had a picture of her on it. 'Hero PC rescues child from household blaze.' It was dated 1975, and it was the night of the fire. She remembered the journalist coming to interview her, she had felt sick the entire time. She was anything but a hero.

Tears stung her eyes now as her mother reached out her hand and took hers.

Jo scanned the floor. Every mention of her in the local paper – every commendation or event she had attended – her mother had cut out and saved. The shock of seeing her mother's pride in black and white took her breath away. Why had Olive never told her how much she cared? Why had she always been so critical of her, if she was so proud?

'I never knew you had these, Mum,' said Jo, as Megan bent down and helped to pick them up.

Megan began to read the cluster of articles dedicated to her mother.

Olive opened her eyes slowly and looked around the room, then turned to her daughter. She examined Jo's face for a while, then smiled. 'You came.'

'I'm sorry, I got held up,' Jo said, her voice shaking, unable to stop the tears. The emotion of the past few hours was spilling out of her. She didn't want to talk about Charlie, but she couldn't prevent her grief taking over her. She didn't know how or what to feel. She was still in shock.

Olive held out her other hand to Jo, and she took it. 'I'm sorry I wasn't a better mother to you, Jo. I just felt like a bird whose wings had been clipped for most of my life.' Olive struggled to catch her breath. 'I was angry a lot of the time. And jealous of your independence. I'm so proud of you, I wish I was brave like you. I'm a coward,' Olive said quietly.

Megan reached out and put her hand on her mother's shoulder. Then she took the book and started gently flicking through the pages.

'It's okay, Mum,' said Jo. 'Don't upset yourself. You weren't a coward, you were anything but. I would have loved to know about your life at Bletchley.'

'It's all in the notebook. Daisy can tell you about it.' Olive closed her eyes, she seemed sleepy.

The two women sat for a while, holding hands.

'I told Charlie that Jack wasn't his father.' Olive struggled to catch her breath for a moment. 'I wish I hadn't. He took it badly.'

Jo nodded. 'Was this Charlie's father?' she said, pulling

375

out the picture at the front of the notebook which Megan now had in her hands.

'Yes, he was a Canadian dispatch rider I met at Bletchley Park. He really broke my heart, and I never got over it. Jack knew Charlie wasn't his, and he looked so like Samuel, it made it very hard to forget. Jack took it out on Charlie, he didn't mean to, but he did. It was hard for everyone.'

Jo nodded, unable to reply, dropping her head and wiping away the tears.

'Dad was terribly proud of you, Jo. And so am I,' said Olive, clutching Jo's hand tight. 'Can you do something for me?'

'Anything,' said Jo.

'Stop being so hard on yourself. All you ever wanted to do was help people, Jo,' Olive said quietly. 'You need to be kind to yourself too, you know.'

'I'll try, Mum.' Jo turned away and walked over to the window. She looked out on to the garden, where an elderly couple were sitting on a bench together, companionably.

'Is Charlie coming back soon?' Olive asked.

Jo bit down on her lip, and turned round to see Megan leaving the room. 'Yes, he'll be here later, Mum.' The couple on the bench were smiling at each other, they had probably been married for fifty years, thought Jo. And now they were about to say goodbye. She felt a pang of jealousy that she would never feel that love. Her career had been her great love – her career, and Charlie. She turned away, ashamed for staring.

'He's been here a lot, he's very good to me,' Olive said quietly.

'I know, I know he is.'

'I hope you don't mind, I've left something to my carer,

Daisy, in my will, she has been ever so kind to me, and she doesn't have much. They pay these girls so badly, and they work so hard.'

'That's kind, Mum, of course I don't mind,' Jo said.

'Come and sit with me,' said Olive.

Jo frantically wiped the tears away, before walking back to her mother's bedside.

'I want you and Daisy to be friends,' said Olive. 'Promise me you'll look after each other.' Olive paused for a minute, catching her breath.

Jo sat her up and gave her mother some water.

'You're both very good at pretending you're okay when you aren't. You're both very similar, it's why I'm so fond of her.'

'But she was nicer to you.' Jo smiled.

'It's easier to be forgiving of strangers,' Olive said, squeezing her daughter's hand. 'Promise me.'

'I promise,' said Jo, nodding. She had never felt so close to her mother before this moment. Perhaps, if she hadn't been so stubborn, so focused on her career, so hell bent on climbing to the top. Perhaps, if they had spent a little more time together, just the two of them. Perhaps.

Olive smiled, as Jo took her mother's hand again and squeezed it tight.

'I love you, Mum.'

'I love you too,' said Olive, as she closed her eyes, her breathing soft and shallow, until finally she fell asleep for the last time.

Epilogue
Jo, Megan & Daisy

Autumn 2015

Jo and Megan looked up as the door of the warm café opened and Daisy walked in.

She looked around, before her eyes fell on their table and she walked over.

'Hi, Daisy,' said Megan warmly, standing to greet her as Jo followed suit.

'Can I get you ladies some tea?' said a girl with a friendly smile, walking over and clutching a small notebook.

'Tea for three, please,' said Jo, as Megan and Jo nodded.

'Megan, you remember Daisy from Downside, you two must have met several times when Olive was a resident?'

'Yes' said Megan, nodding gently, 'I'm sorry I didn't get to speak to you at Granny's funeral. Thank you for coming.'

The three of them sat together in the corner of the café, smiling warmly, as if they had always known one another.

'How are you feeling, Daisy?'

'Better, thank you. A bit nervous about today.' Daisy restlessly fiddled with the toggle on her duffel coat.

'It'll be lovely,' said Megan. 'Mum's been working hard, putting the word out, to make sure Holly has the send-off she deserves.'

'I'm sorry about your uncle, Megan. I can't forgive him

for what he did to Holly, but I know you both loved him. And in the end, he got me out of Morgate House.'

Jo and Megan exchanged looks.

'It's still hard to get my head around what he did,' said Megan, 'but I think my relationship with Mum has been better since he died. I miss him, but he was such a big character I think maybe he came between us more than I realised.'

'He was very charismatic, which is why he was able to do what he did,' Daisy said quietly.

'My father was very hard on him. I guess I know why now,' Jo mused. 'I'm not excusing it, but it does explain quite a lot. It must have been hard raising a child who wasn't yours. A child who belonged to a man your wife yearned for.'

'Samuel . . .' said Megan.

'Did you know, I went to see Mrs Price?' said Daisy. 'Lorna Price, who ran Morgate House. Turns out she was at Bletchley Park with your mother. She knew of Samuel.'

Jo stared at Daisy. 'That's incredible.'

'They were both from Sussex, so perhaps they travelled on the train together,' Daisy suggested. 'Mrs Price said that Olive told herself Samuel didn't know about the baby, but apparently he did. Her husband, Geoff Price, told him. He didn't want to know, he had a wife in Canada. He never had any intention of being with Olive.'

'I guess it's easier to pretend someone loves you than face the truth. But unfortunately, it was Charlie who suffered the most. My dad took out his frustration on Charlie – he looked so much like Samuel, it must have been like living with him. Nothing Charlie did was ever good enough.'

'And nothing you did was good enough for Granny. The sun always rose and set with Charlie,' added Megan, sadly.

'I know you had a complicated relationship, but she did talk about you a lot, Jo,' Daisy reassured her. 'She loved you very much.'

'Thank you for taking such good care of my mother,' said Jo.

'Yes, thank you for making Granny so happy,' Megan added. 'She really cared about you very deeply, Daisy. We wanted to let you know that she left you something in her will. Some money, a deposit for a place of your own.'

'What?' said Daisy, in complete shock.

'She – and we, for that matter – don't want you renting a flat any more. We want you to have a home, so you don't have to worry.'

'I can't accept this, it's too much.'

Megan started to cry at the sight of Daisy's tears.

Jo continued. 'My mother got a lot of money for her house, and we don't need to spend it on her care now, so we'd like you to have some of it. To be paid properly for looking after her so beautifully. She would have wanted you to have the money, you've earned it.'

'There's something else.' Megan smiled, handing Daisy a tissue.

'She wants you to have her motorbike,' Jo added, handing Daisy a letter in Olive's handwriting. It was wrapped in one of Olive's favourite headscarves.

Daisy looked down at the letter, and ran her finger over Olive's writing. 'She wanted to ride it round Europe. I've never ridden a motorbike,' she said, laughing.

'Well, I guess you'll have to learn.' Megan smiled.

Daisy untied the scarf and opened the note, reading it through her tears.

Live your life, dear Daisy, for you and Holly, no one else can do it for you. Don't leave it too late like I did.

I will miss our chats, my dear friend,

Fondest love,
Olive

Jo put her hand over Daisy's before she tied the cobalt-blue silk scarf around her neck. 'You look beautiful, Daisy. I'm sorry I let you and Holly down,' she said, handing over Holly's St Christopher necklace. 'This is to keep you safe on your travels.'

'You didn't let us down,' Daisy said, taking the necklace. 'I don't blame you for the fire, Jo, you were trying to help us. I blame my father. He would have killed Mum one day.'

The three of them sat in silence, finishing their tea.

'We'd better go,' said Jo, summoning the waitress for the bill. 'We don't want to be late.'

Slowly they stood and walked out of the fog of the café into the autumn sunshine. They walked in silence for a while, their strides in sync. Megan looked at her mother and smiled, then linked her arm through Daisy's.

'I'm nervous there will be no one there,' said Daisy as if Megan's gesture had given her the strength to be honest. As they turned the corner, they could see Rottingdean church, and the sun burst through the clouds as Daisy's eyes fell on a scene that took her breath away. At the entrance to the church were a throng of what looked to Daisy to be over a hundred people, milling around, hugging and chatting.

'Oh my God,' said Daisy, starting to cry again. 'Are they all here for Holly?'

'Mum asked Eve to spread the word on Facebook to the Morgate House children,' said Megan proudly, as Stan walked towards them holding Phoebe.

'Holly thought she had no one who cared about her,' Daisy said, as Eve emerged from the crowd and waved to them.

Behind her stood a figure Daisy recognised very well. A man she had longed to see over the past weeks, who she desperately missed.

Julian turned and smiled at her. His beautiful green eyes crinkled in the sunshine. He looked gorgeous in his long black coat, and he'd shaved his goatee beard and had a haircut for the occasion. She smiled, and he winked at her. It was all she could do to stop herself rushing over to him.

Jo put her arm around Daisy. 'Holly was loved. You are loved.'

'And now, it's time to live life for both of us,' said Daisy to herself quietly.

The three of them held hands, and made their way towards the entrance, as the church bells began to ring.

Acknowledgements

As always this has been a collaborative process. Listening to people's stories is the best part of my job and I'm always humbled by how much time – and detail – friends, and often strangers, are willing to share with me.

Firstly I'd love to thank my mother in law, Sue Kerry, a former Woman Police Constable and Detective Constable in the Major Crime Branch who helped me hugely by sharing her experiences in Sussex Police from the 1970s onwards.

Huge thanks also go to Neil Holland for his recollections of life on a Sussex pig farm during WW2, and also to his daughter Sally Holland for arranging our meeting.

I'm very grateful to Dee Wilmott for sharing her wealth of knowledge gained from volunteering at Chestnut Tree House, which provides wonderful care for children and young people with life limiting conditions in Sussex.

Understanding motorbikes was a huge leap, which Martin Gegg and Mark Fielder of the Brooklands Museum Motorcycle Team helped me navigate during my day with them at Brooklands Motorbike Museum. They gave me so much time and thought and cracked more than one plot twist. Thanks also to Beatrice Meecham in the Curatorial Department at Brooklands for putting me in touch with Martin and Mark.

Thank you also to Matt Hawkins for describing his passion for riding motorbikes so eloquently and helping me understand the appeal of something I've always feared.

Also thanks go to Chris Balkham for explaining the mechanics of a motorbike to me so patiently.

Praise goes to the team at Bletchley. Your work in saving Bletchley Park from redevelopment and preserving it so beautifully as it was during WW2 is nothing short of miraculous. I loved walking around the campus, the main house and the huts, which are all spectacularly frozen in time.

Finally, thanks to my agent Rowan Lawton and my wonderful, passionate and patient editor Sherise Hobbs and all the team at Headline for your talent and hard work.

Thank you to my beautiful friends for your unwavering support; Rebecca Cootes, Jessica Kelly, Claire Perry-Riquet, Harriet De Bene, Clodagh Hartley, Kate Osbaldeston, Marita Stark, Claire Quy and Jo Bish. I love you all. A shout out to Katie and Rachael at Gower Heritage Centre for your kindness and talent. Huge thanks to Lisa, Emyr, Howell, Micah and Awen Jenkins for making us so welcome and also thanks go to all the Llanedi mums, particularly Kathryn and Sienna Hunt, Nicola and River Pugh and Lucy and Summer Wiley for making us so welcome in our new Welsh home.

Huge thanks to my sisters Polly, Sophie and Claudia for always being there. And last but not least, endless love to my gorgeous, resilient, funny, talented girls, Grace and Eleanor, and my husband Steve, for all your love and encouragement and holding my hand through the daily doses of self doubt.

Author's Note

Old buildings which incite memories, and often trauma, are at the heart of all of my novels and *The Girls Left Behind* is no exception. Bletchley Park, famous for being the site where Alan Turing cracked the Enigma code, is the home of the WW2 strand with Olive as our heroine dispatch rider.

Similarly, Morgate House children's home in Saltdean, East Sussex takes us back to 1975 when my protagonist Jo is starting out in Sussex Police as a Women's Police Constable.

Life at Bletchley – for women – was unknown to me before I started my research. Films such as *The Imitation Game* and *Enigma* have taught audiences about the incredible code breaking practices which took place there. Indeed Winston Churchill famously referred to the staff of Bletchley as 'the geese who laid the golden eggs and never cackled'.

But as I discovered on my first visit to the Bletchley site, which is beautifully preserved in time, dispatch riders were the unsung heroes, many of whom were women.

Hundreds of highly skilled riders whose purpose was to transport intercepted radio communications from radio towers back to Bletchley where teams of mathematicians were waiting to decipher them.

They faced exceptionally tough conditions, driving in the dark, with no road signs or street lamps, or even their own headlamps to guide them due to the WW2 blackout.

When I first laid eyes on the 1943 Norton WD16H which was on display in the garage at Bletchley, and read about the female dispatch riders braving treacherous conditions, I was instantly hooked. I love finding lesser-known snippets of history with women as the hidden heroines and here I had a humdinger.

I knew nothing about motorcycles, they scare me to death and I could never see the appeal, but after speaking to several motorcycle addicts and briefly sitting on a Norton myself at Brooklands Museum my mindset was forever changed. I couldn't wait to feature all Olive's adventures, and misdemeanours, in the story.

Similarly, when my mother in law, Sue Kerry, told me about her life starting out in the police force in the 1970s, the blatant sexism astonished me. I couldn't believe the allocation of 'blue' and 'pink' jobs to men and women respectively. All the meaty work – 'crime, fraud, murder' – fell to the men. Anything minor or involving children was always a pink job and, to make matters worse, the role of social services was less defined in those days. Sue recalled a mother being detained for shoplifting and her child sitting at Sue's desk while she rang around trying to find a family member to help. On another occasion her sergeant handed her a baby with a soiled nappy – which she had to change in the staff toilets – and then find a foster family for. She told me that if a foster parent couldn't be found, unfavourable children's homes were often the only option and it was on hearing this that the inspiration for Morgate House, on the cliffs of Saltdean, was born.

Teenagers falling through the cracks at these children's home have always been a common problem for the police. After discovering there was to be an inquest in Brighton for a young lady in care who had tragically lost her life, I went along. It was desperately sad to hear the story of her young life thwarted by the lack of a loving family and it became obvious to me that I had the seeds of my second strand.

People often ask me where I get my ideas from and it is always a spark which seemingly comes from nowhere which then sparkles into life as I begin digging into the past and hearing peoples stories.

The Girls Left Behind was particularly magical, walking around Bletchley was like going back in time. I could feel the intensity, and secrecy in the huts, brought back to life by the crackling wireless, trilling phones and the clatter of old fashioned typewriters.

It is a story about the secrets we keep hidden inside ourselves, sometimes our entire lives, as we wait for the right person to come and unlock them. I hope you enjoy reading it as much as I enjoyed writing it.

We hope you enjoyed reading *The Girls Left Behind*.

Discover more moving and powerful page-turners from
Emily Gunnis . . .

The
Midwife's
Secret

1969. On New Year's Eve, while the Hiltons of Yew Tree Manor
prepare to host the party of the season, their little girl disappears.
Suspicion falls on Bobby James, a young farmhand and the last
person to see Alice before she vanished. Bobby protests his
innocence, but he is sent away. Alice is never found.

Present day. Architect Willow James is working on a development at
Yew Tree when she discovers the land holds a secret. As she begins to
dig deep into the past, she uncovers a web of injustice. And when
another child goes missing, Willow knows the only way to stop
history repeating itself is to right a terrible wrong.

For decades the fates of the Hilton and James families have been
entwined in the grounds of Yew Tree Manor. It all began with a midwife's
secret, long buried but if uncovered could save them from the bitter
tragedy that binds them. And prove the key that will free them all . . .

Available to order now

REVIEW

The Missing Daughter

Some secrets are locked away for years . . .

Rebecca Waterhouse is just thirteen when she witnesses
her mother's death at the hand of her father in Seaview
Cottage. But what else did she see?

Years later, Rebecca's daughters Iris and Jessie know their
mother will never speak of that terrible night. But when Jessie
goes missing, with her gravely ill newborn, Iris realises the
past may hold the key to her sister's disappearance.

With Jessie in trouble, Iris must unravel a twisting story of
love and betrayal in her mother's family history.

Only then will Seaview Cottage give up its
dark and tragic secret . . .

Available to order now

REVIEW

The Girl
in the
Letter

**A heartbreaking letter. A girl locked away.
A mystery to be solved.**

1956. When Ivy Jenkins falls pregnant she is sent in
disgrace to St Margaret's, a dark, brooding house for
unmarried mothers. Her baby is adopted against her will.
Ivy will never leave.

Present day. Samantha Harper is a journalist desperate for a
break. When she stumbles on a letter from the past, the contents
shock and move her. The letter is from a young mother, begging to be
rescued from St Margaret's. Before it is too late. Sam is pulled into the
tragic story and discovers a spate of unexplained deaths surrounding
the woman and her child. With St Margaret's set for demolition, Sam
has only hours to piece together a sixty-year-old mystery before the
truth, which lies disturbingly close to home, is lost for ever . . .

Read her letter. Remember her story . . .

Available to order now

REVIEW